THE OCTAGON KEY

Brian K. Kerley

ISBN-10: 0615665810
ISBN-13: 978-0-615-66581-8

Wolf & Sparrowhawk Wilderness Press

ACKNOWLEDGMENTS

My thanks for the patience, encouragement, and input go most especially to my wife Barb. I would also like to thank our friend Jessica for her proofreading and suggestions. And thanks also to my grandson Brian, for minimizing his distractions during my work and for his patience waiting for me to put a thought to paper before answering his many questions. It is also important to thank my daughter-in-law, Brandi Kerley at Kettle Noir Artistry for such fine cover art. Additional thanks go to my editor Emmy Hammond, and to my fellow writer and map artist, Stephan Coleman.

PROLOGUE

I awoke, floating up from the depths of unconsciousness slowly, void of feeling, in total darkness. Unaware of my surroundings, the first perceptions of my senses came alive with blinding pain. Headache and nausea rushed in like a flash flood. I rolled to my left side retching madly. After a few minutes, or possibly only seconds, my stomach emptied and I had to pee. The ground was damp and I was too weak to stand, so I relieved myself while lying on my side. The air was cool and it felt like I was in a space or enclosure of some sort, possibly a cave. I could not see my hand before my face. The thought of dungeons came briefly to my mind and just as quickly discarded due to the absence of the stench of excrement from human or rat.

Stretching out, I found nothing but sandy dirt and a few fist sized stones. I checked my body; flexed toes, fingers, arms and legs, palpated what could be reached with sore muscles. A bloody wound on the back of my head, above and behind my right ear; it throbbed horribly. My fingers came from the tender spot wet and sticky. Some of it had dried in my hair. I had a knife and an empty sword scabbard on my belt. I also found a water skin and drank from it greedily.

Feeling miserable, blinking my eyes, detecting no change in my vision, I wondered if I might be blind. Then the air moved a feather touch across my cheek and nose, a fresh, after-rain smell with a hint of human stench and blood. My head hurt badly, but I tried to piece together where I was and how I got there. Nothing came; my mind was blank. Fear crept up on me. I fought it back and took a few slow breaths and began to collect my thoughts. Through the pounding pain in my head, I focused on the slow, steady rhythm of my respirations. After some minutes had passed, my pounding heart slowed to an almost normal beat. Fear wasn't gone, but it was held at bay. It was then that I realized I had no idea who I was. I'm not sure how long I lay there before I either passed out or drifted off to sleep. If indeed it was sleep, then it was dreamless and I felt no passing of time when I woke again. This time I could see.

The light came from above through a small, almost round, opening between rocks and boulders. I could see a gray sky through the hole and moisture around the edges. I was lying about three meters below it on a patch of sandy dirt not much bigger than a man's height across. My left shoulder was damp from the rain falling through, so I sat up and scooted over. The dizziness; the cost of that move was great and nearly overwhelmed me. With gritted teeth, holding back bile, I waited for my world to stop spinning. When it finally slowed down, I blinked a few times and took stock of my surroundings.

Next to me was a dented helmet, a simple conical type with a chain mail neck flap. Surrounding me were huge boulders, so that I assumed it would be an easy climb out.

Then the pounding in my head returned with a vengeance. Along with it came nausea that kicked me with dry heaves. Recovering from that unpleasant episode, I slowly got to my feet and leaned with hands on knees, gritting my teeth against more heaves and fighting back for balance while the vertigo slowly passed.

I finally stood up, stretched cramped muscles, and grimaced with the snap, crackle, pop of joints. Even though I didn't know who I was, I knew I was getting too old for whatever venture had brought me to this circumstance. Inspection of my surroundings brought me to a two-handed sword lying to one side between some rocks. It was too long for my scabbard, so I tucked it through my belt, tossed the helmet up and out through the hole and began to climb out. It was no easy affair, climbing out while feeling sick with the pounding in my head. I managed to make it to the top without falling.

Blinded, my eyes slowly adjusting to the brilliance, I saw a body near the hole, lying face up and collecting flies. It was barely out of reach. I looked the other way and saw another corpse a little farther off, and from it a light breeze intensified the smell of blood, excrement, and rot. My fingers found purchase in a crack near the first body and I began to pull myself out. I was almost to the point of swinging my leg over the edge when my fingers slipped from the crack. I grabbed at the dead man's boots, thus saving myself from falling back into the hole. I swung my leg over the edge and pulled myself out into the damp morning air.

The rain had stopped. There were patches of fog in the distance and low clouds hid the peaks of the nearby mountains. I stood up and found myself on a hut-size boulder amid other large rocks on a steep barren slope that led up to a small mountain. Below and to the sides of my rock were three more bodies and down the slope about a quarter mile there was a forest of spruce bordering a small creek. The bodies were all dressed alike wearing chain mail and helmets. Blue tabards with white trim displayed the crest of a golden bear standing on two legs. The same crest was displayed on their shields. Their swords were a single-handed double-edged type. The only other weapons they had were dirks. If they had had bows or crossbows, it would have been my carcass lying on a rock, collecting flies.

I retrieved the scabbard and shoulder belt for the claymore. It was next to, assumingly, my pack, bow, and an empty quiver, all lying in a neat pile. I donned the belt, positioning the long sword on my back, then went to the body near the edge of the boulder. He was lying on his side in a pool of blood with a short sword protruding from his left middle. I grasped the hilt, levered him onto his back and pulled it free, then wiped the blood off on his tabard and slid the blade home in my scabbard. His pockets rendered a few coins, which

3

I kept, and a grouse's foot, which I let him keep. The other body gave up a leather purse full of silver coins and a few pieces of gold, which of course went in my pocket. I then checked my bag.

The pack had a half a loaf of stale bread, some cheese, and some jerky. It also contained a medical kit, and a bottle containing tincture of opium. I took two gulps of the latter for pain, a bite of bread and chased it with some water. I also found a strange item shaped like an octagon box in a small leather pouch. It was a finger width thick, almost the size of my palm, dull gray and very light, with a small hole in the center. Returning it to the bag, I tied the drawstring to my belt and stowed it in my trouser pocket. I got up and put the pack on my back, then slung my bow and quiver over my shoulder and began my climb down off the boulder.

The next soldier I came upon had a smashed face and the back of his head was crushed. A round shield with the badge of a hawk ringed with an octagon sat next to him. Assuming the odd shield was mine, I slung it over a shoulder and pillaged the body. The other two men were killed with arrows. One had an arrow through the shield, pinning it to his chest, and the other had an arrow in the throat. I relieved them both of their coins and the arrows and took a good helmet and a chain mail shirt. I continued down the steep slope feeling weak and heavily burdened, but stopping here and there to retrieve an arrow when I could find one undamaged.

Exhaustion and vertigo made me wonder if I was going to make it to the creek. Being exposed and out in the open made me feel vulnerable as well. I had thought of returning to the hole, but whoever sent that squad may soon be sending another when this one didn't report. Also, the close proximity to rotting corpses would be very unhealthy. My head still hurt badly and it was all I could do not to lose my lunch. Vertigo overcame me halfway down the slope, so I sat on a rock to catch my breath.

Again, I racked my brain, but recalled nothing; no idea who I was, where I was, who they were or why they wanted me. I heard a horse neigh further down in the trees, which confirmed my suspicion that the dead soldiers were horsemen. They carried no spears, bows, or lances, which meant they were traveling light and with urgency. They appeared to be a household troop or guard of some sort.

I must have been aware of the pursuit and chose the high rocks to make my stand, probably hoping to discourage them with arrows. When they got closer I apparently got serious and dispatched two of them. Running out of arrows, I unstrung my bow and placed it with my pack. By the signs, the guess would be that the first one eventually attained the top and met his demise with my short sword that I stuck in his ribs for safe keeping. Then I probably threw my shield as another was showing his face near the top. By the way his body was laid out he looked like he caught the spinning disc square on the snout and smashed his head on a rock when he was slammed back down slope. At this point I would have drawn my claymore, tossed the scabbard aside and engaged the leader last. He had two cuts on his sword arm and his shield was broken, but the killing blow was a thrust left of center. At this point the signs left me unsure of how I got my head injury. Perhaps the man I pierced with my short sword was still alive and bonked me on the head when I skewered his sergeant and then tossed me in the hole before he died. Of course, he did all this while holding my sword with his ribs. More likely I yanked my claymore free of the sergeant's belly and stepped back into the hole like a dolt, smacking my head during the fall. I like the first story better. However, the second one is more plausible.

I resumed my descent, but rested again for a few minutes at the creek. The pounding in my head slackened a bit; the pain medicine was kicking in. Filling my water skin and one more from my pack, I scanned the trees for their horses. Using a stick to aid against the swift current, I crossed the knee deep creek. Sloshing up the bank with soaking wet feet, I smelled the horses. A short way into the trees there were five mounts tethered in a small clearing; all were sorrels and of medium build.

I rummaged through saddle bags and gear looking for clues and finding none. All of the saddle blankets were blue and white and bore the badge of the golden bear. I removed all of these, put them in a pile and then cut new saddle blankets from their bed rolls. I was in the process of re-saddling all the horses when another horse with plain trappings came trotting across the clearing and right up to me. This horse was black with a white rump and black spots. It nuzzled me with its muzzle and I could not resist scratching behind its ears. This was obviously my horse, even though I had no recollection of this animal. I found various personal effects in the saddlebags, but nothing jarred my memory. Among those effects, I found accruement bearing the hawk and the octagon. I found a map, but I was still clueless without a reference point. I led the horses down to the creek for water then mounted the dark one. With my pack tied to the bedroll behind the saddle, I rode north.

I soon came to a well-traveled road. By the signs I was pursued from the northwest. There were tracks going southeasterly, but none going the other way. Now came my moment of decision. Shall I continue on my route that I was traveling to who-knows-where or do I go back the way I came and maybe find out who I am? The problem being, that is also the direction from which a squad of men came to capture or kill me. I could be an outlaw. My description might be posted with local authorities. To dally could mean death, especially when leading five stolen horses and tack. Curiosity overcame good sense and I decided to travel the road to the northwest.

Muddy roads and less than pleasant weather plagued me. Even with an oilcloth cloak, the rain, which at times was a torrential downpour, found its way to soak me to the bone. The horses were miserable and I became ill, I think from my wound, because it swelled and became more painful. The headaches were bone crushing; I was dizzy, had no appetite, and drifted in and out of consciousness. I encountered no one and I think I spent two horrible nights on the road, but it may have been three. The whole journey was like a vague memory of misery.

I felt as if I had been in the saddle for an eternity. The rain had finally stopped and a patch of blue sky popped out here and there. Sunset was approaching and the thought of another night on the road filled me with dread. My shivering returned. Then the smell of wood smoke gave me hope and made me cautious. I should have been more alert and left the road, but it was all I could do to stay awake, much less focused. I turned down a path that led to the north and fell asleep. I woke briefly to a beautiful woman with long, curly blond hair. My exhaustion overcame me and I felt myself slipping off to oblivion. No not now, I shrieked to myself, and then all went black.

The man's subconscious story telling ceased. Being unconscious was not the same as sleep. He slept now, a deep and restful sleep, full of dreams of the mysterious woman with the curly blonde hair.

The healer, exhausted from listening so long in the mind speech, lay down on a rug on the floor. She covered herself with a blanket and slept. Her dreams were not as peaceful as his.

CHAPTER 1

He opened his eyes, blinked, and stiffly rubbed away the sleep. He was in a small cottage; very neat, clean and organized. Light came in through small windows in each wall. A woman with long golden locks stood at a counter across from him facing the other way. Even though she wore a simple dress, her striking figure was obvious. She was cleaning a kettle while watching small birds feeding on crumbs and seeds on the windowsill. She stopped, raised her head and turned and looked at him with deep blue eyes. He was in that sluggish state when one wakes normally from a deep sleep. When she turned, her beauty took him by total surprise. For some reason he didn't understand, he felt he should know her.

"You're awake I see," said the lady.

Her voice was like music. Here was a woman that could ambush a man's heart as well as his desires. He recognized her. The fog of sleep inertia vanished like vaporous morning mist warmed with new sun. He spoke while lying on his side. "It was you that I saw before I passed out." He slowly sat up on the edge of the bed and lightly touched his bandaged wound. A wave of vertigo and nausea hit him, and then it passed after a couple of breaths, but the beating of a drum remained in his head. "I don't remember . . ." His eyes met hers again. "Who am I?"

"I don't know," she replied, though she had her suspicions. "You are lucky to be alive." She knew his story. He shared it when he was unconscious. For him it summed up his entire known life. He thought he had told his tale to her, but the memory of the telling was vague and he didn't realize that he had told it with his mind while he was comatose. For him, the recounting of his story was like a foggy dream. He discounted the vagueness to fever and exhaustion. If asked, he would say that he was very tired when he spoke of his adventure.

"I remember talking to you . . . I think," he continued hesitantly, staring off at nothing with furrowed brows and squinted eyes. "But I can't recall anything beyond a few days ago."

She had read about amnesiacs and even encountered two during her profession as a healer, though that was long ago. "Your memory may never return to you or you could wake up tomorrow and be fully restored. It could come to you a little at a time, all at once, or not at all. For now it is important that you rest, eat, drink lots of water and get a little exercise. You have lain in bed for two days with fever."

His face relaxed when she spoke and he felt little butterflies in his chest when their eyes met. "I need to find out who I am, and why someone wants me captured or dead. I don't even know what kind of man I am. I could be a criminal for all I know."

"Just that you ask shows you are concerned. A criminal would not care. I am a very perceptive woman and I sense that you are a man with good intentions. That is more than I can say for some of the folks around here. Confused ideas of ethics are common everywhere but let us save philosophical discussions for when you are feeling better."

"I will heal quickly." The corners of his mouth turned up slightly, "For you."

"A charmer you are." She smiled at him briefly then grew serious. "My name is Dalla. Make yourself at home. I must now go into the village and get some information, primarily about you and your pursuers. No one knows you are here and your horses are hidden out back. Stay here and rest. There is food in the cold-box under the house, help yourself. I put the trail rations you had in your pack down there as well. There is tea in the cupboard or coffee if you prefer. I will be back in a few hours."

The man's eyes lit up at the mention of coffee. Coffee was an expensive import that even peasants considered a necessity worthy of spending one's last coppers on. "Thank you," he paused, "for everything. But before you go, please tell me why you are doing all this for me?"

"I am a healer, it's what I do," she answered seriously, then stepped out the door.

Dalla followed the path to the main road which led into the village. It was about a twenty minute walk and today was a crystal clear spring morning. In the southern regions it would be full summer and hot with the solstice only a week away. The incessant rain of the past week had finally passed and there was not a cloud in the sky. The sun had been up for several hours, though it never got dark at this time of year, and there was still a slight chill in the air. Walking distractedly, she contemplated the day the man rode into her life.

Two days ago Dalla had found him on this very path not far from the main road. She was out gathering herbs and fresh fiddlehead ferns for a salad. The man was shivering, spattered with blood stains and smelling like he needed a bath. He slumped in his saddle and led a string of horses. The stranger obviously needed aid and she hadn't wanted anyone to know he was there. She sensed something special about him when he passed through the village before and her perceptions now warned that caution was needed. Besides that, noses that belonged elsewhere would start lewd stories of her Spartan life.

Discovering a head wound after a quick assessment of his condition, she took the reins and led the string into the woods to her cottage avoiding trails and other houses. She pulled him off his horse and dragged him inside. The man was heavy for his build, nor did his chainmail help her effort. She tied the horses far enough out back not to be spotted should someone come to her cottage. Returning to her patient, she removed his armor and bloodstained clothes and placed him on her bed. Dalla surveyed him for other injuries, finding mostly bruises and scrapes. She heated water, then cleaned and

10

dressed his head wound and very carefully got a few spoonfuls of medicinal herb tea into him without his choking.

She bathed his fevered body. Dalla had enjoyed this immensely. It was not often that she saw a naked man with as fine a body as his. He was a handsome man of his late thirties; however, in his present condition he looked pretty rough. He was a medium to tall man and well-muscled, though not overly so. He had numerous scars on his body which bespoke of his experience as a fighting man. His dark curly hair was shoulder length and he had a full beard trimmed short.

His fever had grown worse as she worked. Using a candle, she checked his pupils for reaction to light—they were unequal and sluggish. His condition degraded rapidly—the pressure in his head had to be relieved. She didn't have the tools to drill holes in his skull for such a procedure, but steps had to be taken or the man would die. Dalla had sat down on the floor assuming the lotus position. It had been a very long time since she had melded with another mind.

She meditated for a few minutes to reach the trance-like calm needed to enter the wounded warrior's mind. She took his hand and felt the heat enter her hand and travel up her arm. Her world of senses became a world of two. Like stepping slowly into a wall of water, she felt what he felt, once she submerged into his mind. It took a moment for her to adjust. It was cold. The room seemed chilly because he burned with fever. Casting aside distractions, she concentrated. With perceptions stretching forth she found intelligence, an educated mind, but injured. Her job was to guide him and give him her strength, lead him to self-repair within himself. She/they found a swollen area in the hippocampus region of the brain; an area responsible for long term memory and emotions. Here she helped him calm the tension and boost the circulation, which assisted the herbs she had given him to reduce the edema and inflammation. The intracranial pressure dropped and they began to breathe better with a less erratic pulse. She then led him to the hypothalamus, caressing it with signals to lower the fever to safer levels. The man's body and mind relaxed noticeably and his sweating stopped. It was then, with melded minds, that she asked him what had happened. He shared, without reservation, all that had happened since his waking in the hole. He spoke without words and she shared his pain, empathy and frustration. He could read, write, wield a sword and do most any skill learned in life, but he had no memory of who he was or where he came from. It was as if he began life a grown man less than a week ago. She ended the meld and gazed at the stranger one more time. She then, regrettably, clothed him in his undergarments and left him to rest. He slept then, a deep and restful sleep.

She watched over him for the next two days, sleeping on the floor next to him, covering him when he had chills and sponging him with a cool wet cloth when his fever returned. She made a poultice of moldy bread and herbs that was alternated with a black salve when she changed the dressing. She did her best to keep him hydrated with water, broth and tea of white willow bark and yarrow. When he groaned with pain she gave him poppy tea. She washed and dried his clothing, scrubbed the rust out of his chain mail with sand and oiled his weapons. Most everything he had was soaking wet and had to be dried out. When she came across the octagon key, she recognized it immediately.

A thousand images raced through Dalla's mind. Memories came to her of hope and defeat, unity and betrayal, progress and destruction. The healer quieted her mind and pushed these thoughts aside. She wondered if he was a descendant of the one who took it into hiding. It had been a long time since she had seen the key. Dalla had given unheeded counsel that it should be destroyed. She put the octagon key back in the pouch and restored it to his, now clean and dry, trousers pocket. She said nothing to the traveler about the key and wondered if he knew anything about it before his amnesia. It had been left in the care of a man who swore his family would guard over it and keep it hidden, but that seemed ages ago. She shook herself out of her memories and deep thoughts and returned to the present.

Dalla enjoyed her walk. The air smelled fresh and the birds were singing. Several birds followed her, flying from limb to limb. Removing a piece of bread from her pocket, she tore it up and left a trail of crumbs in her path. The birds ate and sang as they followed.

Their music was sweet. Dalla calmed as she walked communing with nature, but her mind drifted back to the past when she first came to the village.

She had come to Mentin about ten years before in a small cart pulled by a pony. She had been traveling with musicians and stopped at the inn for the night. When she heard of a boy with the pox she decided to stay a few more days to help the sick child. The band continued on to Three Rivers without her. The boy lived and his parents were very grateful as well as very poor. She declined their offer of payment, but they insisted that she take a few chickens, which she happily accepted. A few of the locals asked her to stay as they had no healer.

She agreed to stay for a little while, so they told where there was an old cottage that lay empty and abandoned. She took up residence there, but she never felt fully accepted by the village. They were quick to come get her when they wanted her services as a healer, but they were just as quick to talk about her behind her back.

She bartered her services, occasionally taking a small coin or two, more for appearances than anything else. She always had money to pay for things she needed; never paying in gold, she always used silver or coppers. Some of the rumors implied that she had a fortune buried somewhere, while others scoffed at this because she lived such a frugal life. They were a backward bunch of miners and trappers. Only a few had ever traveled more than fifty kilometers their entire lives. Some of them accused her of sorcery, especially when a pig died or a calf was stillborn. She never wished any ill of these people, but their gratitude was short lived whenever she saved one of them from sickness or death. Being beautiful and single didn't help either.

Never having a close relationship with any of them, she was often accused of having bedded any number of men, married or not. It was just typical village rumors brought on by boredom. Some of the folks were whispering about her use of magic. "It is strange," they would say, "that she never ages and never marries, she doesn't look a day over twenty-six." There was also a religious faction in the village that found fault with her for not contributing to their temple, and their priest accused her of being a non-believer and a witch. Her beliefs she kept to herself.

Dalla arrived at the village and went directly to the inn. It had warmed considerably, so she had shed her light sweater and tied it about her waist. She wore a simple long, gray dress hoping to look nondescript. Even in the plainest clothes, her striking beauty and long, wavy golden hair would catch anyone's eye. However, when she wanted, she had a way to avoid notice. Stepping inside and waiting a minute to let her eyes adjust to the darkness, she went to the empty common room and took a small table in the corner. Bart, the innkeeper, saw her enter and immediately prepared a cup of tea and brought it over to where she sat. He sat down across from her with his own cup of coffee.

"Good afternoon Dalla," greeted Bart. "It's nice to have some decent weather for a change eh?"

"Indeed," replied Dalla. "Did you find out anything about our mysterious traveler that passed through last week, or the men chasing him?"

"Not much about him. The men chasing him though belong to Jarl Bamsen from the city of Kabula, third or fourth cousin to the king of Abezda. The golden bear standard is his that those men carried. The captain leading them is called Sigurd. He has offered ten pieces of gold for the traveler or an heirloom that he supposedly carries. Should they not find this man, they seek to capture a woman and her daughter believed to be in Border City, so they can be ransomed for his heirloom. The mother, a dark-haired woman of about thirty years is named Anisha and her ten-year-old daughter is Aideen."

"The mother and child, where are they from?"

"They reside in Border City. It is believed they are under the guard of mercenaries. Why, I don't know."

"You said, 'not much,' about the traveler. How much is not much?"

"He is just a man on the road home from visiting family in Three Rivers. He commands a free company of border patrol defending against Kandian bandits and raiding parties. His name is Imar."

"Imar you say?"

Bart nodded.

A look of concern crossed her face. She asked, "The son of Amir?"

He shrugged. "I don't know."

"What relation is Imar to the mother and child?"

"Could be husband, could be brother, I don't know."

"You did well, Bart," said Dalla, handing the innkeeper three silver coins. "How did you get all this information?"

Bart grinned as he put the coins in his pocket. "I hired out two guides to Captain Sigurd and ordered one to desert after a couple days of gathering profitable news. I gave him a bonus when he got back. Fresh news brings people to my bar. They drink, talk and spend money. The news will eventually get twisted into rumors. When that gets old all they have left is local gossip. Then I have to buy more news or make something up."

"You're good, Bart. By the way, I have some horses and tack that were once the property of Jarl Bamsen, five to be exact. I would like to trade." Dalla saw the questions in Bart's eyes and stopped him before he spoke. "You are better off not knowing, at least not now. If you don't rob me blind in the trade, you will have my word that I will give you the full story someday. That is, if I live to tell it."

Bart closed his mouth and smiled. He smelled a profit and couldn't resist a little larceny from time to time.

CHAPTER 2

"Lady Akala, I hate to trouble you this early in the morning, but Lord Townsend is here to see you. He claims his business with you is quite urgent and cannot wait for a more respectable hour."

Akala answered mumbling, waking from a deep sleep. "Is he out of his mind? It's barely even the crack of dawn." Akala liked her sleep, and to be rousted before the sun rode the tree tops would cause a foul attitude that could last for hours, if not all day.

Dorfin knew his employer well. After seeing to his duties, he would avoid the lady of the house for at least three hours. "I'm sorry My Lady, I tried to dissuade him, but he would hear none of it. It was all I could do to prevent him from pushing past me and pounding on the door to your rooms."

"If he did, he would leave bleeding," muttered Akala. "You did well Dorfin," she said louder. "Have his royal rudeness wait on the east balcony if the weather is pleasant. I will join him shortly."

"As you wish My Lady," replied Dorfin, hoping the weather was not pleasant. He would love to leave the pompous Lord Townsend out on the east balcony with torrents of rain and howling wind. Unfortunately, the weather in Port Augustus was usually fair at this time of the year.

Dorfin led Lord Townsend to a small table on a balcony overlooking grass covered rolling hills. Above the hills a few stratus clouds had turned red from the sliver of the upsurging sun. "I shall bring coffee My Lord. The Lady Akala will be with you shortly."

Townsend was less than pleased with the delay. "I must speak with her now. I haven't the time for pleasantries."

Townsend was a nobleman from a long line of noblemen and he was sure to remind everyone of that fact constantly. He owned most of the docks as well as more than half the warehouses, taverns and brothels of Port Augustus and he was one of the most devious men Dorfin knew. The aging lord was as ruthless as his father had been and just as despicable. Tall and lean with short gray hair, he towered over most men and expressed his wishes without manners, decency, or respect, unless of course he wanted something of his equals or those of higher station. He was suspected of dealings with organized crime, drank excessively and had a taste for women of all ages. Townsend was also married to a noblewoman of a high ranking family, whom he abused terribly. He was a man who sought power, wealth and pleasure and cared nothing of who got hurt or killed in his pursuit of it.

Dorfin's morning was off to a staggering start. It seemed that irritable attitudes abounded around him. He was tempted to dose the coffee with something that would send his lordship running to the privy. "My Lord, Her Ladyship hurries for no one, but herself. To rush her will cause an opposite effect."

Dorfin returned a few minutes later with coffee. Townsend was pacing back and forth on the balcony with a worried look of deep concentration when Steward Dorfin arrived and poured him a cup of coffee. Townsend changed back to his normal look of imperious disdain. He took the cup and turned his back on the steward without a word and stood at the marble rail quietly sipping the strong black liquid.

Dorfin's face rarely showed emotion and he showed none now. Dorfin was a lean man of medium build, mid-forties, brown hair tied back and running about a third of the way down his back, with brush strokes of gray at his temples. He was always fastidiously clean shaven and well dressed, with never a hair out of place. He had served the Lord Travin and Lady Akala as steward for more than five years and was the most diplomatic man they knew. He was an ideal choice to represent them in business and politics, since neither of them had the patience or temperament to put up with bureaucratic nonsense. The lord and lady had the final say on large decisions, but the tedious day to day business was handled by Dorfin and he handled it well. He never lost his temper and his face remained as impassive as a rock. Only those that knew him well could spot his hidden mirth by the twinkle in his eye and that twinkle glittered brightly and unnoticed as he stoically excused himself from the Lord Townsend's presence.

Akala Murdoch did not like waking early—not one bit. She especially did not like it when it was because someone she despised demanded a meeting. It was obvious to her that Lord Townsend desperately wanted something. This contemptible man was suspected of sending pirates after her ships as well as pilfering cargo loads coming across his docks. Not only that, she tired of his constant attempts to lure her to his bed. She usually handled this with a reminder that she kept a sharp blade close to hand and would give him back his manhood in a jar. She was a no nonsense type of woman.

Taking her time getting up, she put on a robe and went to her mirror. Even though she was a woman in her mid-fifties, she looked to be no more than forty-five, but at times felt much older. She had led a rough life adventuring with her husband Travin, but they came to riches later in life. She knew what hard work was, could ride with the best of men, steer a ship, and navigate by chart and compass or stars. And, though known only to a few, she was expert with a rapier. Akala bore the scars of numerous battles fought by Travin's side. She dressed in such a way as to cover those scars and kept her past to herself. She brushed her long, brown, silver streaked hair, and tied it high on the back of her head. After drinking a glass of cold water that Dorfin had left by her door, she went to see what was so blasted important that she be disturbed at this unholy hour.

"Lord Townsend, what's so urgent that you need my audience before the sun rises?" Akala stepped onto the balcony and directed a level gaze at Townsend. It was obvious by her look that she was not happy.

"Please excuse me Lady, but it is imperative that I secure passage for one on this very tide to North Harbor," said Townsend with a sincerity rarely seen.

Akala grunted under her breath and replied, "You don't need me for that. See my agent down on the docks to book a voyage." She wrinkled her brow and added, "Not only that, high tide was about an hour ago, leaving you maybe a few hours to catch the ebb and I have no ships departing for at least two more days and none going to North Harbor for another week. Why such urgency?"

"I just received intelligence of an alarming nature that requires immediate action. I must move swiftly to avoid disaster. It is imperative that I send an emissary to North Harbor at once."

"Why should I be concerned if you lose money on a business deal? You are constantly cheating us. It would delight me to delirium to see you lose a few gold crowns. Not only that, one of our ships was due to arrive on this tide from North Harbor. Your spy on my ship; what is his name? Oh yes, Able Seaman Baker. He is probably the one that brought you this urgent information."

"Akala," replied Townsend, dropping the formalities, "I have no spies on your ship, or anywhere else for that matter. Word came to me by horseman."

"I find that doubtful, knowing your penchant for lying. I have been aware of your spies for some time; though I'm sure I haven't ferreted out all of them. Back to the subject matter at hand; I have only two ships in port right now, one in dry dock being refitted, and the one that just came in. It would be nearly impossible to re-supply and send it back out on the same tide. It would also be foolish of me to send out an empty ship for only one passenger, and short on food and water as well. The cost for such an endeavor would be extreme and more. More, I am sure, than you would be willing to pay. Not only that, the crew needs rest and a good break that they duly deserve. What business requires such urgency?"

The Lord Townsend, a man of good posture, usually puffed up and full of himself, slumped in defeat knowing that he would have to dig deep into his coffers in order to get the charter he desired. "My business is my own; however, I do need a ship and no others are available. I must hire yours."

"I'm afraid it's out of the question," replied Akala. "As I said, there is no time to resupply and catch this tide. The *Bedford Lee* is probably still unloading cargo. I can have the ship ready for you on the next tide, but my crew will deserve a bonus and adequate compensation for a back to back voyage without shore leave. Furthermore, there will be an additional cost to re-supply at another port enroute and you will be paying the charter for both directions."

"You are going to charge me for a return voyage when you will probably have a full load of cargo out of North Harbor anyway?" Townsend's eyes bulged with indignation and his sincerity soon slipped away. "You are trying to take advantage of me and my situation."

Akala could have purred at Townsend's discomfort. "Ah, you don't like it much when the shoe is on the other foot, do you? This endeavor seems to be quite valuable to you, whatever it is. The price will be double for to-and-from routes plus supplies at Seal Bay, as well as all additional expenses to be borne by you. The ship shall not depart before the evening tide."

"That's outrageous! I will pay standard charter rate for a round trip if the ship will wait in port for my emissary, and resupply costs are a ship's expense."

"These are emergency rates. Take it or leave it. If you want standard rates, you can catch the scheduled voyage next week. Perhaps you can find another ship, but I believe all the merchantmen are currently engaged. You may get lucky and see if some fool decides to buck tide and wind and row into the harbor in the next hour or so, or you could try to persuade a man-a-war under the King's flag to aid you," suggested Akala.

Akala saw alarm rise in Townsend's face for an instant at the mention of 'man-a-war under the King's flag.' He quickly replied, "I don't think that is a good idea. The Admiral would never involve himself in anything other than business of the realm."

"I will cut your slack sails and deal you straight on the square," said Akala, her seafarer's jargon coming to her more naturally than the social graces of polite society, which more often than not she chose to ignore. "Rates stand as they are, to be paid in full before departure. The crew gets a day off in Seal Bay to resupply and blow off a little steam. If Captain Einar feels he can leave safely on this ebb, then so be it, but the decision is his."

"Done," answered Townsend. "I agree to your terms, even though you are robbing me blind. I had better be on my way. Good day Akala, I will see myself out."

"Good day Lord Townsend. I will send men to your estate shortly to procure payment and send written orders to Captain Einar." *That was way too easy*, thought Akala. *I wonder what that snake is up to.* She watched him walk briskly away and swore to herself to be more cautious next time.

Lord Townsend hurried to the stairs and across the foyer and out the front door, which Dorfin held open for him. "Good day My Lord," said Dorfin, as impassive as ever as he watched the nobleman vault into his saddle without a word and fly down the hedge-lined drive in a full gallop. He nearly made it to the gate when he suddenly pulled up short, quickly dismounted and ran into the shrubs. Groans emitted from the verge shortly thereafter.

Dorfin heard a light chuckle behind him.

Akala said, "That was worth getting up early for. Dorfin, you're terrible. You may want to dump the rest of that coffee out before someone else helps themselves to a cup. You couldn't have done it to a man more deserving. I'm afraid he's still rather full of it though. Did you listen in on our conversation?"

"Of course My Lady, I have already dispatched Captain Coulig and five men at arms to procure payment as well as two more to find Baker and bring him here. I have also taken the liberty to write orders for Captain Einar and the *Bedford Lee*," replied Dorfin, removing a letter from inside his coat. "It just requires your signature and any additional instructions that you may have."

"Good work Dorfin," said Akala admiringly, signing the orders and returning them to Dorfin. "Dispatch these orders immediately and add to them that the captain and crew of the *Bedford Lee* will get double pay and an extra half share for any freight and/or prizes hauled or appropriated on this cruise. They can take what cargo is left unloaded to Seal Bay and sell it there if it will help them make sail on the morning tide. Have the courier tell Einar we will try to get more information to him before he departs. Failing that, have him check with our shipping agent in Seal Bay."

"I was going to deliver the orders to Captain Einar myself."

"Oh no Dorfin, I need you here to extract information from Able Seaman Baker."

CHAPTER 3

Captain Einar was less than pleased. He had been sleeping for only an hour when a messenger from his employer woke him with orders to set sail with a passenger on this very tide if possible. He tipped the messenger a few coppers and sent him to find as much water and food as could be found at this time of the morning and brought to the dock in the next forty-five minutes.

He had left his first officer, Hawkins, in charge of offloading the cargo and now joined him on deck and briefed him on their orders. "Mr. Hawkins, you seem pleased with this venture. I wish I could share your enthusiasm."

"What's not to like, sir?" The tall clean-shaven young man replied. "A bonus, double pay and an extra half-share sound very profitable what with pirates and Kandian merchantmen we can take. We will be light, fast and very maneuverable. The advantage is ours. We barely outran pirates just yesterday. It would be nice to give them a fight."

"Yes, but we are merchantmen first and privateers second. Not only that, I doubt our passenger would be pleased with a raid, since it seems Lord Townsend is in an all fired hurry to get his man to North Harbor. However, if he is a land lubber he won't know why we are acting as if we're lumbering along like we're fat with cargo at sight of another ship. Although, I see no harm in cautiously slowing down to check out enemy ships that may want to take us. Of course we will only be attacking in self-defense if that should happen. Either way, we had best brief the crew to keep their traps shut."

"As good as done sir, I also took the liberty of sending a party ashore to gather up the rest of the crew on shore leave."

"Very good Mr. Hawkins, keep two booms working and take on what supplies you can while offloading cargo, but bring all to a halt in an hour and a half from now if we have our passenger. If he hasn't boarded by then, continue the transference of loads, obtain more supplies and plan to sail on the next tide. Send for me when our guest arrives."

"Aye Captain," answered Hawkins.

The captain was summoned less than thirty minutes later. He was out on deck before the passenger stepped off the gangway. The man was tall and appeared to be thin. He wore a burnous of the desert people, all black with the hood pulled over his head. What little could be seen of his face and hands showed him to be of dark olive complexion. He stepped on deck and stood silently saying nothing.

"I take it you are Lord Townsend's emissary," greeted the captain. The man said nothing and handed the captain a letter from Lord Townsend's steward vouching for his passage as Khaled. "You don't talk much, do you, Khaled?"

Khaled answered only with a slight bow.

"Mr. Powell," Einar called to a sailor, "Show our guest to a hammock on the crew deck."

"Aye Captain," replied the crewman. "This way," he said to Khaled. He led the desert man below decks to a spot along the hull. "You'll stow your gear there below your hammock. It can be cramped aboard ship. You'll need to keep your things picked up at all times and stowed away. Now if you'll excuse me, we'll be making ready to shove off." Powell turned and went topside to resume his duties.

The *Bedford Lee* departed Port Augustus at low slack tide without a moment to lose. If it had not been for a light morning breeze pushing from shore to sea, they probably would not have made it out of the bay before the incoming tide. Once out of the bay, they turned northwest and set all sails.

The *Bedford Lee* was a square rigged ship with a number of triangular lateen sails rigged fore and aft, which increased her maneuverability and allowed for a better tack into the wind. The ship also had top gallants deployed above the top sails, which added greatly to her speed. Captain Einar favored these new developments when outrunning pirates or when on the assault. He preferred not to attack unless he was sure of winning with minimal casualties. The ship was thirty-eight meters from bow to stern with a light catapult and ballista on the bow and another pair on the stern. There were seven ballistae that could be moved from side to side amidships. All weapons were kept covered and battened down until needed.

Murdoch shipping had an agreement with the Kalusian Admiralty to attack only pirates or Kandian ships since they were at odds with Kandia. There had been no land battles in a long time, but the two countries were constantly harassing each other's ships at sea. Sedar was not so lucky. Both Sedar and Abezda were often plagued with border skirmishes and raids. However, there had not been an all-out war in many years.

The crew of the *Bedford Lee* was well trained, well paid, and very loyal. There were exceptions, of course. Able Seaman Baker did not work well with the others. On shore, he didn't socialize with the other crewmen, choosing instead to go off on his own. He never shared anything of himself and he would get indignant when asked. He was constantly asking others about their business though. The other crewmen began to resent him for it, even though he worked hard and carried out his duties efficiently. Captain Einar was relieved when they set sail with one crewman short. *Morale will improve without him*, thought Einar. Still, he wondered where Baker went off to that he couldn't be found so soon after leaving the boat.

Oh well, thought Einar as he stood on the quarter deck. "Three points to larboard and slack the mainsail a bit. I'm going to catch a little shut eye," Einar said to Hawkins. He could hear Hawkins barking out his orders and the callbacks repeated down the line as he took the few steps down to his cabin below the poop deck.

Hawkins was a little shy on sleep himself, but he was energized with the prospect of action and wealth. They probably wouldn't take any enemies until they dropped off the passenger, but the return voyage might be promising. He loved a good adventure, especially if it involved danger. Seeing to the off-load and on-load simultaneously with a time limit put him into a bit of a stress that always seemed to heighten his senses and efficiency. As soon as the captain gave him his instructions, a plan was laid in the back of his mind that would give the ship the most profit and the greatest advantage should they be blessed with battle. *Planning was everything, if you had time*, thought Hawkins. Knowing that there was the possibility of keeping some of the cargo because of departure time, he first offloaded the furs, spools of hemp rope and then ores of iron and silver. These items were bulky or heavy and would not bring as much profit up north. While booming these items of freight onto the dock, they boomed back onboard barrels of oranges, lime juice, salt pork, live chickens, rice, and kegs of water. There were still some provisions on the dock when they shoved off as well as some cargo in the hold, but they could use that cargo on their cruise and what they did not use could be traded at Seal Bay.

It was a fine morning to be at sea. Hawkins went to the starboard side and faced into the morning sun and breathed in the wind on his face. They were presently on a northwest heading and making an easy pace with a quartering wind on the tail. Times like this were good for thinking. He considered their passenger. His brow knitted at the thought of that dark enigma. *Emissary my butt*, thought Hawkins. *The man speaks little, walks without sound and his very presence makes the hairs on one's neck stand erect. The man is an assassin or I'm a jackal in a surcoat.* Remembering back to childhood was difficult for Hawkins and much of it was blocked. He recalled an image of riding beside his father in a caravan while crossing the desert. There were men that would show up out of nowhere, seemingly out of the sand. They would check papers, inspect the pack animals, and talk with his father in their accented dialect. Sometimes they would take something for themselves. Other times coins would exchange hands. His father told him they were buying water at the next well, without which they would surely die. "If we took water without permission, they would take our goods and enslave us all if they didn't just kill us outright, so let us count our blessings," his father would say. Sometimes, traveling with these desert men, there would be a silent one dressed in black. His father had warned him that they were especially dangerous. "Assassins," he'd said. "Once contracted, only death can stop them and they are very hard to kill. They are expert at killing, kidnapping, and extortion. Some of the more important leaders hired them as body guards."

"Ship ho," called a top-man from aloft, stirring Hawkins from his memories.

"Where away?" he queried.

"Off the port bow," the crewman called back, "a sheet on the horizon and moving south."

Hawkins strode forward to the port side. "Rouse the captain," he told a seaman and to the helmsman he ordered, "Ten points to port Mr. Jensen, but gently." Hawkins was pumping with adrenaline as he glassed the horizon. *Barely three hours out to sea and already some action. Maybe*, he thought.

"What do we have, Mr. Hawkins?" Einar asked a few moments later standing next to his first mate, a glass to his eye.

"She's just now hull up Sir, and turned just slightly toward us not two minutes ago."

"Could be pirates," stated the captain flatly, "Beat to quarters Mr. Hawkins, and slow us down a bit, but be ready for speed. I want to see if she's low enough in the water to be worth taking. Half furl the topsails and ready them and the top gallants to full on my order. Set four ballistae to port and three to starboard. Ready the forward catapult and ballista with shot and the aft ones with fire."

"Aye Captain," answered Hawkins. He began relaying the captain's orders with obvious enthusiasm. Grapples were set and stowed along the gunwales, crossbows and cutlasses were handed out, bailers soaked the deck against fire. The crew was astir with action and excitement.

Khaled came up on deck and stood quietly amidships, forward of the quarterdeck. He was armed with two scimitars, one on each hip, a brace of throwing knives on his chest and two black sticks on his back placed in a V formation, each three and a half centimeters in width and no longer than a man's arm. Sensing the mood of the crew, he fought to suppress his excitement. His rigid training had taught him not to show emotion, but he could not hide the glassy gleam in his eyes. Had he been a wolf he would have licked his chops.

"They are pirates for sure," said Powell, pointing from amidships. "Look, they're turning nor'east to intercept."

Einar watched the other ship through his glass, still unsure if he would fight or flee. If they had stolen goods aboard, a profit could be made from that and the bounty from the prisoners once they were found guilty of piracy. The ship would bring partial claim and the crown would claim a stout percentage as well. It could be months before a settlement, but the crown would eventually pay a profitable sum for prisoner bounty and the ship, providing the ship was still seaworthy. The reverse was possible as well should the company wish to buy out the crown's claim and thus obtain a ship for a fraction of the market value. Then there is the time involved.

Einar could see crossbowmen in the tops of the other ship and men loading ballistae along her starboard side as the ships came closer together. She was ahead and to port of the *Bedford Lee*. The other ship began furling its topsails to slow for the intercept. "Now," shouted Einar, decision made that instant. "All sails full! Steer head on. Forward battery, aim for the sheets, fire when you have a shot." He had at that instant planned to slow them down and make a run for it.

The *Bedford Lee* leapt forward and turned smoothly, closing the distance rapidly with accelerating speed as if to ram. The other ship was taken by surprise, thinking they would slow to grapple, and now they were in a hurry to unfurl their sails and turn to port away from this aggressive predator that only a moment before had seemed easy prey. Before the pirate vessel could turn three points, the *Bedford Lee* let fly with shot, first from the catapult followed by a barbed bolt from the ballista. The hooked shaft stuck high in the sheet and tore a long rip as gravity pulled the weighted shaft toward the deck. The combined shots shredded the enemy's top and mainsail and the topmast splintered and was tipping over with men falling from the tops when the second shot rent several holes in the split main sail. The pirates returned ballista and crossbow fire from their broadside, two stones making holes in the *Bedford Lee*'s fore staysail and the foresail. Crossbow bolts struck wood, but not men.

"Hard ah starboard," shouted Einar. The *Bedford Lee* swung hard, now close enough for men on both ships to cast insults and fowl promises back and forth. "Give 'em the broadside," ordered the captain. The port battery fired shot from the ballistae and bolts from crossbows as they pulled away from the damaged pirate ship which was turning west to catch the wind full on their tail to make a hasty retreat. The *Bedford Lee* pulled away fast to the north.

"Good fight, men," Einar told his crew. "We'll let 'em go lick their wounds. We have a mission at hand and I doubt there would be much booty to gain if we gave chase. She was sittin' pretty high in the water."

Kahled, clearly disappointed, found a spot out of the way and sat cross legged facing the east. He closed his eyes and his moving lips uttered no sound as he prayed to his nameless god.

The enemy ship turned north after building speed and gave chase, but the *Bedford Lee* had all sails full and left the pirates far behind, soon to be lost on the horizon. They continued north. The damaged sails were replaced, once the horizon was empty of ships, and the old ones were repaired while underway.

CHAPTER 4

The two men sent to find Baker had come up empty handed. However, Coulig seized him at Lord Townsend's estate. The squad arrived to transfer payment, as agreed by Townsend and Akala, when they spotted Baker sitting by a fire drinking wine in a room just off the foyer. After greeting Townsend's steward Mels, and taking a small chest containing payment, Coulig went to Baker and said, "Lady Akala wishes to see you."

Baker looked first curious and then suspiciously asked, "What about?"

"I don't know," said Coulig. "I just know that Jax and Brin were sent to bring you to see her at once."

"Tell her I will come by later."

"I think you should come with us now."

"I'm off duty and I'll go when I please." Baker now had an edge to his voice.

"Take him," Coulig ordered his men.

Baker found himself with the points of five spears pointing down at him in his chair.

Mels spoke up at that point. "I will remind you Captain, that Baker is a guest of Lord Townsend and you are in his domain."

"Of course, you have my apologies, but our first loyalty is to the House Murdoch and Baker is in the employ of that House. We will go now and Baker will go with us."

"So be it," said Mels, wanting to avoid hassles. "Just go quickly before his lordship returns. He will be less than pleased when he hears of this and I may be in need of a job."

"I am sorry for any trouble this may bring you, but we have our orders."

They left without incident. Baker came peacefully and without restraints.

Able Seaman Baker sat at a table in a recreation room adjacent to a barracks on the Murdoch estate. Two men at arms stood behind him. Coulig sat at the head of the table to his right and Dorfin sat across from the seaman.

"Mister Baker," Dorfin began, "we know you have been in the employ of Lord Townsend while employed to us. There is no use denying you are his spy, especially since you were found at his estate shortly after you went ashore. We have more evidence as well. You are a chronic gambler, always broke and you are well paid on the Bedford Lee. What is it? Do you owe Townsend for gambling debts or are you just greedy?"

"My business is my own," said Baker. His red hair was damp with sweat and his freckles seemed to get redder. He scratched his scraggily beard and said, "I'll visit who I please when I please."

Coulig coughed the word, "Bullshit," drew his dagger and a stone and commenced to sharpen it. Each stroke was slow and deliberate. The implication was not lost on Baker. Coulig was a stout man of medium height, but an imposing figure because of his muscular girth. He kept his brown hair tied back and his close trimmed goatee sported several gray hairs. His scarred face was stern and brooked no nonsense even when he smiled.

"We want to know what information you brought to Townsend that made him charter a ship for immediate departure." Dorfin looked at the silent Baker. He did not care for the man. He smelled of sweat, stale wine, and a trace of urine. It was rare that he was not dirty and slovenly dressed. Most of all, Baker was disloyal. "You will tell us. I personally dislike torture, even though I find it useful. I would prefer not to go to that extreme, but we will do what we feel we must."

"There's no need for that," said Baker, losing his bravado. "I was at Lord Townsend's to visit one of his servant girls."

"Captain," Dorfin said to Coulig, "Have your men hold Baker's arm with his hand flat on the table."

Coulig nodded to his men and they complied. The struggling Baker looked alarmed, but still said nothing. Coulig grinned and said to him, "I hope you don't talk, at least for a while."

Dorfin's face was emotionless. "Captain Coulig, if Baker does not start talking in one minute, cut off his thumb and then each finger for every minute he stays silent." Dorfin said this as impassively as if he were ordering a fish dinner.

Coulig stood and stuck the point of his dagger into the table next to Baker's thumb, slowly pushed the blade against his knuckle, and stopped. Baker was clearly frightened now. "Stop, I'll talk, I'll talk, please don't, I'll talk," he cried. "I never thought any harm would come from just passing a little information now and then."

"Release him, and give him some water," said Dorfin, glad that his bluff had worked.

Coulig pulled his knife point from the table, sat down and resumed honing the edge. The guards let go of Baker and one of them scooped a cup of water from a barrel and set it on the table. Baker took a drink of water and began. "About two years ago a man passing through town lost his horse in a dice game. It was at one of Townsend's casino taverns, so the debt was to his lordship. He bartered information for the return of his horse and a gold piece."

"What has this to do with this morning's departure?" Coulig growled.

"I thought it best to start from the beginning. If I had just said that the artifact is no longer in Three Rivers, you would have asked, 'What artifact?' And then you would have told me to start from the beginning anyway."

"True," admitted Coulig grudgingly. "Okay, you're telling us that Townsend actually paid a piece of gold *and* a horse for information?" Coulig scowled at Baker. "What convinced him this information was so valuable or that he was speaking the truth?"

"The man had a book, a very old book. The pages were disintegrating, but there were colorful images like I have never seen before. The illustrations weren't just color drawings nor painted; they were as if the images were captured from a glass or a mirror and placed on paper. Even faded, the pictures were very realistic. The man claimed that there was knowledge of great science in this book. Townsend bought the book."

"Why did Townsend show you this book?" Dorfin asked.

"He didn't," replied Baker. "I got curious. I listened in on the conversation between the vagabond and Townsend. I had been collecting a few coins from his lordship for bringing him some news or other when the traveler was brought before him. That's how I knew about the book. Another time I was waiting for him in his study and did a little snooping. I picked the lock to his desk drawer. That's where he kept it. The book nearly fell apart in my hands, so I had to use extreme caution looking at it. I could barely make out some of the pages and the words I didn't understand but for one or two here and there. The language was foreign."

"Did this unlucky gambler have a name? Where did he get this book? And what does this have to do with Townsend's dealings in North Harbor?" Dorfin was beginning to wonder what they were getting into.

"You know my days here are done now. When Townsend hears of this I'll be put to the whip or worse. He isn't beyond murder you know. I will have to go far away." Baker was in a sad state. When his comments were answered with silence, Coulig resumed sliding his blade down the sharpening stone. Baker shook his head and continued. "The man's name was Harris or Harrison or something like that. I don't remember for sure. A black man he was; darker black than any man I have ever seen, medium build and height, a little to the tall side. He claimed he got the book in a trade with someone from far to the east across the great desert."

"It was shortly after this that Townsend sent for a historian. I was at sea then, so I don't know who he was or what was learned, but as soon as I came into port, Townsend sent for me. He told me about a device that he desired greatly. He said he learned of it in an ancient book and would pay dearly for this relic or for information on its whereabouts. He told me it may be thought to be a museum artifact or family heirloom. Months went by with very little turned up, at least on my part. Then about six or seven weeks ago he sent for me again. He told me that he had information on the item he sought."

"It was in the keeping of a man in Three Rivers, a city far to the north. Townsend hired some mercenaries to go and retrieve it. They were to send word to him of its acquisition, or any problems acquiring the device. Send word they did. The man in Three Rivers is named Amir. The device has been in his family for a long time. When Townsend's mercenaries went to him he told them it was not for sale. They insisted . . . firmly. He told them that he no longer had it, but would say no more. They searched his house and found nothing. They learned that he had family in Boarder City, so they were going there to find Amir's son, Imar. They were to go by barge on the Daishon River as far as Daishon Ferry. From there Boarder City would be a little over a day's ride by horse."

Coulig looked at Dorfin with concern. Dorfin, without the slightest change of expression, gave a slight shake of his head. "Go on," he told Baker.

"When I was in North Harbor on my last cruise, a little over two weeks ago, a messenger sought me out and told me this news. Imar is nowhere to be found. A Jarl named Bamsen learned of this device somehow and sent some of his men to search the roads between Three Rivers and Boarder City to find Imar. Failing that they were to take his family hostage. That is what I told Lord Townsend this morning when I arrived. He was quite distressed and sent for someone he referred to as his emissary, and then departed for the Murdoch estate."

"Tell us about this emissary," said Dorfin.

"Pure evil," Baker shuddered. "He only looked at me and I felt cold to the bone and my hairs stood on end. That man gives me the creeps. Khaled is his name." Baker made a sign to avert evil. "He comes from the desert, a member of an elite guild of assassins. Many of their order are religious fanatics to the nameless God and Khaled is as fanatical as they come. They have been known to kill whole communities and call it spiritual cleansing. They normally kill for money, half of which they give to their guild. They do other jobs as well; theft, extortion, torture, etc. I heard he arrived three days ago. He has no particular target that I know of other than the retrieval of the relic. I heard Townsend doesn't want him killing anyone unless it is absolutely necessary to get the device." Baker forced an irritating little grin. "The price goes way up if he kills and Townsend is rather close with his coin."

"What can you tell us of this device?" Dorfin asked. "What does it do? How does it work?"

"I know very little; only that it will fit in the hand, has eight sides, is smooth to the touch, and gray in color with a small hole in the center. There are images of it in the book. It is supposed to unlock a door to a vault containing knowledge, power, weapons, and wealth. I don't know how it works or what it does beyond that. I have told you all I know, I swear it."

"Okay," said Dorfin. "You can go."

"My life is worth spit once Townsend hears of this, at least here in Port Augustus. I didn't think I would cause any harm with a little extra work in the information business. Is there any chance I could still work for you in another port?"

Dorfin thought about this for a moment and said, "You are embedded as a spy for Lord Townsend. Let him think you still are. These men here are sworn to secrecy, so no one needs to know that you told us anything. If you want to redeem yourself, then work for us as a spy, a double agent so to speak. We will employ you here or send you out on another boat. You will continue to report to his lordship and pass information that we approve as well as some misinformation. And you will report to us all you know of his activities."

"Are you out of your mind? Townsend will have me flayed if he finds out."

"Then pray that he doesn't," said Coulig with a nasty grin. "If you don't do this work for us, we'll make sure he finds out how talkative you really are. Then you'll have to leave town for sure, maybe even the country."

"Alright, alright, I'll do it," said Baker unhappily, "but if I get the slightest hint that he knows about this, then I'm gone."

"Makes sense," said Coulig. "I could just cut your throat now and save you the worry and misery."

Baker blanched.

"Your first assignment is to steal the book," continued Dorfin calmly, ignoring the exchange.

Baker looked as if he would pass out, pee his pants, or both. "You really *are* trying to get me killed."

Dorfin continued, never changing his bland expression. "Bring it to me and me only at any time day or night. When I am finished with it, you will then return it with no one the wiser. That will be all for now." He paused in thought a moment, then added, "Except for one more thing. His Lordship will know we hauled you off for questioning. We must make it look like we punished you for some indiscretion aboard the *Bedford Lee*."

"Coulig," Dorfin said to the captain of the household guard, "have your men rough up Seaman Baker a bit. Please try not to overdo it. A few marks from a cat 'o nine tails would be a nice touch, but it is up to you as long as he can walk out of here when you are done."

Coulig looked as happy as a boy with a new puppy. "I would be delighted," he said.

Dorfin left the room, ignoring Baker's pleas for mercy.

CHAPTER 5

Dalla returned to her cottage mid-afternoon with Bart's nephew and two horses. Through the pounding in his head the wounded warrior heard them coming up the lane. He looked out the window and saw Dalla riding a brown and white paint. Next to her was a young man in his late teens riding a black and white paint and leading a buckskin packhorse laden with two full panniers. Imar decided it best to stay out of sight, so he sat down and kept his ears open. He could hear them talking out in the yard.

"Just tie the horses over there, if you would, please, James," said Dalla, dismounting and walking to the back of the cottage. "I'll be right back with your uncle's horses."

"Of course, Dalla," replied James, watching her walk away. "Take your time."

Dalla returned a few minutes later with the five horses that Imar had brought with him. She tied the lead horse to a tree next to a shed. Then, after going in the shed, she came out with two saddles. James followed suit and brought out the other three. They worked efficiently getting the saddles on the horses, James stealing a peek at Dalla as often as he could. They were almost finished when James said, "I hope you are not away a long time in Three Rivers, Dalla. You will be missed. At least I will miss you."

"That's very sweet of you, James," said Dalla.

"Bye Dalla," he said with a red face as he mounted the lead horse and rode off down the lane.

Dalla went inside the cottage. Looking directly at her guest she bluntly said, "Your name is Imar." Then she told him everything she had learned from Bart; about Sigurd and his heirloom, and about his family in Border City that they planned to take hostage. After she was finished she recounted what she had heard of him when he came through the village a week and a half ago. "You came to the inn apparently tired and hungry, like most travelers. You arrived in the evening, put your horse up at the stable and paid extra to have him brushed down and fed grain. You didn't give your name, but the hostler heard you call your horse Cerus. You went to the inn and rented a room for two nights. You took a hot bath, ate a big steak dinner, drank some ale and went to bed. It appeared that you weren't in a hurry, nor did you act as if you were being pursued. The next day you slept late, ate another large meal and bought supplies for the road. You spent most of your time resting and eating. The next morning you were up and on your way at dawn."

Imar sat there thinking over what Dalla had told him. His brows were knitted and he stared at a nail head on the floor sticking up just high enough to snag on one's foot stockings. He racked his brain for a recollection of any kind. He just stared at the nail head, thinking . . . thinking . . . thinking he should fetch a hammer and pound the nail back in. "Nothing comes to mind. I am still blank. At least I know my name and my horse's name, but there is no recognition for either."

Dalla had hoped that what she told him might jar a memory out of his head. "Maybe you are trying too hard. You look like you are in pain again. How are your headaches and appetite?"

"They both come and go. The headache came about an hour ago and chased away the appetite."

Dalla went to a cabinet, took out a bottle of laudanum, and poured out a dose in a very small tin cup that looked like an oversized thimble with indented lines of measurement on it. She handed him the medicine. "Here, take this. We have more to talk about."

Imar took the tin and tossed it down like he was doing shots in a tavern. "I figured as much, after seeing you arrive with new mounts and sending off the horses I took in battle." He looked down at the empty measuring cup and then back up at Dalla. "May I have another?"

"Well, I can't know what you are feeling and it affects everyone differently." Dalla took the tin and poured him half as much as last time and handed it back. "Be warned, opium is a good pain medicine, but it is also very addictive."

He tossed the second one down as quickly as the first. "You say I may have a wife and daughter, or that they may be my sister and niece, in a place called Boarder City, as well as family in another city called Three Rivers. There is also a lord that wants me or, more likely," Imar put his hand on his pocket and felt the object beneath and said "something I have in my possession." The movement did not go unnoticed. "And," he continued, "that there is another that is holding my family as ransom for my person or my property." He continued, "It is frustrating not to know who these people are, my family, who I am, whether or not I am married or single." At this he looked into Dalla's sapphire eyes and she into his brown puppy dog eyes. The gaze was only a few seconds. They were aware of their quickened pulses and the cottage seemed to get warmer. Each of them felt the mutual attraction and they were both aware that it could be forbidden.

They looked quickly away at the same time. Dalla got up and opened a little quick access door in the floor to her cold box and took out some cheese, bread, and a jar of pickles and began preparing a meal. Imar took some kindling from a box next to the hearth and began building a fire more for something to do than for any need for warmth. The opium was dulling his pain and making him talkative. He spoke while he worked. "I could go to Three Rivers and find out who my family is there. You said my father lives there and his name is Amir." He tried to remember, but the effort made his head hurt, so he relaxed and abandoned the effort. "My father could be in danger," he stressed, "but the family I have in Boarder City is in danger for sure, so that is where I go." Imar had a man's natural instinct to protect women and upon hearing of ladies in need his decision was made instantly.

"We go," said Dalla.

"It is too dangerous. I would like very much for you to go with me, but you have a life here and I would not want anything to happen to you."

"Nonsense, I'm going. My time here is finished, something I wish not to explain right now, so it is time for me to move on. Not only that; with your memory loss, you need a guide and a nurse. I travel the same direction as you and I need the protection of your sword on the road. The fates have brought us to the same path, so for now you are stuck with me."

"Oh dear," Dalla's expression changed as did the subject. "I forgot the pack horse. Would you please go out and unload the poor beast and put the gear in the shed."

"Of course," said Imar, feeling like he had been outmaneuvered. He lit the fire using a candle that was burning on the table and headed out the door after replacing it.

"Oh and while you are out there," Dalla added. "Would you give the horses some grain and slay us a chicken for dinner?"

"Sure. Is there anything else?"

"No, that ought to about do it. Thanks."

After dinner they discussed supplies and preparations. Dalla briefed him on the geography along their planned route. They went over his map and he asked her for details of river crossings, creeks, canyons and mountain passes. They talked for hours. He asked about politics and who ruled where, what, and how. He asked about the economics of this land and that land. Finally they were both too tired to continue any longer.

Dalla checked his wound and was pleased with the way it looked. She decided to leave the dressing off for the night, so it could get some air. Imar insisted that he would sleep on the floor and Dalla would have her bed back. She argued of course, the healer wanting comfort for her patient, but Imar wouldn't hear of it. He went to the corner, grabbed some blankets and made a bed on the floor next to her bunk. He then banked the fire with a couple of rounds for the night, and went to bed. His head no sooner hit the pillow then he was fast asleep.

Dalla sat there for a little while after blowing out all but one candle. It was time for her to go again. The village people were suspicious. Some were already whispering that she was a witch or a sorceress. Soon enough religious fanatics would be shouting it while bearing torches and throwing stones. The local priest was just the type of rabble rouser to lead such a mob. Most of their gods were of nature and harmless enough, but some of their idols were depicted in the armored trappings of war and held wicked weapons. It was just a matter of time before this rural ignorance became serious and that time was near. She would avoid trouble and leave so that no one would get hurt.

She looked down at the man sleeping on her floor. *A gentleman for sure*, she thought. *Most men would have told me that 'slaying chickens was a woman's work' and damn few would have taken the floor when a bed lay open.* Some would even have insisted she join them, although they would soon learn to regret it. Dalla, though nonviolent, was not without her defenses. Her mind ran through memories of long ago. Then she thought of the current circumstances, and considered the impending journey with both anticipation and trepidation. The key was strong in those thoughts of past and present, and she doubted Imar knew what he had. He needed rest, but there was no time to take for it. A head injury such as his was a serious thing and would bear watching. The key could change this world, possibly destroy it. Dalla finally stopped thinking so hard on weighty matters, and meditated to slow her racing mind. Within a few minutes she went to bed and slept an uneasy sleep.

The sun dawned on another beautiful spring morning, but colder with a touch of frost. After a breakfast of fresh chicken eggs and toasted bread, the day was spent preparing for the long journey. Dalla went into the village to give away a few things that they would not be able to take with them and to promote the false tale that she would be traveling northwest to Three Rivers to visit family. She had also made arrangements for someone to come get her remaining chickens after she left. When she returned to the cottage Imar was organizing his gear. They killed and cooked two chickens for the trip, baked two loaves of bread, and added this to the cheese, wine, and coffee Dalla had traded for the day before. They had three riding horses and one pack horse. The extra riding horse would share the burden of carrying some of the gear unless the need for another riding horse became necessary.

They were up before the sun the following morning. Imar wore black suede knee high boots with cross-tied laces worn outside his brown double knee leather pants. He had on a black long sleeve shirt of cotton under a tunic of forest green with a vest of stiff dark brown boiled leather with steel rings fastened to it for armor. The rings were sewn on in such a way as not to jingle. Imar saddled and loaded the horses while Dalla dressed and prepared a hearty breakfast. Being practical, she put on tight fitting black leather pants and a sleeveless dark blue tunic over a light blue long sleeve top. When Imar came in for breakfast he had trouble keeping his eyes off of her. She smiled at him as she served him his plate of eggs, ham and potatoes. The smile made his heart pound. He concentrated on his food.

As soon as breakfast was finished, the sun rose and they boarded up the windows and door and laid boards with spikes sticking up around the cottage to discourage bears from being bears. Grizzly and black bears alike were known for breaking into unoccupied houses for a free meal and some mindless maliciousness, and thus wreaking havoc and causing much damage. Once in a while, though rarely, a bear would tear its way into an inhabited dwelling. Most people kept a spear handy, but Dalla had a way with animals and kept no weapons other than the knives she used in her kitchen. After the cottage was secured, she took a bag of bread crumbs and filled the bird feeders around the yard for her birds. Before she had finished, several gray jays and a few chickadees and red poles swooped down to be first in line for the treat. "I will miss you my friends, please don't follow me today." After throwing some scratch out into the chicken pen, she took a last look at what had been her home for the past ten years and then mounted the brown paint she called Bell.

"Let's go," she said. They departed down the lane to the road.

When they got to the main road, Imar turned left to go southeast toward Boarder City and Dalla went to the right with the other two horses. They had planned this to reinforce her story of traveling to Three Rivers. Even though it was early, there was a good chance she would be seen leaving the village, so if questioned they could report that she departed alone to the northwest. Her friends advised her of the danger of a lone woman on the road, but they also knew she had an uncanny knack for avoiding trouble. She went past the inn and stable and saw no one, but when she went past the blacksmith's shop she saw that Harry the smith was building up the fire in his forge. She waved to him when he looked up. "Take care, Harry, and say good bye to Gina."

"Be careful Dalla, and fare you well," replied Harry.

Dalla left the village behind and continued for a half an hour before she came to a creek. She turned south up the creek and kept the horses in the water so as not to leave a trail. After about a half mile she turned east. The woods were thick and she had to dismount. The way was difficult and slow going, but she soon came to a firewood trail that looped around behind the village. Before long, Imar appeared ahead, riding up to meet her. He had done the same thing, only from the other side of the community, using caution to hide his tracks. They followed Imar's route back to the main road.

It was a cool morning and clouds were gathering. "You can smell the moisture in the air," said Imar, "my shoulder is a bit stiff as well."

"It will rain before the day is over I'm afraid," replied Dalla. "I am not fond of camping, I must admit. I can rough it with the best of them, but I prefer comfort if I can get it. That's why I secured us a tent."

"After my miserable journey in the rain, I could kiss you for that tent." Once he said it, the thought of kissing Dalla came to his mind. It was a pleasant thought, but he tried to suppress it. He could be married, even though he didn't know for sure. Imar was attracted to Dalla. He hoped the lady he was going to rescue was his sister, or if she was his wife, perhaps his memory would return soon and overpower his enchantment for the healer. Dalla was having similar thoughts. It had been a long time since she felt this way about a man. She too suppressed those thoughts, or at least tried to, but the memory of washing his naked body kept coming back to her mind like a repetitious song. They thrived on each other's company, yet felt awkward at not being able to express themselves as is natural between man and woman.

The day wore on and they stopped for a short break early in the afternoon to rest the horses and have a lunch of cheese and bread. It had started to rain. It was a light rain, but enough that they prudently donned oil cloth cloaks. The road began to gently climb in elevation and though it was raining, the air was pleasantly mild. At one point they encountered a cow moose with a young calf crossing the road. The woods were beginning to become slightly less dense, with areas of sparsely wooded taiga and small lakes and ponds. They rode on till dark, which at this time of year at these latitudes, was quite late. They ate cold chicken and set up camp out of sight from the road and slept in comfort on caribou hides in the tent.

The nights never got truly dark at this time of year, only dim. Whenever Dalla peeked at Imar from her woolen blankets she would find him looking at her. Once in the night she woke to find them holding hands. She gazed at his sleeping form, watching the rhythm of his breathing and wanting to wake him with caresses of affection. She went back to sleep without releasing his hand.

They got up early the next morning and built a small fire for coffee. It was foggy and damp and neither of them felt like eating, so they loaded and saddled the horses and moved on. They carried extra coffee with them in a ceramic jug insulated with wool cloth. As the morning grew older and the fog burned off, the day began to warm. They shed their cloaks and ate cheese and bread while they rode. They saw numerous hawks and at one point a large set of bear tracks. Luckily the tracks didn't have feet in them.

Imar's headaches became infrequent and less intense. Enjoying themselves immensely, they talked from time to time. Dalla did most of the talking, since Imar had no memories to draw from. He did have some philosophical views, and these he shared. He wondered if he had had these same views before his memory loss. Most of the time, they seemed to forget about the seriousness of the mission. Their attraction for each other grew. Under different circumstances, it would have been a romantic journey, but in a way, even though they were properly distant, it still was. Imar looked at Dalla often when they rode close and imagined pulling her off her horse into his embrace. At times he could almost taste her lips before shaking himself from his imagination. His thoughts, and more so, his restraint threatened to drive him mad.

The rain had let up, but the mosquitoes had come out in full force. While riding, Dalla retrieved one of her medical kits from a saddle bag and took out a bottle containing oil of citronella. She applied the repellant to all of her exposed skin and then handed the bottle to Imar, who reined in.

"We should put some of this on the horses," he said while applying the lotion to his face, neck and the backs of his hands. He dismounted and rubbed a little oil on Cerus's muzzle as well as a bit around his ears. Imar then went to each of the other horses and did the same. He climbed back into his saddle and they rode on, but even though the bugs weren't biting, they were flying into their eyes and buzzing in their ears. What had been just an annoyance became a black cloud of buzzing misery.

"These mosquitoes are driving me insane," Dalla shrieked at the pests, waving her hands in front of her face and swatting at her ears. She had another method of dealing with pests, but she did not want to expose Imar to too much of her talent too soon.

Imar handed the reins of the pack horses over to Dalla. "Here, take the horses and kick 'em into a trot, I'll catch up."

Dalla took the reins and kicked them not into a trot, but a full gallop. Imar steered Cerus over to a willow bush and cut two leaf laden wands, then rode to catch up with Dalla. Once he caught up he slowed them down to a trot, took the reins back and handed her a wand. At a trot the bugs were less intense, but still bothersome. The leafy wands worked well to fan in front of the face and around the head, which helped with keeping some semblance of sanity.

After an hour of this it became quite warm and muggy. Between the heat and humidity and battling mosquitoes, it was not turning out to be a pleasant day. Dalla was beginning to question her decision to go on this journey, but she also knew that if the key came into the wrong hands the world would become far more miserable than her discomfort on the road. Another two hours of anguish had passed when out of the east blew a cool and refreshing breeze. It was a relief that instantly soothed the body and the mind. The wind took away not only the mosquitoes, but some of the clouds as well. Sunshine broke through, albeit intermittently, lifting their spirits and seemingly the horses' moods as well.

They paced themselves for Imar's sake. He no longer wore a bandage, Dalla deeming the injury healed enough not to need it anymore. He grew stronger with each day. He still had headaches, but they became bearable and he used the pain elixir less often.

They traveled without encountering anyone for three days. On the morning of the fourth day they passed the spot where Imar had turned off the trail and fought with Bamsen's men. It was, for now, where Imar's life began. Shortly after that they met a trader traveling to Three Rivers with his two sons. He and his younger son of middle teens rode in a loaded wagon and the other well-armed son of late teens rode point on a white mare. Traders such as these carried supplies to many villages that were not on the river system.

Dalla had seen this family before in her village of Mentin. They had come from Boarder City. They spoke briefly, sharing road conditions mostly. Both parties were glad to hear that there had not been any recent raids from Kandia and neither had reported any rumor of highway robbers. Daishon Ferry was operating, but there didn't seem to be much of the community about. Many of the winter trappers were probably out mining now that the creeks were open and most of the ice melted off. The teamster still thought it strange that the ferryman and innkeepers were the only ones he saw, and they were unusually tense and quiet. Imar and Dalla did not say anything of themselves other than that they were going to Boarder City. The teamster seemed relaxed as this man and woman did not seem a threat. The boys glanced often at Dalla and no one could blame them, but Imar knew that trouble could come if they encountered any dishonorable men on the road.

Imar noticed that they were wearing what appeared to be scarves made out of cheese cloth, only of finer mesh. "I can't help but notice your scarves. I have not seen anything like it."

"Nor have I," added Dalla. "Does it cool you in the heat?"

The teamster smiled and, reaching back, pulled the garment up and over his head and face, tucking the edge in his collar. "It is a hood made from mosquito net. They have been selling like worms at a fishing derby. It works great to keep out the bugs. Breathable and see-through, I have them in white, like these, black, blue, and forest green."

"We'll take two," said Dalla and Imar at the same time. They looked at each other and started laughing. The other three travelers joined in as well.

The young man sitting on the horse spoke up after chuckling. "You must have encountered a nasty patch of the little demons. These hoods are truly the greatest invention of all time. I go nowhere without one. I hate mosquitoes more than anything. They work well with gnats too."

"I think we will take four instead," said Imar, "one blue, the rest black. How much do I owe you?"

The trader took out four hoods from a box behind him under a tarp. "That will be one silver and eight coppers."

"How about I give you two silvers and you throw in two extra hoods in black," bargained Imar.

"Done," said the trader.

After making the transaction they said their farewells and went their separate ways. As soon as they started their horses into a walk, Imar handed the blue mosquito scarf to Dalla. "This one will look good with your blue tunic." He put a black one around his neck and put the rest into a saddle bag as he rode.

Dalla thanked him and put on her scarf, opting to leave it on her neck, since the bugs weren't bad just then. The road began to wind up into some hills that jutted out from the rugged Abezda Range, always to their right. When they started out, the foothills of these mountains were only a few miles away. Now, with the exception of the finger ridge they were ascending, the base of that massive range was about twenty kilometers away. When they reached the top of the sparsely wooded ridge they looked down at the Daishon River and the ferry that their road led to. An inn sat next to the ferry landing. Spread out in the vicinity there were a dozen or so cabins as well as a few other buildings for workshops and storage. They started their descent as it was nearing sunset, both of them looking forward to a hot meal, bath, and a bed. Dalla reined in. "Wait," she said with a distant look on her face.

Imar stopped and looked at her. "What is it?"

Dalla didn't move and barely even breathed for a minute before answering. "Something is not right. Remember what the teamster said? There was no activity, no people outside. I sense several people and danger as well. We must be cautious."

Imar handed the reins to the pack horses over to Dalla. He reached behind him for his chain mail and pulled it on over his head, then strung his bow. His long sword was hung on his saddle, the short sword on his hip. He loosened both in their sheaths then hung his quiver of arrows in front of him. He then handed his shield to Dalla, put on his helmet, nocked an arrow and led the way down to Daishon Ferry.

CHAPTER 6

The pleasantly warm afternoon so common to Port Augustus summers was accented with a few clouds which drifted lazily across the sky on a light wind out of the west. The Murdoch estate covered a hilltop which allowed a view of the mountains to the east, the ocean to the west, the bay and city to the south and the lush forested hills to the north. The Lord Travin and Lady Akala Murdoch chose the location for the view as well as the tactical advantage of high ground. Travin and Akala hired free men and used no slaves or indentured bondsmen to build their estate; however, Akala was in charge of design. Architects reported to her and her alone. In the beginning they would come to Travin, if he was not at sea, but he would have none of it and would send them to see his wife. It was on the south terrace where Akala was tending her garden that Dorfin filled her in on Baker's story.

"I wish Travin were here," Akala said softly. She was trimming yellowed leaves from various flowers and vegetable plants. Her garden was a place of reprieve where she could think, meditate, and relieve stress. She refused assistance from servants, but enjoyed Travin's help when he was home to help her. He had taken a ship to the south several months ago to secure produce to supply the winter market. No word of him had come despite the many inquiries she sent out with nearly every merchant marine she knew. She was contemplating another dedicated search, and this time leading the crew herself. Now her daughter and granddaughter had probably been taken captive for some item possessed by her son-in-law.

Dorfin sat in a lounge chair enjoying the sun. "You might want to prepare yourself for the possibility that Lord Travin and his crew may have perished."

"No," Akala paused, contemplating his words. "I think I would feel it if he were dead. I think something has happened to him though, and I feel the need to take action. I really didn't need this other crisis to complicate things. After the matters at hand are dealt with, I would like you to take me up to the hills to inspect our project. I may have to use it to aid my husband. But for now I need to focus on Anisha, Imar and little Aideen."

"That is true. Travin is on his own for now, if he is still alive, and it will be difficult finding him. He did say it would be a long trip and winter sea travel can be quite challenging. I think we should address the current situation first. Of that at least, we have some information. Imar is a capable man, but this assassin concerns me."

"I could kick myself for letting Townsend manipulate me. And he puts my family in danger with his schemes," Akala said vehemently. She took a breath, let it out slowly, and then continued in a more self-rebuking tone, "I saw a profit at his loss and swooped on it just to get even for past indiscretions." Her ire returned with vengeance. "If anything happens to them I will cut his eyes out." The rollercoaster her temper rode coasted now on level rails. "I am not sure what we should do. Travin would know, but he is not here. We haven't a ship for pursuit and if we send riders to Seal Bay, the *Bedford Lee* would be long gone by the time they got there." Her anger returned to its former fury and she said, in a low growl of determined vengeance, "Upon the spirits of my ancestors I swear, Townsend will pay for sending an assassin after one of my family."

"We could step up the work on the *Coastal Raider* currently in dry dock," said Dorfin, "but if we wait for Baker to bring us more information, we can at least be armed with knowledge. Imar is one of the best weapons masters I have ever seen and, I hear, a good tactician in charge of a company of loyal men. He is our best hope."

Imar had served the Murdochs as Captain of their Free Companies as well as weapons master in charge of training their men-at-arms and archers for many years. Before that he had sailed with Travin and Akala in their adventuring days before they came to Port Augustus with their purchased titles of nobility. Technically he was a lord too, but he preferred not to use the title his acquired wealth had brought him.

He had returned to his childhood home a few years ago when his father was injured and needed his aid repelling Kandian raiders on the border of Abezda. Imar took his wife Anisha and daughter Aideen with him to the frontier. Anisha had not wanted to go. She had grown accustomed to the rich living of the aristocracy and enjoyed the city life, but Imar had a call of duty to answer and Akala reminded her daughter of a wife's duty to her husband.

"You are right, Dorfin. Imar is a good man, intelligent, and very good at what he does. He always had an uncanny insight that saved our lives more than once. Anisha and Aideen will be alright if he can get to them without mishap. I only wish we could warn him somehow. A wizard would be nice if we could find a real one. The city is full of charlatans. I wish I knew where to find Ivan. He is the only real wizard I ever met and that was a long time ago."

"I heard he was on the Island of Renauld, but that could be rumor."

Akala tossed the yellow leaves along with a few weeds into a compost barrel then began seeding a freshly tilled bed with radishes. They were both quiet for a few minutes while Akala worked the seeds into neat rows. Then she stopped, stood and looked at Dorfin. "No, we have to help them if we can. Anisha and I may not see eye to eye, but she is my daughter and little Aideen is at risk as well. We are a long way away with less than reliable information. We need to send some men we can trust to free my daughter and granddaughter if Imar hasn't done so by the time they get there."

"We can certainly spare them," said Dorfin. "We haven't had any contracts for our soldiers yet this year, but if anything came up, it would probably be up north in Sedar on the Kandian border. Our reputation for having some of the best fighting men has spread far.

Even the King has been talking about hiring a company of our military advisors, but he hasn't coughed up any money yet."

"Good," said Akala. "Let's double the crews doing the refit on the *Coastal Raider* and get her in the water. Find her captain." She scrunched her brows and suppressed a wicked little grin, and then added, "Captain Beros will probably need sobering up. Tell him he can have any modifications he wants for speed and weapons. That way we can have a ship ready to go. Have Coulig assemble a platoon of marines to go with the ship. Send someone, by fishing boat if you have to, over to Renauld Island to find Ivan. When and if Baker comes through, I want to see this book."

"I will make the arrangements." Dorfin stood up, smoothed back his hair and turned to go, but stopped when Akala spoke again.

"I'm tempted to go," she said. "I am just getting too old for these adventures, and the last thing I need is to go charging off to another Anisha crisis, which seem to draw to her like lightening to a metal rod. She is my blood, but she would probably rather I send gold than come myself. No, Dorfin, my husband needs me and I must find him. Imar and Anisha need men with swords. After this business is set on course, we need to search for Travin."

Akala resumed her gardening. Dorfin knew she had a lot on her mind and figured she would probably spend the rest of the day puttering in her garden. He left her and went to find Coulig.

All of their men-at-arms were also skilled bowmen. That was something Imar had insisted on as weapons master. Every soldier had to shoot each day for one hour. Coulig spent more time than anyone else on the archery range, so that was where Dorfin went to find him. He was not disappointed.

Coulig greeted Dorfin when he approached after letting fly with a shaft from his longbow. "Care to wager a few shots Dorfin? I am feeling a bit tired today, you may have a chance to beat me."

"No one could beat you even if you were blind drunk. Nice grouping by the way." Dorfin noticed that three arrows were stuck in the same hole and two of them had damaged fletching.

"Thanks," said Coulig. "What's up?"

"I need you to find Beros."

"He's drunk somewhere or sleeping it off. That, I would bet on."

Dorfin told Coulig of Akala's orders and the plan to send men to Abezda. "Beros is a good seaman and a worthy captain. We need to find him and get his ship afloat as soon as possible."

"I'll get right on it," said Coulig.

Dorfin then went to see the harbor master and made arrangements for the refit of the *Coastal Raider*. By the time he got back to the mansion it was dark. He met with a lady friend that owned a bakery, and they enjoyed an agreeable meal together. After a relaxing repast he retired early. He was in a deep sleep when he was wakened by a servant shortly after midnight. She told Dorfin that a smelly seaman by the name of Baker insisted on seeing him at once. The maid was less than pleased with the interruption, and just wanted to go back to bed. The steward dismissed her, and went to receive the informant.

Dorfin found Baker at the front door. He reflected that the girl's assessment of the sailor's odor was accurate. The maid had refused to let him in. Dorfin nodded to a watchful sentry standing in the shadows and then led Baker to the study. He sent for Akala. She came to the study a few minutes later looking alert, but tired. Baker had the book. He removed it from a cloth bag and placed it carefully on the table. "Townsend was furious that you had interrogated me, but he seemed to believe me when I told him that I had said nothing." Baker had a black eye and a swollen lip. "The bruises convinced him, but Coulig didn't have to be so thorough."

Dorfin ignored Baker's whining and examined the book. It was large, thick, and had a hard cover of dark blue with circular, unreadable markings. Dorfin carefully opened it to the first page.

"That's my book," said a voice from a dark corner.

Dorfin, Akala, and Baker all nearly bounced out of their bodies. Baker jumped so high he could have latched on to the ceiling. Akala turned toward the voice with eyes wide and heart pounding, a dagger in her hand. No one saw her draw it. Dorfin recovered first and calmly asked, "Who are you?"

"My name is Ivan," said the stranger, stepping into the light. "I heard you were looking for me."

CHAPTER 7

Coulig took Jax and Brin with him to look for Beros. They went at night thinking the young sea captain would be easier to find. He loved beer, music and women, and not necessarily in that order. When in port he would often sleep all day and party all night. He had many girlfriends and was always on the lookout for more. The ladies were attracted to his long curly red hair and his charismatic zest for life despite the black leather patch he wore over his left eye. He often rented a room near the waterfront taverns so that his female conquests would not know where he lived. Beros always seemed to have lots of friends when he had money and was buying rounds at the bar. He had just as many enemies; primarily the husbands of women he had dallied with. Beros enjoyed a good fist fight and never pulled a blade unless someone else drew steel on him first.

Port Augustus had more than fifty establishments selling alcohol. There were brothels, but the port had a number of freelance prostitutes working the streets and taverns as well. Beros rarely hired professionals for his needs, so Coulig, Jax, and Brin concentrated the search on places that had music. They avoided the upper class places frequented by the aristocrats and started with the seedier places of evening entertainment.

The night was wearing on past midnight and they were beginning to wonder if they would find the wayward captain. They had looked through a dozen places without luck. The formidable trio strode the streets without hassle, making inquiries as they went. Edged weapons were discouraged in the drinking establishments and were required to be checked at the door or, in the smaller places, at the bar. Most people kept a knife concealed, because it was, after all, a rough town, especially at night. Coulig, Jax, and Brin carried wide, forward curving blades in shoulder holsters under their tunics as well as short batons made of hard wood. They appeared unarmed, but being dangerous looking fighting men, no one gave them trouble except for the occasional drug peddler offering herb or opium. Prostitutes offered their wares as well, but the men were on a mission and ignored all dealers and whores.

They were walking down a hill on a boardwalk that led to the docks when they heard music. It was a slow melody played by a band that knew their business. All of the other places they had been to were noisy with raucous crowds overpowering the music. This place was quiet, but for the sweet soothing notes being played. Jax was fond of music and was known to play the strings from time to time. He looked up at the sign in front of the door that was hanging over the walkway. "The sign of the Blue Crab, I will remember this place. Let's go in."

Just as they walked in, a young lady in a white gown with tawny hair and golden skin began to sing. She stood in front of the musicians and every eye was on her and every mouth was shut. Her voice was like cool spring water to a parched soul. Her accompaniment was a clarinet, guitar, violin and a percussionist. The drummer was at rest and the young lady sang of two people falling in love and the joy of raising a child. Then the song changed and the drummer began a steady beat to words that bore the threat of war and the man going off to do battle to protect his family. The music built up with cymbals adding to the force of the music and song. Jax felt his blood coursing through his veins and he was ready to run home and grab his sword. The crowd was getting pumped with adrenalin as the angelic singer sang of heroes and the clash of weapons on shields until the battle met its peak with the crescendo of the music. The battle slowed and died down with the music and the crowd followed. The percussionist quietly played on only one drum now with the strings winding down to the slow melody and the clarinet amplifying the grief of the moment as they played with sorrow. The young vocalist sang of the hero who was both husband and father, being carried home on his shield. Some in the audience were openly weeping while some of the men tried to hide their tears pretending to have gotten something in their eye. The hero was delivered to his family and his sword was given to his son, a son too young to lift a blade or even know what it is for or why. The lady sang quietly, her voice trailing off as the song ended. The clarinet and strings stopped playing one by one till only the violin played the last dwindling note drawn on till barely audible, then silence pervaded the room.

Seconds passed and not a soul moved and then all at once the crowd burst into applause and deafening cheers. Jax, the hairs on his body stood on end throughout the entire performance, wiped the moisture from an eye and clapped like he had never clapped before. The vocalist and the band bowed and took their leave of the stage as the audience yelled for more. Jax was cheering above the others. He had to speak to the angel with the voice from the heavens. He started to push through the crowd to find her, his mission forgotten, when a hand on his shoulder stopped him.

Coulig was attached to that hand. His other hand was pointing to the back of the room next to the horseshoe shaped bar. There was Beros, back against the wall, an arm around the shoulders of a scantily clad girl of middle teens with a tankard in the other hand. Three men faced him with clubs. Coulig, Jax and Brin approached them and they heard Beros say with slurred speech, "I assure you, sir, she told me she was seventeen."

The three men were the girl's father and two brothers. They were not happy with her recent behavior. Ever since she was twelve she had had a tendency to be too friendly with the boys and now at fifteen she was downright promiscuous. They'd had a tough time keeping up with her; running off, lying about where she was going or who she was going to see. Local custom considered youth to have the right to choose at seventeen since this was the age when all males were expected to serve at least two years of military duty. However, whenever there was a need for a draft, that age was lowered to sixteen. That is why Kalusian law allows youth their freedom to leave home at sixteen.

The girl's father was tired of the constant disruption his daughter was causing in their lives, and now he was looking at someone his own size that he could vent his frustration on. "You say that with your arm still around my daughter."

"Oh Daddy, I'm going to be sixteen in a few months." The girl wasn't pressed quite as close to Beros as she had been when her father and brothers had showed up.

Beros then looked beyond the men and squinted, trying to focus. He recognized his friends and burst into a smile. "Hey guys," he yelled over the din of the crowd, "I didn't exshpect to shee you here. Let me buy us sall a round." He then turned to the father and said with his arm still around the girl, "You too, what'll you guys have? It'ss on me."

The three men all turned before Beros finished his words and brought their cudgels up. Coulig, Jax and Brin, now shoulder to shoulder, spread out as Coulig called out, "Batons." The trio moved with military precision as each stepped back with the right foot while reaching under their tunics with left hands and drawing out sticks a cubit in length. They displayed no fancy spins, just held them forward at an angle to the right with the right hand balled into a tight fist and cocked ready near the chin and close to their hidden blades.

The father, standing center between his sons, turned his head without taking his eyes off of Coulig and said to his daughter, "No more lip girl. See the trouble you've caused, again." He said this firmly with enough volume to give power of command to his voice. "You will extract yourself from that man and go wait for us by the door." When he didn't hear her move, he sharply barked, "Now!"

Beros was draining his tankard during this exchange and set it down on the bar as the girl was making to go. "Wait," he slurred. "How's za 'bout a little kissh before you go?"

That was more than her father could bear. He turned around and let fly with a right hook that landed squarely upside the head of the smiling Beros. Beros smacked against the wall and then crumpled like a sack of rocks.

The girl shrieked at her father, "I hate you!" She ran off and out the door. The father turned back to Coulig, his cudgel again at the ready.

The spectacle had drawn the attention of three quarters of the patrons. A few bouncers arrived at the scene, but they prudently held back. A little action was good for business with the Blue Crab's clientele as long as it didn't get too bloody. Coulig admired the way the girl's father handled the situation. He pitied the man as well. His brother was going through the same thing. He silently vowed, if he ever married, that he would insist his wife bear only boys.

The father said, "I came only for my daughter and if that man is your friend, his scruples could get him killed one day."

"You are right," answered Coulig. "He is indeed our friend and, in my opinion, had more coming than just a smack upside the head." He then holstered his baton and when the father lowered his stick Coulig motioned his men to do the same. The brothers relaxed their guard as well. The crowd was disappointed that there was no fight so they went back to their libations. One bouncer stayed nearby to be sure things remained peaceful while the others went to their regular positions. "Now if you will excuse us, we will see to our friend."

The father said to his sons, "Let's find your sister and go home." With that they departed in search of the little misfit.

Brin squatted down and tried unsuccessfully to revive the comatose Beros. "He's out cold. We'll have to carry him."

"Bring him," said Coulig. "We'll hire the first wagon that will take our coin."

Brin sat Beros up and from behind slipped his arms under his and locked his hands on his chest while Jax took the legs facing away. Together they lifted him and carried him out the door feet first with Coulig following close behind.

CHAPTER 8

They all stared at the tall, black cloaked stranger. He had bushy salt and pepper hair and beard with the salt warring for dominance over the pepper. He was not exactly tall, but he seemed to stand taller in their presence. He wore a wide brimmed black hat, a black oil cloth coat, and black leather lace up boots. He stepped up to the table, removed his hat and looked at Akala with eyes so dark they were nearly black. "Akala, last time I saw you, your hair was light brown, almost blonde. And you were thinner and perky."

Akala lifted an eyebrow and put her dagger away. "I was younger then. You have not changed one bit, neither in looks nor in dramatic entrances. You're just as blunt as I remembered as well." To Dorfin and Baker she said, "Gentlemen, this is Ivan." Then without finishing introductions, something dawned on her. She turned back to Ivan and asked, "How could you possibly know we were looking for you?"

"It has been a long time," replied Ivan, evading the question. "It is good to see you again. I sensed your need a month ago and . . ." he paused. "I heard the key has been discovered and figured I had better get back to work. I set out immediately and just now arrived. I was tempted to visit the king, but like all kings, he is a moron. We may have to involve him and other monarchs before this is over, but let us try our best to avoid any government for now. They tend to be greedy idiots and only mess up anything they touch. Now if you would be so kind as to introduce me." Ivan looked directly at Dorfin.

Akala had been trying to do just that, but could not get a word in with Ivan's long winded oratory. Not to let a pause stand open, she proceeded with introductions before the wizard started off on another extended spiel. "This is my steward Dorfin." Akala gestured toward her right hand man.

"Dorfin son of Alfin," greeted Ivan. "It is a pleasure to meet a fellow student of higher education. Studious achievement is rarely seen in the highborn."

Dorfin did not flinch or bat an eye. "The pleasure and the honor are mine," he said with a bow.

Akala and Baker watched in stunned silence. Akala knew little of Dorfin's past. Her years as a privateer taught her a certain etiquette of not asking of a person's history, instead letting people share what they wished. The comment, 'highborn,' Akala stowed away in the back of her mind. After a few long seconds, she turned to Baker and said, "This is . . ."

"Baker," interrupted the wizard with an inflection of contempt, "I know, I know, the traitorous, double agent, seaman and backstabbing thief. Not to mention foul smelling scoundrel in need of a bath."

Baker stopped short of a bow, slumped his shoulders at the insult and then self-consciously sniffed an armpit and began making excuses. "I beg your pardon sirs and lady; I've been busy of late and have had little time for a bath. I will wash up just as soon as I return this book to his lordship."

Ivan never took his eyes off Baker. "The book is mine. Why should I let you take it?"

"Lord Townsend will have me flayed should he find it gone," whined Baker.

"Why should I care?" replied the wizard.

Dorfin spoke up at this point. "He could be useful."

"My, aren't we optimistic?" Ivan was enjoying himself at Baker's discomfort. "You know it is difficult for a spy to sneak around when his stench can be detected a league away." The wizard wrinkled his nose. "Oh I know. I was just having a little fun. I can steal it back later anytime I want. If you wish, I will do it when this scoundrel is out of town."

"You said 'key' a moment ago. Were you referring to the artifact that is causing my family such grief?" Akala had had enough bantering and wanted answers.

"One moment please, my dear," said the wizard. He turned and looked Baker in the eyes and locked his gaze. He then made a pass with his left hand, fingers splayed, in front of Baker's face in a downward motion and quietly spoke, "Sleep."

The seaman's eyes drooped and his legs turned to rubber as he crumpled on the floor. His soft snores attested that he was safely asleep.. Ivan then turned and went to the book. "Now we can begin. This book once belonged to the leader of a great and very powerful nation." He then opened it and gently flipped several pages till he recognized the page he was looking for. "There, that is the key, artifact, device or whatever you want to call it."

Dorfin and Akala leaned over, one on each side of Ivan, and looked down at the color picture of a gray, eight sided object. There were words printed on the page, but Akala couldn't understand them, apart from an occasional word or two. Dorfin was able to read more of it with some understanding and was showing an intense interest such as Akala had never seen him openly display. Ivan turned the page carefully. On the next page were pictures that showed the key in a wall slot next to a large door. The slot had a panel next to it with twelve squares, three columns of four rows, each no bigger than a fingertip. Above the slot were two small lights, one red and the other green. "That is called a key pad," said the wizard. "It works like a combination lock, but it is worthless without the key."

"It seems to me that you have a lot more to tell us," said Akala. "If this is your book, you can probably tell us what we need to know. Asleep or not, I would prefer not to discuss this further in the presence of Baker. I think we should send him on his way and, for now, let him return the book, so as not to cause suspicion in our new spy."

"I agree," said Dorfin.

"Well said," replied Ivan. He went to the sleeping Baker, leaned over him and spoke softly. "Listen carefully, Baker. When you wake you will return this book to Townsend and then immediately seek out a bath and scrub yourself clean." He waved his hand in an upward diagonal motion and said, "Wake." He then reached down and tweaked the seaman's ear, which was answered with a shriek of pain. "Time to be on your way, your smelliness," he said. "Now get your butt up and out of here."

Baker got up and yawned with a stretch, went to the book and put it in the cloth bag he had brought it in. He looked dazed and confused with sleep inertia. He gazed about the room with glassy eyed bewilderment. He checked the bag again to be sure he had the right book then said his farewells and departed.

As soon as Baker walked out the door Ivan said, "Good riddance." He then turned to Akala and said, "Shall we sit in some comfort and refreshment while I share the history of this relic?" Ivan removed his coat and hung it on a peg by the door then took the most comfortable looking chair and began unlacing his boots.

Akala nodded to Dorfin, and the steward left the room. Akala looked at the wizard. He was wearing the same attire that she remembered him in years ago; only his clothing now appeared newer. His black pants were loose fitting soft cotton and his tunic was black wool with gold stitching worn over a black turtle neck shirt. He sat at the head of the small table and Akala took the chair to his left. "It amazes me how you show up when you are most needed. I have never known a wizard with your powers."

"Most of it is perception and illusion, my dear," replied the wizard. "There is really no such thing as wizards, though I like to encourage the belief because it creates a certain awe of my reputation. I am just intelligent and well read. I am also much older than I look, so I have the wisdom of age, which is actually where the word wizard comes from. A true wizard is just a very old scholar and not a magic wielding warlock."

"I saw you put Baker to sleep like it was nothing, not to mention your timely arrival when I just spoke of you this very morning."

'My dear, Baker was already tired. All I did was to give his mind a suggestion to do what it wanted to do anyway. And my perceptions along with news of the land encouraged me to travel here. Your mentioning it this morning was just coincidence."

Akala wasn't convinced. In the past, she had seen Ivan do things that could not be explained with logic. Dorfin came in carrying a tray with a decanter of red wine and three glasses as well as a plate full of cheese and crackers. He set down the tray, filled the glasses and took the seat opposite Akala.

Ivan seemed quite pleased as he drank down half his glass and began munching a cracker with cheese on it. He washed it down with the remainder of his wine and refilled his glass. "Ah," he exhaled with relief. "I think I will live now." Akala and Dorfin each took a sip of their wine and sat patiently waiting for Ivan to begin. "First," began the wizard, "I need you to tell me all you know about the key and anyone who may know what the book contains."

Akala told him all that had occurred since early that morning when Townsend arrived wanting a charter, including Baker's story and their plans to assist her family. Dorfin added a few details that Akala had missed.

Ivan listened quietly, interrupting only to verify some details in Baker's interrogation. When they had finished, the wizard said, "The wayward gambler that Baker spoke of was Sumas. He was a former colleague. Now he is an adversary. He stole my book a long time ago. Now he seems to be out in the world stirring things up."

Akala asked, "How do you know it was him?"

"Baker's description of him as 'blacker than any man he had ever seen'," Ivan replied. "My other colleague would appear as whiter skinned than anyone else. Where we came from there were distinct racial differences that aren't seen anymore. Call it racial blending. There are still differences, but not as many and not as pronounced as in Earth's earlier days. In the old days—the very,

very old days—human features were fairly unique to an area of the planet, exceptions being travelers and migrations. A race of people may have been black, white, yellow, brown or olive skinned. They may have had bony, narrow, flat, wide or sharp faces. They also might have had almond eyes or round or been known for tallness, shortness, blonde hair or dark. Now you see a blend of all and a mixture of differences in every land without uniqueness other than that caused by weather and personal trades."

Akala stored this away for later. Right now she just wanted to help her family, so she asked another question to head off an extended oration. "Do you have any way to get a warning to Imar?"

"I am afraid I would have to know where he was and even then it could take time and probably fail." Ivan sat there for a minute then said, "I will try to contact my colleague in Abezda, but don't get your hopes up. I have not communicated with her for a long time. For now though, I need to give you both some history." He took a sip of wine and began, "A long, long time ago there thrived an advanced civilization, so advanced, it made us now look like groveling mammals trying to best our neighbors for a bushel of nuts."

"Yes, we suspect that much knowledge was lost in ancient history," said Dorfin. "There are thousands of fictional stories of the time before. There just isn't much evidence to substantiate proof of that advanced time."

"All fiction is based on fact to some degree, my dear fellow, and there is evidence," replied Ivan. "That book you saw tonight is from that time. It was, in its time, called a hard copy manual for the leader of a powerful country. It was a union of lands, so to speak. Together this union encompassed an area many times larger than the kingdom of Kalusia. Other great nations of that world were also run by elected officials. Most of the countries with kings or queens were managed by parliaments instead of absolute power being wielded by an individual. Monarchs were just powerless figureheads."

"Books from that age are rare; most of them have been lost to the ravages of time. There used to be great libraries that had sealed chambers for storing books of antiquity against the elements that would cause decay. There were other chambers, shelters, and underground fortresses as well. Some of these places were built to protect people from elements of weather as well as from the effects of great weapons of mass destruction."

"A number of years ago an archeologist found one of these places. It was a special chamber built for the man who ruled much like an emperor, except that this leader would be voted to rule for a few years at a time and then a new one would be elected. The chamber became his tomb and all that remained of him was his bones. It was there that we found the device we now know is a key. No one could figure out this device until a collapsed passage was discovered adjacent to this leader's final resting place. That passage led to a cavern, and in that cavern was a door with an octagon slot the size of the device. It was then that we knew the artifact was a key. At the very moment the key was placed in the lock, the keypad lit up and the lights above it illuminated the room. No one could figure out the combination to the keypad and the door was impenetrable, at least to any tools we possess today."

"Excavation was tried all the way around to find another way in, but all attempts failed. The walls of this fortress are thick with layers of concrete and alloys that we also found to be impenetrable. Mathematicians were summoned to figure out the code, but they hadn't a clue where to begin, not knowing how many digits the combination would be. After almost a decade, a man and a woman that had been working together trying to figure out the combination finally succeeded in cracking the code. What they found inside was beyond the wildest dreams of the most outlandish science fiction writers known today."

Ivan had their complete and undivided attention. He loved storytelling as much as he did the sound of his own voice. If left unchecked, he would still be rattling on after everyone had retired to bed. Neither Dorfin nor Akala moved. Each sat with their hands on the arms of their chairs, quietly listening to what the wizard claimed was a true history that neither of them had heard before. Ivan paused for another cracker with cheese, polished off his second glass of wine, and poured himself another before resuming his tale. "Inside was a lift that went even deeper into the very bowels of the earth. It led to a place where politicians and generals could survive a great cataclysm and still direct the machinations of war. The place was built with a nuclear power source with a half-life of a billion years. That means that the energy is weakened by a half every billion years or so. There is still an abundance of energy for powering heating, cooling, lighting, lifts, and most importantly, computers."

"What are computers?" Dorfin asked this with a slight knit on his brow. Facial expressions on Dorfin were as common as flying pigs.

"Ah, where do I begin? Computers were one of the greatest tools of the prehistoric age and probably its downfall as well. It was on these computers that a select few of us had learned about the prehistory, the history of the world before the unwritten beginning of this age. Computers were an access point to nearly all the world's information; books, communications, problem solving, and much, much more. They allowed you to talk to someone far away and look at their holographic image as if they were in the room next to you. It was an age of information, but it was also an age of both production and destruction. One could ride in an automobile, much like a carriage, that could speed you down a smooth highway many times faster than a running horse. People would board aircraft that could fly miles above the surface at speeds ten times faster than an automobile. There were hand held weapons that could kill from distances far greater than the stoutest bow as well as powered missiles that could destroy entire cities on another continent. Cities that would make Port Augustus look like a peasant village. Some of the missiles would carry plagues, some had chemicals that would make the skin blister and the membranes bubble till the victims would choke on their own puss. What evil possessed them to produce such weapons and, much worse, deploy them, I can't imagine. The most devastating of all was what they called the nuclear bomb. This dreadful device could be attached to a missile that could fly for hundreds of miles and strike a city with the heat of the sun burning millions instantly to ash. Then the aftermath of such an explosion would cause the burning radiation to travel on the air contaminating land, food, water, people, animals and everything it touched causing horrible deaths far from the explosion site."

"May all the gods help us," exclaimed Akala. Her face was pale and she looked like she was going to be sick.

"Maybe the gods did help us by putting an end to such evils. Back then, most people believed in only one god, but they fought over his name and who he favored," reflected the wizard briefly before continuing his story. "There were also many good achievements back then as well. Medicines and surgeries and huge hospitals were extremely advanced. People lived long lives, diseases were cured, arms and legs could be replaced, vision and hearing restored. There were still wars, but most of the world lived in peace until near the end of that great age. People prospered and famine was rare. Unfortunately, with that prosperity came pollution as a byproduct."

"The air, land, and water all became polluted by industry and from mining fuels needed for energy to heat or cool for comfort and in some cases, survival. Energy was desired for many things, most especially transportation. Energy burned had polluted the air. Great factories pumped toxic smoke into the atmosphere and dumped toxic waste into the rivers and oceans. Food that was grown had toxins, the beasts raised for food became sick and unsafe to eat, and the fish from the sea became unhealthy to eat and eventually died off into extinction."

Ivan paused, took a sip of wine and continued, "All this brought diseases and famine back with a vengeance. Medical technology, as advanced as it was, could not keep up with such epidemics. People became desperate. They were sick and hungry and still greedy for their lost prosperity. Wars broke out all over the world. Billions were killed and much of the earth became uninhabitable. Nuclear ballistic missiles were not launched, but chemical and biological weapons were, and a few small nukes called 'dirty bombs' were deployed. Wars and mayhem took out three quarters of the population. Disease and famine killed half of the remaining souls on the planet. Survivors formed into bands that raided each other for food and supplies. Some escaped to wilderness areas to hide from the insanity and attempted to live off the land, but game animals carried toxins too and were dying off as rapidly as people. Some small communities moved underground and learned to farm fungi for sustenance and various meat animals were raised in tunnels. The world was devastated. The progress of humankind had nearly caused its own extinction. A fraction of one percent of the planet in its prime may have survived."

They sat in silence for a few minutes digesting the wizard's words. Dorfin had a thousand questions in his head and the more he heard, the more questions came to mind. "How long ago did all this happen? Where is this chamber of knowledge? Who all knows of this? What do . . .?"

"Stop," Ivan interrupted, holding up his hand palm outward in the universal stop sign. "Let me finish." Ivan lowered his hand to his glass and took a drink before going on. "This is a very brief telling of a very long story and thirsty work at that, so please have a bit of patience. As soon as the keypad was found, it was obvious proof of technology beyond our modern yet primitive ways. The archeologist in charge of the dig, Welker, had his team swear to secrecy. He sent for me and other men and women of reputed knowledge from around the continent. The location was in Eastonia. Welker did not trust monarchs, politicians, or government of any kind even though his funding came from King Anders of Eastonia. Welker and I were in total agreement when it came to government."

"Wait a minute," Dorfin knew his social studies and thought maybe Ivan was mistaken. "King Anders died sixty years ago. That would make you at least eighty-five at the youngest. You don't look a day over fifty. How can that be?"

"Clean living," answered the wizard before he drained his third glass of wine. Ivan grinned as he filled his glass again. "Actually, I am quite a bit older than that, but that is an explanation that will have to wait."

Akala had been working this thought in the back of her mind. "Come to think of it, you didn't look a day over fifty back when I saw you last. That was twenty years ago."

"Anyway," Ivan said, changing the subject. "We spent months studying all we could from the databases as well as exploring the underground fortress. We did all this in secrecy, but word got out and back to the King. Anders was furious of course, but we fed him a line of bullshit that we were preparing a special presentation just for him and the vain moron gobbled it up. We scholars and scientists were originally ecstatic about this discovery, but I and one other saw the danger of this knowledge as well as the danger of the weapons and certain substances we found there. We debated back and forth for bringing this technology to our primitive world for the good it could do, against sealing it away from a world not ready for it. I argued that history tends to repeat itself and so long as greed was part of human nature, this knowledge was dangerous. It was Anders that made the decision for us."

"King Anders wanted to enlarge his kingdom and elevate his status to emperor. His first thoughts were to train his army to use these new weapons and then destroy the capital city of Medimia as a demonstration of his power. We had to work fast to stop such lunacy, but we weren't unanimous in the decision to seal up the fortress. One of our people betrayed our plans to Anders. We locked up the fortress and gave the key to Hamish, a man that was both scholar and warrior. He vowed to keep it hidden at his frontier home and told none of us exactly where that was. Anders' troops were on the way and as much as Hamish wanted to stay with us he knew his mission was to protect the key, so he departed. We had brought out explosive devices with us and blew up the tunnel leading to the entrance chamber with the lock and keypad. There were originally nine of us and now we were seven with Hamish gone and Sumas going to Anders. By the time we got to the president's tomb we were met and taken prisoner by the King's men."

"Hamish got away. I'm sure he had a time of it, for Anders turned his kingdom upside down looking for him. The king sent spies all over the continent, but failed to turn up a trace. Hamish was the finest woodsman I knew and the smartest weapons master to wield sword or pen. Sumas became chief advisor to the king who in turn funded his research in finding another key or another way in to the fortress. We were afraid that there may be other places in the world like the underground fortress. Those of us with good sense hoped those places would stay buried forever. We were tortured for Hamish's whereabouts, but all we knew was that he lived on the frontier since he was at the University of Sedar when he was asked to come to Welker's dig. Three of us escaped. I managed to steal Welker's book back from Sumas, but the sneaky devil stole it back later. Welker was one of the four that didn't get away."

"From the histories I learned that after the age of information, humankind devolved through an age of destruction to a primitive state. Climatic changes, earthquakes and continental shifting occurred while humans scrabbled for survival living in tunnels deep below the surface, on the brink of extinction. I don't know how long men and women lived underground before surfacing as hunters and gatherers, but some knowledge was retained. That knowledge was passed down though most was lost without the ability to apply it and without the tools or equipment it required. Evolution to surface cave dwellers came next followed by huts then houses. Expansion to areas once uninhabitable became possible again."

"It was the beginning of the second Dark Age. Education ceased for many years and evolution had to start from scratch. Time passed, the earth healed and much of the climate and geography had changed. Some animals became extinct while new ones evolved. People farmed and raised animals. Communities grew faster than the first time, probably because knowledge of steel was handed down, so there was no bronze age. Gun powder, which you have not heard of before, was forgotten and not rediscovered."

"Warlords sold protection, mainly from themselves, and acquired fertile lands and called themselves barons, who in turn attacked other barons and stole more lands and then called themselves earls or kings. It is still argued who the first king was, but that was roughly the beginning of the new calendar. That start was debated at a conference of kings about two thousand years ago in the year 3685 and now at least a dozen countries are on the same calendar and date. Evolution climbed with only a trace of past knowledge and without the help of certain discoveries. For example, the written and spoken language is vaguely similar. As with the book, you were able to read some of the words. Now we have colleges and universities all over the continent and most cities have schools for the commoners. It is rare to find someone over the age of ten that cannot read and write."

Akala stood up and stretched. The men stood too, as gentlemen should when a lady stands. "It is very late and past even my bedtime," she said. "Ivan, you have told us much and given us a lot to think about. We must talk more on this when we are fresh and well rested. Let us meet tomorrow, or should I say later today? I'll see you late morning, after breakfast." She turned to Dorfin, "Give Ivan any room with a bed for now. We can set him up with better accommodations tomorrow." Then to both of them she said, "Goodnight gentlemen." Akala was out the door as they were returning their goodnights.

CHAPTER 9

Imar insisted that Dalla stay far enough back to be cautious, yet close enough that he could come to her aid if need be. The descent was to the east, a little over a mile long down to the ferry. The river was fed from a glacier in the Abezda Range and flowed north past the village before making a bend around the northern tip of the ridge they were now descending. The Daishon River then flowed its snake-like route northwest to the city of Three Rivers, where it joined the Kand and Benshi Rivers. The road was fairly straight as much as the terrain would allow as it tracked down a draw toward the ferry on the south side of the inn. The trees were very sparse with a number of dead and silvered spruce trees indicating that a forest fire had cleansed the area some ten to twenty years before. There was a fairly good view of the community, but the willow brush was thick and chest high except in the immediate vicinity of the village. Brush that thick could hide a platoon, if not a whole company, easily.

The ground rose on both sides of the road. Just ahead of them the terrain flattened out where the inn sat along the bank of the river. Dalla's warning had heightened Imar's senses, which were now on full alert. They were in a very bad position for an ambush. Imar stopped and signaled Dalla to do the same. They were only half a kilometer from the inn, but Imar was considering going back and finding another route. He scanned the hills and listened, barely breathing. Dalla was right, something was wrong. There were no sounds; no people talking, no dogs barking, no birds singing, nothing whatsoever. He heeled his horse lightly to urge him into a slow walk and motioned Dalla forward. She gave a slight shake of her head and then glanced up the slopes on each side of the road. Imar saw it too, a slight showing of blue less than twenty meters off the road to the left. He saw nothing on the right.

As they walked their horses down onto the flats and into the yard of the inn, Imar could see into the stables off to the right. The mews were full of horses. Before he could dismount, a lean man wearing a blue and white tabard with a golden bear emblem on his chest came out of the inn. He wore no helm and his weapons were sheathed. Imar raised his bow and drew back in one fluid motion.

The man smiled and raised his hand palm outward. "That won't be necessary." At that moment four men appeared, two from around each side of the building with shields up and swords in their hands. Imar looked back and saw two more on each side of Dalla. One of them was taking her shield from her and the other had his sword pointed at her belly. Two men with crossbows leveled at them were coming up the road from the way they had just come. Another came out of the stable. Imar wanted to attack, but knew it would be Dalla's death if he did. He cursed himself for foolishly walking into a trap. Inwardly he blamed his head injury for robbing him of simple strategy as well as memory.

Imar relaxed his bow and put the arrow away. The man said, "Wise decision. You must be Imar, son of Amir, and you," he said, slowing his speech to peer at Dalla, "are from Mentin. I remember you when we passed through. What is your name?" He retained the decorum of a gentleman as he appraised her, unlike his men whose lascivious stares were uncomfortably rude. A piercing look of disapproval from the man caused his men to instantly avert their eyes and assume bland faces.

"I am a healer," she said, stepping down from her horse. "My name is Dalla." Healers had a reputation for being noncombatants and their abilities were prized in all the known lands. Even in war, a healer taken prisoner was usually given better treatment. There were exceptions, of course, but it was common courtesy for a healer to declare their trade in case their services were needed.

The man answered, "I am honored to make your acquaintance. I am Sigurd, captain of the guard to Jarl Bamsen from the city of

Kabula." The captain had a dark complexion, a friendly face and a well-trimmed mustache.

Imar dismounted and one of the guards relieved him of his sword and dagger. "Your men tried to kill me. Why?"

"I do apologize for that," answered Sigurd. "You have something my Lord Bamsen wants. He wants it very badly—badly enough to kill for it, I'm afraid. My men's orders were to not use force if it could be avoided. They were supposed to bring you to me, so that we could negotiate a price for your property. It is obvious that their overzealousness got the better of them. I must tell you that I was quite angry with you for killing my men. However, I would have done the same thing had someone attacked *me*. I underestimated you. We went back for them when they didn't meet us here, and I must say your skill at arms is impressive. Your trail was lost to us, wiped out by heavy rain. I bet we just missed you. After cremating our dead we went southeast to Boarder City. Finding that you had not arrived there, I deduced that you must have gone the other way, so we decided to wait for you here, since you would have to pass here to go home."

"What is it I am supposed to have that your liege wishes to relieve me of?" Imar was glad this conversation was at least civil. He had expected to be run through or at least tortured while Dalla was raped.

"Come, come," said the captain, "I am sure you know what we seek. You must be tired and hungry. Remove your chain mail and let us go in and have food and refreshments while my men search your things. We can talk over dinner. The innkeeper and his wife stayed behind along with the ferryman." Then in a mock injured tone he added, "But the whole village thought us a threat for some reason, and escaped to the woods. We have the inn to ourselves." The captain was quite jovial. He acted as if he were receiving guests, rather than taking prisoners. "Our hostess has prepared us a fine moose roast for dinner and the innkeeper is quite skilled in the art of making beer."

Imar took off his helm and hung it on his saddle, then draped his mail shirt over the cantle and handed his sword sheath to the man who had taken his weapons.

They went inside the inn. The captain led them to a table in the center of the room. Four guards, two with crossbows, took up positions around the room. Imar had a reputation with them after besting five of their comrades. The other guards took the horses to the stable and began dismantling their gear to search for the octagon key. To the back of the main room was a bar, behind which stood the innkeeper. Behind him there was a wall with a door to the kitchen and a window with a wide shelf for setting plates of food. Through that window Dalla could see the innkeeper's wife preparing dinner. The couple looked distressed, both casting a fearful glance at the captain when he entered the inn and a look of concern at Dalla and Imar. Under normal circumstances the innkeepers probably would have greeted them with the open friendliness common to rural communities. However, despite Sigurd's amiable attitude, there was an air of oppression bearing down on the couple as if they carried the weight of slave chains upon their shoulders. As soon as Sigurd, Dalla, and Imar took their seats, the innkeeper brought them beers in pewter mugs and placed them on the table. He did this without a word, but made eye contact with Imar and gave the slightest shake of the head. He then excused himself and went to the kitchen to help his wife with dinner.

"I have a proposition for you," Sigurd said after drinking down half his beer in one draft. "My orders are to appropriate a family heirloom of yours by purchase or force. Your father does not have it. A contingent of hired swords got to him before we did." Sigurd noticed Imar's eyes widen slightly at this and added, "He's fine, the mercenaries roughed him up a little, but he is okay. He wouldn't tell anyone anything, but the housekeeper that lives next door was quite the chatter box. It seems that you had left your father's house before the mercenaries arrived. That means you must have the item we seek."

Imar had put the key, as Dalla called it, down his pants, as most men are hesitant to search another man's crotch. He was now

77

secretly wishing he had hid it under a rock before they came down the hill. "How can you be so sure? My father may have just hidden it well."

"I doubt it. The mercs found nothing, but after questioning the neighbor, they took a riverboat to here and then rode on to Boarder City, where they hold your wife and child. They wish to use your family to bargain with you. We had orders to do the same, but your villa is very defensible. We were just there and decided to come back and wait for you here. We would not be able to take them with only ten men. Kendal is the mercenary captain with at least a dozen men under his command. He told the lieutenant of your border patrol that he is an old friend of yours and that something is afoot that requires the protection of your family. He allows no passage in or out of your villa. Your men are there keeping a wary watch until your return."

"That still isn't proof that I have the item." Imar shifted slightly in his chair. The key was causing him some discomfort. He took a drink of his beer to hide a movement that reduced the pinching in his nether regions. *Wife and child*, thought Imar. Now he knew for sure that he had a wife and daughter. None of this was bringing his memory back. He tried to stay focused on his current situation, but his mind kept coming back to his feelings for Dalla. She was always there, always on his mind even though he now knew he had a duty to his wife and child.

"True," replied Sigurd, "but the house keeper seemed to be quite the busy body. She told us that she overheard a conversation between you and your father. She said that he gave you something of great importance that has been in your family for a long time. And, he told you to guard it well. That is why I am sure you have it." He looked up and smiled. "Ah, dinner," said the captain, "it smells wonderful."

The innkeeper came out of the kitchen carrying a huge cast iron pot steaming with the aroma of roasted meat. He set it on a table next to them, removed the lid and began cutting meat that literally fell apart. His wife took the empty beer mugs and replaced them with glasses of blueberry wine. "I'm sorry the carrots and potatoes are last year's and came from a jar, but I made gravy to help the taste. There is also fresh bread." After serving the three at the table, the innkeepers set up a buffet on the other side of the room for the soldiers. They came in, took plates and ate in silence. Then the ones standing guard were relieved so they could eat.

Imar and Sigurd were ravenous. They did not speak during dinner. All that could be heard from them was sounds of munching and the moans of delight that hungry men make when sinking their teeth into succulent meat. Dalla ate like a bird and took only one small helping whereas the men filled their plates three times. Dalla's mind was racing with the new revelation confirming Imar's marriage. It depressed her. She had thought that she had prepared herself for this possibility, but she obviously had not. She was saddened almost to tears which only made her mad at herself. The fates just didn't seem to be in their favor. *How can the chemistry between us be denied?* It had been such a long time since she had felt even the feather touch of love and now she saw her hopes turn to smoke and drift away on the wind. She looked at Imar. *Men,* she thought. *Look at him wolfing down his food as if he hadn't a care in the world. Didn't he hear that he's married to someone he doesn't even remember? And he acts as if we weren't prisoners, hoisting beers with our captors and wining and dining like they were good buddies.* Dalla became as angry with Imar as she was with herself. She was mostly angry for being angry. Dalla knew she was being foolish. After all, she was beyond such immaturity, but then again, she just couldn't help herself.

They all complimented and thanked their hostess for the fabulous meal as she cleared the table and brought out more wine. Imar noticed that something was bothering Dalla, but he didn't have a clue as to what it was. He tried to make eye contact, but Dalla wouldn't look at him. *It's as if she were mad at me,* he thought. *What did I do?* Imar sighed and thought, *Women. Did the Gods make them all difficult?* He wasn't sure where that thought came from, since he had met only two women from the time his current memories began. He turned to Sigurd, "You said you had a proposition for me. What did you have in mind?"

Sigurd ran a hand over his short cut hair, looked at Imar with piercing dark eyes and smiled. "You could join forces with us. Together with your men in Boarder City we can rescue your family. After that, travel to Kabula with us and meet my Lord Bamsen. You can bring as many of your men with you as you wish. I'm sure you would want to leave enough to keep the lands free from Kandian raiders, but you and your men would be welcome. You can bring your wife and daughter if you wish or you can bring your, ah, healer."

A couple of the guards snickered at this and Dalla's face reddened. She had been a bit pensive during dinner, but now she was angry. "I am not *his* healer," she retorted with a hiss. She took a few seconds to cool down and regain her composure. "I travel with him as a friend and a friend only. His injury required care and I desired protection on the road. We travel the same direction and it behooves us to travel together." She said it calmly, but coldly. She was not pleased with herself for losing her temper. She hadn't lost control since she was very young.

"If I agree to this," Imar said to Sigurd, hoping to avert any unpleasantness, "what is to stop me from turning on you once I rejoin my men?"

Sigurd laughed at this, "Your word, of course. I was told to offer you as much as fifty pieces of gold for your heirloom. After seeing your estate, I knew you wouldn't take it. You are rich, by rights a lord. You have the wealth of a Jarl and serve as a mercenary captain. You should be a general in the King's Army," Sigurd said, slamming a fist down on the table for emphasis. "I learned that you have estates in Kalusia as well. Great wealth came to you while adventuring at sea. You attended the university at Port Augustus while working as weapons master for Murdoch Trading and Free Companies, and then you married the boss's daughter, which connects you to even more wealth. You came up north to take over for your father when he was hurt in a skirmish with Kandian raiders. Your father has retired in luxury, thanks to you. You live well, but risk much living in this northern frontier when you could retire to your southern estate and trouble yourself with nothing more than seeing to the condition of your vineyards. You are obviously a man of honor and duty. A man like that would not break an oath even to his enemies."

"There is more I need to know," Imar said. "Why is this heirloom that I supposedly have desired so much? What does it do?"

Sigurd leaned forward and spoke seriously but more softly, "It is supposed to give access to weapons far superior to what we have." The captain patted the sword at his side as he said, "It is supposed to be a key to a vault somewhere far to the east. The vault is bigger than a castle and all underground. It is full of very powerful weapons that can crush whole cities from long distances."

Dalla didn't like what she heard. Far too much was known about the octagon key and the underground control center that it could unlock. Things were worse than she had thought. She had to stay near the key and make sure that the vault was never opened.

Dalla remembered that Bart had sent two spies as guides with this party and only one returned home. The other was nowhere to be seen. "Captain Sigurd," she said, turning to their captor, "You said the ferryman remained here. Also, in Mentin, Bart the innkeeper said he had sent out a guide with you. I have not seen either of those people. They didn't appear for dinner. Are they ill?"

Sigurd's jovial attitude vanished in an instant. "The ferryman is being detained in his quarters. I am not very pleased with him. Not to worry, his health is fine and his meal has been taken to him. On our return back here from Boarder City, he sabotaged the ferry and we had to swim our horses in this frigid glacier melt water. As soon as we recovered from hypothermia, I sent two trackers after him. He was found and put to repairing the ferry. I will keep him detained until we get back across the river."

"And your guide?" asked Dalla.

"That lying innkeeper in Mentin convinced me that the road was awash with rock slides and mud bogs. He said his guides knew all the bypass trails. The road was fine, except for a little mud here and there. I paid him for two guides that weren't guides at all. They were sent as spies to gather information that he could sell. The first one deserted three days out of Mentin. The other I seized and took prisoner. Come with me," Sigurd said as he stood up.

He gave some orders and one of his guards led them down a hall to a back door. The other three guards followed behind Dalla and Imar. The lead man took a torch from a basket by the door and lit it with a flint when he stepped out into the dimness. There was no darkness at this time of year, but the late hour and the heavy overcast made having a torch helpful. They all stepped outside and fanned out around the torch lit spectacle. Bart's guide was tied with his hands above his head and his back to the pole that was supporting him, with his feet just a hand's breadth above the ground. It was raining lightly and the man was shivering. He was stripped to the waist and had burns from hot irons all over his chest and arms. His face was swollen and his lips were bloody. He was covered with hundreds of mosquito bites and had a dozen of the blood sucking pests feasting on him as Dalla and Imar took in the ghastly spectacle of what men could do to another human.

"What cause have you to treat him like this?" Dalla was outraged. "Please, I beg you to cut him down at once and allow me to help him."

Sigurd nodded to his men. Two of the guards cut the man's bonds and he crumpled to the ground with a moan. "I do not tolerate spies or dishonesty," replied the captain. "I suppose he has learned his lesson. He is free to go home now if he wishes."

"This is brutal and beyond necessity." Dalla went to the man on the ground and began checking his pupils with the torch she took from the guard. "I need my medical bag, the black leather bag with my gear. This man needs to be taken in to a bed at once."

Sigurd had one of his guards go get her bag. The soldier returned with the bag as the tortured man was carried into a room on the first floor. After placing him in bed they left Dalla to treat the man's injuries with a guard posted in the hall. Sigurd led Imar out to the main room at the base of the stairs. "Separate rooms have been assigned to you. The healer will stay in the room adjacent to the spy.

You will stay in a room upstairs. There will be guards in the hall outside your door and also posted in the yard as well. My men did not find what we seek, so I expect it is on your person." Sigurd had regained his friendly demeanor. "Consider my proposal. Your skills and reputation precede you. With advanced weaponry we could bring peace and civilization to the world. Power and glory can be ours for the taking."

"And if I refuse?" Imar asked cautiously.

Sigurd replied emotionlessly. "You will be strip searched, beaten, and tortured like the man down the hall, maybe killed. Your friend the healer will be given to my men when I am done with her and we will go on this quest without you. Good night, Imar. Think well on my proposal, I expect an answer in the morning." With that, the captain walked off while the guards escorted the fuming Imar up the stairs to his room.

Imar lay on his bed fully clothed in the dark. His head ached and the darkness was soothing. It was normally light throughout the night in the northern regions at this time of year, but the heavy overcast made it darker than usual. One could still see with some difficulty without a torch. He remained clothed so he would be ready for action should he decide to attempt escape. The darkness could aid him in such an endeavor.

He had so wanted a bath and a good night's sleep in a bed. Now it seemed that both would be denied to him. There were two men on guard outside and two in the hall. Sigurd wasn't taking any chances. Four out of ten men for a duty guard meant long shifts between relief changes. They would probably change the guard two or three hours after midnight. Near that change the guards would be most fatigued. He would have to take out the two in the hall with stealth. If he failed to do it quietly, he would have to fight all ten. They would be groggy with sleep, but still very poor odds. The alternative was not pleasant either.

Sigurd was such a friendly and likeable man on the outside, but ruthless and power hungry on the inside. Joining him was the last thing Imar wanted to do, but doing so would save Dalla. Well, it would save her if Sigurd was a man of his word, which Imar was hoping he was. If an agreement was made to go as far as Bamsen's Keep in Kabula, he might be able to break away with the aid of his men. What Sigurd had done to that poor young man was just plain malicious. There were times for torture, but inflicting pain and permanent scars for no gain other than spite was just sadistic.

It was just past midnight and Imar had not decided for sure what he was going to do. He still wore his hard leather vest armor. The metal rings would provide protection with the close-in fighting that would come in the hall, but he had no knife, not even a stick. His room had been cleaned of all potential weapons, including the curtain rods. He was pondering all this when he heard the latch on his door move.

Imar was up in an instant, moving like a cat; he positioned himself behind the door. *What luck,* he thought, *if only one comes in I will dispatch him and then deal with the other in the hall one-on-one.* The door began to slowly open, his body tensed like a coiled spring, his mind set to reach from behind, grab a chin and back of the head and snap the neck. As the body cleared the door he moved and stopped mid-strike, seeing curly golden-blonde hair before him. He put his hand on her shoulder and she turned and looked at him with her finger to her lips. He had a thousand questions on his mind, but they all went on hold for a few seconds as he admired her beauty in the dim light. She held his gaze for a moment then embraced him with the side of her head against his shoulder. He was aware of her breasts against his chest and he felt himself stirring and remembered he still had the key in his trousers. She raised her head and neither of them could hold back. They kissed, not just a kiss, but a first kiss, long and deep. Time seemed to stop. They enjoyed the moment while they stood on the edge of danger as if alone on a mountain top, melding their spirits in passion yet still aware of their peril. When they finished, they came rushing back to more than one reality.

Dalla spoke in barely a whisper with her lips touching his ear, "We mustn't do this, and we can't do this, but my heart wants it badly." She still embraced him, her body pressed close to his. "You are a married man. This just isn't right even though it feels thus and we have more pressing concerns at the moment. The guards are asleep, a deep sleep. However, I cannot vouch for those still in their rooms. We must be quiet and not talk until we get to the stable."

Imar nodded and they broke apart and stepped out into the hall. Both of them felt the pang of loss when they pulled away from each other, as if their souls were joined for that fleeting moment and then torn savagely apart. The taste of the kiss lingered on their lips as they focused on the mission at hand. They padded silently down the hall past the slumbering guards and descended the stairs on the sides of the steps so as to prevent the boards from creaking. A few of the steps did creak, but what little noise was made was drowned out by the snoring coming from the guards upstairs. They made their way outside into the wet night. More snoring came from each end of the building where the other two guards on duty slept soundly. Imar was very curious about this but prudently set his questions aside for a more relaxed time, if they weren't caught.

When they got to the stable, two men were busy muffling all the horses' hooves with grain sacks. One of them was Andrew, Bart's guide. His one eye was swollen nearly shut and he moved with pain, but he was mobile and ready to leave. The other man Imar had not met and assumed he was the ferryman. They all nodded wordlessly to each other.

Imar and Dalla's horses still had their saddles on, accounting to the laziness of Sigurd's men. Imar's claymore was still in its scabbard on Cerus and his chain mail shirt still lay across the back of the saddle. They still had to pack their gear and they did so quickly and quietly. Imar found his short sword, dagger and shield against the wall and reclaimed them as well as one extra shield for Dalla. When all was ready they came together and spoke their plans barely above a whisper.

"I will take their horses," Andrew said, indicating the mounts belonging to Sigurd's men. "They cannot follow you on foot and will want to regain their mounts."

"I won't have it," Imar said with fierceness in his voice. "Those men will track you down and kill you."

85

"I insist," said Andrew. "I probably would have died if not for the intervention and medical care your lady administered to me. That is if Sigurd didn't change his mind and kill me anyway on the morrow. No, I will take their horses and hopefully lead them away from you. With them on foot and me mounted they won't have much chance of catching me either as long as I keep my pace. When I get back to Mentin I will sell the horses. Ten horses should fetch a tidy sum. I also intend to demand a hazardous duty bonus from Bart. After that if Sigurd wants me he will have to look to the sea, for I intend to go to North Harbor and find a ship that is in want of a stout hand."

Imar smiled, partly because Dalla didn't object this time to the young man's reference to 'your lady' and also because this youth had grit. "Very well then, I am honored to have met you. I wish it was under better circumstances. If you ever wish a position in my company of soldiers, there will be a place for you." They gripped forearms in the fashion of soldiers as Imar said, "Safe journey to you, Andrew."

Andrew led the ten horses at a slow walk out of the stable and up the road toward Mentin.

They waited a few long agonizing minutes, until he was out of sight, and then the ferryman spoke. "The innkeepers departed in a canoe just before you came down. I will take their horses to them down river. Now follow me." With that he led three other horses down to the ferry.

Imar handed Dalla a shield and motioned her to go first. While they were waiting for Andrew to depart up the hill, Imar put on his mail shirt, but this time he put on a dark brown sleeveless tabard over it with an emblem of a hawk outlined by an octagon embroidered in tan. Next came his helm, followed by his short sword, and then he placed his claymore across his back. He fastened metal grieves to his boots and stood tall in his battle finery. Imar looked good and felt good. The weight of his accruements put him in his battle glory and his adrenaline soared. Dalla led the horses down to the ferry while Imar strode to the side between the inn and her. The weight of his shield felt good on his arm and he drew his sword which felt good in his hand. Dalla sensed his mood and began to move the horses faster, well aware of his rising bloodlust, so common to northern warriors. The ferryman was aboard his vessel untying the lines.

Imar stopped and turned toward the inn.

Dalla said, "Oh no, please don't."

Imar shouted at the top of his lungs, "Sigurd! I have your answer! You can kiss my arse and taste my steel!"

The guard on the porch leapt to his feet as did the one at the back of the inn. They were confused, but to their credit, they didn't just charge to their deaths when they joined each other at the front of the inn. They locked shields and slowly approached this formidable warrior with the wolfish grin on his face and the fire in his eyes. Sounds were coming from the inn and Dalla was tugging on the horses with all her might, loading them onto the barge.

The ferryman helped her. "Is he out of his bloody mind?" he asked as he tugged fiercely on the reins. "I thought the man had some sense about him."

Dalla kept her mouth shut, but her sarcastic thoughts rolled on. *A sword in hand and blood flowing from brain to crotch, a man will do the most foolish things.*

Imar charged with his shield out front and his sword held high. The men braced themselves against the impact, but Imar's momentum could not be stopped. As he broke between them he sliced low to the right under the man's shield, his blade finding flesh below the chain mail skirt—it cut into the man's knee. A scream rent the air as he turned and caught a sword from the left on his shield. He faked a low thrust then spun an arc and came over his opponents shield and sunk the point into the man's neck. Imar roared with battle lust.

Men came charging out of the inn half-dressed, carrying shields and swords but no armor. Imar cut down two in an instant. The others stopped at Sigurd's shouted commands. "Halt you fools. Form up or die! Shield wall, shield wall, you idiots."

Dalla called out to Imar as the ferry was pulling away from the shore. "Imar, you must come now!"

Imar could hear the ferryman's steps on the deck as he pulled on the line that propelled the boat across the river. He turned and ran for the craft. When he got to the shore there was a meter of water between him and the ramp. He didn't stop, but leapt for the boat. His foot landed on wet wood and he slipped, skidded, tripped and did a face plant on the deck. He quickly got up and helped Dalla raise the ramp. As soon as it was up, two cross bow bolts struck the stern. They were now several meters into the river, so Imar turned around, dropped his breeches, lifted his mail and shined them a moon. He smartly pulled his trousers back on and he and Dalla held up their shields to protect the horses and themselves from more bolts seeking flesh.

Sigurd shouted across the water, "I will have my revenge, Imar, you can count on that!"

Imar answered back, "Thanks for dinner, Sigurd, and you were right, the beer was excellent!"

CHAPTER 10

Do you hear me? The mind speech was meant for only one to receive.

I hear you.

I have been trying to contact you for a while now.

I have been busy, my mind distracted. The key is known about and sought for.

Tell me something I don't know.

It is with Imar Amirson. I am with him now. Where are you?

I am in Port Augustus trying to hitch a ride and bring you some help.

It is needed, but where will you send it?

Where are you?

We are approaching Boarder City to free Imar's ransomed family, but there is a problem. Imar was injured and lost his memory. Jarl Bamsen of Kabula knows of the key and has sent troops to get it and we have made an enemy of one of his captains. A mercenary may be holding Imar's family as ransom for the key. All roads are becoming dangerous and I am not sure where to go.

Here is more news to brighten your day. A Hamaudi assassin has been sent to North Harbor to retrieve the key. You must not let him find you. Do not go to North Harbor or Kabula. He will probably travel straight to Boarder City. If you go to Three Rivers you go away from where we need to go and what we need to do as well as box yourself in.

You are a bundle of good news. We should have destroyed it long ago.

I am tiring and haven't the strength for argument in this manner of communication.

I will convince Imar to go to Valekrie. Border fighting has been nil lately. It is our best route at present. We need to get the key out of the North.

I agree. I will meet you there and bring friends. It is good to talk to you like this again. It has been a long time.

Yes it is, and it has been too long, but He could be listening and I perceive his hand is in this.

Yes, my perception tells me He is involved as well. Let us limit our communication to only when absolutely needed. Contact me when you get to Valekrie. I will be there. Good bye, for now.

For now, good bye.

CHAPTER 11

Akala was up earlier than her normal time. She hadn't gotten to bed until late the night before and her sleep was restless and full of nightmares of people disfigured from disease fighting over scraps of tainted food. She woke often through the night and each time she went back to sleep, the next dream was as bad as or worse than the last. Tired of tossing and turning, she finally decided to get up and go downstairs to the dining room.

The Murdochs had two dining rooms, one for large parties such as feasts and banquets, and the other smaller and more practical dining room, which most aristocrats kept for their servants. Travin and Akala rarely used the big dining room except for parties and often ate with their servants. This was unheard of among the aristocracy, but the Murdochs had a fairly relaxed relationship with the help. Whenever a new employee was hired, it took a while for them to overcome their shock of sitting at the table with the lord and lady of the house. For a servant to be asked for an opinion was often met with apoplexy until the new member loosened up and got accustomed to their employers.

The common dining room was next to the kitchen and had huge glass doors that faced the west, allowing a spectacular view of the ocean. In the evenings thin drapes were pulled shut to limit the sun's intensity in the room, but mornings needed no drapes and when warm enough, there was another table outside where one could breakfast while enjoying the fresh ocean air.

It was at this outside table that Akala found Dorfin and Ivan drinking coffee. Akala never touched the stuff, opting instead to have just water first thing in the morning. After the normal greetings she sat and looked at her glass of water. She found it difficult to imagine a world where fresh water was unsafe to drink, where clean filtered water was a prized commodity, bottled and sold for premium prices. She pondered this and other things Ivan told them of the world before. No one spoke for a while; the men sipped their coffee in silence and gave Akala time to wake up at her own pace. Dorfin warned Ivan to wait for Akala to gather her thoughts and not to start the morning off with a lot of talk. He advised the wizard to let her start the conversation. Ivan had no problem with this; he was, after all, considered a very wise man.

After about twenty minutes of contemplation, Akala finally spoke. "Why wasn't this key destroyed? It seems that as comparatively primitive as we may be now, we would be far better off without this advanced technology that you spoke of. Powerful people would become more powerful. That much knowledge taken on too soon could destroy the world again and possibly faster than before."

"Human nature I guess," answered the wizard. "We wanted to embrace the good things and study the histories and sciences, so we thought that some day humankind may be ready for such knowledge. Throwing it away has its risks as well. There is also the possibility that other keys may exist. We had little time when we abandoned the control center, so we did what we thought best before our enemies gained access. I still fear that another way in could yet be found."

"This knowledge could cause wars just for the key," said Dorfin. "What should we do?"

"We need to join up with Imar, son of Amir, son of Hamish and keeper of the key. He needs all the help he can get protecting it from those who would take it for their own ill purposes. I think getting it out of Abezda and hidden again is best for now. After that we can decide what should be done with it."

"Can we keep ahead of others that want the power? What if one or more monarchs get wind of this and decide to take the key with a thousand or even ten thousand spears at his back?" Akala was genuinely worried. "Shouldn't we enlist the aid of our king and get the support of his army?" Akala realized the contradiction of her words as soon as she said them.

"I have never met a politician I could trust," Ivan said evenly. "Even King Gerald would find it difficult to resist the lure of power. He seems a decent enough man, far more fair handed than his father. No, I think it best to leave rulers and politicians out of it for as long as possible. We don't want to start a war. It is bad enough having poor relations with Kandia, all these skirmishes and sea battles may very well build to a full scale war without us mentioning advanced weapons. A small protective force will move faster and quieter. Disguised as a caravan of traders, we can move across the continent without drawing much attention."

"Move across the continent?" Dorfin inquired. "What are you talking about? I thought you were concerned with just hiding it for now. Do you have other plans?

"Perhaps," answered the wizard, stroking his beard. "Something will eventually have to be done with it. It is very hard to destroy—it's been tried and failed—and would probably require nuclear power to do it. That kind of power can only be found in the fortress. Not only that; I'm not so sure it should be destroyed. The knowledge the key can open is vast. In the end, the octagon key will have to go to its home for use or destruction. And the power is there in the fortress, not in the key. We still need the key, but for now let us get it away from Abezda and Kandia."

Akala turned to Dorfin, "Any word of our wayward captain?"

"Beros was brought in last night," answered Dorfin. "I would suspect he is probably being rousted as we speak. Coulig will brief him on his mission. Crews and shifts have been doubled on the *Coastal Raider*. Beros will be supervising the rest of the refit and adding whatever modifications he wants. If he doesn't get too ostentatious, the work should be done by late tonight or tomorrow morning. She will be ready for launch on the morning tide."

"Good," said Akala, "Beros can take her out on a test run tomorrow and depart for North Harbor or, better yet, Kabula the following day."

"Valekrie," said Ivan.

Dorfin and Akala turned and looked at Ivan. Dorfin's face showed no expression, but it was obvious his mind was working while he waited patiently for an explanation.

Akala was not so patient and had no intention of waiting. "Damn it Ivan, you are doing it again. You're withholding information. Spit it out." Akala was always a bit snappish when she got up early and this was the second day in a row of not sleeping in.

Ivan raised his eyebrows, held his hands palms out and looked apologetic. "I meant to tell you as soon as I had an opportunity. I made contact with my colleague in Abezda last night after we all retired. It was not easy, I will have you know." Ivan lowered his hands and poured himself and Dorfin more coffee from a silver pot. "Conditions have to be just right and both parties must be open to telepathy and then there is the possibility of being overheard," he said, defensively. Then he added apologetically, "I have been very much out of practice as well."

"Ivan please, enough excuses," Akala was in no mood to be put off any longer. "Just tell us what you know."

"Yes, of course," Ivan agreed. "My colleague is with Imar, as is the key. Imar was injured and has lost all memory of his past. It is called amnesia. Enemies pursue them for the key. Enemies before them ransom your daughter and granddaughter for the key. They approach Boarder City to free your family even though he no longer knows them. Their best route now is to come south. We must meet them in Valekrie and bring them here. Then Imar will have to decide whether to give up the key to a king or travel to the East and open the fortress himself. I would opt for the latter, but then you know my opinion of politicians."

"You speak as if we can just sail into an enemy port and tie up to the dock. Not to mention the long journey Imar will have to travel through enemy territory to get there." Akala paused a moment. Her temper was replaced with seriousness. "So Imar has lost his memory. Will it return? What about his skills?"

"People with amnesia sometimes will regain their memory a little at a time or all at once and sometimes not at all. They usually still have their skills and are even surprised by them when used. Imar is still a weapons master, even if he does not know it. I suspect he realizes his skill. Sometimes an amnesiac just needs to see something or someone to bring back those memories. I knew of a case where a man took a rap on the head and his memory returned as soon as he regained consciousness."

"So, he may not remember my daughter when he reunites with her. That ought to be interesting," Akala said sardonically. "I'd love to be a fly on the wall at that meeting." She turned to Dorfin. "I suppose if they must go to Valekrie, then to Valekrie we shall send the *Coastal Raider*. Have Coulig warn the warriors going on this mission. They need to know where and how far they are going and what may be expected of them. I want only volunteers for this mission, preferably old friends of Imar."

Dorfin nodded and departed to find Coulig.

Akala went to the kitchen and returned with an orange and some yogurt. "Care for some breakfast Ivan?"

"Dorfin and I had a fine breakfast of ham, eggs and cheese before you were up, thank you."

"You are welcome. Help yourself or have the cook prepare you whatever you wish to eat. You look a bit thin and if you are going on this quest, you could use a little meat on your bones. Now tell me about your colleague in Abezda and whoever else that could possibly listen in on your thoughts. Are they wizards like you?"

"My colleague in Abezda is Dalla, and I am sure she would rather be referred to as a healer. The other I speak of possibly listening in on our telepathic communication is Sumas. I mentioned him earlier." Ivan frowned when he mentioned the latter. "Dalla is a good person and the most skilled physician you will find on this planet. None of us are really wizards, as I said last night, we are just special. It is a long story and I am sure you have much to do to prepare for the journey."

"I am not going." Akala peeled her orange as she spoke. "I love my daughter, but she would only find fault with me traveling half way around the world to her aid. She would rather I send money, horses and men. Not only that, I have to find Travin. Anisha and Aideen have Imar to rescue them and I am sending a platoon of fighting men to their aid. I am getting too old for battles anyway and I need to organize a search for my husband. The mission preparations are in competent hands, so I have time for your long story."

"Very well, I will tell you some of it. It will explain a few things, such as my long years and boyish good looks." Ivan said this with a wry grin while stroking his black and gray beard.

"In the age before, when prosperity was high and technology was at its peak, science bloomed in so many areas. One of the areas was genetic enhancement. I was one of many people that were reconstructed genetically with altered DNA and born from a test tube. I know those terms are foreign to you, so please excuse me. What that means is that I was born with technology to have special abilities. I was one of the first special born, Sumas and Dalla came later. We have extremely high intelligence, powerful perception, telekinetic and telepathic abilities as well as slow ageing long life. Our metabolisms operate much slower and more efficiently. There are a few other things that we can do and some of us have specialties. Our learning abilities are endless. There were about two hundred of us that were committed to cryogenic chambers."

"What is that?"

"Cryogenics has to do with the science of freezing people for later reanimation. It was originally developed for space travel to distant star systems that would take years of high speed travel to get to."

"Space travel," Akala repeated, unsure she had heard correctly. "You mean like to fly to the stars?"

"Yes, but we're getting sidetracked. We can discuss that another time. Anyway, it was Welker, the archeologist I mentioned last night, who found Sumas, Dalla and I, as well as a few others. He discovered the underground fortress a few years after he found us and it was only three years later that the code was cracked to gain access to the vault. He figured out how to activate the machinery to reanimate us."

"Our cryogenic chambers were nuclear powered and could sustain power for a billion years or more, which was lucky for us. Unfortunately, the shifting of the land masses over the centuries caused many of these places to be damaged, including ours. A few of us survived, but most of our colleagues in the same chamber did not. The place was filled with the rubble from years of earthquakes. It was by pure chance that we survived at all. There were other places, but the ones we found were destroyed. We finally gave up looking for other cryogenic labs. It is possible, I suppose, that there could be others like us that survived and are living elsewhere in the world."

"Explain 'telekinetic,'" asked Akala. "I've never heard that word before."

"Telekinesis is the ability to move objects without physical touch," Ivan explained. "One just uses the mind to make it happen. There was a time when such practices were considered acts of the occult. It was supposedly demonic mumbo jumbo and thought to be nonsense or blasphemous by some religions. People were encouraged to believe that such acts were either impossible or that the power to do it came from an evil and all powerful being like a demon or a devil. That belief stemmed from an earlier age of ignorance and naivety."

"There was a scientist that demonstrated the bending of a spoon with her mind, but belief in the impossible proved more powerful and she was laughed off as a charlatan. You see, a person educated with facts and evidence can hold a belief without any proof whatsoever and that belief will sit rock solid in their mind."

"Eventually telekinesis was scientifically proven by a neurologist. It was widely known that humans use only one quarter of their brain. I have met quite a few that use even less. This neurologist found a way to stimulate other regions of the brain that would normally lie dormant. She had numerous failures, but when she suppressed areas controlling memories, thus blocking beliefs, she succeeded. Unfortunately the test subjects could not survive long under such stimulation nor could their stimulated abilities work when their memories containing beliefs were restored."

"The other problem was that a test subject was bound by a harness of wires that kept them fettered to a huge machine. This research was closely followed by a genetic engineer that eventually teamed up with the neurologist. Together they were able to alter human DNA—the building blocks of life—enough to genetically enhance a human to be born with the ability to use almost all of the brain. These children were taught to be open minded and encouraged to embrace possibilities in everything. They were taught that the impossible was just something that hasn't been done yet. When you believe that nothing is impossible, then you are capable of accomplishing most anything."

Ivan stopped. "I'm getting ahead of myself again. DNA is like the building plans for each and every living organism. Everyone has a different DNA, so to alter it changes the genetic foundation or in other words, it is like changing and strengthening your inherited traits and natural talents. With enhanced talent in a child that isn't suppressed with teachings of 'you can't do this' or 'you'll never do that' their mind is free to embrace positive belief in themselves.

Akala was listening while she ate. "I get the picture, sort of. Please, go on."

"It was a major medical and scientific breakthrough," Ivan continued. "When I was still very young, I was paraded before the world as a manmade prototype genius. Scientists marveled over me and my abilities, but all sorts of religious factions called me an abomination against God. They demanded my destruction and claimed God would punish my creators. After that I was hidden away and eventually forgotten. I buried myself in study and research.

I outlived my designers and worked with their protégés in the same field of research. By then the world was on a downward spiral to destruction."

"That was when I led a team in developing more people like me. By the time my children, so to speak, were mature adults we tried to assist and advise world leaders and corporations on ways to clean up the planet as well as negotiate peace in war ravaged regions. We were, for the most part, ignored. We were the smartest and most gifted people on earth, yet impotent. Cleaning the planet would cut into profits and was not cost effective. Wars were for minerals and that meant profit, except for the ones doing the fighting. The soldiers were given empty promises from politicians granting them rewards that would come either in this life or the next. For every holy man that truly prayed for peace, there was another claiming his God wanted war."

Akala could hear the frustration in Ivan's voice. His head was bowed and he looked into his lap as he remembered the grim past of long, long ago. She reached over and put her hand on his arm. "What did you do?"

"We gave up." Ivan raised his head and continued with only a hint of grief in his voice. "We turned our minds to space travel and exploration, hoping to find another habitable planet for colonization. A few missions were launched, but shortly after that all resources were needed for wars and survival on earth. We sealed up our labs and ourselves and went into the deep freeze of cryogenic sleep as the world got flushed down the proverbial toilet."

Dorfin and Coulig rode down to the shipyard to check on the progress of the *Coastal Raider*. They had hoped to take Beros with them, but he was gone when they arrived at his house. A neighbor told them that he was up early and would be seeing to his ship should anyone ask. They tied their horses at the shipbuilder's office and walked down the hill between rows of boats on blocks that were stored in dry dock. These were mostly single masted fishing boats ranging in size from seven to thirteen meters in length. Most of these boats were being worked on by the owners themselves and a few were being prepped for launch with wheels or log rollers for moving to the water. After passing two rows of fishing boats they came to the warships and merchantmen at the water's edge. These ships, because of their size, sat in a cradle at the top of ramps dedicated to each individual vessel. Each ramp had its own cradle and each cradle was mounted on wheels and attached to a large winch that could be powered by men or horses. The cradle could accommodate anything from a fishing boat to a large ship with a beam of twelve meters in width. Blocks and lines would be used to keep the vessel upright and secure. Ships larger than that had to be secured to a shallow dock at high tide and hull work would be done during the low ebb.

Beros could be heard directing his crew over the noise of the busy shipyard when Dorfin and Coulig strode up to the ship. The crew was in the process of stepping a new main mast that was being raised like a flag pole with lines and pulleys anchored off the cradle. When the mast was tipped up vertical it dropped into its slot and was lowered through the deck and set in place with an audible thud.

As soon as the mast was secure, Beros went to the rail and spotted his friends. He smiled and gave a shout of greeting, then climbed onto the top of a ladder with both hands and feet on the ladder rails and slid to the ground in the time it would take to sneeze. He walked up without any signs of the previous night's intoxication. His cheek was, however, a little red and swollen from the fist of the man that had objected to him groping his daughter.

"Nice boat," Coulig greeted.

Beros lost his grin and looked as if he had been insulted. "Ship, Coulig, it is a ship, not a boat."

"What's the difference?" Coulig liked messing with his friend. He knew very well the difference and that dedicated seamen were very proper and exact with nautical terms.

Beros shook his head and spoke patiently as if speaking to a young cabin boy reporting for his first cruise. "A boat is open without decking and can be carried on a ship, but a ship cannot be carried on a boat. One must speak with respect when referring to one's home, conveyance, and livelihood, especially when in the presence of such a fine ship as the *Coastal Raider*. To do anything else could bring bad luck."

"I never knew a seaman that wasn't superstitious," Coulig replied. "When will you put her in the water?"

"The hull just got a fresh coat of tar and paint yesterday morning, so we could launch on the afternoon tide. She was cleaned up, painted and refitted for commerce. All I did was change some rigging to make her a fast little man-of-war. For a twenty-six meter brig, she will be a force to be reckoned with. She now has four catapults on each side with as many ballistae and two sets fore and aft."

"When will you be ready to depart?" Dorfin asked.

"If the test run goes well, we can shove off for North Harbor on the morning tide."

"Your destination has been changed to Valekrie." Dorfin spoke as blandly as if he were talking about the weather.

Beros didn't waste time searching Dorfin's poker face for any hint of humor, so he turned to the grinning Coulig. "You aren't really serious, are you? Please tell me you're joking."

"Sorry, my friend," answered Coulig. "Imar has enemies behind him and his best chance is to go into Kandia and meet us at Valekrie. If it's any consolation to you, I will be going with you as will twenty-five of my best men."

Beros shrugged. "Who knows? We may even live to tell about it."

"The *Bedford Lee* will have a two day lead on you," added Dorfin. "You may catch up with her since they will be stopping in Seal Bay. Your chances are slim of intercepting her, but if you do, have Einar clap irons on his passenger and bring him back after assisting you at Valekrie. I sent a pigeon to our shipping agent in

Seal Bay, so he may know a little should you meet. Hopefully he will already have the assassin in chains."

"All this good news is more than I can stand. I had better get back to work. I think I will load a few extra barrels of naphtha." Beros turned to Coulig. "Have your platoon come to the dock about two hours before dawn." He then bid his friends a good day and ran up the ladder like a monkey up a tree. Before his feet touched the deck he was barking orders to his crewmen.

The *Coastal Raider* launched on the afternoon tide without incident. They had to tack against the afternoon breeze coming in off the ocean as well as buck the incoming tide. It took some skill to get her out to deep water, but she did well for the conditions. After a few maneuvers to break in the new rigging and to get a feel for how she handled, Beros ordered the sheets furled to come to a full stop. The ship drifted on rolling seas of no more than a three foot swell. Beros stood on the quarterdeck next to his first mate. "Let us smash a few timbers, shall we Gavin! Away the rafts," he ordered excitedly.

"Aye, Captain," answered the first officer. "Launch the rafts!" Gavin shouted as he strode amidships on the rolling deck, his black braided ponytail swaying with each stride. His skin was dark brown, almost black, and his hair was shiny, straight and hung to his waist in a single braid. He was lean with corded muscle and stood well over two meters tall. He joined the men standing ready with the three crudely made rafts and helped them swing the boats off the deck. Once the lines were clear of the third and final launch he called back to the captain, "Rafts away!"

"Give us some sail," ordered Beros.

"Unfurl the sails!" shouted Gavin, as he went aft and ran lithely up the narrow steps to the quarterdeck.

The ship leapt forward once the sheets were shook out and made fast. Beros ordered the decks dowsed and buckets with lines attached were cast over to scoop water from the fast moving sea. They came about, all hands working in concert with the captain directing his orchestra of crewmen with well-timed orders. The men responded with precision that gave harmony to the ship's movements. They came head on to the targets now spread out, each with small masts and sheets to practice aim.

On the first pass they missed completely with shafts and stone splashing around the rafts. On the next pass the forward ballista made a hit with a shaft and another hit with shot, but the four pound stone of the catapult only grazed the target. The starboard battery destroyed a raft which was followed by cheers from that side of the ship. They went past the flotsam of wreckage, leaving two targets still afloat.

"Okay, last pass men," Beros said as they came about. "We have the feel of it now, so let's give it some fire." Orders were relayed down the lines. Cloth wrapped ballista bolts were dipped in naphtha as were cloth wrapped stone for the catapults. Small casks filled with naphtha were loaded in the catapults first and the clothed stones readied for the second loads. The rafts had drifted apart a fair distance, so Beros directed the quartermaster to steer dead on the one to the right. The first raft was dowsed and lit only a minute before the port battery set the other raft ablaze and the aft catapult broke them up with two shots just before they turned for home port. Cheers erupted all over the ship and Beros ordered a double ration of grog to every hand. The crew took up a song as they sped into the bay with the wind at their back and the high tide at slack. The sun slipped behind the westward clouds, bringing an early sunset.

The next morning was dark, cold, and wet. A steady rain had been falling since midnight. Port Augustus was known for fair weather at this time of year, so all but the arthritic were taken by surprise with the unseasonable storm. Whitecaps could be seen in the bay, but the horizon was dark and the severity of the sea could only be guessed. A somber mood prevailed amongst the crew. Coulig and his men seemed to be less than pleased to be departing in foul weather aboard a boat of any size, but especially one of only twenty-six meters. Ivan seemed a bit grumpy and went below as soon as he stepped aboard. Coulig and the wizard were assigned hammock places in Beros' quarters and the soldiers were billeted on the crew deck.

"Are you sure this is wise?" Coulig asked Beros after they shoved off. They were still in the bay and the deck was swaying badly enough to make walking difficult. Crewmen, ordered to batten down, were tying tarps over hatches, stringing out safety lines, and securing anything that could move. His men-at-arms had gone below and only essential personnel were working topside. Ivan was nowhere to be seen.

Only Beros seemed to be looking forward to the high seas with anticipation. "The *Coastal Raider* is a stout ship. She can handle it." Sheets of rain were whipping across the deck, stinging their faces and pelting their tarred jackets. Waves were breaking against the bow sending spray up half the mast height. "It's going to get a little rough once we clear the breakwater and make for open sea. You might want to tie yourself off or go below." Beros handed Coulig a safety line and tied another about his own waist.

Coulig took Beros' advice and tied himself off. "What do you mean, 'going to get?' It's rough now."

Beros grinned largely. "It's going to get a lot rougher." He took the helm and steered out to deep water before turning northwest. The wind was howling out of the south, sending them fast before the wind with only the trysail up to hold course and some semblance of control. The sea anchor was deployed to slow them down and give a little stability. It was a wood and cloth conical affair cast off the stern to be used as a brake in bad weather. Green water was crashing over the bow knocking men off their feet, the safety lines keeping them from going over the rail. Beros handed the helm back to the quartermaster and shouted orders over the wind to make adjustments to keep the course and prevent the ship from breaking apart.

Coulig had had enough of holding on to the rail for dear life and made his way below decks to get out of the weather. He latched both arms around the port stair rail and scooted down the steps on his backside, coming to the end of his safety line at the bottom of the gangway. He looked around for another line, not wanting to release his grasp on solid wood. His backside was bruised from the abrupt pitching of the deck. It seemed that he went up when the boat went down and they would come back together with a smack. Then a wave would crash against the side, smashing him into a bulkhead, followed by a deluge of sea water trying to wash him over the side.

Every muscle in his body ached, and he was a man accustomed to rigorous weapons training. Looking up at the front of the quarter deck he saw Beros with his hair plastered to the side of his face, gripping the rail. He was laughing and shouting, sometimes orders to his crew and other times at the iron gray sky, calling on the gods and asking if this was all they could give. *Madman*, thought Coulig. *I went to sea in a tempest with a madman.* He spotted another line on the main deck, just out of his reach, stretched out his foot and snagged it with his toe.

He got the new line tied around his waist while keeping an arm looped through the railing, but the other line holding him to the quarterdeck was too tight and swollen to untie. He drew his dagger and sawed at the line. He was through two strands and halfway through the last when he was slammed with green water coming over the port rail. The line snapped, the dagger went flying and the ship pitched to starboard. Coulig held his breath as he slid down the deck underwater toward the starboard side. He rolled over on his belly and grabbed his lifeline, amazed his fingers found it under the flood of dark seawater. Grunting with the yank at the rope's end, he let out his breath as the water passed over him and back to the sea where it belonged. Pulling himself hand over hand he came closer to the door to get below. The deck righted itself, but he dared not try to stand and was glad he hadn't when the boat pitched to port. He slid with the movement, but held his grip on the line.

Coulig finally made it through the door and inside. He knew he would later regret losing his dagger, but right now he could care less. Working vigorously, he untied his line with numbed, rope burned hands, tossed it out and shut the door. He lay there a few minutes panting on the stairs inside the gangway that led to the captain's cabin or around the corner and down a few more steps to the crew deck. He braced his back on the wall and pressed his feet against the opposite wall to hold himself in place. Coulig was not a religious man. He often had doubts about deities and even considered atheism, but he was also prudent and decided not to take any chances. He sent a prayer off to every god he could remember hearing about as well as a few requests to the spirits of all his ancestors.

Getting to his feet, he made his way down to the crew deck and wished he hadn't. Coulig was a veteran of many battles. The mutilations he had witnessed in numerous shield walls had not prepared him for the scene he now experienced. The stench assailed his nostrils, turning his stomach over before his eyes registered the scene.

The deck was crammed with men sitting or lying in vomit. Hammocks were impossible to stay in but for the few that had tied themselves in, and they swung and bounced violently sending anyone flying that came close. Everyone else sat on the deck and wedged themselves together or against the hull to minimize the violent shifting of the ship in the angry seas. Nearly everyone was puking or retching with the dry heaves. Water from above decks found its way down, mixing with and diluting the vomitus that sloshed against everyone there. There was a small toilet hatch in the bow, that could be used in calmer weather, but even if it were not sealed tight now, there was no way it could accommodate all those in need of expulsion. Coulig gritted his teeth against the bile coming up his throat, but could not hold back his breakfast or his dinner from the night before. He apologized to Brin, whom he sprayed before he could redirect the projectile of his stomach's contents. Brin was too miserable with his own seasickness to care at the moment. Coulig left that vile scene and went up to the captain's quarters, wedging himself in a corner to ride out the day that seemed an eternity.

The storm raged on all day and into the night. Sometime after midnight the seas seemed to slacken and Coulig drifted off to an exhausted sleep. When he woke, Beros was sleeping in his bunk and Ivan was dry as a bone and snoring in his own hammock. Sunlight shone through the cabin's stern window, now uncovered. Coulig's clothes were still damp, so he went to his pack below his unused hammock and changed into dry attire after washing up. He went topside to find calm seas, a blue sky with a few small clouds, and sunshine. Some of his men were up, as well as some off duty crewmen who were busy washing gear and stringing up clothes lines.

Gavin, first mate and duty officer on the morning watch, greeted Coulig. "Top o' the mornin' to ya Captain."

Coulig looked up at the tall, dark man on the quarter deck. He looked like he had a fresh shave and his long handlebar mustache was well trimmed. He wore a bright red shirt with loose bloused sleeves and a black vest. His baggy trousers were bright blue and tucked into his boots. Most crewmen wore ankle high boots of oiled leather and gum soles for gripping a wet wood deck. Gavin's boots were much the same, but his were red and came halfway up his calves. Coulig went up on the quarter deck and greeted him. "Good morning. I didn't think we would live through that storm. I have a renewed respect for men of the sea now and I will be very happy to get my feet on firm ground again."

"We all think that when we're in a bad storm, except Captain Beros of course. He seems to go a little crazy in the nastiest storms. He does that in battle too."

"How far have we come?"

"We should be a day off of being abeam Seal Bay."

Coulig was surprised. "I thought that was a four to five day sail."

"It is when you're not scudding before a demon's wind. We made good time of a miserable journey."

The next few days were calm, for the most part, and uneventful. The seas kicked up with the wind a few times, but nothing like the first day. A few of the soldiers had reoccurring bouts of seasickness and those unlucky souls were teased by their comrades mercilessly. Poor Brin was one of the few that would often sit in misery on the leeward so he could lean over the side and feed the fish. Jax acquired his sea legs early on and quickly developed a love for the sea. He learned all he could about the ship and crewman duties. It was not long before he was climbing the rigging, walking yard arms and sliding down the lines. Sometimes he would save a piece of bacon just so he could sit by Brin and eat it. Of course, that was too much for poor Brin and over the rail he would heave. Brin tried grabbing the agile Jax, but he was too ill to succeed. He swore he would get even with his friend one day, probably on shore.

Ivan spent much of his time telling stories to anyone who would listen. He carried a little three legged folding stool in one hand and a pewter mug of grog in the other. He would sit anywhere that he wasn't in the way so long as there was an audience for his tales. If it rained more than a light sprinkle he would go below and return with his wide brimmed hat and coat with his mug topped off. Anytime there was excessive work to be done on deck, Ivan vanished in an instant.

Coulig and Gavin drilled the crewman and soldiers together so that they would be used to working as a team. Beros set out a target raft once a day for archers and crossbowmen to practice shooting a moving target from a moving deck. The most agile would fire arrows or bolts from the tops. They would then practice maneuvers with catapult and ballistae. They all became confident with their improving skill and morale was high.

Beros watched Coulig and Gavin's joint training and was glad the two got along well together. He was also pleased that the soldiers and crew were melding into a team that would be able to fight together in harmony. Valekrie was an enemy port. Kandian navy and pirates alike would love to take the *Coastal Raider*. They all knew that they would have many enemies, the closer they got to their destination. Beros kept the grog rations moderate. He wanted the men to socialize and blow off a little steam at the end of a watch, but he also wanted to keep fights to a minimum. Vigilance and sobriety were needed as well.

Ivan ignored ration rules altogether. It was suspected that he had fashioned his own key to the liquor locker. He even joined in the sword practice from time to time, surprising everyone with his skill after downing three mugs of grog. Beros was contemplating this while watching sword practice on the main deck when he heard a shout from the crow's nest.

"Sail ho!" cried the lookout.

CHAPTER 12

Einar walked down the hill to the docks after his visit to the shipping agent. It was a nice day and walking helped him think. The air was fresh and the sun warm. He relished both, especially after riding the storm from hell that brought him to Seal Bay in record time. Einar was a sensible man of middle years. He loved the sea, but would prefer to sit out violent storms in a sheltered cove or, better yet, with his wife in front of their fireplace. He was clean shaven and his graying hair was thinning on top. He was getting thick in the middle and kept promising himself that he would do more walking when he went ashore. He had meant to walk to the shipping agent's office as well, but the hill got the best of him and he hailed a cab before making it halfway. It was downhill back to his ship, so he told the carriage driver not to wait.

A message had just arrived via pigeon from Port Augustus. It was some most unsettling news about his passenger and orders to intercept the *Coastal Raider* to assist on some fool's errand at Valekrie. The last place on earth that Einar would have wanted to go was Valekrie. *Well, orders are orders*, thought Einar. *Maybe I should retire. I'm getting too old for such nonsense.* Einar was not afraid to fight, he just preferred to choose the battles he knew he could win, nor did he care to fight unless there was a considerable profit. Einar ran a tight, well-disciplined ship, avoided danger when he could, and practiced good planning. He was not prepared for this news. He looked again at the message.

PAX KHALED: ASSASSIN → ARREST HIM. C-RAIDER DEPARTED MON.→ ASSIST AT VALEKRIE.

How he was supposed to take a Hamaudi assassin by surprise, he did not know. Finding the *Coastal Raider* would be difficult as well. Sailing into Valekrie seemed to him pure insanity. Best chance would be to go into the area at night and drop anchor in a nearby bay or cove and watch for the *Raider* there. Einar picked up his pace, a plan formulating in his mind. Before he left the shipping agent, he not only made arrangements to sell his cargo, but to buy additional weaponry and ammunition to include two pallets of three gallon casks of naphtha. If he was going to Valekrie, he was going armed to the teeth. He went to the warehouse as directed by the shipping agent and showed the manager the invoice for a ballista and eight catapults with ten kilogram capacity. Naphtha casks, ballista bolts, crossbow bolts, shot and cable were also on the list. The warehouse manager assured Einar that his order would be filled immediately and delivered that afternoon. Einar then returned to his ship and told Hawkins about their new mission.

Hawkins was normally delighted to hear of prospects of action, but Valekrie didn't seem to please him. "Sounds more like a suicide mission than a profitable venture to me."

"I'm not exactly overwhelmed with joy either," replied Einar. "How many men are ashore?"

"Twenty-five have taken shore leave sir, including our passenger. The purser is securing additional supplies as well."

"Don't let any more crewmen leave until our new weapons are installed and provisions and munitions are stowed. How do you think we should capture this assassin?"

"It would be better to kill him if it is possible," Hawkins answered. "Hamaudi assassins don't stay captured for long and they are very hard to kill. If we try to take him prisoner we will probably lose men. If we leave him behind or try to kill him and fail, he will have his revenge."

"Alright, let's depart tomorrow as planned and take him prisoner once we get to deep water."

The *Bedford Lee* set sail the next day on the afternoon tide. Einar was still trying to decide how to go about capturing Khaled without any losses. He was discussing this with Hawkins when the ship's cook overheard the conversation when he came to get the captain's choice for evening meal.

"Beggin' yur pardon sah," said the cook, "but 'ow 'bout I slip a little somethin' in 'is meal to 'elp him sleep?"

Einar and Hawkins looked at each other with expressions that said, 'Why didn't I think of that?' "Excellent idea, Mister Kensington," said the captain. "See the doctor and make it so."

It was thus that Khaled found himself in shackles late the following day. He accepted his situation without word. He was given a bucket to use as a privy and was brought meals and water. The chains allowed him to stand or lay on his hammock, but kept him out of reach of anything that could be used as a weapon. Khaled remained quiet, watchful, and kept his ears open. He eventually learned that the new destination was Valekrie and that his target was coming there. This news pleased the assassin. He smiled inwardly then meditated in prayer, giving thanks to the nameless god that his quarry's soul would soon be set free. In his prayers he asked that a few more souls might get in his way, so that he could set them free as well.

While enroute the crew stayed busy with sword and crossbow practice as well as ballistae and catapult drills. Grog rations were watered down and good meals of fish and chicken were served to keep up strength and morale. The first day out they had roast mutton. There were a few ships that steered close enough to inspect them, but when the new armament was glassed by the curious they quickly changed their course and gave the *Bedford Lee* a wide berth. Einar didn't order any attacks either. His officers glassed every ship they saw, hoping to find the *Coastal Raider*. The weather was getting cooler and wetter. They experienced occasional rain as they traveled north. Einar planned to find a cove to hide in during the day when they got close to Valekrie. They could probably pass for a Kandian ship at night if there was enough cloud cover. In this seasonal daylight, without cloud cover they would be doomed.

CHAPTER 13

Imar and Dalla traveled through the night after leaving Daishon Ferry. They had only gone a few hours before the light of day increased, if only slightly. Gray gloom and intermittent rain pervaded the land with tenacious grip. They were both very tired and needed to get some rest, so they moved off the road to what they deemed a safe distance and found a small clearing in the thick spruce forest in which to set up their tent. Imar took the time to cut some branches to camouflage the tent and set tripwires to cookware to warn them should they have visitors.

They slept until midday. When they woke, Dalla rubbed the painted emblem of the golden bear off her shield with sand. Then she used some fresh herbs and some coffee grounds boiled down to a paste to paint a tree with many branches on her shield. When she finished her art work they ate a meal of cooked oats then broke camp and resumed their journey. They had not gone far when they heard riders. After the events of the previous day they decided not to take any chances, so they took cover off the road. They were lucky that they were in a wooded patch at that time, since much of the terrain sported wide areas of treeless bogs overrun with hillocks and tussocks, which made for difficult walking for both man and horse. The riders were traveling west and all were wearing brown, but neither Imar nor Dalla could make out their sigil. After the riders passed they continued on the road with eyes and ears open.

Dalla had a lot on her mind that she needed to share with Imar. Until now, she had thought it best to keep quiet about her role with the key, but now forces were in motion to take it and she felt that she needed to stay close to it. While they rode, Dalla told Imar about the octagon key as well as where and when she was from. It was a long story and Imar listened quietly as he rode beside her. She told him of the great marvels of technology as well as the destruction that came from the byproducts of that technology, how humankind went back to a primitive state and began evolution all over again with only a remnant of handed down knowledge. She gave him the history of the key along with her role, Ivan's, and that of their colleague and betrayer, Sumas.

"This is quite a bit to take in," said Imar. He briefly entertained the thought that Dalla may be mentally unstable. She seemed rational though and the story was too farfetched to be made up. He decided to accept her story and consider the possibilities of gaining access to such knowledge. A weapons cache of such magnitude would be a great treasure indeed. He also considered the doom that would come if an enemy were to find it first. "That would make you at least seventy-five or eighty years old, or at least that old since your waking from the freeze sleep. You don't look a day over twenty five and if I understand correctly, you were older than that when you went into this cryogenic chamber." Imar knew that by rights he should discount this wild tale as preposterous, but for some reason that he suspected was being blocked because of his amnesia, he believed her story almost as if he had heard it before in some forgotten dream. "Does that mean you are a sorceress?"

"That is a misused term. No, I am not a sorceress. I can use most of my brain, that's all; most people use only one quarter. That is how I put those guards into a deep sleep. It is how I perceived danger when we went down the hill to Daishon Ferry. Ivan and I can sometimes talk with our minds, though it is not always possible or easy. We spoke early this morning in that manner. He is coming with friends of yours from Port Augustus to meet us in Valekrie. From there we need to travel to Eastonia and destroy the key and the vault. What you need to understand is that what you carry in your pouch is a key to vast knowledge, for which this world may not be ready. The advanced weaponry that the key can unlock may lead to vast destruction."

Imar didn't respond. He thought about all that Dalla had said. He thought again that she may be somewhat deluded, but he thought he knew her better than that. Going to Eastonia with the key seemed a good idea; he was not sure that destroying it was. He would think on it. For now his mission was to rescue his family, even if he didn't remember them.

Dalla explained to Imar about DNA and genetic enhancement as Ivan had told Akala. The brief version of the history of the old world and the new one took most of the day. Describing who she was and where she was from took just as long.

"You said that three of you escaped King Anders' imprisonment," Imar said. "If Sumas had joined Anders and you and Ivan got away, then who was the third?

"That would be Sumil," answered Dalla. "He was the twin brother of Sumas. Sumil looked like Sumas, but all likeness stopped there. Sumil took his brothers betrayal very badly. He was very weak from the depression it brought on him and it was all Ivan and I could do to escape with him. He didn't speak for weeks. Once we got out of Eastonia he finally spoke. He told us he had had enough of power plays, kings and betrayal. Sumil said his good byes and walked south. We never heard of him again."

Imar and Dalla had only snacked through the day and when evening came they were both in need of a meal. They began searching for a place to camp when they heard riders again. Imar led them off the road, but there wasn't much cover. The riders were getting closer, so Imar chose a low spot. They dismounted and got the horses to lie down. It looked like the same party that had passed them before, but this time they were spotted. The riders turned off the road and came toward them.

With a nudge from Imar, Cerus stood with Imar astride his back. The riders were too close for them to run or for Imar to don his chain mail. "Get on your horse and ride," Imar said firmly to Dalla. He then looped his arm through his shield straps and drew his long sword. Dalla climbed into Bell's saddle, but didn't ride off. Her perception told her that these men were friends. Imar rode out to meet the approaching six men and noticed that they were smiling and had not drawn their weapons. They wore tabards like his, bearing the hawk within an octagon.

The leader was a man slightly younger than Imar and of similar build, but with light brown hair and beard. He held up a hand and called out. "Captain, it is good to see you. We have been searching for you." He glanced at Dalla and raised an eyebrow.

"Do I know you?" Imar looked puzzled. "I am sorry, but I sustained a head injury and barely survived. In the process I have lost my memory. If it weren't for this young lady, a healer, I would surely have died."

The men looked at each other. The leader spoke again with knit brows. "I am Olaf, your lieutenant and second in command. We have much to talk about, namely your wife and child." Olaf glanced again at Dalla.

"This is Dalla," Imar introduced. "She is a healer from Mentin and as I just said she saved my life. She has been a good guide and companion and nothing has happened between us beyond friendship." Imar could tell by the looks on their faces that this needed saying. He also suspected that they probably didn't believe him. "I have had news that my wife and daughter have been taken under house arrest by mercenaries claiming to be my friends."

"That is true, Captain," replied Olaf. "Their leader is called Kendal. He is an old comrade of yours, and has taken over your villa supposedly for the protection of your family. No one is allowed in or out. I remember him from our adventures years ago. He was a good friend back then, but now I don't know. People change. We didn't storm the gates because your villa is defensibly formidable, and we weren't sure if he was telling the truth."

"Without my memory I have no way of knowing whether or not he or anyone else speaks the truth," said Imar. "For now though, it is late. We are tired and hungry and need to set up camp." Imar pointed to a hill a little farther off. "Let us set up camp behind that hill and out of sight of the road. We have enemies behind us, so your company will be a comfort."

Before going any further, Olaf insisted on introducing the other men. "Captain, these are your men. They are not only your men; they and I are your friends." Imar sheathed his sword, hung his shield on a saddle hook and dismounted. The five soldiers dismounted and approached Imar. Olaf then began introductions indicating each man with an open hand. "This is Hager, also a lieutenant." A stout man with a serious face stepped forward and grasped forearms with Imar in a bone crushing grip.

Imar did not recognize this burly man, but Hager looked into Imar's eyes with intensity as only a close friend, or rather, a brother in arms would do – a brother that has shared combat, stood side by side in a shield wall, bled together and worn the blood of their enemies together. Neither man spoke. Imar began to see images in his mind that he couldn't touch, couldn't make out. Vague fleeting phantoms of memory, almost within reach, that vanished like smoke on the wind when Olaf spoke.

"This is Vidar." Olaf introduced a tall man wearing dark brown braids as well as two small braids in his beard.

Vidar took Imar's forearm and smiled. "It is good to see you again, even if you don't remember us." Then he took on a serious look. "I hope your memory returns soon."

"Pleased to meet you, again, and thank you," replied Imar.

"I am Rolf," said the next man in line. A young, happy faced, red haired man stepped up and grabbed Imar's arm. He couldn't wait any longer.

"And these two," Olaf went on, "are Aksel and Egil." Barely more than boys, they were both thin, but beyond that they were opposites. Egil had dark hair, nearly black, with the fuzzy beginnings of a thin mustache. Aksel, on the other hand, was a towheaded blonde without the trace of even fuzz on his face. Imar grasped arms with both of the young men and then Olaf spoke again, this time to Dalla. "Lady, you have brought our friend and captain

117

back to us, alive and healthy. For that we thank you. Consider us at your service."

Olaf and his squad struck their right fists to their left chests and bowed to Dalla. She was still sitting on her horse and feeling pretty special at that moment. "Thank you gentlemen, but I am very hungry as well as road weary. Shouldn't we make camp?"

They set up the tent on the back side of the small hill Imar had indicated. They found the hill was shaped like a crescent on the side opposite from the road with a flat area for the tent on the bank of a small lake. It was an ideal spot for a camp. Birch trees covered the hill with a few spruce intermingled. A thicker patch of forest could be seen on the far side of the lake where a bull moose waded amidst the lily pads. Mosquitoes were out in full force, so Imar shared the extra bug hoods. Even though there weren't enough to go around everyone took turns escaping the pests. The weather turned clear, so the night would not be dark, just a twilight dim enough to make their small campfire difficult to detect.

Dalla built the fire while the men set up the tent. The tent would sleep four, so they strung lines and draped a couple of tarps to form an extension that would keep all of them out of the weather should it cloud up and rain. Aksel and Egil had gone to the forest when they heard the clucking of spruce hens. They returned in less than a half an hour with five grouse which they set by Dalla, since she was preparing a meal of bread, cheese and fresh picked fiddle head fern.

Dalla looked at the birds and then at the two young men. "Nice birds, but you forgot to clean them."

Aksel stammered, "We thought that if we shot them you would . . ." Dalla's level gaze stopped him from finishing his sentence.

Egil reached down and picked up two of the birds. "I think we had better clean them, Aksel."

They carried their prizes to the lake arguing over who should clean the last bird. The men were amused with the exchange. Vidar showed the boys a fast method of de-breasting grouse and within a few minutes mouths were watering with the aroma of roasting bird.

Imar and Olaf spoke by the fire long after everyone else had gone to sleep. Imar told Olaf all he knew about his heirloom and his life since his memory began. Olaf told Imar all he could about his family, his villa, Boarder City, and his company of professional soldiers. Hager, Olaf and Imar had left Boarder City together years ago seeking fortune and adventure. They worked for Travin and Akala for many years and returned home wealthy men when Imar's father Amir requested their aid. Amir had injured his sword hand and asked Imar to take his place. They were not the king's soldiers, but contracted by the king each year for a considerable sum to protect the border from raiders. Amir moved to Three Rivers for retirement and better medical care than the frontier town of Boarder City could provide. He stayed active in negotiations on behalf of his son's elite forces.

Aideen, Imar's daughter, was a highly energetic little girl with a flaming interest in everything. She had long dark hair, piercing dark eyes, and preferred to play stick swords and dress like a boy, to the great distress of her mother. Anisha, Imar's wife, was somewhat short with brown hair. Olaf spoke with some reservation about his friend's wife.

"What is it? What are you not telling me?" Imar asked.

"I would rather not say." Olaf could have kicked himself for not hiding his thoughts better. "It is just that she can sometimes be a little curt with servants and soldiers."

Imar tried to get Olaf to elaborate, but his lieutenant would say no more. Imar grew solemn and asked, "What of my mother. I have heard about my father, my friends and some of my history, but nothing about my mother."

Olaf looked at his friend, and sadness crossed his face. "There was a time when we lived in a small village not far from the city. We were children then, barely even fourteen years old you were. I was twelve. Our fathers were out on patrol when the raiders came. Most of us children hid in the woods. You stayed behind to protect your mom."

"She had been sick, food poisoning I think. She was feverish and could not move very fast. The raiders pillaged our community, took our livestock and our harvest, and then they torched our homes. The rest of us found safety in the forest, but you and your mother were still in the open when they found you." Olaf's eyes tightened at the corners as if he held back tears. "You were a fair hand with a sword even at fourteen and you made your first kill that day. More than that actually, you killed three of them before you were knocked down and disarmed. They tied your hands, planning on taking you prisoner, probably for the slave market. Your mother screamed when they knocked you down. Then they turned on her."

"We were just women and children hiding in the woods fearing for our lives, fearful for what was happening to you and your mother. We were all too scared to move, except Hager. He tore free of his mother's grasp and ran screaming out of the woods. A boy too small for the sword he carried, taken by the berserker's rage. The raiders laughed at him. They laughed until he hacked off the hand of their leader and sunk his sword in the belly of another. They disarmed and bound him too and kicked him repeatedly where he lay on the ground. Then they made you watch. We all watched. It was horrible. I still hear her screams."

"A shout went up. It was the patrol. It was our fathers. Your dad led the charge on his great antlered moose. They came to save us, to save you, and your mom. But it was too late. Before our fathers fell upon the Kandian demons they ran her though. They killed her, after they used her, before she could be saved. The patrol killed them all. That wasn't enough for your father though. He hacked their bodies to pieces and scattered them for the beasts of the woods and the birds of the air. He would not allow them to be burned."

Olaf exhaled heavily. "You did not speak for weeks. When you did, you told Hager and I that you would teach your children to fight before they could walk, so they would not be taken as dishonorably as your mother had been." Olaf hated telling this sad story, but his friend had a right to know. "This is a depressing tale. But know this: I may not think much of your wife, but your daughter at ten years of age is better with sword or bow than many a young man of eighteen years."

Olaf left Imar to his silent contemplations. He woke Egil to take the next watch and went to bed. Imar lay awake for some time thinking about Olaf's words before he fell into a troubled sleep.

They were on the road early the next morning. Imar sent Aksel and Egil to find out where Sigurd was and what he was up to. He warned them to use stealth and avoid contact. Imar and company rode hard all day using a method of walk, trot, gallop, run, then back from run, gallop, trot, walk. This method allowed for the best overall rate of speed without overworking the horses. They took short breaks to rest the mounts and their backsides, but they ate up the distance in good time. As they got closer to the city, they encountered people on the road with increasing frequency.

Olaf had briefed Imar on the layout of his villa during one of those periods when they were walking the horses. None of them could think of any way that they could assault the villa without endangering his family. Imar had to talk to Kendal. He wanted to take Dalla with him. Her abilities might be able to detect lies and warn him of danger, but he didn't want to expose her to any possible threat. Also, it probably wasn't wise to arrive home to one's wife after a long road trip and present a beautiful young lady as one's traveling companion. Imar may have lost his memory, but he had not lost his senses.

They arrived at the gates of Boarder City in the late afternoon. Imar was surprised to find not only a large frontier city, but a defensible one as well. The city was walled with granite and had only two gates. The gates were manned by soldiers of the realm. These were usually men enlisted for a two year term and of minimal training at arms. The garrison at Boarder City never helped Imar's contracted men, even when local villages were being raided. The garrison commander claimed that his duty extended no farther than the city walls. If the city fell under attack, then his men would fight, but keeping raiders at bay was what Imar's warriors were hired for.

The city itself had not been attacked in thirty years. The locals were thankful for Imar's men that wore the badge of the hawk within the octagon. The townspeople and the surrounding villages considered the king's soldiers to be worthless. That sentiment also extended to the government in general. Taxes, as far as the citizens were concerned, were a waste of hard earned money.

Imar gave the key to Dalla for safe keeping and went alone and unarmed to his front gate, where he demanded to see his family. He was let right in and escorted toward his house when a fair haired man of thirty some odd years came out of the house and greeted him in the courtyard with a strong forearm grip.

"Imar," said the man, "it is good to see you again."

Imar was confused. This man was friendly. Stories were that he had pressed his father hard for the key and taken his wife and child hostage. "Kendal?"

"I haven't changed that much. Don't you remember me?"

"Where are Anisha and Aideen?"

"Would you like to see them? Come on." Kendal led Imar up a half a dozen steps and into the house followed by the two guards. Imar counted six men in the courtyard plus the two watching him. Upon entering the double doors, he saw two more in the foyer. They walked down a long hall and entered a room full of toys and overlooking a garden. A middle aged lady was sitting in a chair knitting, and a young raven haired girl was playing on the floor with little toy soldiers set up on a mock field of battle. Kendal cleared his throat a moment after they entered.

The little girl looked up and her eyes lit up with delight. "Daddy, you're back!" Aideen came running across the room and slammed into Imar with a big hug. "I missed you so much."

Imar squatted down and hugged his daughter while wracking his brain for a memory. Unrecognizable phantom images danced around in the foggy darkness of his mind, much like what he had experienced with Hager. Something was there. He could almost put his finger on it and then the images shattered when a woman walked in and spoke.

"It's about time you got back." The tone was sharp and sarcastic. Anisha looked at the nanny with tight squinted eyes and made a motion with her head.

"Mom, please be nice. I'm so happy to see Dad again. It has been such a long time." Aideen turned back to Imar. "How is Grandpa doing?"

The nanny interrupted. "Come Aideen, your parents have grown up stuff to talk about. Let us go to the kitchen and get a snack. You can see your father later."

Aideen didn't look happy, but she complied without a fuss. "Okay, Greta." She let go of Imar and said, "I'll see you later, Daddy."

"See you later, Aideen," Imar said as Aideen and Greta went out the door.

"Where in hell have you been, Imar? You were supposed to be back a week ago. People have been looking for you, you idiot. People that want to buy some worthless heirloom that your father gave you." Anisha was about to say more, but Kendal stopped her.

"Why don't we sit and talk about this," said Kendal. He led them down the hall to another room. Imar was confused. Anisha didn't treat him like a wife should a husband. Olaf had warned him that she was curt with the help, but she seemed to be outright rude and not just to the servants. She scowled at the nanny and didn't say a word to Aideen.

They went down the hall and into a room with swords, shields and halberds on the walls in between tall shelves stuffed full of books. There was a table in the center of the room with six wooden chairs. On the far end of the room were four soft padded chairs covered in caribou hides with matching foot stools. Each table had a reading lamp made of carved diamond willow, which was not needed at the time because of the light coming in through the skylights directly above the chairs. The chairs faced inward in a circle and beside three of them was a glass of wine. Kendal indicated the chairs and said, "I took the liberty of having some wine poured when I heard you were at the gate. You have an excellent selection in your cellar, Imar. It must have cost a king's ransom to get so much of such quality to this remote frontier city."

Imar said nothing, but nodded as they all took their seats.

Anisha grunted something under her breath. She took her chair and drained her glass. As soon as her empty glass was back on the table, a teenage servant girl came from the doorway and poured her another. "Leave the bottle and leave us. And be sure to shut the door," Anisha snapped at the girl. "I'll have you whipped if I catch you eavesdropping." The girl set the decanter down on Anisha's side table and quickly exited the room, quietly closing the door behind her.

Imar looked at Anisha. *She would be pretty if she didn't wear a perpetual frown and scowl at everyone*, he thought. *Maybe she was having the cramps or something.* "Aren't you being a little rough with the help?" Imar tried to say this gently, seeing Anisha's foul mood.

Anisha turned on him—her face was livid. "What's it to you, you're never here to deal with them."

"I can see why," Imar retorted. "I get better treatment from my enemies."

"Please, please," said Kendal, "let us try to be civil here. We need to discuss the device."

Imar, relieved at the interruption, said, "I agree. Before we go on I must tell you something of importance. I hope you will not use this against me and be honest with me instead. My wife, at least, has a right to know." Imar paused. He looked at Anisha and Kendal and saw that he had their undivided attention. "I lost my memory— completely. I don't know either one of you. At least I have no memory of anyone or anything. I was attacked by Jarl Bamsen's men. I received a severe rap on the head and remember nothing before that. I nearly died from the injury and would have if not for a healer of unusual skill."

Imar then briefed them on the events that had brought him back to his home; the waking in the pit and the miserable journey back to Mentin, Dalla finding out who he was and that his family was in danger, and the offer from Sigurd and the fighting escape. Imar looked at Kendal. "I was told you were hired to ransom my family. I was also told you were an old comrade and here to protect my family. Which is it?"

"Both," said Kendal.

"Wait a minute." Anisha had been itching to speak up since the first mention of Dalla. "You say this healer traveled with you here. Why? What does she have to do with any of this? Have you been sleeping with her?"

"No, I have not slept with her. Dalla told me my name and that I might be married. That possibility alone was enough for us to be properly distant. It was later on when Sigurd confirmed to me that you weren't my sister, so nothing happened." Imar thought it wise not to mention the kiss. He had not bedded Dalla, so he didn't feel like he was lying, but now after meeting his wife he was beginning to regret not giving in to his passions with the healer even though it went against his morals.

Anisha grunted, but said nothing.

"Do you still have your skills?" Kendal was sitting forward in his chair, looking at Imar curiously.

"I seem to. It may have been the battle rush, but I bested Sigurd's men with ease. Now tell me who you are and why you are here."

Kendal sat back in his chair and said, "We met a long time ago sailing with Captain Travin as privateers and treasure hunters when we were young. You taught me the sword. At seventeen you were the best swordsman anyone had ever seen. You told me your father was your teacher and even better than you. You used to tell stories of your father patrolling the border on a great bull moose trained for battle. Anyway, you loved the sea and I did not, so after a few years of gathering wealth and experience I went to Sedar and became a mercenary. I eventually came to lead a free company much like what you lead here. King Bertil of Sedar has paid well in the past, but of late there has been little action on the Kandian front. I have heard the same here, a strange peace without a treaty. For some reason Kandia has been quiet. Bertil hasn't needed us for several months, so when the time came to renew our contract he sent us packing."

"I was contacted by Lord Townsend from Port Augustus. He had a small job that could be handled by a half a dozen men, so I left one of my lieutenants in charge and went to Port Augustus to check out the job. He wanted me to go to Abezda and buy or steal an heirloom that was supposed to have some sort of magical power. I don't believe in magic, but I do believe in money, so I took the job. I convinced him to hire a twenty man troop. I got half down and will get the other half when I bring him the device, as well as a big bonus. He wanted me to go to Three Rivers to get the device from a man named Amir. I learned when I got to Three Rivers that Amir was your father. I also learned that Jarl Bamsen had taken an interest in this device as well. Your father told me nothing, which was fine. His housekeeper told us everything we needed to know, and then some. It was all I could do to shut her up. I never did succeed at that. When we left she followed us down the lane chattering non-stop. I asked your father to ransack his house and tell Bamsen's men that we roughed him up. I convinced him that we would get to Boarder City as quickly as we could to protect his daughter-in-law and granddaughter, since he was unable to travel. He said you could take care of yourself, but you needed warning. I sent two men by road and the rest of us went by ship up river. I have not heard from my men that I sent by road. I have heard by pigeon that Bamsen is coming here with eighty horsemen. He wants the device."

"Why was my father unable to travel?"

"He broke his leg," replied Kendal. "He said he fell off his horse. My guess is that he fell out of bed. The chatterbox neighbor seemed awfully affectionate for just a housekeeper."

Imar sat there a minute wondering if Kendal was telling the truth. "So you came here to help me? What about Townsend's retainer?"

"Imar, think about what that thing is worth. Townsend has spent a small fortune just looking for it. He would pay a larger fortune to get it. Bamsen would pay dearly to get his hands on it as well. We could auction it off to them and be rich."

"By the look of things I am already rich."

"You idiot," Anisha snapped. "We could be richer. We could leave this middle of nowhere frontier and live on our southern estate like royalty. Why should you lead this rabble for guard duty? You should hire it out and spend your time gaining the king's favor at court."

"I don't know who I am or even much of what I was, but I do know that I have no desire to involve myself in politics or court intrigue. Besides, there are more important things than money. The device is a key that can unlock knowledge this world probably isn't ready for and great destruction could come of it. I have no intention of selling it to some power hungry lord."

"What do you plan to do with it?" Kendal hadn't thought that Imar would sell out, but he had hoped. He needed money in a bad way, but he didn't want to betray his old friend.

"I plan to go to Eastonia and find the vault this key opens, once I see to the safety of my family. From what I understand, it is more like an underground fortress as big as a large city. Dalla knows its location as well as the codes needed for entry. She will be our guide. As to what I do upon entry, I'm not sure yet. I am curious, yet curiosity killed the cat, as they say. I may decide to destroy the place. It seems to me that this place would provide more power than what any one man should have. However, such knowledge would greatly benefit the world if used properly. For now though, it is not safe for me to leave my family here, especially with Bamsen on his way, so they will come with me to Valekrie. There we will go by ship to Sedar. Anisha and Aideen will go on to Port Augustus and stay with family."

"Valekrie," exclaimed Kendal. "That bump on the head has rattled your senses."

Anisha was silent for a change. She liked the idea of going south. It would also give her time to convince Imar to sell the key or better yet, use it to become king or even emperor. Failing that, she may be able to steal it when they parted company. She could sell it to Townsend herself when she got to Port Augustus. Anisha's thoughts went to a deep and very dark place. A plan began to formulate in her mind. A sale to both Townsend and Bamsen, with conditions—the possibilities were endless.

"I could use your help," Imar said to Kendal. "Trade still goes on between warring kingdoms. Monarchs don't like it, but they tax it heavily, so they profit. That is why Boarder City thrives." Imar was thankful for Dalla's lessons in social studies. "We can travel as merchants with a few wagons of goods and an armed escort. We may even make a profit. I need to go to Eastonia. What say you?"

"Okay, I will join you, so long as I profit somewhere along the line. I go only as far as Sedar for now. However, Bamsen will easily overtake us if we plod along with wagons. We would be better off waiting here and facing him, with all your patrols called in, or leaving now with a pack train and forget the wagons. My guess is that Bamsen is at least three to five days out."

Imar sat there thinking with his fingertips touching, thumbs against his chin and elbows on the arms of his chair. He began formulating a plan.

Imar sent for Dalla, Olaf and Hager. Introductions were made. Kendal greeted them with the openness that would be expected of a friend's friend. Anisha already knew Olaf and Hager and her treatment of them bordered on rudeness. Imar was surprised at this and wondered what he saw in Anisha to marry such a woman. She treated his friends no better than she did the servants, which was bad enough. When Imar introduced Dalla, Kendal nearly tripped over himself with niceness, but Anisha was barely cordial.

"Pleased to meet you," Dalla said straightforwardly.

Anisha sniffed and said, "I suppose I must thank you for saving my husband's life. I'm sure you saw to his every need."

Dalla was no fool. She heard the implied slight against her and instead of replying with a catty rebuttal she went the other direction even though it left doubt on all ears, except Imar's. "It was no trouble at all. My ministrations on Imar gave me great pleasure. I have not been as pleased to treat a man in many years."

Anisha looked shocked and everyone looked at Imar's reddening face. Kendal looked jealous and Hager seemed as if he wanted to slap Imar on the back and congratulate him. Dalla enjoyed the effect her reply had had on everyone, especially Anisha. "I was just having a little fun. Imar was a complete gentleman; our relationship is no more than patient/healer and friendship."

Anisha pursed her lips and in a frosty tone said, "Well, if you will excuse me, I have other matters to attend to." She walked off rather briskly.

Dalla didn't need her perception to tell her to watch her back. *That could have been handled better*, but she just couldn't help herself. *That bitch had it coming,* she thought.

Imar took Dalla, Olaf, Hager and Kendal to his study, where they made plans for the journey and preparations to deter, or at least slow down, Bamsen. Vidar would be put in charge of buying trade goods and Rolf would purchase pack horses. Aksel and Egil, when they returned, would assist Vidar and Rolf with any grunt work that was needed. Kendal added five of his men to help them with the preparations. Imar would only bring five of his friends, since his contract with the king required that he keep a company of one hundred men at Boarder City, and he did not want to deplete the border defenses. Kendal had twelve men remaining, since two had disappeared. He would leave orders for them should they show up after the party had left.

Imar asked about this. "I thought you had twenty men."

"I charged Townsend for twenty. I brought fourteen with me," replied Kendal. "Times are tight; I have to cut costs wherever I can."

CHAPTER 14

The morning was chilly for a mid-summer day. Smoke came from chimneys all over Boarder City. People knew enough to build very small fires that wouldn't last, because the day promised to be warm. A small kindling fire would be enough to take the chill off first thing in the morning. There wasn't a cloud in the sky. That would change when the day grew hot, pulling moisture skyward to form the clouds into towering cumuli.

Imar's company of border patrol had a training ground near his estate that had stables and corrals that would be used for a staging area. It was here that Rolf brought pack and riding horses that he had chosen for the mission. Vidar set up wall tents in the staging area for storing supplies and equipment needed for the journey. Once essential supplies were acquired, Vidar began buying wholesale goods to be used as trade in Kandia. It was mid-afternoon when he began haggling with dealers for goods. The weather had turned warm and for people not used to it, it would be considerably hot.

Vidar used the warm temperatures to his advantage. He visited trappers and fur dealers. He made some excellent deals, far better than he would have been able to in colder weather. After that he went north of town to a mining camp to purchase gold. He was able to obtain numerous sacks of nuggets and gold dust. He also haggled for un-refined dirt containing gold. Buying dirt with gold in it was a tricky business. One could either do very well or get cheated badly. Miners loved to sell gold in this fashion because it was less work for them and sometimes they made a better profit by salting the dirt with gold dust. Vidar was well aware of this practice and knew to take samples off the bottom instead of from the top where the miner would want to test the specimen. He returned to Boarder City with a fully loaded packhorse of gold and gold dirt.

As evening fell so did the temperature. It was not a cold evening, but cool and comfortable after a hot day. The mosquitoes were out in force, so people sought the comfort of their homes. Very few citizens were out in the streets and the ones that were walked quickly and with purpose to stay ahead of the buzzing pests.

The villa sat upon a hill where one could look above the city rooftops and over the defensive wall from the upstairs veranda. It was on the west side of this high veranda that Imar paced back and forth with impatient frustration for any sign of Aksel and Egil. Dozens of citronella candles were placed along the rails to drive off the bugs. Imar's eyes burned from the fumes, but at least he didn't have to swat mosquitoes. He had not seen Anisha or Dalla since the day before. He spent the afternoon with Aideen practicing with wooden swords and trying to catch up on his life. Aideen was a smart little girl. She was very intuitive, which aided her skill with the sword. She had a way of anticipating the next move in order to adequately block almost any strike coming to her. In a real situation she would have trouble defending herself against the strength and reach of a larger adversary, but her reflexes were extremely fast and she could return a thrust or a slash with lightning speed after parry or riposte.

Aideen explained things to her father that surprised him, but helped him understand more about his wife. Imar had a great relationship with his daughter and a worthless one with his wife. He spent a lot of time with his company of soldiers or out on patrol, just to get away from the foul tempered, nagging Anisha. She spent very little time with her daughter, but was jealous of what Aideen had with her father. Imar hated the constant verbal abuse that he was bombarded with from his wife. If it were not for that, he would have spent more time at home with his daughter. Aideen understood this and looked forward to the day when she was big enough to go out on patrol with her father. The little girl would have liked to have a better relationship with her mother, but she couldn't stand the verbal abuse any more than her father could. Instead, most of the day was spent with her nanny reading books and playing battlefield tactics or practicing with wooden swords.

Imar stayed out on the veranda watching for Aksel and Egil until an hour before midnight. With summer solstice past, the nights were getting longer, if you could call an hour of darkness long. He was about to call it a night when Dalla appeared. She looked beautiful as always, but tired and mentally drained. "What's the matter? You look distraught," said Imar.

"There is an army coming from the southwest. I feel the presence of hundreds of people and they are stressed. I sense Aksel and Egil are in danger and riding for their lives." Dalla spoke confidently. Concern filled her face in the dim light.

Imar sensed it as well, but he had to ask, "How do you know?" He had been feeling the same thing and wondered if it was truly his perceptions or if his mind was playing coincidental tricks on him.

"I can feel it with my perception. Trust me on this. Please make preparations."

Imar did not hesitate. He left her to find Olaf, to have him call in his patrols for the city's defenses. He also went to Commander Trotter of the city garrison, but the commander would do nothing without proof of an attack. Olaf sent riders out to the remote line camps within a day's ride to order all patrols to make haste to the city immediately.

Imar was standing on the west battlements with Kendal an hour after midnight when two riders approached on lathered horses at a full gallop. Behind them a dozen riders pursued, firing arrows. Imar could not make out who the fleeing riders were, but he knew it was Aksel and Egil and their tired mounts were losing ground rapidly.

"Open the gates," shouted Imar to the gate men, "and be ready to close them on the double when those two men come through."

Aksel and Egil raced through the gates at full speed. The guardsmen slammed the gates shut and barred them hastily. One of the horses had an arrow in the rump and both men had arrows stuck in their leather armor, but without harmful penetration. Once they dismounted Imar removed the arrows from their stiff leather back plating.

"Follow me," Imar said as he ran up the stairs two at a time to the battlements. Aksel and Egil's pursuers sat their horses about seventy-five meters from the gate. The glint of chainmail could be seen in the dim northern twilight aided by the many torches and watchfires along the wall. Imar took up his bow from where he had left it leaning against the wall, strung it and nocked an arrow with a bodkin head. Bodkin arrowheads were used for penetrating armor. Imar had twenty men with him on the wall and could hear Olaf marching double-time toward him through town with another twenty. Hager was at an outpost and, hopefully, riding toward the city with his platoon. Imar signaled his men and they all stretched their bows. The riders saw this and turned their mounts to ride away. At that moment Imar called out, "Loose," as he released his arrow. Twenty arrows took flight in unison. The riders were whipping their horses into a dead gallop in the opposite direction, but arrows took down half a dozen men and injured a few of their horses. To their credit, their comrades came back for the wounded and carried them out of range.

"Nice shot," said Kendal. "At least you still remember how to shoot."

Imar ignored the compliment and turned toward Aksel and Egil. "Report," he commanded briskly.

"We found Sigurd and his men traveling on foot this side of the Daishon." Egil spoke confidently and smiled. "They were still wet from their swim. We left the road and watched them pass to the east. Sigurd had a face that would make a cat puff up and run. He made four of his men run circles around them as they walked, all the while berating them for falling asleep on duty. We followed them, but kept our distance and pulled back even farther at night in case they thought to ambush us. When they got about forty kilometers from South Road, they took a trail across country and joined South Road at Lynx Pass. That is where they met up with Jarl Bamsen's army."

"How many?" Imar asked.

"We're guessing one-fifty, maybe two hundred strong, all on horse. That was only what we could see. There may be more." Aksel spoke this time, not as confidently as Egil, but he wanted to put in his piece as well. "We were spotted and the men came after us. We rode like the wind, but their horses were fresher and they kept getting closer. When we neared the gates I felt the arrows striking my back and I thought I was a goner. If you hadn't given us these stout boiled leather vests we would be dead. Thank you, Captain."

"Good job, men, and you're welcome. If they would have been closer and using bodkins your armor would not have stopped the arrows." Imar was proud of these two young men that were barely more than boys. "Get some food and some rest. Report back in four hours."

They both saluted with a fist slammed to the left breast and departed to the compound's mess hall. Olaf came up to Imar and saluted as his men positioned themselves on the wall. "Hager should be here by morning," said Olaf. He looked out to the west and saw the enemy's lead elements setting up camp. "It is light enough for an attack at nearly any hour this time of year, but they look like they are going to settle down for the night and wait till morning."

"I want one quarter of our available men to rest in shifts until an attack. Position sentries all the way around the city walls, I don't want to overlook any blind spots."

"It's already done, Captain."

"Good. And have that worthless garrison commander position his men on the south wall. That is if the standing army at our front gate is enough proof for him. How many do we have mustered?"

"We have forty-five men, and if you count the city garrison, that makes it seventy swords inside the walls. We have four catapults and two trebuchets being readied to stir up some havoc. Fire crews are going through the city looking for volunteers and urging citizens to wet their roofs."

"Outstanding," Imar exclaimed.

Bamsen's army set up camp on the west side of the city. Enemy patrols were dispatched to the east side to discourage reinforcements from entering the city. The main army set up camp first and then bedded down for the night after setting out pickets. By morning the first supply wagons began rolling into the camp with additional units swelling the numbers to roughly three hundred swords plus support crews. Imar had stood out on the wall all night glassing the army, looking for strengths and weaknesses. Bamsen's tent was set up in the center surrounded by the pennants of his captains.

"Why don't they attack?" Olaf was standing next to Imar on the wall. "I am surprised he's committed an army of this size. He must want that key pretty badly."

Imar brought the glass down from his eye. "They will form up units after they finish morning meal. We are undermanned here and need our men from the field. I hate to weaken our defenses from the wall, but let us buy Hager a little bit of time by shaking things up a bit."

"What have you got in mind?"

"Get me a dozen bowmen on horses right away. I intend to interrupt their breakfast."

Olaf looked incredulous for a split second and then saluted and went off to gather the men for the sortie. In less than fifteen minutes Imar was astride Cerus with twelve men behind him armed with bows, arrows ready.

Imar ordered the gates opened and kicked Cerus into a gallop. His men followed him in two by two formations. They charged to the center of the front line. Calls went up in the enemy camp to sound the alarm and men scrambled to grab weapons to meet the unexpected threat. They were totally unprepared for an attack, being overconfident with the size of their force. Imar and his men fired their bows in rapid succession, riding down more men than they shot with arrows. Casualties were minimal from the arrows; however, more than a few were wounded and the disruption was total. Imar led his men straight into the camp and then curved an arc to the left and ran back out toward the gates of the city. All of his men came out without a scratch.

Imar pulled aside just outside the gates as his men went back into the city. He sat his horse and looked at the camp, happy with the chaos that he had caused. He saw a man walk out in front of the camp, away from the confusion, and look at him. Even at this distance he recognized the man as Sigurd. Imar watched Sigurd raise his fist high in the air and then extend his middle finger upward in an act of defiance. Imar chuckled, turned and walked Cerus through the gates, which were then closed behind him.

The men in the sortie were cheered when they came back into the city. Once they saw to their horses, they resumed their places on the wall. When Imar dismounted from Cerus he saw Dalla worriedly waiting for him. He walked up to her and asked, "What's wrong?"

"We can't be delayed with this. We must leave in order to meet Ivan's ship at Valekrie." Dalla had more to say, but Imar cut her off before she could finish.

"If we left now we'd be easily taken and Bamsen would have the key." Imar looked at her and could tell that something else was bothering her. His eyes narrowed and he knit his brows. "What is it?"

"Sumas is here."

"Sumas? *The* Sumas you told me about? What is he doing here?"

"I suspected his hand in this all along, but now I sense his presence. He is here, with the army. That is how Bamsen knew to march before Sigurd could send a pigeon with your denial. He must have known somehow that you couldn't be bought, and so convinced Bamsen to take the key by force. I don't know, we all have our specialties and no two of us are alike. We must try to guard our thoughts, at least until I can figure out how to shield them."

A runner came up and interrupted them, nearly out of breath. "Captain, Lieutenant Hager has just arrived at the east gate with forty men." The runner gasped out the message. "He was delayed because he made a detour to gather more men. They were also harassed by Bamsen's patrols."

Imar had no sooner thanked the messenger when Olaf called down from the wall. "Captain, four men on horses approach under the banner of the golden bear. They are stopping midfield."

Dalla's eyes looked as if she were looking a long way off. "Sumas is with them…Sumas, Bamsen and Sigurd. I should go with you."

"No, it is too dangerous. Not only that, your beauty is distracting and I need to think clearly. Does Sumas know you are here?"

"I am almost sure of it." Dalla couldn't help but appreciate the compliment even though they were in the middle of a crisis. Her smile was like the radiant rays of a bright sunrise after a rainy night.

"Well, stay out of sight anyway."

Hager joined them just as Imar, Olaf, and the garrison commander, Trotter, were riding out the gate to meet with the enemy. Sigurd was there with the Jarl and his standard bearer. Three of the four were wearing chain mail, but no helms or shields for the parley. The fourth man wore no armor. He was a black man, bald headed and without facial hair. His skin was darker than any black man Imar had seen, at least since the beginning of his short memory, just as Dalla's skin was the fairest of any white person he had met. Imar wondered at this and tucked it away for later speculation. The man wore a long black riding coat, open in the front, and his garments were all black as well. He wore a short, thick gold chain on his neck and had piercing green eyes. Imar knew this man was dangerous. This was Sumas.

After making the introductions, Bamsen spoke first. He was a big man and overweight. Imar felt sorry for the man's horse. His long brown hair was braided and his beard was cropped short.

Bamsen controlled his rage with difficulty. "You know what we are here for. Hand it over and we will leave in peace."

"What is he talking about?" Trotter chimed in, "If you have something he wants, give it to him."

"Shut up," Hager said to Trotter.

"No," said Imar. "I will not give up the key. Our city is defensible and we have enough supplies to withstand a long siege. Are you ready to waste the lives of your men?"

"If all he wants is a key . . ."

Hager backhanded Trotter mid-sentence, knocking him off his horse. The garrison commander got up without a word, dusted himself off and indignantly climbed back into his saddle. He gently touched his bleeding lip, but remained silent. Imar and Olaf were relieved by Hager's action. Bamsen and Sigurd looked on with approval, while Sumas appeared to be amused.

"I am accustomed to getting what I want. You are sadly outnumbered and the king is coming to my aid. I sent an envoy to King Thorson telling him about the key and your unwillingness to give it up to the crown. My dispatch indicated that you want the power for yourself in order to have his throne. You are wanted for treason. Give up the key and I will convince His Majesty that it was all a mistake."

Imar was speechless. Bamsen was ruthless and treacherous. He and his family were in deep trouble if the king believed the Jarl. If Thorson was now after the octagon key, that was yet another army that could be sent after him for his heirloom. If Imar left the city, his men would be spared showing loyalty in defending the king's city. Those men going with him, however, would be in exile until Thorson could be convinced of the truth. He began formulating a plan. "It seems as though someone has thought this out very well." Imar looked at Sumas as he spoke to let him know that he knew who was behind this. He turned back to Bamsen and said, "I will not give up the key. When the king arrives, he will have to step over your corpse and pick his way through your dead army, so that I can tell him the truth."

Bamsen's face flushed red with anger, but it was Sigurd who spoke. "I told you, Imar, that I would have my revenge. Before I put your head on a pike, I will make you watch while I ravage your wife and your healer, then I will have my way with your daughter."

Imar had been fingering a throwing star on his belt and when Sigurd made his threat, he flicked the star at him before he finished the word 'daughter.' The star stuck in Sigurd's right cheekbone—he screamed. Facial wounds are known for bleeding profusely and Sigurd's was no exception. With a great deal of difficulty he pulled the star out, cutting his fingers in the process. Blood ran over his hands and down his face and neck, staining the blue tabard covering his chain mail. Sigurd seethed with rage as he cast the scarlet star on the tundra. He had his sword half drawn when Sumas moved an open hand toward him, which made him stop and replace his blade in its sheath seemingly against his will. His clenched jaw and corded neck muscles relaxed when Sumas lowered his hand.

"You deserved that, Sigurd," said Sumas calmly. Then to Bamsen he said, "My Lord, I think we are done here." He looked at Imar with some amusement. "Give my regards to Dalla." He turned his horse and rode back to the encampment.

Imar, Olaf, Hager, and Trotter rode back to the city, leaving Bamsen and Sigurd yelling threats and insults at their backs.

Upon entering the city Imar called a war council at the city hall. Olaf and Hager were there as well as two other lieutenants under Imar's command. One lieutenant as well as another forty men were unaccounted for. It was hoped that they were on their way to Boarder City. Kendal was there with his right hand man, Lieutenant Ian.

Trotter, the garrison commander, was also there. He realized that he was outnumbered in opinion and decided to follow Imar's lead with hopes of saving his city. Dalla was there too, as well as the mayor and several concerned citizens.

Since word was out about the key, thanks to Bamsen and Sumas, Imar thought it best to tell everyone present all that he knew about it. After his briefing, he was bombarded with a multitude of questions, seemingly all at once. Imar held up his hand and asked for silence. He said, "The key was put in my grandfather's care a long time ago, passed to my father, and now to me. It is my responsibility and mine alone, as are any consequences that may come of it. I will leave with the key. Once it is gone, there will be no reason for an army at the gates and if the king is truly on his way, he will see to the safety of his city."

"We must cause as much disruption as we can and disable the enemy as quickly as possible so that I can escape with my family to the north until King Thorson can be convinced of Bamsen's deception. Once the Jarl realizes I am gone, he will have no reason to attack the city, but will instead follow us for the octagon key. My company will still patrol the border, and will stay here to defend the city. I am promoting Lieutenant Olaf to the rank of Captain and Commander of my company until my return. I am keeper of the key and have a sworn duty to keep it safe from those who would abuse its power, therefore those not with me shall not be hunted. I will take my family and a few friends to the northern wilderness until I can be sure it is safe for my family to return. Now, let us plan a defense for the city and a strategy for my family's escape."

The war council was shorter than to be expected. There were of course the usual objections and arguments common to such meetings, but those protestations were short lived and lacked emphasis.

The majority of those with voice were just as happy with Imar's plan to take the desired relic away and, should the army follow him, all the better. The comments settled down rapidly to constructive input toward the defense of the city. Some of the older citizens made quiet observations on this rarity and more than one claimed that they had never seen a town meeting come to agreement and unified cooperation so quickly.

The plan was to bombard the enemy with catapults to push their lines back into the wetlands and bog them down, or make them concentrate on the firm ground of the road and thus narrow the range of target area for ballistae fire. Then the longer range trebuchet would scatter and confuse them. With luck this would bring their patrols watching the east side to their aid, allowing Imar's and Kendal's men to make a tactical withdrawal out the east gate. Most of Imar's company would assist Trotter's garrison defending the west wall while the rest would go with Imar. Once his family was a safe distance away he would send his defensive escort back to the city's defense with word that the talisman was gone.

After the council Imar held a private meeting with Hager, Olaf, Kendal and Dalla, and told them the real plan.

CHAPTER 15

Anisha was frantic. Imar had sent word of pending evacuation. She was supposed to pack light, only what could fit on a pack horse. "Yeah right," she said when she read the note. Anisha had her household staff hustling and bustling to pack things she absolutely could not live without. She insisted on two wagon loads, even though Imar was explicit about only one pack horse. Aideen was far more practical. She had a sack of personal effects—to include a few toys—and a belt pouch as well as her bow and arrows, a light two handed katana her father had given her and a buckler. The girl also had a small helmet lined with sheepskin that spent more time hanging on her saddle than on her head. She dressed in brown leather breeches, a black cotton long sleeve top and a dark brown boiled leather vest with the emblem of the hawk encircled by an octagon in tan, just like her father's. With the sword worn across her back and a thin black headband on her brow, Aideen looked like a cute little warrior. Smiles at her appearance hinted at the assumptions of her dressing up to imitate her father, which was partly true in her case. However, it was not just looks. Even though the child was not really a warrior, Aideen was quite good with her weapons, for a ten year old. Many hours of training and playing with practice swords would at least allow her to defend herself and hopefully escape a dangerous situation.

Anisha had her two wagons packed so heavily they were almost overloaded. She was about to send a servant out to get another wagon when the first stones from Bamsen's catapults began crashing against the city wall. The earth shook with the impact of the large stones. Anisha opted to forego the third wagon and had Kendal's soldiers take the other two to the east side of the city where Rolf and

Vidar waited with the pack horses and extra riding mounts. Aideen went with them, riding her pony alongside of her mother's baggage train.

Imar had not seen the catapults in the enemy camp before now. He was hoping to attack first with his own artillery, but now that plan was changed to a counter attack. He had his batteries aim for the enemy catapults, but the stones were falling short, only to be picked up and returned to them with accuracy against the weakening wall. An occasional stone would miss the wall and smash through the roof of a house or nearby building. A siege tower was being constructed in the enemy camp and Imar was certain that Bamsen would attack upon its completion.

Dalla had been watching the trajectory of the stones launched by the city catapults. The azimuth was correct, but the altitude angle for the given power of the arm and weight of the projectile was wrong. She knew that the artillery sergeant would not listen to a woman, so she spoke to Imar instead. He went with her to speak with the sergeant in charge of the catapult battery.

The catapults were sitting four abreast in an open area behind the wall and in front of a pile of stones ranging in weight from ten to ninety kilos. A spotter stood on the wall relaying hit locations in relation to the intended targets. The catapults and the two trebuchets were city property and manned by garrison soldiers.

Imar walked up to the sergeant in charge. "Sergeant, your shots are falling short, except for the few that are going long."

"I'm sorry sir, but we have had no training in artillery. I have asked the commander repeatedly for permission to train on the equipment, but I am always denied. He says it has been years since the city has been attacked by a full size army, so the need is small. I'm sure he is regretting his words now."

Imar wanted to say that the garrison commander's an idiot, but decided to hold his tongue. "Sergeant, we can help you if you are willing to listen."

"We will gladly take any help you can give us."

"Sergeant, this is Dalla. She is a mathematical wizard and a genius at physics. Follow her directions to the letter and you will not regret it."

The sergeant looked skeptical. "Okay, captain, we will give her a chance."

"Good," Imar said. He left them and went to speak with the sergeant in charge of the trebuchets.

Dalla had already sent for a scale which was just arriving. "It is important to know the weight of each projectile," said the healer. "By doing so, a correlating tension can be applied to the arm in relation to the angle set on the mechanism. Once the shot placement for a given weight, tension, and angle is established, add or drop corrections can be made by calculating the weight ratio as it applies the settings on the catapult."

The artillery team looked blank.

The sergeant said, "Clear as mud."

"Let me demonstrate," said Dalla. "Take that twenty-one kilo stone on the scale and put it on the number two catapult with the tension cranked down to the fifth notch on the tension gauge." The trebuchet sergeant arrived just then to observe. Dalla handed both sergeants a chart she had made with stone weights, tension settings and angles with resulting distances and then continued with her demonstration. "Now set the angle to twenty degrees. That should come close to the enemy's number six catapult. An 'add' or 'drop' signal relayed in meters from your spotter can be adjusted by tension and degrees of angle. Okay, you are ready to fire."

The sergeant gave the order to fire and the stone launched high into the air. It seemed to slow at its apex and then sped up as it began the downward descent and was lost to view to those on the ground behind the wall. The men on the wall began cheering and the spotter yelled, "It's a hit, it's a hit, it's a direct hit!"

The stone hit the enemy catapult and smashed the forward framework and left front wheel. Bamsen's men worked fast to block up the frame, where the wheel collapsed, and repair the damage with cross braces. The catapult was back up and working in twenty minutes.

The sergeant of the trebuchets ran back to his unit to begin firing. The catapult sergeant thanked Dalla and in short order had all four catapults launching stones with deadly accuracy. They began covering the stones with cloth soaked in naphtha, ignited just before launch. All six of Bamsen's catapults were eventually smashed and burning and the siege engine became nothing but scattered logs.

Bamsen withdrew his army back out of range of the city catapults. Then the trebuchets began launching basket loads of stones ranging in weight from one to four kilos. Each volley carried at least twenty stones. This barrage caused a great number of casualties and scattered the enemy into the soggy wetlands. Supply wagons were abandoned and many of them were destroyed. Troops were slowed in the wetlands and struggled to get onto the dry and already crowded road.

Olaf sat his horse behind the gate, ready to attack with thirty bowmen on horses. Imar gripped his forearm in soldierly fashion. "Good hunting and farewell, Olaf."

"Good luck to you, Imar, and good journey. You have been a good friend. I hope your memory returns soon. If you ever need me or the company, send word. Fare you well, Imar." Olaf paused, his decision made to say something to his friend. "One other thing you should know." He paused again even though he knew he needed to say what was on his mind. "You married Anisha out of duty and responsibility. You and she were having a fling, nothing more. She got pregnant with Aideen, so you married her, more out of honor to her parents I think than her. You never really loved or even liked your wife. In fact, you barely tolerated her. Your daughter you love with all your heart and she is nothing like her mother. If anything, she favors her grandmother."

"Thank you, Olaf, I appreciate you telling me."

"Beware of Anisha, Imar. She is treacherous and will do anything for her own gain or pleasure. If only you had met the healer first. The way you two look at each other, it's obvious you and Dalla are in love." He paused, then looked his friend in the eye and gripped his arm again, "Goodbye, my friend." Olaf turned and yelled to the gatemen, "Open the gates!" The gates swung open and Olaf spurred his mount with a battle cry and out the gates they went in a thundering charge, thirty men shouting as they raced to the confused enemy in two by two formations.

Imar climbed onto Cerus as the gates closed and rode to the east side of the city where his family and friends waited for him with Kendal's company, plus another thirty of Imar's men. Imar thought briefly on Olaf's words about his wife. It was frustrating, this memory loss. When he came upon his evacuation party he put his contemplations on hold.

Rolf and Vidar were with the pack horses. Aksel and Egil were helping them double check cinches. Hager, Dalla and Kendal were at the head of the line and Kendal's men were positioned on each side of the line. When Imar rode up, everyone standing climbed into their saddles. Aideen sat her horse next to Anisha's carriage, which was positioned ahead of two heavily loaded wagons. Thirty additional mounted warriors were standing rear guard.

Imar was less than pleased when he saw the wagons and carriage. He rode to the carriage and spoke to Anisha with quiet, but barely controlled anger. "I was explicit about traveling light with no wagons. We are fleeing for our lives, not going on a summer holiday."

Anisha retorted with her usual insults and superior attitude, but Imar rode off to the head of the line with Aideen riding alongside him.

"All of Bamsen's patrols have gone to reinforce his main host," Hager reported.

"We have an open road," said Kendal. "If we're going to go, we had better get going now."

Imar nodded, looking none too happy with his wife. "Open the gates," he said to the gatemen. "And shut them as soon as we pass."

The east gates swung open and the caravan headed out on the east road. The day was warm and the mid-afternoon clouds were gathering rapidly and building into towering thunderheads. The party was moving at a fair pace, but Anisha's wagons were ponderously slow. They came to North Road ten kilometers east of the city and Imar called a halt to wait for the wagons. He fumed at the delay. As soon as the wagons caught up they proceeded north into the rolling hills patched with forests of black spruce. After another ten kilometers the wagons were once again falling far behind. Imar didn't call a halt this time.

"Aideen, would you ride back and ask Aksel and Egil to report to me in the front, please?"

"Sure thing, Daddy," replied Aideen. She wheeled her horse and galloped full tilt down the line to the pack horses. The wind caught her raven black hair to match her horse's tail, like twin pennants. She rode with a smoothness that would allow a glass of water to balance on her head with nary a ripple. Aideen returned a minute later with the two young men, each saluting fist to breast as they approached.

Imar spoke to them quietly, so that Anisha or her attendant, Missy, would not overhear them, since her light carriage was right behind them in the front to avoid road dust. "I want you two to go back to the wagons and unload them as we travel. Leave one quarter of the load and do it quietly."

"Yes, sir," replied Aksel and Egil together with grins and salutes. They turned and rode back to the wagons with teeth clamped to restrain themselves from whoops of joy.

"Not a word out of you either," Imar said to his smiling daughter.

"I won't say anything, but she's going to blow her top."

It was not long before the wagons were able to catch up.

The sky was mostly covered with dark clouds, the air became cooler and the trees were buffeted with occasional wind gusts from the convection of the towering cumulus. Large rain drops were beginning to fall sporadically with audible splats. Everyone not in a carriage donned oilcloth cloaks. Imar sent for the lieutenant leading his thirty extra men.

"We are about to be hit with a downpour, Lieutenant Cole." Imar's statement was reinforced with a flash of lightening followed a few seconds later by the booming of thunder. "This is where we part company. Assign five men to take the carriage and wagons north to create a false trail. They are to continue for three days or until Bamsen's men catch up with them, then they are to abandon all and evade the enemy. The rest of you are to make haste back to the city and give aid to Captain Olaf."

"Yes, Captain," the lieutenant saluted, "and safe journey to you."

Anisha took this change very badly. When she saw her near empty wagons she went ballistic. It was in the middle of her tirade that the clouds burst with heavy rain that rapidly turned into a torrential downpour. Missy put on a cloak before she stepped out of the carriage; the girl tried to put one on her mistress, but Anisha threw it on the ground in a fit of rage. She was soaking wet in seconds.

"Anisha," Imar yelled to be heard over the storm and his wife's tantrum. "We are going across country. The wagons and the carriage cannot go over uncut terrain. That is why I insisted on packing light on horse only. Your wagons and carriage will provide a nice false trail for us, so for that I thank you. Now you can either mount up on a horse or I can have my men tie you across the back of one, but we leave the road now while this storm can cover our tracks."

Anisha answered in a low growl. "You wouldn't dare."

Two men brought up horses for Anisha and her maid. The maid didn't hesitate to vault into the saddle.

Imar retorted loudly to Anisha, "Try me."

Anisha, soaked to the bone, picked up the oiled cloak and put it on, then climbed into the saddle with a face of pure hatred directed at Imar.

Imar's party then turned off the road and went east, picking their way through thick brush and patches of forest. Five of Lieutenant Cole's men took the wagons and carriage north with the drivers riding mounts in tow. Cole waited until both parties were on their way then rode back to Border City as fast as the weather and the road would allow.

CHAPTER 16

The city catapults and trebuchets had ceased firing when Olaf's archers sallied forth against Bamsen's floundering troops. Thirty horsemen rode full speed in a tight two by two formation, like a speeding shaft flying to its mark. The disorganized army had little time to form up a proper defense. However, a group of fifty men still on firm ground managed to assemble a shield wall between their troops in the bog and the onslaught of terror racing toward them. Another smaller shield wall of approximately ten men formed up on the road to protect a handful of archers and crossbowmen. The larger group bristled with pikes with the butts braced in the ground, ready to receive the charging horses.

Olaf's sortie closed the distance rapidly, and began firing arrows in rapid succession over the shields and into the muddling troops scrambling to get onto the crowded road. He veered left away from the road, leading his men with practiced skill along the front ranks, firing arrows that fell like raining death upon Bamsen's army. Olaf then turned back toward the city and slowed his horsemen to a trot and then to a stop with a line formation of all abreast facing the enemy as they rested the horses.

It was a very warm day, but towering cumulus formations were beginning to build into thunderheads, thus cooling the temperature to a more comfortable level. Enemy patrols were coming around from all areas of the outer wall to reinforce their battered comrades. The shield wall was growing and the beleaguered army was getting organized as disciplined officers began forming the army into a phalanx that slowly marched out of the bog and toward the city. Olaf led another charge, but the arrows just bounced off or stuck in the shields. An occasional foot was pierced and twice a shaft found a throat. Olaf led his men back to the city and prepared for the coming attack.

The sky had darkened and the smell of rain was in the air. Dark, heavy clouds roiled overhead. Flashes of lightening followed by the booms of thunder repeated with less time elapsing between each episode as the storm moved toward the battlefield. The phalanx moved toward the city like a slow moving armored bug. Arrows from the wall bounced off shields held overhead that encased the hundred men marching toward the city's gate. Catapults from the city lobbed stones over the wall now that Olaf's men were clear of the field, but the phalanx was too close to the wall and the projectiles fell harmlessly beyond the encroaching menace.

The phalanx stopped before the huge wooden gates as a few drops of rain began to fall. Stones rained on the enemy as well, thrown from the catwalk above the gates. The defenders began carrying up bigger stones from the catapult arsenal and dropping them on the host with noticeable effect, but the process was slow and the dead or wounded were quickly replaced.

At the forefront of the phalanx a fire was started with an indistinguishable dry substance. As the flames grew, more of the volatile powder was cast onto the gates. Olaf was ready for naphtha, having ordered buckets of sand to be staged above the gates after wetting them down. Water thrown on naphtha can spread flames, but this was not naphtha. However, buckets of water worked to quench the strange burning powder. Men on the catwalk poured water on the flames, but for each bucket of water poured from above, a bucket of powder was cast upon the fire causing a large flare-up with each cast. Twice a small explosion occurred with the joining of powder and fire, thus injuring a few of the attackers. The gates held firm, but they were weakening.

The defenders began carrying more water than stones and it seemed a losing battle, when the enemy then seemed to run out of fuel for the flames. The gates were still burning on the lower end when a cloudburst, seemingly sent by the gods, poured rain in a violent downpour that extinguished the fire in seconds. The defenders cheered along the wall, but the clamor of the storm muffled their shouts of joy.

The exuberance along the wall died with the booming of a ram smashing against the charred and weakened timbers. The enemy at the gates came well prepared to force entry into the city. Defenders hurled rocks on the shielded men, but the ram swung back and forth in rhythm to the low enemy chant. Olaf formed up a shield wall behind the gates with Trotter's men on the flanks, ready for the inevitable sundering of the timbers. Men futilely braced logs against the splintering barrier, while men in the shield wall said prayers to their gods or made gestures of luck as others made signs to avert evil. Then the booming stopped and a man on the wall called for Olaf.

Olaf ran double stepping up the stairs and looked to the north where the man was pointing. Lieutenant Cole was riding hard with his men in five by five formations, shields up and swords bare. The phalanx set down the ram and turned to face the immediate threat.

"Archers," Olaf called. "Fire when they break. And watch your aim that you don't hit our own men." Olaf ran down the stairs to join his men, the news of Cole's attack racing ahead of him. He took his position in the shield wall, locking his shield over on the right and under on the left. "Open the gates," he shouted. The men bracing the gates with logs pulled their timbers away while four men lifted the heavy cross brace out of its slot. It seemed to take forever as Olaf watched the gates swing ponderously outward into the melee of embattled phalanx and cavalry. The scene was one of savage chaos and bloody pandemonium. Sword in hand, axe men behind and chaos ahead, Olaf shouted, "Attack!"

Bamsen sat his horse in the pouring rain between Sumas and Sigurd with eighty horsemen standing ready to charge into the city. The jarl was obsessed with the power the octagon key would bring him. Thorson could keep his kingdom and his crown, as could all the other kings in the world. Kings would bow down and grovel before him when he became emperor; maybe some would even call him God.

"Lord," said Sigurd, "the men are being torn to shreds. Shouldn't we reinforce them or call a tactical withdrawal?" Sigurd knew better than to use the word retreat with his liege.

"Bamsen," Sumas said, without bothering with formalities, "pull your men back or you will have no army left. You will be weakened. The key is gone. You would do well to trust me on this. When the king arrives, he will not only want the key for himself and pursue it, he will have your head for attacking his city. Pull your men back and send out trackers to pick up the trail. Do it now or I will go on without you." Sumas said this quietly, but the force of his words carried power.

Bamsen turned and glared at Sumas with undisguised rage. Any other man would lie bleeding on the ground, his head rolling away from his twitching corpse for speaking to him like that. Sumas was dangerous and Bamsen knew it. "Go reinforce a withdrawal of the army." Bamsen said this to Sigurd between clenched teeth, never taking his eyes off Sumas. "Leave me ten trackers and catch up with us as soon as you withdraw. Send home the wounded, the wagons, and a small guard unit to escort them."

Sigurd saluted and left to pass on the orders, then rode to the rescue of his defeated comrades with seventy horsemen.

CHAPTER 17

Imar dozed in the saddle as he rode at the head of the pack horses. They had been on a fairly good road in Kandia for a week and a half, traveling southeast. Kendal rode at his left and Aideen at his right. All of the company wore the simple garb of traveling merchants. The men still wore swords and thick boiled leather vests and carried their bows, but no other armor and no emblems. All other accruements of war were bagged and stowed away on pack horses.

The party spent four days, after leaving North Road, picking their way through trackless terrain. The first day Imar insisted on silence as he led them single file on a zigzag route to the east through the pouring rain. He had not slept for two days and was tired from the battle as well as the escape. Anisha broke the silence once, pushing Imar's foul mood beyond its limits. He threatened to gag her if she spoke again.

Anisha remained silent after that. Imar had surprised her with his ferocity. She thought it may be his amnesia that made him a little different. He seemed the same as before in most ways, but there were differences and he often appeared to be deep in thought as if something troubled him, especially when he looked at the healer. Anisha wasn't quite sure what to think of Dalla. She was beautiful to be sure, but she seemed confident and carried a hidden power in her words when she spoke. When Dalla looked at her, she felt as if the healer was reading her mind. It gave her goose bumps. The only other time she had experienced that in another person was when she had met Ivan the wizard when she was a young girl.

It had been two weeks since fleeing Border City and so far, no sign of pursuit, nor did they encounter any signs of Kandian raiding parties. The few villages and settlements they had passed through were unusually peaceful and shy of young men. The mornings were clear and beautiful, warming quickly and becoming hot in the afternoon followed by thunderstorms lasting into the night. The road led through the mountains and into a valley where they came to a small town with an inn. Imar decided that everyone needed a break. He rented every room at the inn, ordered baths for all and had the innkeepers prepare a huge buffet for his people. The horses all got a good brushing and a generous helping of grain. Kendal prudently sent out two men to scout the back trail and appointed a guard duty, but rotated the men on short shifts, so that everyone could enjoy a restful night in a soft bed.

There were two to three beds in each room. Anisha insisted on her own private room and no one objected, since no one wanted to be her roommate. Kendal offered to share his chamber with Dalla, but she roomed with Aideen and her new nanny, Missy. Imar and Hager roomed with Kendal instead. The baths refreshed everyone, most especially the ladies, and the buffet was a feast after so many days on the trail.

Imar went to see the blacksmith first thing in the morning and showed him the octagon key. "Can you make a copy?"

The blacksmith scratched his bald head and replied, "Sure thing, but it will take most of the day if I start now. I'll have to make a sand mold and pour a non-ferrous alloy and then polish it as it cools. It'll cost you three silvers."

"Then make two." Imar handed him the coins. "And here is an extra silver to tell no one."

The blacksmith agreed to the terms and asked Imar to leave the octagon disc with him, but he refused. Instead he waited while the smith packed the key in sand and carved a pour-hole and vent-spout in the mold. The smith then separated the frame, removed the key and handed it back to Imar.

"That should be all I need for now," said the blacksmith. He put the mold back together, scooped some coal into his foundry, and began tossing scraps of grayish metal in a crucible. "Check back with me this evening."

Imar went back to the inn and sat down to breakfast with Hager, Kendal, Dalla, Missy and Aideen.

Kendal said, "No sign of pursuit on our back trail. I think we should stay here another day and then hit the road tomorrow."

Imar was relieved that he didn't have to make up an excuse to wait for the blacksmith to finish his project. "Good idea, Kendal. I think we could all use the rest. I'll have Vidar do a little trading with our goods so we can look the part and maybe increase our profits a bit."

Dalla looked at Imar, raised one eyebrow slightly and smiled.

Imar's heart melted whenever she smiled at him. Her look made him feel like she knew what he was up to. He turned to his daughter and said, "I saw some kids outside. Why don't you go out and make some friends? I think you can take a day off from lessons and go play."

"Thanks Daddy," Aideen replied joyously as she shot out the door followed by her grinning nanny.

The past couple of weeks had been long and tedious with little time to sit and relax and certainly not comfortably indoors at a table. Imar had been withdrawn and often deep in thought while torn between avoiding Dalla and wanting to talk to her, be next to her. He was trying very hard to be properly distant, being a married man, but his attraction to her only seemed to grow stronger.

Anisha was different. Imar had no emotional difficulty avoiding his wife, except that she would often approach him with some sort of trivial nonsense that she demanded he rectify, as if the world depended on his immediate action. He was becoming annoyed with her with increasing frequency. From all that he had heard from friends, he and his wife had no relationship at all. Aideen even told him he would be happier married to someone else, and should that ever happen he should take his daughter with him.

"Come," said Hager to Kendal. "Let's go tell the men that we will be staying another day. They can use the time to dry out our wet gear."

"Good idea," said Kendal, grabbing another biscuit before going out the door with Hager.

"Hagar," Imar stopped the burly man before he went out the door. "Have Vidar and Rolf gather some news. It is strange that we haven't seen any signs of bandits and this village seems to be devoid of men."

"True," said the taciturn Hagar. "I have noticed the high ratio of women as well. I was thinking that retirement here would be nice. I will tell them to ask around."

Imar raised one brow and smiled, unsure if his serious friend was joking or not. As soon as Imar and Dalla were alone, he looked around the room to be sure no one else was there. "That was the most I've heard out of Hagar at one time."

"He does use his words sparingly," Dalla agreed. "But he uses them well."

Imar reached in his pocket and removed the pouch holding the octagon key and gave it to Dalla. "Put this away and keep it safe. I am having a couple of fakes made; I will carry one and stash the other."

"So that is what you were doing this morning. It is probably a good idea." Dalla took the key and put it away in one of her pockets. "The lure of power has been known to overwhelm the best of people."

"There is something else . . . ." Imar let his unfinished sentence hang while he struggled for the words.

Dalla reached across the table and put her hand on Imar's, perceiving what he wanted to say. "Imar, I have feelings for you too, like I have not had in a very long time. We are doomed to misery unless you can come to terms with Anisha."

Imar's heart began to pound with Dalla's touch, but her words brought him back down to Earth. "You are right of course, even Aideen said as much." Imar stood up and said, "I will talk to her now." He looked into Dalla's eyes with longing, then turned to go in search of Anisha.

All that Imar knew of the people in his life was recently learned from the teachings of others and from his own observations since his memories began just a few weeks ago. What he knew of his family, friends, and acquaintances before his amnesia was an accumulation of information built up and stored over a period of years, a lifetime. All that knowledge was beyond his reach now and possibly gone for good. This lack of accessibility to his memories was difficult to deal with not only for him but for the people in his life, who saw the same man they had always known, except that his actions and reactions to different instances had unexpected results because of his inability to remember. This was often puzzling to his friends and family, even with the knowledge of his amnesia. Dalla was different because she came into his life after his amnesia and had no expectations based on previous acquaintanceship.

If Imar had retained his memories, he would have sent someone else to Anisha to request an audience, but not knowing this he went to her room and knocked smartly on the door.

Anisha was accustomed to luxury. The past two weeks in the saddle had rendered her sore and exhausted without any conveniences other than what the trail could offer. She was sleeping in and didn't hear Imar's knock on the door. It was a deep sleep, but when Imar knocked a second time and louder, she woke with a start, and realized with the amount of light coming through the window, that it was mid-morning. Anisha was grateful for the slight reprieve from the dreadful saddle.

"A moment," Anisha said, getting out of bed and shuffling to the door as she put on her robe. "Imar," she said when she opened the door, "give me a few minutes and I will be ready to go."

"We are staying another day to rest."

"Thank all the gods and their angels too." Anisha was extremely pleased with this news, but then her brows lowered and, had her eyes been daggers, Imar would have been skewered. "Then why in all the seven hells did you wake me?"

"Anisha, we need to talk."

Anisha looked at Imar, saw the seriousness on his face and nodded. "Come in." She stepped back and took a seat on the edge of the bed.

Imar shut the door behind him, pulled up a simple wooden chair and sat facing her. "I feel as if I were born fully grown a few weeks ago. All I know of our marriage is what I hear from people who know us. Please tell me if I am wrong, but it seems that our marriage is one of convenience rather than one of love. We have a beautiful daughter that I love dearly even though I feel as if we just met. You and I have little else in common. We don't get along and from what I hear, we never have. Your family is very well off, so you would be well cared for if we were to dissolve our marriage and go our separate ways."

Anisha just sat there looking at Imar as the seconds ticked away. Imar was about to say something more when Anisha lifted one brow slightly and spoke. "It's the healer, isn't it? You want to bed her and your precious honor won't allow it while you are wed to me." Anisha let out a short little chuckle. "Go for it Imar, just be discreet. I'll not have you embarrass me with scandalous rumors. I have certainly seen to my needs, as you would know if you had not lost your memory. We hardly need a divorce to enjoy a little diverse entertainment. At least, I certainly do not."

Imar was stunned by her words. His morals were deeply ingrained in him, so deep that even total memory loss could not change the way he lived, the code he lived by. He barely knew this woman sitting before him and what he did know of her he neither liked nor trusted, yet he was married to her. Not knowing himself—the person he was before his head injury—he couldn't fathom what had possessed him to stay with this woman for so many years, even considering his duty to his daughter. "Anisha, I want a divorce."

"No."

"But, why not?" Imar was getting nowhere with this and felt he knew the answer already.

"You really don't know?" Anisha chucked again and her eyes sparkled with intensity beyond just delight, with sheer determination. "Power, my dear Imar—power, and vast wealth. I have great plans for you. Did you think I would be satisfied as a captain's wife in a frontier border town? I trapped you with a child because you have charisma and you are a born leader. Not only that, you shared with my parents the greatest treasure find known to man. With your wealth and ability to lead, I had planned to help you become the most powerful lord of Kalusia, but now with the octagon key you can become a king or even emperor with the wealth it will bring and I shall be your queen. Whether we take the power the key may unlock, or we sell it and use the money to raise an army matters little to me, but we are in this together and we shall be great." Anisha spoke with fierce fanaticism that matched the insane illumination in her glassy-eyed stare. When she finished speaking, that light held for a few seconds then slowly faded to her normal look of haughty disdain. "No, Imar, I'll not give you a divorce and I do want you to consider what you hold as well as the quest you will be embarking upon. If indeed the key can unlock such vast weapons, then why not take them and use them? I personally think we should sell the key to the highest bidder and then steal it back. We could buy a kingdom outright or take one of our choosing with an army of professionals." She waited a moment, and then emphatically added, "Power and riches, Imar, power and riches."

"This is madness. I am not of any royal line to be a king, nor do I want to be. I have plenty of wealth and can find or earn more if need be, so if it is power and riches you want, then name your price and give me a divorce."

"I'll not be humiliated with you leaving me and running off with the healer or anyone else for that matter. Till death do us part, Imar, and I'm holding you to it, so go fall on your sword if you want a divorce, just so long as you give me the octagon key first."

Imar stood up and fought for control over his anger. In combat when battle lust was upon him he still kept his head and calculated his moves and tactics with practiced skill, but this woman with just a few words could make his temper burst like a berserker's. With tightened facial muscles and gritted teeth Imar said, "We will speak on this again."

He turned and went out the door, pausing for half a second when Anisha, as always, had to get in the last word. She answered him in a voice that dripped like honey, laced with sarcasm, "Of course, my husband; anytime."

Imar slammed the door and retreated down the hall. His boots echoed loudly as they pounded the wooden floor.

CHAPTER 18

"Where away?" shouted Beros in answer to the 'sail ho' shout from the tops.

"Starboard bow, ten points off the sprit."

Gavin left Coulig on the main deck, where they were training the men, and vaulted up the starboard stairs two at a time to join Beros on the quarterdeck. "Do you think it's the *Bedford Lee*?"

"Too soon to tell, she's not flying her colors. Set a course to intercept and beat to quarters."

"Aye Captain," Gavin struck his fist against his chest in salute, turned, and began barking orders.

Catapults were readied, ballistae cocked and armed. The decks were doused with buckets of water and crossbowmen climbed up into the rigging. The ship came into view just as another shout came from the tops, "Land ho."

Everyone aboard the *Coastal Raider* saw a distant bluff beyond the ship in question. That was not all they saw. Beyond the ship they were closing with, another ship came into view just as the second 'ship ho' call came from aloft. Both ships turned toward the *Coastal Raider* and hoisted the colors of Kandian freebooters—pirates. Gavin looked to the captain. A number of other eyes on deck looked to the ship's master as well.

Beros studied the ships a full minute, which seemed an eternity, before speaking. "Hold this course and keep the speed, the wind favors us. We'll hit the first ship with the starboard battery and steer to give the second ship hell from the port. Then we'll make a run for it. I'd rather not try to take two ships by ourselves. Let's give 'em some flame in their sheets. Maybe we can slow 'em down enough that they won't chase us."

The distance to the enemy ship closed rapidly with the wind blowing straight on the stern of the *Coastal Raider*. Her bow danced lightly on the swells, casting up spray in an even rhythm that kept time to a war chant sung by Coulig's men. The ship's crew joined in the cadence and morale soared along with a strong dose of adrenaline. The men had trained and bonded into a well-coordinated fighting team. They anticipated the two to one odds much the way a hungry tiger would look at a wounded gazelle; only this was no wounded prey that they approached, but two fully armed and dangerous enemy ships that would happily kill them all or sell them into slavery.

The first ship began firing ballistae bolts that fell short. The bolts carried no flame which indicated their adversaries meant to capture them. The two converging ships fell into range a few seconds later and a flaming bolt from the *Coastal Raider* set ablaze the enemy's foresail. Just as the two ships began to pass, each opened fired with broadsides. Bolts and stones struck wood and rent sails, men were wounded and more of the enemy sails caught fire.

Coulig, arrow nocked in his bow, drew and fired a clothyard shaft, timing his release to the peak of a swell. The arrow sped across the distance, barely missing shafts and stones from both batteries, and met its apex halfway over the water before arcing down to strike the helmsman dead center in the throat. The man fell dead on the helm, turning the wheel with his fall and causing the ship to veer off to port while her crew turned their fight to the flames in their sheets. A top-man could be seen cutting the foresail down as they tacked into the wind.

The *Coastal Raider* turned slightly to port. The crew cheered and all near Coulig slapped him on the back, but the cheers died as they neared the next enemy ship. The enemy captain was not about to let his ship fall to flames as easily as his comrade. Flaming bolts fell aboard both ships, but as they closed with their adversary the enemy crew began furling their sails and slowing to a drift. Each ship began firing their port broadsides with stones, bolts, and flames. The *Coastal Raider* caught fire in her mainsail and as she sailed by, the enemy hooked her stern with grapples that pulled the pirate ship in tow.

Before she turned, Beros saw '*Northern Demon*' painted on her stern. "Cut us loose and replace that sail. We could be in trouble here." Men were already cutting down the burning sheets. The fire had spread into the main topsail, so that nearly all the sheets on the mainmast had to be replaced while under fire from the enemy. The *Coastal Raider* slowed considerably with the loss of her mainsail and the drag of the *Northern Demon*. Men hacked at the grapples on the stern under the rain of bolts and stones. Casualties were mounting on the stern deck, but only one grapple remained. The *Northern Demon* unfurled her sails while under tow and as she gained speed the last grapple went slack. A crewman tossed the line off the stern.

"She's gaining on us, Captain, and the other ship is getting her wind as well." Gavin pointed, ducked a bolt and pointed again. The other ship had turned in pursuit under three-quarter sail and would soon have full sheets. The *Northern Demon* was pulling up on the starboard stern and trying to set fire to their mizzen as well as harassing them with bolts.

Beros shouted to the men replacing the main and top sails. "Hurry up with those sails, lads, or we'll all be working the mines under a Kandian whip."

The crewmen of the *Coastal Raider*, as well as Coulig's marines, held shields or wore chain mail—some did both. Many of the shields bristled with bolts. Ivan strolled up onto the quarter deck without a shield or armor and seemingly without a care. He acted as if he had just woken up from a nap. No one really took much notice of him. Everyone was busy firing arrows or bolts, catapult or ballista. Missiles were flying all about, but none ever came near Ivan.

"Hard a port," shouted Beros. The *Coastal Raider* turned left and the *Northern Demon* turned to intercept.

"Ah, Captain?" Ivan spoke as calmly as if he were commenting about the weather. In fact, in a way he was.

"Not now, Ivan. I'm kind of busy at the moment." Beros scratched under his eye patch, and then held up his shield to catch two bolts. He broke off the shafts with a sweep against the rail. "Forget their deck, set fire to their sails," Beros called to the men on the aft ballista.

"Why don't you head toward that thunderstorm to the north? That is where the *Bedford Lee* is coming from." Ivan spoke a little louder this time, but just as calmly as if he were discussing crackers over tea.

Beros, Gavin and the helmsman looked to the north. Gavin raised a glass to look and Beros gave the order for a hard turn to starboard. "Is it her?"

"Aye Captain, it is the *Bedford Lee* and she never looked finer than she does right now."

Even though a light wind was blowing from the south, the *Bedford Lee* came running before the wind caused by the down drafts of the thunderstorm that she left in her wake. Out of the north she came, white sails full and spray splashing white off her prow. With the black cloud above and the grey rain behind, she danced on the rolling seas with a bolt of lightning flashing and the boom of thunder announcing her arrival. It was a glorious sight to the embattled crew.

The *Northern Demon* was keeping pace with the *Coastal Raider*. Both ships had replaced their worst sails, but a multitude of holes and rips kept either vessel from attaining full performance. The battling two were also losing speed because of the contending winds coming from the storm. The other enemy ship was also gaining on them. The dueling ships each caught flame in the sails, but battle ready crews were quick to douse the flames. To change a sheet now would lose the fight. To lose the fight would lose the mission. Imar's family, and friends would all be left to fend for themselves in an enemy port and the crew of the *Coastal Raider* would be killed or enslaved.

The dead were dragged out of the way, and the wounded went below to have bolts removed, wounds stitched and burns dressed. Those that were able returned to the deck to help where they could. Bandaged men weren't allowed in the tops and some could not draw a bow, but they could shoot a crossbow. A few of the wounded had to have help cocking the mechanism, and then they would use the rail as a rest to steady their aim.

Another grapple hooked the stern and a harpoon from a ballista sunk in the hull at the water line out of reach. "They mean to board us," shouted Beros. "Our friends are almost here. Let's hold 'em off a few more minutes." Beros turned to Gavin and said, "Ready three casks of naphtha, one aft on the starboard battery and two on the stern. Have 'em aim for the base of the mainmast and fire on my order."

Crews aboard the *Northern Demon* cast and hooked more grapples and were heaving on the lines, drawing the ships together. The *Bedford Lee* was bearing down on the two embattled ships fast and looked as if she meant to ram them. Boarding parties were swinging across on lines and landing on the quarter deck and amidships. The clamor of steel and the battle shouts of men began.

"Now," Beros gave the order to fire. Gavin lit a cask and the gunner launched the catapult in concert with the other two. No time could be spared to watch the flight. No sooner than the fiery keg launched, Gavin parried a slash with his torch and answered with a thrust from his cutlass. Battle aboard the *Coastal Raider* was pitched.

Ivan stood center on the quarterdeck and watched the flight of the flaming kegs. He had assumed a state of calm amid the chaos of bloody battle. His legs moved with the swaying of the deck, but his body was still as he peered at the projectiles. Like small comets they flew in formation to the apex of their flight, then one of the little comets broke formation and took its own course toward the rear of the target ship. The other two continued their natural course and hit their mark amidships at the base of the mainmast and exploded with fire that spread up into the sail and out on the deck. The third cask, on a mission of its own, curved around the main spar and struck the helm in a burst of flame.

The enemy captain watched this strange flight, as if the burning cask flew toward him in slow motion, with his feet glued to the deck. In truth the burning missile took only a second to fly its arc and slam into the helm. The helmsman was totally engulfed in flame, but the captain had little time to consider this because half his body was burning with the flaming liquid as well. He ran to the rail, feeling the heat and searing pain on his left side. The stench of burning flesh, his flesh, was thick in his nostrils as he dove over the side into the quenching relief of the cold sea. Other crewmen aboard the *Northern Demon* were doing the same, flaming bodies diving overboard. Some were saved by comrades that smothered the flames with wet sail cloth. Others died screaming.

On the *Coastal Raider* the battle paused when the kegs exploded with a mighty boom followed by a wave of heat. That momentary pause was interrupted with the ramming of the *Bedford Lee* crashing between the ships, snapping the lines and smashing timbers and rails. More than one set of eyes noted the two areas burning on the pirate ship. The *Bedford Lee* pushed the two ships apart, knocking all hands off their feet. As she passed between the two vessels, she opened fire with catapults upon the flaming *Northern Demon*, smashing her mainmast which toppled flaming off her starboard side into the sea. The *Bedford Lee* then left the two ships adrift in her wake to sail forth into battle with the other pirate vessel approaching from the south.

Beros wasted no time getting to his feet. He looked across the short distance to the quarter deck of the *Bedford Lee* and caught the eye of her captain, Einar. He struck his fist to chest in salute and nodded a 'thanks.' Einar returned the salute and then turned his attention to the engagement of the other pirate vessel under full sail. Beros, too, had pressing matters at hand.

Outnumbered now, their ship disabled and in flames, the boarding party surrendered. The clang of cutlasses hitting the deck was heard in a wave, starting with the leader when Beros put the tip of his blade to the man's throat as his defeated adversary struggled to his feet.

Gavin put the quartermaster in charge of securing the prisoners. He then led a rescue party in a longboat to look for survivors. Beros turned to watch the *Bedford Lee* turning around and returning. The other pirate vessel, with her sister ship in flames and two battle ready enemy vessels to fight, chose discerning discretion over half-witted honor and prudently turned tail to seek the safety of deep water on a southwesterly tack.

After the battle, crews from both ships rescued survivors from the *Northern Demon*. A few hearty souls were taken from the ship along with what booty could be salvaged before the flames overwhelmed the men fighting the fire. Kalusian merchantmen and Kandian pirates fought the flames side by side, but the effort was futile. Flames had engulfed half the ship. Most of the cargo from the forward hold and all from the forecastle was taken as the men retreated over the bow into longboats. Only eight pirates were taken from the burning ship and another twelve were plucked from the sea. Of the boarding party, fifteen survived the raid aboard the *Coastal Raider*. An estimated fifty pirates and another eight men from the *Coastal Raider* died or were lost at sea.

The wind kicked up and the rain poured down hard as both ships set a course for a hidden anchorage Einar had found. The *Bedford Lee* trimmed sails so that the *Coastal Raider* could keep up with her tattered sheets. Both ships were taking on water from the ramming damage, but it was manageable though it kept men busy on the bilge pumps and buckets.

The *Bedford Lee* and the *Coastal Raider* anchored in a quiet cove not more than a few hours sail from Valekrie. The day was dark with a low overcast and the rain was constant, not like the downpour that hit them after the battle at sea, but a steady rain that showed no promise of letting up. Repairs had been underway for three days, and hunting parties were successful bringing in fresh meat and water for resupply.

A fine table was set aboard the *Bedford Lee* in the officers' mess. Ivan pushed his empty plate back and drained his glass of wine. He raised his empty glass and nodded to a crewman standing by with a decanter. It was a huge decanter, more like a jug, to supply the needs of this thirsty crowd. "We are no more than thirty kilometers from Valekrie." Ivan paused while the crewman filled his glass halfway. Ivan lowered his brows at the man and hefted his glass. The crewman topped it to the brim with a grin and returned to his post in the corner. "I think we should send a party overland to meet our people. They must be close."

"Can't you do your wizard thing and find out where they are?" Coulig was on his third helping of venison and barely stopped eating to talk.

"I could contact my colleague, but our enemy has the same talent. He could sense our location and the gist of our thoughts. If he is in the right frame of mind he could listen in, so to speak. I think it better to wait until Dalla contacts me. That will be our clue to sail into port."

"A fool's errand," said Einar.

"I agree," chimed in Beros. "There could be two hundred ships wanting our blood. We need good intel and a plan."

"Why can't we just have a few hearty souls bring them back here overland? This is an ideal hideout. A whole armada could sail by and never be the wiser to us," said Hawkins.

"I fear we have little time to dally here once our friends arrive." Ivan put down his glass and spoke very seriously. "I sense tension in the masses, as if everyone for hundreds of miles were stressed. Not the kind of stress one feels when applying for a job or thinking about what they will tell their landlord when they are broke and the rent is due. I perceive a mounting tension like what people feel when preparing for battle. I have the feeling that Kandia is mobilizing for war. We must proceed with great caution. Valekrie could be in a state of readiness."

"That's just wonderful. How are we going to pull this off? If the navy is on alert, we are going to have a rough go of it sneaking in past sentry boats," said Gavin.

"I have an idea," said Einar. All eyes turned toward him with mouths shut. "We send in two teams. Coulig and his men go in and skirt the city, avoiding local contact. They go north and meet our friends then link up with the second team at the harbor. Our second team, led by Hawkins and Gavin, will go into the city. They will gather information and prepare a diversion in case there is trouble. Our ships, disguised as Kandian merchants, sail into the harbor at night and meet up with the teams and sail out. We will probably have most of the fleet hot on our tails if we aren't caught."

"Not bad," commented Beros, "not bad at all. I like it. We'll have to work out a few details, but I like the idea of tying up at the dock, taking on our people and sailing quietly away. I hope we can get away with it."

"We have another problem that needs to be addressed," said Einar. "We have thirty-six prisoners. We don't know how big Imar's party is. It could get a bit cramped if he has a large group. The Hamaudi is too dangerous to set free, but we may need to cut the others loose."

"Are you out of your mind?" Beros was incredulous. "Those prisoners are the only profit we may see from this venture."

"We have several bales of seal skins taken from the *Northern Demon*," countered Einar. "That'll bring us a little something. I'm just saying that we might not have room. I doubt Imar would travel through Kandia with less than a dozen swords for company."

"All right, but let us wait till we know for sure and then dump only what we have to."

"I should know something when Dalla contacts me," Ivan said. "If you must, you can set the prisoners free here when we weigh anchor. That way, by the time they get to where they can start any trouble, we should be long gone."

"Okay, that works for me," said Beros.

"Me too," added Einar.

"Be advised," Ivan warned. "When Dalla does contact me, Sumas will come. And he won't come alone."

CHAPTER 19

Imar rode in front with Hager, Kendal and Vidar. "We have been on the road for nearly two weeks since leaving the inn. Every town, village and settlement is devoid of young men."

"Haven't seen hide nor hair of any bandits either. This land is rich with them. Or at least it was," said Kendal.

"We have made small profit as well," said Vidar. "The army is about a week ahead of us scooping up men from fifteen to fifty. Three quarters of all food stocks, blankets and half the tools have been appropriated, leaving women, children, old men and cripples with little to live on. I have sold all of our bulk supplies, but these people have little left to trade with. I feel sorry for them."

Imar smiled. "I'm glad you cut them a deal. If I'd handled the trading, I would have just given them the goods."

"I don't feel *that* sorry for them. We still have our gold. I have distributed that amongst our personal gear. As we get closer to our destination I will sell off our extra horses. We have several unburdened pack horses as it is now that can go at the next village."

"Riders," Ian called from the rear. Kendal's lieutenant and the two rear guards had formed a blockade while others took up flanking positions around the party.

Imar rode back to Dalla, his questioning look clearly obvious to her.

The healer answered his non-verbal question. "They are friends."

Imar nodded, rode back and joined Kendal to meet the two riders, now slowing their horses to a stop.

Recognition was made and the men were off their horses grasping arms and slapping backs. The flanking guards held discipline, but still called out greetings to their friends they had thought lost. They were Kendal's men that he had sent from Three Rivers, but hadn't made it to Border City by the time Imar and Kendal's company had left.

"Hey everybody," Kendal introduced them to Imar's friends and family, "this is Olsen and Grenek."

Waves and nods were exchanged. The men remounted and the party continued to travel down a gentle slope.

The road ran straight and wide. A light breeze rustled the leaves of the birch trees and cooled the otherwise hot day. For such a good road, Imar thought it strange that there was no traffic. He called for vigilance and Kendal ordered a debriefing from Olsen and Grenek.

Vidar rode point with one of Kendal's men. Behind them riding five abreast were Imar, Kendal, Hager, Olsen and Grenek, followed by Anisha, Dalla, Missy and Aideen. Rolf led the extra horses while Aksel and Egil took flanking positions with Kendal's men. The rear guard crept up closer than they should have. They wanted to hear the news their friends had brought.

Olsen was one of those men that could talk for an hour without drawing breath, while Grenek was the quiet type that would only nod or grunt an affirmation from time to time. He did this while Olsen rambled on while gesticulating with his hands.

"We were at a tavern, not two days out of Border City, asking if Imar had passed through. There were five men at a table wearing Bamsen's colors. One of them looked at the sketch we had and said he saw our man in the stables just before they came in. We fell for it. We no sooner stepped into the stables and they had the drop on us. We were taken prisoner. And treated none too well I might add."

Imar asked, "Was the leader a dark, narrow faced man named Sigurd?"

"Yes, and may his testicles wither to dust. A mean streak runs in that one. We were bound and kept that way except to eat. Questioning was an upside down affair involving a whip."

"That's his style. Did he burn you with a hot iron too? It is one of his favorites."

"No. We didn't really know that much, so we told him what we knew. He seemed satisfied with that and sent us to Kabula under the guard of a squad. We no sooner got there and a mobilized army departed for Border City flying Bamsen's colors. Kabula was a ghost town after that and Bamsen's castle was just as sparse. We were locked in the dungeon to be sold as slaves when the army returned. That's probably why they bothered to treat our wounds from the whip. We saw our jailer only once a day for our bread and broth. We used our spoons to grind the mortar out from around the bars in the window. We were lucky to even have a window. It was pretty small too. I doubt I could have squeezed though if I hadn't lost weight from poor prison rations. Once outside we went into town and spent a couple of days eating our fill and getting our strength back. We found an inn keeper that was no friend of Bamsen. He offered us credit. We took it. Then we snuck back into the castle to retrieve our arms and personal effects, as well as our horses."

Kendal had an amused look on his face. "Did anyone object to your requests?"

"Not a peep once our hands were filled with cold steel," said Grenek flatly. His face seemed impassive, but for the tightening around his eyes and intensity in his gaze that indicated he wasn't finished paying for his hospitality.

Dalla felt the wave of emotion that rolled from Grenek's aura like a boulder dropped into a still pond. It caught her by surprise. She gripped her saddle rim as the force of it hit her. It passed as swiftly as it had come. Missy and Aideen looked at her with concern.

Dalla shook her head and signed that she was okay. Anisha cocked an eyebrow, harrumphed, and returned her attention to Olsen's story.

"We escaped about a week after the army departed," continued Olsen. "After retrieving our effects we paid the innkeeper and headed north. We were almost to the pass when we had to evade Bamsen's returning army. First were the wagons, wounded, and support troops. They were torn up pretty bad. Then we had a break and crossed over the pass. Two days later the rest of them came. They appeared to be making haste. We found out why when we got to Border City."

Everyone within hearing range was listening intently while they rode. Aksel and Egil had crept up with a couple of Kendal's men to catch what they could of the story.

"King Thorson was there with half a thousand troops camped outside the gates. Actually, his Majesty was in the city at the finest luxury inn. It took us two more days to get into the city what with security checks and repeating our story a zillion times. Engineers, compliments of his royal highness, were repairing the wall and replacing the gates."

"Did you meet up with Olaf?" Imar asked.

"Indeed we did. We first went to the commander of the city garrison, but he was as useless as tits on a boar. Commander Trotter was too busy groveling to the king to spare any attention on us. Thorson tired of that right off, or so we heard. The king appointed an aide to hear out Trotter's petitions mainly for keeping him out of his Majesty's way."

"Sounds like Trotter alright," added Hager.

"Olaf gave us the short version of what happened. He re-equipped us and sent us on your trail right away. He said that Thorson got word from Bamsen of Imar's so-called treachery, but the king didn't believe it. King Thorson never trusted his cousin and figured Bamsen was playing him for the jarl's own gain. Because of that Thorson thought it wise to bring five hundred swords. When he got to Border City and saw the damage wreaked by Bamsen, he was pissed. At first he wanted Bamsen's head, but one of his advisors, a priest at that, reminded him of some law that prohibits him from killing any royal family. I think Thorson may still make an exception for his cousin, but for now the king has bigger fish to fry."

"What happened to Bamsen?" asked Imar.

"He followed your false trail for only a day before he realized he had been duped. He didn't have time to look for you. He got wind of the king being only a day or two off and thought it wise to high tail it back to Kabula. Olaf grabbed some prisoners while harassing Bamsen's retreating army. He put them to the question." Imar's face darkened, so Olsen amended, "Olaf convinced them to cooperate by giving them fair treatment. In fact, the prisoners preferred their incarceration to Bamsen's army. In the end, they signed on with Olaf in your free company."

Imar was pleased with the way Olaf had handled the interrogation. He did not care for torture unless lives were at stake. He wondered if he had always felt that way.

Olsen took a long pull from a water skin. "Thirsty work, all this debriefing." He cleared his throat and looked at his captain. Kendal got the hint. He reached in a saddlebag, pulled out a wineskin and passed it to Grenek, who in turn and declining to drink passed it on to Olsen. He took a couple hefty swigs before Kendal prompted him to go on with his debriefing.

"It seems that Bamsen's wizard advised him to take ship and go south while the king cools off. He is still obsessed with finding you and getting his hands on your heirloom though. How many swords he's taking with him and what destination he's going to, he is keeping secret. Rumor among Bamsen's men is that he will try to intercept you at Valekrie."

Hager groaned and shook his head.

Kendal whistled and said, "How could he know?"

Imar turned and looked back at Dalla. "Sumas? Could he know our minds?"

Dalla paused for a moment thinking, then replied, "It is possible that he may have intercepted my communication with Ivan, but that was weeks ago. We planned to not use that method until we reached Valekrie. I have also been keeping my mind shielded. His perceptions are very strong, but he should not be able to penetrate my barrier." Dalla paused, wrinkled her brow, and pursed her lips. "Although," she reflected. "He may have become stronger than he was when I knew him years ago."

"You told me that all of you from the past have a very high intelligence. Could he have figured out our route through deductive reasoning?"

"That would be my guess. Once he realized that our trail going north was false then the only other way to go would be east, and then south overland through Kandia or head for Valekrie and take a ship south. If he doesn't catch us at Valekrie he will make for Seal Bay or Port Augustus. Sumas knows me. He knows that I would advise you to take the fastest and shortest route out of the northlands."

Everyone listened to Dalla with profound respect. Anisha was aware of the healer's charismatic hold on the company as well as her intelligence, but she was beginning to feel as if she had underestimated that intelligence. She took note to self to use extreme caution when making plans to further her ambitions, especially if she was anywhere near Dalla.

"There's more," said Grenek. "Better tell 'em."

Olsen nodded. "I was getting to that." He took another swig from the wineskin and stowed it away in his own saddlebag. "The king has intelligence reports that Kandia is mobilizing for war. They are going to march on Kabeka. Bertil is concerned that Drayden may want to move his Kandian troops through his kingdom, which of course means an invasion of Sedar. Bertil is waving the treaty again, but this time more frantically. King Gerald of Kalusia is on the way and may already be in Seal Bay. Thorson was preparing to go when Bamsen started stirring things up, so he delayed in order to deal with Border City. He's probably halfway to Seal Bay by now."

"Wow, this is great news," said Kendal. "My free company is probably employed again. I bet my coffers are overflowing with Bertil's coins."

Hager grunted. "Yea, except that we'll have to pass through a hostile army to get to an enemy port in order to get there."

"Well at least I'll die knowing I'm rich."

"There's more," said Olsen.

Everyone looked at Olsen as if he had brought enough news. The only one that seemed to take the news as good was Kendal, but even he was not looking forward to Valekrie.

"Well, it seems that Thorson has taken an interest in your heirloom, Imar. He thinks that a device that could unlock such power should be given freely to the king; all for the good of the kingdom of course. He insists that you meet with him at Seal Bay. He was planning on sending out search parties, but we have about a two day lead on them."

"Wonderful," said Imar. "This is exasperating. Everyone wants the damned key. I should melt the thing down."

"It's been tried." They all turned to look at Dalla. Anisha resented the fact that when the healer spoke people listened. "It is made from a substance not found on this planet. Astronauts brought it back from an exploration mission."

Everyone but Imar looked clueless at Dalla's words. Imar made the mistake of looking into Dalla's eyes. They locked only for an instant. It was enough to quicken both their pulses. They broke the contact as quickly as they had made it, hoping no one had noticed. It was only a second, but the separation made them both feel hollow. Having feelings that they wouldn't allow themselves to express was wearing them down. Even pushing those emotions into the back of their minds, up like a spurting geyser they would emerge from the subconscious with only the slightest provocation. A glance, a scent or the sound of the other's voice would yard out those feelings from the heart. Dalla's extra senses were strong to begin with, but Imar was finding his perceptions to Dalla's presence growing with each day. Imar cursed himself and swore to be more careful. No one acted as if they had noticed.

Anisha missed nothing.

Imar spoke up to cover his blunder. "This changes everything. We must, at all costs, avoid everyone but our closest friends." Imar wished he could remember who his closest friends were. He called a halt, pulled Cerus ahead and turned the horse around to face his friends and family. "You all know what the key is," he patted his belt pouch where he kept the fake, "at least vaguely. And that it's very valuable. King Thorson wants it and Jarl Bamsen is obsessive about getting it, as you have seen. Word is out and every king, lord, adventurer and treasure hunter on the continent will be looking for us to take it. I am not even sure what I'm going to do with it, other than put it in the lock it was designed for. But I do know that I will not hand it over to anyone who seeks it for power or profit, at least not without a fight. That goes for any one of us who may be entertaining illusions of running off with it." Imar glanced briefly at Anisha, who returned his look with a steady gaze. "I cannot promise you anything beyond a soldier's wage in my free company and a share of any spoils that we may gain along the way. But if you ride with me, I will demand your loyalty and will consider you oath bound to me until this quest ends. If you have any doubts about giving me your loyalty, over and above your loyalty to the King, speak now and I will free you of your obligation to me and send you off with coin and provisions."

Silence followed. No one moved. Neither bug nor bird stirred in the heat of the day. A horse clopped a hoof and another swished a tail, breaking the silence. Imar turned to Kendal. "Your men are sworn to you and in this, you to me. You took a job with Townsend, which will put you at odds with him unless you decide to turn on me once we get to your home base in Sedar. I need to know if I can count on you and for how long."

"You are my friend and Townsend can go to hell," said Kendal vehemently. "This news of war means my free company is fully employed and probably recruiting. I will return Townsend's retainer, now that I am sure to have it and more in Sedar. Of course you have our loyalty, but I can only go with you as far as Seal Bay. Once there I must see to my company and tend to this business of war."

Imar nodded. "I understand. Thank you."

They continued their journey south, passing though small hamlets and villages sparse of men. Many of the crops they passed were fallow or tended by women and old men. Orchards that had any fruit or nut near harvest had been picked clean. Each day they grew wary and sought cover off the road when one of Kendal's scouts returned with word of a patrol ahead or behind. The frequency of patrols increased and everyone in Imar's party became tense and jumpy.

The evenings were getting darker earlier. Dusk was a couple hours before midnight, earlier when the sky was clouded—indication that summer had passed its zenith. The days were still warm, but the mosquitoes were less prevalent, only to be replaced by gnats. Everyone in the party had bug hoods to escape those voracious pests that seemed to take chunks of flesh greater than their own body mass.

They started each day early and took only short breaks for meals and to rest the horses as well as their backsides. They ended each day a couple of hours before dark far enough from the road to not be heard or spotted by their fire. Tired as they were, Imar and Aideen spent thirty minutes each evening practicing the sword while the others tuned their skills at arms. He also showed her take-downs and throws and had her practice her kicks. Even though her bow was small and light of draw, she was becoming a competent sharp shooter. She proudly contributed several grouse to the evening fare during their journey.

Anisha didn't approve of Aideen's martial arts training or her hunting, but seemed content to practice avoidance and keep her thoughts to herself. Much of her time was spent quietly studying Imar and Dalla. There were times, of course, that she couldn't help making a snide remark or returning a comment or question with sarcasm. The rest of the party gave her a wide berth, trying not to look too obvious.

Dalla rode with Aideen and Missy most of the time. She wanted to be next to Imar, but did not want to appear inappropriate. They spent the evenings together as well when Aideen wasn't playing 'whack your daddy,' as the girl called it, with her practice sword. The three shared a tent as well. Anisha insisted on her own tent. This was fine with them. Anytime Anisha joined them their normal chatter ceased and conversation became strained and guarded. Just before bedtime in the tent, Dalla guided Aideen and Missy in methods of meditation as well as in lessons using the senses to feel human and animal presences in one's proximity. Aideen was showing promise at being particularly gifted at this. Her range for detecting mammals could already reach several meters beyond their camp. She was even able to detect mice in the food bags, and pinpointing the exact location of the sentries was becoming easy.

One evening after practice when Missy was having difficulty getting Aideen to be quiet and go to sleep, Aideen said, "Dalla, I want to go to Eastonia with you and my dad. I don't want to go with my mother to Port Augustus."

Dalla took a breath and sighed. She had grown quite attached to this little girl. Even knowing the dangers of their quest, she felt sorry for the girl's life without her father in it. She had heard good things about Aideen's grandmother though. "That is not for me to decide, but wouldn't you like to see your grandma?"

"Of course I would, but I am learning so much from you and my dad. Grandma only practices her sword when no one is around to see. She doesn't even know that I know she can use one. My mother rarely sees me and then it's only to tell me not to have fun."

"Your grandmother knows the sword? I'm impressed. How do you know this?"

"When I was little I used to watch her and my grandpa practice in their great hall. They didn't know I was there. It was a couple years ago when we were visiting. I was very good at sneaking in and hiding under a cloth covered table. One time I saw them fencing naked. That really embarrassed me, so I snuck back out."

Dalla and Missy were both amused with this little tidbit of information. Dalla now wanted very much to meet Akala. She seemed to be a remarkable woman. "The dangers of our quest are great. I doubt your father can be convinced to take you with him, but it is up to you to ask him. You must also accept whatever answer he gives you."

"But he may listen to you."

"It is well past your bedtime. Past all of our bedtimes and we have another long day tomorrow, and I fear a wet one. The weather is changing. Now go to sleep."

"But . . ."

"Sleep," Dalla said in a monotone, waving a hand at the talkative little girl.

Aideen fell asleep instantly. Missy, while sitting up on one elbow in bed, also fell asleep at Dalla's word and gesture. Dalla reached over across Aideen and gently pushed the nanny over onto her back. Missy snored quietly like a purring cat. Dalla smiled and followed them in slumber.

As they traveled south the weather turned cooler, overcast, and occasionally rainy. One could almost smell the sea in the air. They knew they were near Valekrie.

CHAPTER 20

"What of our project up in the hills?" Akala asked as she harvested radishes and carrots from her garden.

Dorfin was reclining with a cup of tea and enjoying the afternoon sun. He liked this method of giving his employer the daily report. Such comforts would be gone soon enough with the change of season and the weather it would bring. "Nearly finished, my Lady, we just need to choose someone to train in systems and operations."

"True. I'd hoped to use one of the engineers, but we need to keep them all busy shaking out the bugs, so to speak, if it is a success."

"If it is a success, and I trust it will be, we will need them all to build more and fast what with all this talk of war."

"There is profit in war. I just don't want to hire our soldiers out to a king that wants to chase down Imar for the key."

"It is a hard choice, but I think they all want the octagon key. For now the treaty has Kalusia, Sedar, and Abezda in an alliance against Kandia. Drayden has already dispatched his Kandian cavalry and some infantry units overland to invade Kabeka. A long journey, but he could triple his legions with recruits along the way. Drayden plans on taking Seal Bay by sea and occupying the main caravan route through Sedar. This would not only cripple the alliance, it will give him an easier supply line to feed his troops this winter in the plains of Northern Hamaud."

"What interest could that lunatic have in Kabeka? Half the population are still hunter gatherers and the rest are struggling fishermen." Akala went to a water bucket and rinsed her vegetables then took a seat across from Dorfin.

"Bertil's intelligence corps thinks it is a big ruse and that his actual target is the underground fortress in Eastonia."

Akala sucked in her breath. "Oh dear, word certainly travels fast. I think Imar will have a time of it staying ahead of kings and their armies."

"King Gerald's emissary has been most persistent wanting to hire ships and troops for the upcoming war. I won't be able to put him off much longer."

"What is the current status of our ships?"

"Two are on exploration missions across the ocean. The *Bedford Lee* and the *Coastal Raider* are up north, hopefully on their way to Sedar or here. All the rest, as you wanted, are on merchant missions to the southern continent looking for Lord Travin. I expect any one of them, that isn't working below the waist of the world, to return in the next week or two."

"Send messages to our southern agents to pass word to our captains. Under no circumstances are they to return to Port Augustus. Renauld is still a neutral island country. They can go there if need be or work the southern regions, but under no circumstances are they to come here. I want to keep our ships out of this war for now and focus on finding Travin."

"Consider it done. You know, of course, Gerald will not be pleased."

"Oh well. They're not his ships and it's not his husband we are looking for. I'm afraid that if we don't agree to hire out our vessels he'll just appropriate them by royal order. If the ships aren't here where he can get his hands on them he'll have trouble taking them."

Dorfin's bland expression showed nothing except twinkling irises and a slight tightening of the crow's feet in the corners of his eyes, "How about our troops?"

"I want ten marines assigned to each of our ships. Send enough men south by horse to accomplish this. They can double up on the first ships they meet in Southern Kalusia and Northern Pagentia until they meet up with the rest of our fleet working near the equator."

Dorfin took out a pad and pencil from his vest pocket and began taking notes. "I might suggest you keep some strength close to home in case hostilities find their way to Port Augustus."

"Good idea. Keep a household guard to ward off any nonsense and send a company to our project in the hills to help with construction. Tell them that they will help with the work. They aren't going there just to guard the project—men with nothing to do tend to get into trouble. They can take their families with them if they wish. That should keep them busy, out of sight, and close at hand."

"That will leave only one small company."

"Hire them out to either Gerald or Bertil, whichever one will pay the most. They are for homeland defense only. I want that in the contract. They are not to go on any campaign across the continent. We can add on recruits if there proves to be a need."

"I'm sure both kings will be delighted with your terms," said Dorfin sarcastically with eyes shining in a straight face.

Akala smiled with a laugh. "You mean before or after they come out of their collective apoplexy?"

CHAPTER 21

Coulig swore to himself. He backed out of the alder thicket with the caution of a cat. It was a painstakingly slow process to move through the brush soundlessly, but the enemy picket was less than ten meters away. Half an hour passed before he made it to the team's rendezvous point.

A light drizzle had fallen steadily for days. Even with an oilcloth cloak the wetness found its way through clothes and boots down to the skin. Coulig felt the chill creeping into his bones. Everything he touched was wet. His cuffs acted like wicks drawing the water off the foliage and soaking his sleeves. This made sneaking around in the woods none too easy. He knew it was a matter of time before he would have to wring out his stockings to prevent them from squishing. He wanted to grumble but had to remain quiet, so he clamped his teeth shut and thought of how nice it would be to sit by a warm fire and eat a fat juicy steak.

Brin and Jax had arrived only a minute before Coulig stepped into the circle of spruce trees. They were well concealed and spoke softly in case an enemy patrol or picket may have been missed in their reconnaissance. They all shared similar reports. It seemed that Valekrie was not only occupied with troops, but the surrounding valley was full of camps circling the city.

A day and a half overland to the East Road and then two more days had been spent creeping and crawling through forest and thickets to get past sentries and patrols. Twice the trio witnessed a battalion marching east followed by supply wagons and pack strings.

Coulig thought it best to keep his team small, especially after Ivan's warnings which had turned out to be true. Stealth was needed where force would be futile. "We will have to skirt the valley up on the hillside a good ways to avoid patrols. A little farther north we can intercept the North Road. From there we might find an inn or a village where we can wait for our friends."

"There must be at least two more legions surrounding the city," whispered Brin. "How are we going to get our friends through if the papers don't work? That is, if we find them."

"We'll find them or they will find us," replied Jax. "They have a she wizard with them or whatever you want to call her. She is supposed to be like Ivan. If the papers don't work I'm sure she'll come up with something."

Coulig grunted. "We'll see. Enough talk, let's move."

Brin and Jax nodded and followed Coulig away from the enemy pickets. Out of the valley they went, and into the hills that formed the base of the mountains that reared to the northeast. The valley ran many leagues to the north with the North Road centered in it. The mountains bordered the valley, which was speckled with farms carved out of much undeveloped and forested land.

Coulig silently hoped that Imar and company had not been captured and inducted into the Kandian Army.

CHAPTER 22

Khaled dogged Coulig, Brin and Jax. He was a master of stealth; they never knew they were being followed. They thought him to be still in chains aboard the *Bedford Lee*. He was also a master of escape.

The assassin could have slipped his bonds at any time he wanted. He chose to bide his time instead. To become an Hamaudi Assassin he had to master seven levels of skill, another of which was deception. He let them think he was their prisoner. He listened to men talk. Often their tongues wagged freely in the evenings when drinking the demons' spirits they called grog. From hearing bits and pieces of the plan to find Imar, Khaled knew the man Coulig would lead him to his target.

When the two teams launched for shore in a longboat, Khaled made his escape in broad daylight under the very noses of the crew on watch. Anyone that passed his station below deck would have said that they thought they saw him sitting there in meditation. He had picked the locks on his manacles using a wire buried under the skin of his wrist. The assassin gathered his weapons and effects, and slipped over the side with no one the wiser. He never heard an alarm signaling his escape. Khaled knew his illusion was successful.

The water was numbing cold, but Khaled used a mind trick to ward off hypothermia. That technique would only delay the effects in these frigid waters. He swam on his back below the surface with nary a ripple, using a small blow gun as a snorkel. The assassin made it to shore undetected when the shakes of hypothermia overtook him. As soon as he melded into the trees he ran at a stumbling pace, his coordination impaired from the cold water.

Khaled's quarry had a good lead on him and he needed the run to warm his chilled desert blood. His pace picked up as his core temperature warmed. For a day and a half he followed the two groups.

The next day the away teams split up after coming to a well-traveled road, but not before hiding out in the woods while a large contingent of troops marched east. The larger party went west on the road. The smaller group of three went north into the woods. He thought of following the larger group, killing them all and then returning to his mission, but that would violate the code. He was angry with them for locking him in irons. Then he was angry with himself for being angry. He stopped and knelt in the wet moss and cleansed himself in prayer for dirtying his mind with such selfish thoughts.

After ten minutes of soul purging Khaled resumed his quest, reminding himself that he was hired to get the key. The assassin was not hired to kill unless it was necessary to complete the mission. He prayed that it would be necessary.

CHAPTER 23

An entire day had passed since the away teams had set out overland. Powell had discovered Khaled's illusion when he brought the man his breakfast. He noticed that the prisoner hadn't touched his dinner from the night before. The crewman could have sworn that the Hamaudi was in the exact same position that he saw him in earlier. Fearing the prisoner may have croaked, Powell reached over to put a hand on the man's shoulder. His hand went right through him and the illusion evaporated like mist on a warming day. He ran to tell the Captain.

Einar, Beros and Ivan were discussing tactics for entering the port of Valekrie. They were in Einar's quarters leaning over his map table and looking at a chart of the area when Powell knocked on the door and identified himself.

"Come in, Mr. Powell," said Einar.

Powell came in with his stocking hat in his hands. He was ringing the hat as if trying to get water out of it even though it was dry. He told the two captains and the wizard of the assassin's escape.

Ivan had the crewman tell his story in complete detail and then had him tell it again.

"It is my own fault," said Ivan. "I should have foreseen this. I had heard tales of Hamaudi assassins being trained in illusion, but I did not believe that they had advanced this far."

"We should send another team to warn our men," said Beros.

"I think we underestimated our guest. He probably left shortly after our away team departed." Einar looked troubled and rested his chin on top of clasped hands. "I think both our teams and Khaled are too far away for us to help. I'm afraid, gentlemen, that our people are on their own."

"I will try to warn Dalla when she contacts me," said Ivan. "I just hope my warning gets to her before Khaled does."

CHAPTER 24

Gavin and Hawkins each led four men from their respective ships, the *Coastal Raider* and the *Bedford Lee*. Their plan was to infiltrate themselves into the port community as crewmembers of the *Northern Demon*—the Kandian vessel they had barely defeated and burned to the waterline the week before. Their story was that their bark took heavy damage in its victory over a Kalusian pirate ship that they had sunk at sea. They came to Valekrie to purchase repair materials for their vessel. They were really there to gather intelligence and prepare a diversion for their departure, should they need one.

Gavin had extracted some information from the prisoners they took from the *Northern Demon*. When the decision was made to release the prisoners when the ships departed the cove, Gavin used freedom as a bargaining chip. This brought him a wealth of information that was unobtainable earlier.

Following the road, they entered a valley resembling cupped hands extending from the north with fingers cradling the city and extending into the bay. A short distance from the city they encountered a road block. Gavin was prepared for this. He pulled out a letter wrapped in wax paper from under his tunic and handed it to the sergeant of the guard.

One of the most helpful prisoners from the *Northern Demon* was not only the purser on the pirate ship, but was also a forger by previous trade. Jon was his name, and he became the *Coastal Raider*'s newest crewmember as well as part of the away team. He proved to be a valuable guide.

Jon was from Sedar and had been forced into service by a press gang. He woke one day aboard the Kandian ship with a horrible headache and a knot on the back of his head. This turned out to be a profitable two year employment, even if forced. With his job literally going down in flames, he saw opportunity for new employment with his captors. Jon had never liked the captain of the *Northern Demon*. "The old barnacle was mean as a snake and twice as treacherous," Jon said when interviewed. "But my purse never ran empty."

Jon liked Captain Beros and got along well with the crew, so signing on seemed the smart thing to do. He had warned Gavin about checkpoints and patrols that inducted anyone into the Army without proof of employment. Jon, and Hawkins who also had some experience with altering documents from his caravanning days, worked together to make up papers for the away teams as well as an extra set for Imar's party.

It was one of these letters of proof that Gavin handed to the sergeant. The sergeant looked at the letter and raised an eyebrow at the signature. It was signed, *Captain Rasher, Commander of the Northern Demon.* The sergeant knew and detested the notorious captain. His brow lowered and his face was beginning to form into a scowl when Hawkins sneezed.

Hawkins could tell by the sergeant's face that a hassle was imminent, but he was ready for it and took action. He sneezed, and in doing so he released a few silver coins he had concealed in his palm when they approached the road block.

The sergeant saw the flash of silver and quickly stepped on the shiny coins that fell onto the muddy road. He glanced around at his men, and ascertained that none had noticed the coins. Pleased that he wouldn't have to share, he folded up the letter and handed it back to Gavin. "All seems to be in order. You may go. Good luck finding materials for your repairs. The warehouses are running low and the prices are shooting up sky high."

"Thank you, Sergeant," said Gavin.

The crewmen walked on toward the city. After they had gone a few meters, Hawkins looked back and saw the sergeant kneeling down to retie his boot laces. Undoubtedly it was a ruse to retrieve his bribe.

"That was good thinking, that deal with the coins," said Jon. "I had a couple coins ready myself just in case. I'm glad you spent yours so I could hang onto mine."

Hawkins smiled. "I'm sure you would have billed me for bribes payable if you had dropped yours." Jon had an easy sense of humor. Hawkins liked the young man even though he suspected him of being as much thief as forger. "I grew up riding caravans with my father. Bribery is a way of life in a caravan. You'd never get through customs without passing a few coins under the table."

They took rooms at a seedy inn close to the docks, which had been prearranged with Coulig as a rendezvous point. The inn was a run-down dive. The owner of the establishment had jacked up his prices to the extreme when the port city became overpopulated with troop and ship mobilizations.

The ten men had to share two rooms. They were lucky to get those rooms. The only reason there was a vacancy at all was due to a brawl the previous night in the tavern downstairs. Several men were severely injured and were now billeting at the navy infirmary.

This opened up two rooms at the Orca Inn. There were plenty of takers for the rooms, but no one else would pay ten times the value of the dump. Gavin and Hawkins both haggled fruitlessly, as the inn keeper refused to budge, so out of necessity they paid the exorbitant price.

"Okay guys," said Hawkins. "Split up by twos or go alone. We need information on troop sizes, regiment types and movement not to mention ships and supplies. I think it would help to know the political environment as well."

"Jon has a good handle on that," said Gavin. "He can fill me in with what he knows while we snoop around the taverns for news."

The men chuckled at this. There was no shortage of volunteers to frequent the bars.

"I want someone to find us a building to set to blaze," continued Hawkins. "We will need a good distraction."

Some of the men went to the docks and warehouses while others headed to the edge of town to see what the army was up to.

Hawkins went to the docks. Gavin paired up with Jon to listen to local scuttlebutt in the seaside taverns. Likeable as he was, he was still new, and had been formally employed with the enemy. Jon's loyalty was to his purse and to whoever paid him. Gavin suspected that loyalty would lean the strongest toward the highest bidder. There were some who would see Jon as a traitor, but the young forger had no sensitivities in that area. He didn't look at nationalism the way other people did. He didn't belong to one side or the other even if employed to one of them. Even being from Sedar he thought of himself as human first. 'I'm just a man making my way through life,' he would say about himself, 'and having a little fun along the way.' Jon thought it funny when someone referred to him as a Sedaran.

Gavin and Jon went out into the afternoon drizzle. They were an odd pair; tall, dark Gavin and skinny, sandy haired Jon, not excessively short, but less than medium height. They walked along the boardwalk following the storefront awnings and shop porches to stay out of the rain and mud of the street. The street was rutted with wagon tracks and getting soupy from the heavy hoof traffic. Occasionally a wagon would bog down in the mud and men and horses would struggle to free the heavily loaded wagon from its suction grip. The two men walked by a stuck wagon that men were unloading so they could pull it from the mud. Jon was explaining Kandian politics to Gavin when the teamster of the mired wagon called out to them.

"Hey you two," barked the muddy teamster, "come lend a hand."

Gavin, ready to help, took a step toward the mud covered men to help, but Jon stopped him with a hand on his arm.

"Sorry, sir," replied Jon. "We are on urgent business for our captain. We cannot delay. To do so could mean our jobs and we're not quite ready for a career change into the Army."

"Who's your captain? I could write a pass for your delay."

"Captain Rasher of the *Northern Demon*," replied Jon, watching the burly man's face for the expected reaction.

The teamster's mouth closed and his face lost some color. "Forget it. I'm sorry to hold you up." The teamster went back to his task.

"What was that about?" Gavin asked. "That's the second time the mention of Rasher's name has spurred such a reaction."

"My former employer was liked by no one," replied Jon. "The only reason the Kandian Navy didn't hunt him down and hang him was because he brought in a lot of revenue. He honored his agreement with the former king. He never attacked a Kandian ship of any kind. However, he was known for murdering people that angered him and he angered easily. He raided a lot of ships and the king got his cut. He paid his taxes so that he could boast his fame for taking so many ships. He didn't pay taxes on the stuff he smuggled though, but the authorities were willing to overlook that. They probably feared that he would cut their throats in their sleep if they didn't look the other way."

Gavin shook his head. "You were telling me about Kandian politics."

"Oh yes," replied Jon. "The old King was a tyrant and his taxes were dreadfully high. The country suffered for it. Farmers and ranchers were starving, so communities formed into bands and would raid other communities. After a while there was nothing left to raid. The old bastard on the throne had everything. He squandered the tax payers' money lavishly on himself and on those that licked his boots. He cut taxes to nobles that sucked up to him and stuck it to the nobles that didn't. The small bands of brigands formed into bigger bands and started carrying their raids across the borders. Trade goods already over taxed became even more expensive because merchants had to hire larger armed escorts to transport their wares. Many of these bands had members formally in the military. These men became leaders of well-trained raiding parties."

"There was some talk of revolt," continued Jon. "Then a couple of years ago the old king took ill. He didn't keep as close an eye on his revenuers as he once had. They began to pocket the money, but took less from the taxpayers and gave less to the King. That is when border raiding slowed down. But a year ago the king kicked off and his youngest son, Drayden, stepped up and took the throne."

"Wait a minute. What happened to the crown falling to the oldest son? You know—primogeniture?"

"Drayden had three older brothers. All three suddenly died. One of them drowned, another fell from a high window and the third died in bed from sickness."

Gavin raised an eyebrow and asked, "The fever?"

"No, a hemorrhaging disease caused by a slit throat."

"I see," said Gavin dryly. "Politics seem to be the same the world over. I suppose Drayden's ruthlessness probably prevented a civil war."

"You're probably right. Anyway, political news here can be very entertaining. The first thing Drayden did was lower all taxes. Everyone pays a straight ten percent now, even the nobles, nothing more. This made him a national hero, except with some of the nobles. They learned to live with it though since the commoners were supporting the new King. People could afford to eat again. The next thing he did was start building an army and he hasn't stopped. People have been signing up in droves. Steady pay has a promising appeal compared to the fickle fluctuations in agriculture. Not only that, farmers often found themselves defending their own crops with a bow or spear without pay. If you're going to take a risk anyway you might as well get paid and fed too."

They came to a tavern and decided to go in. There were only a few patrons. A few men were over in the corner drinking ale and throwing knives at a target on the wall. Gavin and Jon bellied up to the bar next to a sailor that appeared to have half a buzz on. Jon ordered ale for both of them and an additional one for the sailor slouching on his stool next to them.

"Thanks mate. Here's to ya," said the sailor, hoisting the tankard and drinking down a third of the mug. He craned his head to look up at Gavin. "Yer a tall one—bet ya bump yur head a lot. I haven't seen ya in here before. Just sail in?"

"Walked in," replied Gavin. "Our ship took heavy damage biting off more than we could chew. We had to beach her, so she wouldn't sink."

"That'd be embarrassing. I hate walkin'."

"You should've seen the other ship. At least we're not decorating the bottom and feeding the fish."

"I'll drink to that." The sailor took another swig along with Gavin and Jon.

Jon set down his mug and wiped his mouth on his sleeve. "We're in need of some hull planking and tar as well as a horse and wagon to haul it with. You wouldn't know where we could inquire about something like that, would you?"

"Ya gotta be kiddin'," chuckled the sailor. "Fat chance ya'll find anythin' that hasn't been propriated fur the war."

"Yea, we've been out to sea for a while and a little behind on news. I have never seen so much hustle and bustle in Valekrie before. I knew there was a war brewing. After all, anytime a new ruler takes over that is usually the first order of business. It keeps the people busy and fills the royal coffers if they're victorious."

"And the people bleed while the nobles get richer." The sailor took another healthy swig and set his tankard down with an audible thud.

Jon signaled the bartender to bring the seaman another brew.

"Mighty kine of ya, thanks again," said the sailor with a bit of a slur.

"Don't mention it. This looks to be one of the largest campaigns in several generations. Drayden seems to be pretty confident if he thinks he can take on the Allied Countries by sea and march his army across the continent. Even with Renauld standing neutral he'll have to contend with Abezda, Kalusia and Sedar."

"Yea, but 'e's turned one of the jarls of Abezda to 'is banner," slurred the seaman. He looked around to be sure no one could hear him rumoring state secrets. "This Jarl not only brought twenny ships 'ere to add to Drayden's armada, but 'e 'as some sort a secret weapon on one of 'is ships."

"Yea, I've heard that before," said Gavin. He kept his deep voice low to encourage quiet conversation with their informative acquaintance. "But half the time when I hear some rumor about a secret weapon it turns out to be no more than some alloy for an arrowhead or a stronger cable on a ballista. I wouldn't give it another thought."

The sailor looked a little indignant at Gavin's comment at first, and then shrugged it off. "Have ya seen dat monster ship tied up at da docks?"

"I saw the masts towering above the other ships. What about it?"

"It's probably da biggest ship to sail da seas. It's heavily guarded and no one can get near it without shpecial clearances and background shecks. It has shtrange hatches along each shide. Rumor hash it that they're doors whish conceal shome short of new type of weapon. She's built with hardwood, very tough shtuff and can probably take a good ramming. This Jarl hash a warehouse to hish shelf and they have been bringing wagon loads from da warehouse to hish ship all day. All of it has been under heavy guard."

"What is the name of this ship?"

"She's called da *She Dragon*."

"The *She Dragon?*" asked Jon.

"No, no, iss da *Shee Dragon*," the seaman reiterated.

"You mean the *Sea Dragon?*" asked Gavin.

"Daas wha I shed. T'was beginnin' ta tink yur deaf."

"It sounds impressive. Good name for a warship."

Jon took another sip of his ale, still on his first one. "What is the name of this Jarl?"

"Baneth, Bamkin, Bansesh . . ." The sailor scratched his head trying to remember.

"Bamsen," said Gavin, a little louder than he had intended.

"Dat's it! Bamshen is hish name."

Their conversation had grown a little louder than either Gavin or Jon had intended. They wanted to keep a low profile, but their acquaintance was very drunk and drunks are not known for subtlety. Normally this would be expected behavior in a bar, but Jon noticed the group playing daggers in the corner looking over their way and muttering to each other. "I think it's time for us to go," he said to Gavin, indicating their audience.

Jon called the bartender over and bought the sailor a double shot of good rum. He wanted to be sure that the sailor was good and intoxicated, thus making it difficult for him to recall their conversation as well as their descriptions. *Although,* he thought, *Gavin would be hard to forget.* The seaman slurred his thanks as Jon and Gavin took their leave.

They continued on their way down the street going farther away from the Orca Inn. "Looks like we have a tail," said Jon.

"I see that," replied Gavin. "Let's go find a place to eat and then give 'em the slip. It will be dark soon and easier to lose 'em then."

They found a mediocre restaurant in an old building with new menus. The prices were inflated but the food wasn't bad. The men following them did not come in. They assumed their tail was watching the front door, so they went out the back when they were finished with their meal. It was dark, not the full dark found at this hour at southern latitudes, but darker than evening twilight. They followed some side streets and alleys, keeping to the shadows when they could. They noticed they were still being followed.

Jon knew his way around Valekrie. He led Gavin down a dead-end alley to a storm drain. "Here, pull up the grate."

Gavin lifted the heavy steel grating and slid it to the side with a grunt. The powerful effluvium made him spit. "You must be out of your mind. This is a stinking sewer."

"You can stay here if you want and wait for our friends that are following us, but I would rather not explain our interest in state secrets." With that, Jon climbed down the metal ladder into the stygian blackness below.

Gavin followed him in and pulled the grate back into place. When he got to the bottom of the ladder he stepped into calf deep water. Being a fastidious man, Gavin cringed, feeling goose bumps run up his spine. His neck and shoulder muscles tightened with the knowledge of the disgusting filth in that water as it soaked his fine red boots and blue silk trousers. He growled when it touched his skin. "This is nasty. I can't see a thing. I am already regretting this."

"Quit complaining," Jon replied in a whisper. "At least you are tall. This water is well above my knees. Here, put your hand on my shoulder. I will lead you. I know the way."

"You mean to say you have been down here before?"

"Yes," Jon whispered with a hiss. "Now be quiet. They are right above us."

They could hear voices up on the street through the grate. They could not make out the conversation, but it sounded like they were arguing. They did hear the words 'torch' and 'stinks' and some distinctly profane vocabulary. Jon decided stealthy movement was a priority. They moved away from the ladder quietly in blackness so dark that they could not see any difference between eyes open and eyes shut. They had not gone far when the sound of the sliding grate, followed by muttered curses, reached their ears.

Gavin followed Jon with one hand on his shoulder and the other hand dragging fingers along a slimy wall. Every now and then his fingers picked up something gooey on the wall. He would shudder, wipe it off on his once bright blue pants, and continue on feeling the wall for stability in the stinking dark. He tried to take short breaths through his mouth, but that only seemed to coat his teeth and tongue with fuzz. Occasionally they would pass an opening and could feel the water moving one way or another. They briefly saw a faint glow of torchlight behind them, but it faded away as soon as Jon took a turn down another passageway and another after that. In a few places the water decreased to ankle-deep and in one place Jon was up to his armpits, which was little more than waist deep for Gavin.

The stench was horrible. At times they each gritted their teeth to keep from retching. Sometimes some indescribable flotsam would bump against them. They could probably guess what it was but neither of them really wanted to know, much less open their mouths to speak. Eventually they started to rise up to a level where the water was gone completely.

It seemed that they were underground for a long time, but in reality it was probably only thirty or forty minutes. The stench seemed to slack off, either that or they were getting used to it, but they could feel some air moving that was slightly fresher than what they had been breathing. They stopped at another metal ladder that they could actually see because of faint light coming from overhead.

Sure that they had lost their pursuers, Jon indicated that they should go up here. Gavin went up first and removed the grate. He looked around and saw that it was an alley similar to the one that they had entered earlier, except that this one didn't have a dead-end. There were apartment windows on each side of the alley above them with laundry hanging on lines stretched between the buildings.

When Jon climbed out he looked around and nodded his satisfaction. "Wait here," he said to the scowling Gavin. The tall seaman was looking not at all happy with him just then. He was a very dark and impressive man. His expression when serious, added to his great height, made him look very intimidating. Gavin had not said a word since the beginning of their navigation through the sewers. Covered with filth and stinking of human excrement, he was not at all pleased. A wandering alley cat stopped mid-stride and looked Gavin in the eye with its glowing green orbs. The cat immediately puffed up and hissed, then shot off like a fur covered arrow. If a group of thieves had entered the alley just then, one look at Gavin would have caused them to drop their weapons and run screaming from the alley.

Jon shimmied up a rain gutter drain pipe and stole some laundry. He had to do this from a couple of different spots to acquire clothing that would come close to fitting each of them. Returning to Gavin, Jon handed him a bundle of clothes. "Here, try not to foul these against your dirty garments."

Gavin returned a level gaze that, had he been a sorcerer, would have fried the young forger to a crisp. Jon led his friend out of the alley and down some side streets to a laundry and bathhouse that was still open. They had to pay extra for their baths because of their filth and to have their clothing laundered was double the normal cost.

They spent considerable time in the baths scrubbing their skin nearly raw and both insisted on changing the bath water twice. Their laundry would not be finished until the following day, so they arranged to have their things delivered to their rooms at the Orca Inn. Jon's stolen clothing was too big for him, but Gavin's was much too small. He looked like a big kid wearing his little brother's clothing. At least they were clean and Gavin's mood seemed to be slightly better, although he still didn't speak much until they returned to their rooms at the inn.

It was late when they got back to the Orca Inn. Everyone was there and greeted them with laughter at their comical appearance. Jon took it good-naturedly with a smile, but one look from Gavin silenced them all instantly.

"What happened to you?" Hawkins asked Gavin. "We were about to come out looking for you guys."

"Jon will brief you," replied Gavin sourly. He went to one of the two bunks and sat on the edge.

Jon told them everything that they had learned and about their trip through the sewers evading their tail.

Hawkins confirmed that the *Sea Dragon* was the largest ship he had ever seen. "She must be about sixty meters. I saw those hatches, though I have no idea what they are for. Could be for ballistae, no way catapults could launch through those doors. There are about thirty to each side. I would like to get onboard, but she's heavily guarded, so I don't see how that will be possible. What did you find out, Jessup? You and Mackey went to the warehouse that's supplying Bamsen's ship."

"Pretty tight security," said Jessup. "There's no way we can get in, at least not in the daytime using the front doors. Mackey got close to one of the wagons, but they chased him off."

"I got a look under the tarp," said Mackey, "but all I saw were rectangular crates and wooden kegs. The kegs could be lifted by one man. The crates took two men to load each one. They were about a half meter by two hands high and two meters long. As soon as it started getting dark, they quit hauling supplies. They keep a guard at the doors and a patrol circles the perimeter."

Gavin seemed to be recovering from his earlier displeasure, especially since the men were reporting their findings instead of making him the center of their comedic ridicule. "Those crates may be the secret weapon our loose lipped sailor was talking about. I think we need to get in that warehouse." He turned to the two men sitting on the edge of the bunk next to him, "Your turn, Muar. Did you and Pat learn anything?"

"We went to the camps outside the city. Pat and I stole some uniforms and wandered around with a clipboard pretending to be investigating a series of defective swords. We got a lot of cooperation. Our story of how this particular batch of steel can easily break ran like wildfire. We were overwhelmed with soldiers wanting us to check their equipment. We finally had to limit our inquiries to supply sergeants only. One particularly nosey captain took an interest in our activities. We were suddenly late to report to our superiors and left. I don't think it would be a good idea for us to go back."

"Okay, enough oratory," said Gavin irritably. "Get on with your debriefing."

"Right, sir," said Muar. He thought it best to use the honorific, since Gavin seemed to be incredibly testy after his ordeal in the sewers. "It seems that half the army and three quarters of the cavalry are marching overland through Kandia to the upper plains of Hamaud. Most of them have already left and the rest should be cleared out of here in the next three days. The rest of the troops will be traveling by sea in the armada. The ships will depart in about three weeks. They intend to attack Seal Bay and occupy it. If they hold the port they can run supply lines and bring support troops to the army in Northern Hamaud where the troops will winter. They plan to invade Kabeka next spring. The Kandian navy will guard the occupied city of Seal Bay against attack from the Alliance. If they can keep the ships of the Alliance busy it will tie up resources for land forces in the counter attack. Drayden wants to take Kabeka, but rumor has it that his eyes are on Eastonia. That was about all we were able to get, sir."

"A campaign like that could last years," said Hawkins. "Drayden will have to hold Seal Bay or he could return home to find Kandia a province of North Sedar or Eastern Abezda."

"Right," said Gavin. "His country will be weakened with most of his troops being across the continent. He'll have to keep his navy wreaking havoc and keep a strong force in Sedar while harassing Abezda's shores and ships. It is a bold move."

"We had better plan tonight's escapades."

Shortly after midnight they went out to pay a visit to the warehouse. They went out in twos and threes. There were patrols of military police, since the city was under martial law for the interim of the mobilization. All the crewmen rinsed their mouths with wine or ale and splashed some onto their clothing, so that they would blend in with the tavern hopping night life. The army guards policing streets didn't trouble them and seemed envious of their partying off-duty comrades. Every establishment serving alcohol was packed with raucous crowds. Every alley they went by had at least one passed out sailor or soldier snoring in drunken slumber.

As they moved away from the tavern strip to the warehouse district they slowly disappeared from public view. One by one they slipped off to back streets. It was still raining, giving them good reason to wear their black oil cloth cloaks and black stocking caps. Once off the main street they each darkened their faces with lamp black and soot.

As planned, one man with a bow hid in the shrubbery across the street from the front entrance to stand lookout on the south side. He was a support sniper. It was hoped that he would not be needed. Two men hid under a garbage wagon on the northeast corner with cudgels. There was another bowman not far off covering them. The third support sniper was stationed to the west between two buildings. The remaining five men crouched in the shadows across from the dark and little used rear entrance on the north side.

Two guards wearing Bamsen's blue and white tabards stood on stationary duty at the well-lit front entrance. A patrol of three men, also wearing blue tabards, circled the perimeter of the warehouse. It was a fairly large warehouse and the patrol was thorough in checking all downstairs doors and windows. They also checked the papers of any people walking by, which were very few except for the occasional reveler walking back to his or her lodging after a night of libations. The circuit took twenty to thirty minutes to complete.

The five men at the back of the building waited like black marble statues, blending with the dark as they watched the patrol make its routine pass. Once the patrol turned the corner on the west side, Hawkins and Muar raced across the backstreet and stood shoulder to shoulder with their hands braced against the building. Behind those two ran Pat followed by Jon. Pat climbed up and stood on the shoulders of Hawkins and Muar. Jon climbed up the human pyramid to stand on Pat's shoulders where he could jimmy the latch of the window. It took him only a few seconds to get the window open, slip inside and close the window behind him. Pat jumped back to the ground and the three men returned to the shadows across the street.

A half an hour later the patrol returned and found nothing amiss. As soon as they turned the northwest corner the crewmen ran to the back door of the building. This time Gavin joined them. Two seconds before they reached the door Jon opened it and held it for them as they entered and closed the door behind them. He had small lanterns for each of them. They were shielded in such a way as to emit a small beam of light in one direction only.

Jon whispered to them as he handed out the lanterns. "I had a chance to look around while waiting for the sentries to pass. Most of this stuff is standard supply for warships and troop support except for the stuff in the far corner. There are crates and kegs there that look like the freight they were loading onto the *Sea Dragon*."

"Lead on," said Hawkins.

Jon nodded and led them over to the freight in question. Gavin grabbed a pry bar and worked the wooden plug from one of the kegs. Shining light into the opening reflected nothing but black. Gavin tipped the keg and poured the substance onto a short piece of broken plank. It was a fine granular media as black as night. They all aimed their lights at the stuff.

"Anyone know what this is?" Gavin sniffed the small pile on the plank and looked around at the blank faces and shaking heads of his fellow crewmen. "It smells almost like medicine. It reminds me of the sick bay after a battle."

"Smells kind of like sulfur," added Jon. "Only it doesn't look like it."

"Pat, Muar," whispered Hawkins. "Bag a sample of this stuff to bring with. Then put the keg back and clean it up like it hasn't been disturbed."

Pat already had a cloth bag and he and Muar took to their task as the rest of them moved on to the crates. Jon went to a stack of steel balls while Gavin set to opening a crate.

"Check this out," whispered Jon. "It's probably ammo for catapults. I could see where being consistently round and equal in weight would be more accurate than stones. Only lead would be cheaper and easier to make. These balls have got to be expensive."

"Let's bring just one," said Gavin quietly. "They look heavy."

Jon nodded and handed the heavy steel ball to Pat, who said, "Why me?"

"Bad back, plus you're bigger."

Pat took the ball and grumbled under his breath just as Gavin got the crate open. They all crowded around with their lights and looked at what was inside. The crate was full of long tubular steel contraptions with wooded attachments that had butt stock similar to a crossbow. Gavin lifted one out and glanced at his baffled mates. The items were chest high to a man, set on end. Hawkins reached into the box and removed a smaller version of the one Gavin held. It was less than half a meter and the wooden end was curved as if to fit the hand.

"We better get out of here," said Hawkins.

"Right," answered Gavin. "I think we have enough samples for this dog and pony show. Let's clean up and go before we get caught."

They were able to make their exit without incident. Jon let his mates out the back door when the sentries passed. He then returned all the lanterns from whence he found them and made his exit out the window. Hanging from the ledge by his fingers, he dropped silently to the ground without help and joined the others.

They split up again after signaling the others standing watch with the call of a night bird. They found their way, one by one, back to the inn. They had all cleaned the camouflage from their faces and faked intoxication as each, in his own time, staggered up the stairs to the rooms.

CHAPTER 25

Imar was riding alone ahead of the others. He often took moments of solitude to reflect on his thoughts. He tried very hard to find his memories, but they always fluttered away out of reach. It was the same thing every time, like grabbing out at a shadow and coming up empty handed. He sought to find his inner self and wondered if he was doing the right thing with his life as he knew it. Dalla came to his mind regularly. Nearly every waking moment she would be in his thoughts and even when he slept, he found her in at least one of his dreams. He wanted badly to be her mate. If he could just convince Anisha that it would be best for all of them. Dalla made him happy, but their union was just not to be. This line of thinking made him miserable.

He turned in his saddle and looked back at her. She was looking right at him. Their gazes locked as they often did. He felt a spinning inside like supercharged butterflies flying circles inside him, while his heart stepped up its pace and he caught his breath like a teenager. He could have sworn that he heard her thoughts say, *Imar, we can't.* He broke off the eye contact, feeling that momentary loss he always felt when he did that. He told himself that he was just imagining it, he couldn't hear thoughts.

Suddenly the hairs on the back of Imar's neck began to rise and he felt an itch between his shoulder blades. He almost felt as if he should dive for cover lest an arrow take him in the back. *Nonsense,* he thought, but he turned in his saddle again. This time it was his wife boring holes into him with her steely gaze. There was no love in that look, nothing at all like what he felt from Dalla. All he saw in Anisha's eyes was ambition laced with evil. He shuddered as a chill took him. *Damned rain,* he thought. He was about to turn back when he saw his daughter.

Aideen was looking at her mother with a very disapproving look on her face. It was almost as if she could read her mother's thoughts. As absurd as that seemed to Imar, he had to admit that his daughter had been displaying some strange talents lately. Or maybe it was just coincidence. Dalla was special and she was teaching Aideen about meditation, perceptions and controlling one's mind. Imar wondered if his daughter was truly learning to have abilities that Dalla had been born with. He turned back to his contemplations.

Imar saw three men step out onto the road. They were a ways up ahead, and he could barely make out their features. They were armed, but their weapons were sheathed. One of them, the oldest and stoutest of the three, waved a friendly greeting. Imar signaled his troop to stop and wait, and then rode on ahead to meet with the three men.

"Greetings, Imar," said the stout one. "My name is Coulig. These are my men, Brin and Jax. I know you and you know me, even though you don't appear to remember me. I heard you were injured and lost your memory."

"I am at a loss. Please forgive me," Imar said. He turned and signaled Kendal and Hager to come forth and join him.

The two came forward followed by two of Kendal's men.

"Akala sent us from Port Augustus. We came here with Ivan," said Coulig.

Several things happened all at once. Imar heard simultaneous shouts of warning from both Dalla and Aideen. He saw Coulig, Brin and Jax look to his right while reaching for their swords. He heard the brush to his right rustle and both heard and felt a thump ahead of his right knee. Cerus screamed and reared as Imar drew his short sword. He felt himself falling out of his saddle rearward. The wind rushed from his lungs when he hit the ground on the flat of his back. His horse fell next to him.

A flash of black robes appeared suddenly and crouched over him. Imar raised his sword, but the man in black was quicker and struck his hand with a black baton, effectively disarming him. The man yanked the pouch at Imar's belt free, briefly felt the shape of the contents, and stowed it away in a pocket. Imar was gasping for breath and his right hand was numb from the blow, but he grabbed his assailant with his left just as Kendal dove from his horse onto the assassin. The man rolled onto his back and launched the mercenary off him with his feet. Kendal went flying.

Imar struggled to his feet, drawing his long sword from over his shoulder as Hager rode by him slashing down on the assassin. Black Robes parried with his right baton, spun and struck the horse's knee with the left. Hager cleaved the baton in half, but his injured horse was driven to the ground. The burly soldier was thrown rolling across the ground and smacked against a tree, stunned. Imar saw a knife handle protruding from Cerus' ribs. The horse was thrashing around and had pink frothy foam around his mouth. Coulig, Brin and Jax were getting to their unsteady feet, apparently stunned by the attacker's sticks.

Imar let out a battle cry and charged as the two men that were following Kendal and Hager rode past him to attack the man in black, one on each side, both of them slashing to halve the man at the waist. The assassin leaped in a forward summersault over the slashing blades, and dropped his remaining baton mid-flight. He landed on his feet in time to cross draw his two swords and block Imar's down slash. The horsemen turned and came back as the assassin traded blows with Imar, but Black Robes suddenly turned and ran from Imar toward them. The man in black simultaneously parried their overhand strikes as they passed, and back slashed his blades into their backs, effectively felling them both.

Imar and Kendal were on the assassin now, blades whirling and full of battle lust, but they could not get beyond the man's defenses. He was simply too fast with his twin scimitars. Hager, somewhat recovered, joined the fray, but the assassin seemed to be playing with them, wearing them down and teasing them with surface cuts. Whirling blades wove patterns that blurred and formed an impenetrable sphere. The man in black saw the rest of the troop riding toward him, and skillful as he was he could not keep this pace much longer. Coulig, Brin and Jax were picking up their weapons and approaching as well. Black Robes wanted to kill, wanted it badly. He had his prize, and could have run off then, should have run off then, before the odds were too great and his mission and life fail. But he wanted the life of the weapons master with the long sword. Desire overcame reason. The man in black disarmed Kendal first, sending his sword flying into the woods, then did the same to Hager. Now one-on-one he would send this soul to his nameless god.

Imar was a master swordsman and fought for his life against an opponent of amazing skill. He knew he had to break free and get away from this man or die. He was tired and breathing like a bellows. Black Robes diverted a thrust from Imar with swords scissoring to the side, then dropped Imar to the ground with a sweeper kick. Imar saw the twin swords raised high and start their descent toward his doom, knowing he could only block one, when in the next instant an arrow was sticking out of the assassin's shoulder. The arm dropped without dropping the sword. Imar saw another arrow hit the other shoulder a second later. That arm fell as well. He recognized the tan and purple fletching on the shafts. They were his daughter's arrows.

The assassin's retained his grip on the weapons, if barely. He looked incredulously at the shafts. He didn't want to believe they were there. When the first arrow struck he knew his desire to kill had overwhelmed his awareness—the second shaft confirmed it. Looking up at the source, his emotions of regret and self-flagellation changed to indignant rage. The Hamaudi was wounded by a girl child. Imar's sword slashed empty air where the man in black had been. In a flash the assassin was gone, fleeing into the woods.

Imar was surrounded by the rest of the troop a second later as he got to one knee. He was not ready to stand. Aideen flew off her horse and slammed into her father with a bone crushing squeeze. Once Imar caught his breath he asked no one in particular, "What in the seven hells was that?"

"His name is Khaled," answered Coulig. "When last I saw him he was in chains aboard the *Bedford Lee*. He is an Hamaudi assassin."

"There is a lot to share. Let's regroup and debrief later," said Imar.

One of Kendal's men was dead. Another was crippled and dying. Dalla knew the instant she knelt by her patient that she would not be able to save him. Those wickedly curved scimitars bit too deep, did too much damage. Both men had severed spines. The first man had bled to death in seconds. He was the lucky one. Dalla's patient was conscious when she got to him and in pain far beyond unbearable. She put her hand on his clammy forehead and immediately went rigid with the rush of pain and emotion she felt from the link. Putting up a block, only to shield from the forceful flood of fear and pain but still allowing her to meld, she guided him to a trance like calm.

She did what she could to make the young man comfortable. It was all she could do for him. His time was near. She knew it, he knew it. Even with the calm she put on him, spasms of pain still shot through the barriers, sweat beaded and rolled off his face as much from shock as from the agony. Teeth clenched and breath ragged, he began to shake. Dalla tried to put him to sleep, but his mind was diverted to fighting the torment. He knew he was going to die very soon, but resisted the peaceful arms of death waiting.

The healer reached in her bag and removed a small vial, syringe and needle. Some of the men watching had seen needles used for medicinal bleeding, but nothing like what she had now. After attaching the needle to the syringe she inserted it into the vial and pushed air in it. Inverting the vial, she drew out a measured amount into the syringe. She tied a tourniquet above his elbow and searched for a vein.

"Gar," she said to him, "I need you to make a fist." He clenched both his fists. He had been a young, healthy man and normally his veins would stand out, but shock was shutting down the circulation to his extremities and his veins were rolling and hiding from view, so to speak. Dalla placed her index finger on his bicep and ran it down across the inside bend of his elbow, muttering soft words that no one near could make out. "There," she said softly as a plump vein rose to the surface. She inserted the needle into the vein, removed the tourniquet and slowly pushed the medicine into his bloodstream.

In a few seconds Gar relaxed. The shakes stopped, his jaw went limp and his breathing slowed. Dalla heard an audible sigh from the others circled around her, but her focus, her empathy was for Gar. Seconds ticked away. Someone asked if he was still alive and another asked if he was going to make it. To Dalla, those voices were like distant talking heard in a quiet forest. Close enough to hear, but too far away to make out all of it.

Gar seemed as if he were asleep. Then his eyes opened and he looked at Dalla. He lifted his hand and she took it. With lips barely moving he whispered only loud enough for her to hear, "Thank you." He closed his eyes, shuddered once briefly and died.

Dalla wept. Her spirit, her emotions, her skills and more she had put forth to give this man some little bit of comfort in his last few moments of life. It drained her. She was exhausted beyond that of the physical being. Her tears ran freely and dripped onto the arm of the man that lay lifeless before her. She barely knew him, yet he was a friend, a comrade. They had all grown some ties traveling together through the Kandian wilderness. He was nice to her, always helpful. Gar had been a good looking young man in his early twenties. He would ask her questions about combat medicine, about this herb or that tincture and whatnot. He told her once that he planned to be a surgeon. That man was now gone. He had thanked her. And Dalla wept.

Aideen helped Imar to his feet. He gave her a powerful hug and thanked her for saving his life. He saw Kendal standing behind where Dalla was kneeling next to one of his fallen men. The others were moving there as well and forming a circle. He had watched her work, applying the skills of her trade. Even with his memories gone he could see that there was no hope for this young soldier. He had seen wounds like this before. He just could not remember them. He watched in silence as she administered medicine to him in a way that seemed strange, but made sense.

As Imar watched he felt something. He couldn't put his finger on it, but he was sure it was coming from Dalla. But there was more. His arm was around his daughter's shoulders. He looked down at her face as she watched the scene before her. She was crying. He felt it from her too. It was all very strange to him, these feelings, this awareness or linking of the spirit or whatever it was. He felt the flow, the sorrow, the pain. He could not explain it or even figure it out, but a tear formed in the corner of his eye.

Dalla knelt in quiet memorial by the body of the man whose spirit had left. She knelt there for a minute or two then rose to her feet, dusting off the knees of her leather pants. She turned and looked at Imar, her face wet with tears, eyes pleading, soul calling. The circle opened and he felt his daughter remove his hand from her shoulder. He felt Aideen's wordless urging. He felt Dalla's wordless calling. She went to him and he went to her and they embraced. It wasn't just an embrace. Their bodies pressed against each other in a way that was closer than just man and woman, more like the joining of souls. Their spirits yearned for each other and in that moment all thought of appearances vanished. They knew they would have to go back to being properly distant after this embrace ended. She pushed her face into his shoulder and sobbed quietly. He rested his chin against her head and held her. Neither of them wanted the embrace to end. Everyone left Dalla and Imar alone.

Several pats on the back came to Aideen praising her for her good shooting. Kendal and Hager took charge and organized the party to move off the road and set up camp.

Coulig looked at Imar and Dalla. Then he looked at Anisha, still on her horse. She knew Coulig. She looked right at him and he nodded to her, but she didn't return the acknowledgement. She lifted her nose a little higher in the air and ordered Missy to find her something to eat, then followed the others into the woods. The veteran shrugged and said to himself, "I guess this will have to wait. It ought to be good though." Coulig, Brin, and Jax, looked confused not knowing what was going on Imar, Dalla, and Anisha. The assassin's arrival was a surprise; he was supposed to be in chains aboard the *Bedford Lee*, but he had just attacked and killed two men. They went into the woods to look for a suitable campsite.

A camp was set a few kilometers from the road. As soon as the fight had ended, Rolf, Vidar, and Kendal's lieutenant Ian took up bows and followed the wounded assassin's trail. Aksel and Egil wanted blood and moved to follow, but Vidar stopped them. At their age they thought themselves three meters tall and arrow-proof. He had seen Khaled's moves and didn't want the rashness of youth getting those lads hacked to pieces. "Stay with the horses and guard the women should he return," Vidar told them. They puffed themselves up with young soldiers' pride and returned, to 'protect the women.'

They constructed two travois to bring the bodies of the fallen soldiers. They also made one for Imar's horse. After cleaning the road of battle-signs, the last men were only a dozen meters into the thick woods when a patrol passed by to the south.

Dalla treated the cuts the men had sustained in the fight with Khaled. Imar replaced his fake key with his only remaining duplicate without anyone noticing. He confided with Dalla what had happened. Coulig, Brin and Jax had been stunned and on the ground when Khaled took his pouch, so they hadn't see it. Kendal saw the theft as he rode the assassin down. He was the only one that had. Imar told his friend that the thief only got his coin purse. He was a very poor liar and Kendal accepted the story with skepticism, but was satisfied when Imar briefly produced the dull gray octagon disk from his pouch.

"You may want to secure that in a deeper pocket or stuff it in your trousers next to your other sword, so that the next time you're thrown off your horse it doesn't fall out in the open."

"You're right of course," answered Imar sullenly.

Kendal realized what he said after he said it. "I'm sorry Imar, please forgive me. Cerus was a fine horse. He served you well for many years."

"Thank you, Kendal. I do regret the loss and had I not lost my memory I'm sure it would be devastating, but I feel as if we were just getting to know one another."

Coulig and Hager joined them as Ian, Rolf and Vidar returned to camp.

"It was a hard trail to follow," reported Ian to Kendal and Imar. "He didn't bleed much—a spot on a leaf here, on a blade of grass there." He handed the broken arrow shafts bearing Aideen's purple and tan fletching to Imar. "We found these at a wide creek. We lost him there. I think he knew we would."

"We looked for signs several kilometers both up and downstream," said Rolf.

"Hamaudi assassins are nothing to trifle with," added Coulig. "Khaled seems to be particularly skilled. Wounded he may be, but we shouldn't take any chances should he return."

"Right," responded Kendal. Then turning to Ian he said, "Double the guard. Set booby traps and make a tight picket."

Ian saluted and went to carry out his orders.

Imar turned to Coulig as Dalla approached. "What is the plan to get aboard a boat and out to sea?"

"Don't let Beros hear you call his ship a boat," replied the stout man. "If he doesn't throw you overboard he will force you to listen to days of lectures on ship nomenclature and seaman's etiquette."

"I'll try to remember that."

"It should come back to you. You spent most of your early manhood at sea."

"Yea...I just don't remember any of it. So what's the plan?"

"Once Dalla contacts Ivan, the *Coastal Raider* will sail in and tie up to a dock about midnight. The *Bedford Lee* will be close enough for support, but she will remain under sail and mobile with weapons cocked and locked. We're hoping to sneak in and out. Failing that, if we're spotted the *Bedford Lee* will try to disable as many ships as she can to discourage or, at least, slow down any pursuit."

"Brave move," responded Imar. "What is to stop patrol boats from sending out an alarm? And if they pass the patrols what is to stop them from seizing the *Coastal Raider* when she ties up to the dock?"

"On our way here we sunk a Kandian pirate vessel called the *Northern Demon*. She was a brigantine not unlike the *Coastal Raider*. Captain Beros is repainting his pretty ship to look like that particular vessel as well as putting the false name on her stern. He's also made a couple temporary modifications to the bowsprit to make her look like the *Northern Demon*. Now that we are in the latter part of summer the night should be good and dark at midnight, especially if this overcast holds. Although," admitted Coulig with a sigh, "I am getting tired of all this incessant rain."

"As soon as I contact Ivan, Sumas will know and he will come," said Dalla. "I have the feeling that he is not far off either."

"Ivan warned us of that," replied Coulig. "We have a support crew of ten men in Valekrie that will be ready to aid us if we need it and to start some fires for a diversion if we need it."

Hager, silent till now, scratched his massive brown beard and spoke up. "There are patrols; we have been dodging them for days now. I expect there will be checkpoints or roadblocks. We will need to appropriate some uniforms to get us through all of that."

"I agree," said Kendal. "We will also need a good story that will seem plausible."

"We won't need uniforms, just unit badges and a banner indicating us as one unit of mercenaries," replied Coulig. "We have a story already. Our men in Valekrie are posing as crew members of the *Northern Demon*. They are using the story that they are there to obtain repair materials for their ship. I have forged documents that will allow us to pass as mercenaries hired on as Marines to the *Northern Demon*."

"How soon do you think we can do this?" Imar liked the plan, but he felt as if they were overlooking something. He decided not to say anything until he was sure of what it was.

"How 'bout night after next? I would like to send Brin and Jax in to tell our people when we will be ready to move. Once we have a confirmation from them we can have Dalla get ahold of Ivan, so Beros can come give us a ride."

"Sounds good to me. It's a date then."

CHAPTER 26

Brin and Jax left the next morning for Valekrie to set the plan in motion. Kendal wanted to build a funeral pyre for his men that had died. Hager and Coulig argued against this because the smoke would draw attention to them, although the two veterans agreed that fallen comrades should not be left behind without a proper burial or cremation. Kendal wouldn't agree to bury his men because their families believed in committing their dead to the flames and not to the ground. Vidar suggested bringing the bodies with them to Valekrie and then finding a crematorium. This too was ruled out because of the questions that would arise and their need to keep a low profile. Dalla spoke up and ended the debate.

"I have a technique for cremating the bodies that will not create much smoke," said the healer.

"I'm all for it," said Kendal, "but how will you do this?"

"I'm afraid if I explained pyrokinesis, you wouldn't understand anything I said. Just trust me and follow my instructions."

"I do trust you and we shall do whatever you ask."

"We will need a slab of rock or a bed of stone to lay the bodies on. Digging the topsoil away from the gravel base will work, but a stone slab would be best for gathering the ashes."

After Imar and his men had finished burying Cerus, Kendal's search detail returned to camp with good news. They had found some flat stone slabs that appeared to be ancient tables or benches from some forgotten time. It was only a few kilometers away. They immediately took the bodies there to prevent further decomposition.

They came to a small meadow of green grass with three slabs of stone in the center, each measuring one by two meters. Surrounding these slabs were what appeared to be old and decomposed wooden benches long since deteriorated to the elements. They placed the bodies on two of the stone slabs. All of their party attended, but only a few were religious. None of those few were of the same religion, so they said their prayers quietly to themselves.

After a few minutes of quiet meditative memorial, Dalla stepped up between the two slabs and held a hand a half meter over each body. Her eyes closed, face calmed, and her body stilled. A shimmering field of sparkling air surrounded each of the bodies. Gasps of surprise startled the still air. A few men made religious signs to avert evil. The field intensified, making it impossible to make out what lay on the slabs other than the general outline of the men. The shapes within took on a reddish glow that grew brighter and brighter. Smoke rose from the shapes and swirled within the shimmering field, but no vapor escaped the barrier. The red hot bodies coalesced into blue then to light blue then became white hot, but no heat could be felt outside of the sparkling dome. Faces turned and hands shielded eyes from the white hot brilliance. The smoke inside was consumed. In seconds the brilliance faded to nothing leaving only the lightly shimmering dome and the ash inside it on the slab. Dalla moved her hands and the domes disappeared.

"You may now gather up their remains," said Dalla.

No one had seen anything like this before. It frightened them, but they had come to know and trust Dalla. "It isn't magic," she told them. "It is a natural process of channeling energy that very few have learned to do." They appeared skeptical; some of them were convinced that she was a sorceress. They were also glad she was their friend. After some hesitation she assured them that it was safe and that the ashes were cool enough to touch.

All of Kendal's men stepped forward with hastily made whisk brooms constructed that morning from dried grass. The ashes of each man were placed in oiled leather bags and the two bags were ceremoniously carried by Ian and handed to Kendal.

The mercenary captain spoke ritual words. "These remains shall be carried in reverence and honor to their families and their stories shall be told and songs shall be made of their deeds."

They all turned and left the meadow and returned to their camp. Garments were mended and swords were sharpened. Kendal's men wore uniforms different from that of Imar and his men, but they had armbands enough to go around for everyone. Armbands were common for mercenary units, especially when taking on recruits when time didn't allow for uniforms. Kendal and Imar decided it best not to display Imar's badge of the hawk in the octagon, so they opted for Kendal's badge of the winged lion.

The anticipation of their final journey into Valekrie was causing some tension. It was a normal reaction and they did their best to relax. They ate well, drank moderately, played card games, dice games, and told stories. There was a light breeze and the mosquitoes were minimal. Even the gnats seemed to be less than usual. As evening came on the clouds broke up and some blue sky appeared. A little bit of sunshine broke through and lightened their moods as none of them had seen the sun for at least a week.

Aideen found her father sitting with his back to a tree watching Dalla and Missy prepare dinner with the bumbling aid of the well-meaning Aksel and Egil. She took a seat next to him and asked, "Who was that man that tried to kill you? I mean, I heard his name was Khaled, but maybe I'm not asking the right question. I just don't understand why somebody would pay somebody to kill somebody else."

"It *is* kind of complicated, isn't it?" Imar paused a moment. "I suspect that he was hired to take the octagon key. Gar and Anton got in his way, so he killed them."

"Yea but, he thought he had the key when he took your coin pouch, he could've just run away with it then and not kill anyone."

"You're right, Aideen," Imar agreed seriously. "Khaled could have gotten away after he threw Kendal off him. He is very good with his weapons and he seemed to be enjoying himself."

"It is more than that. I have heard you and other soldiers talk of the battle rush, but you are always protecting people. When you fight, you're trying to save someone. It's kind of like a game to see who will win, except that people die. You play to win and to live. You're not playing the game only to kill, like him."

Imar looked at his daughter. Her insight at only ten years old amazed him.

"I felt…" Aideen stammered for the right words. "I felt, could almost see, something very dark around him, no, maybe in him. Dalla calls it an aura. It was dark and it made me shiver. Khaled was happy when he killed those men. His eyes were glazed and shiny when he took their lives and he looked crazy when he held his swords over you. Khaled got Hager and Kendal out of the way so he could kill you alone. He wanted very much to kill *you*."

"Well I'm very glad you stuck some arrows in him."

"Yea but, if he only got a few coins then he didn't get what he came for. He'll be back. Maybe I should have killed him."

Imar put his arm around her shoulders and pulled her to his side. "You didn't want to kill him though, did you?"

"No," she answered, staring at her boots. "I don't really want to kill anybody. I just wanted to stop him. I aimed for his shoulder. I think if I had aimed for his middle I would feel really bad no matter if he lived or died."

"You have the heart of a protector. I hope you never kill anyone. And more than that, I hope you never want to." Imar let that thought sink in for a few seconds then added, "Besides, he is wounded now. I don't think he will bother us for a while."

Aideen knitted her brows and tilted her head slightly. Then she raised her head up and turned to look her father in the eyes. "There is something you aren't telling me." Her words trailed off as she peered deep into the windows of his mind. "He thinks he has the key." It was a statement, not a question. "You had a fake one and that's what he got."

Dalla looked up from the cook fire. She was too far away to hear them, but she could feel the gist of their thoughts. Imar didn't see her appraising look. He looked at his daughter incredulously. He wanted to deny that she could read minds, but he had seen things lately that could argue that point. Now Aideen really was reading his mind. Unless Dalla had told her, since she was the only one he had told about the duplicates, but that was very unlikely.

"You seem to have a gift, my dear. Now listen to me very carefully. This is very, very important. You must not breathe a word of this to anyone."

"Except Dalla, right? You tell her everything anyway, don't you?"

Imar took a breath and let it out through pursed lips. "Yes, I trust Dalla; and I trust you too not to talk about this to anyone, not even Dalla. Someone might overhear you, so promise me—not a word."

"Okay Dad, I promise."

"Good. Now go get something to eat. I'll be right behind you."

Brin and Jax returned to camp a few hours after sunrise. They were tired, wet and hungry. The nice weather they had had the previous evening was gone, replaced by the same old dreary overcast and drizzle the locals referred to as the Valekrie rain festival. It was held all year long. In the winter months, wet nasty snow mixed with rain to the accompaniment of howling winds were the norm, and the summers much the same, but without the snow.

Coulig shook his head and smiled when his men walked into camp. "You two look like a couple of soggy doggies." He built up the fire and dished them up a couple of bowls of hot oatmeal from a pot by the fire.

Most everyone who wasn't on guard duty was sitting on logs under a rain fly near the fire. They made room on a log for the sodden scouts to soak up some heat and rest.

"Looks like we're on for tonight," said Jax, taking a bowl. "Hawkins and Gavin have a target in mind to set on fire. Ironically, it belongs to Jarl Bamsen. King Thorson is not going to be very happy when he hears of his cousin's treachery."

"If Bamsen is here, then so is Sumas," said Imar. "We need Dalla to contact Ivan to signal our ships, but that will alert Sumas which will bring Bamsen down on us—so much for sneaking out of town."

"There is no way we can change the plan now," said Coulig. "We are running out of time." He turned to Brin and Jax. "Continue your report."

The two men ate and debriefed between mouthfuls of gruel. The good news they brought was that nearly all of the troops and cavalry going by land had departed. With the lessening of congestion, security seemed to let up a little bit as well. Hawkins had arranged and paid for a dock to be reserved for the so called *Northern Demon* due to arrive at midnight. The two men described Bamsen's huge warship and the items the team had stolen from the warehouse.

"Did you see these things yourself?" Dalla had a serious look on her face.

"Yes, ma'am," they both replied at once.

"Please describe each item in as much detail as you can."

Aideen stepped up and handed Dalla a tablet that she had been practicing some long division on. "Maybe they could sketch some drawings of these things for you."

"That's an excellent idea. Thank you, Aideen." Dalla took the tablet and pencil and handed it to Jax, since he had some artistic talent.

Brin described everything in as much detail as he could while Jax sketched rough images of the items in question. Jax added a comment here and there while he drew. Every now and then Dalla would stop Brin and question him in order to get more detail. After Brin was finished with his description Jax handed Dalla the tablet. He had made drawings on more than one piece of paper and in Dalla's opinion, they were very good.

Dalla looked at the first drawing. Imar, Kendal, Ian, Hager and Coulig all crowded around her to look at the sketch.

"This is a musket," said the healer. "And the smaller one next to it is called a pistol. These are firearms, gentlemen. With the black powder that you described used as a propellant, these guns can shoot a lead ball with more power and accuracy than an arrow. They have a flintlock mechanism that fires a primer charge in a flash pan which sets off a propellant inside the gun. This creates an internal combustion that builds pressure rapidly and pushes the lead ball out through this metal barrel," she said, pointing at the sketch. "The pistol works in the same way except it is not as accurate because of lower pressures due to the shorter barrel and shorter distances between aiming points on the weapon."

She had their undivided attention. Everyone crowded around to see the sketches as Dalla spoke. Even Brin and Jax stood up, although they stayed by the warm fire to dry out. "This invention and these discoveries occurred in the history of my world long before I was born. They will eventually make armor obsolete. A musket ball will part chainmail like butter at much greater ranges than a crossbow, but a ball can penetrate a shield and breastplate as if they weren't even there. You have already seen the disadvantages of wearing heavy and cumbersome armor. That is why most of you choose the comfort of thick leather with rings and save the chainmail and plate armor for heavy fighting. Without armor a soldier can move faster without tiring as quickly. Without armor you will find that your big heavy swords will be too slow to move and the advantage will shift to the lighter sabers and rapiers with a couple of pistols tucked in your belt." Dalla saw the alarmed look on the warriors gathered around her and added, chuckling, "Worry not, gentlemen. This isn't going to happen overnight, so don't go trading in your broadswords and chain mail just yet."

"A dagger can be fixed on the end of the musket," continued Dalla. "It is called a bayonet. After the shot is fired, if there isn't enough time to prepare another load, the musket can then be used much like a spear." She looked at the next drawing depicting the big steel ball. "This ball is a projectile fired from a very big gun called a canon. It is filled with black powder and sealed so that it does not explode when fired from the cannon. See this indentation here." She pointed to a spot on the sketch. "The fuse is attached here and when fired from the cannon the discharge lights the fuse. If the fuse is cut to the right length and timed just right the cannonball will explode when it hits the target or shortly after. Those hatches in Bamsen's ship along the sides are gun ports for the cannons. If there are thirty on each side that means there are at least sixty guns on that ship and I would suspect an additional five more in the bow and another five on the stern."

Everyone started talking at once. The talk got louder and louder. The news was very alarming to them. They could see where this technology would allow the enemy to triumph against incredible odds. Imar held up his hand and asked for quiet without much luck.

Hager then let out a bellow that blasted everyone to silence. "Let us keep this down to a low roar shall we, so we can figure out how we are going to handle this." He turned to Dalla, speaking in a soft voice rarely heard from the surly warrior. "How is it that we have not heard of these weapons before? I could see where this black powder would have many uses besides warfare. I mean if I recall my history lessons correctly, all of our modern weapons that we have now evolved from hunting spears, bows, and big knives. Now we have good steel swords, catapults, ballistae and trebuchet. Centuries have passed to bring us to what we have now. How could Bamsen's engineers come out with something like this all of a sudden?"

"It wasn't Bamsen. It was Sumas. He's been tampering with the natural order of history and evolution. He is using Bamsen as a tool to get what he wants. Sumas gave Bamsen this technology for the advantage it will give him in seizing the octagon key. Failing that, he can use the black powder for its explosive force to blast his way into the fortress at old DC. I will have to discuss this with Ivan, but I'm sure he will agree that we will have to share some of our knowledge to balance the weaponry on the battlefield. If we don't do that, Bamsen and Drayden will grind the Alliance into dog meat. Sumas acts like he is working for Bamsen, but he is dangling the Jarl's strings like a puppet. If they succeed in gaining access to the fortress, Sumas will toss both Drayden and Bamsen aside like an old tool. He means to become the ruler of the world. He would have the power to destroy millions in an instant and he wouldn't hesitate to do it if anyone opposed him."

"We will have to alert Ivan at the last possible moment," said Imar. He turned to Coulig and asked, "How long will it take for the *Coastal Raider* to come in and dock?"

"I'm not sure," answered Coulig, turning to Jax. "What do you think? You seem to have picked up a number of skills as a seaman on our voyage here. You'd probably be a better judge of it than me or Brin."

Jax answered without a moment's hesitation. "No more than two hours if they buck tide and wind Captain, maybe forty minutes to an hour if they don't."

"We need to plan to have Dalla contact Ivan an hour or two before midnight tonight," said Imar. "We will also have to have a defense prepared, because we can be pretty sure that Bamsen will attack us and we must hold that dock until we can get aboard the *Coastal Raider* and sail out of here."

"Wait," Dalla spoke up. "We need to raid that warehouse and get as many of these weapons as we can and then destroy the rest. We need these guns and munitions as models for the Alliance or it will be crushed."

"There isn't much time," said Kendal. "We need to send Brin and Jax back in to tell the team our plans, so they don't torch the warehouse tonight."

"No way," argued Coulig sternly. "My men are exhausted. They need rest. Exhausted men make mistakes, and mistakes in this business can get them killed." Brin and Jax started to complain, but he halted them with an upheld hand and a look that could sour fresh milk. "I won't have it. I will go instead."

"You are right of course," apologized Kendal. "Please forgive me. Take Ian with you. You shouldn't go alone."

Coulig looked over at Kendal's lieutenant and asked, "Are you up for it, Ian?"

"I'm game."

"Good, let's go. We're burning daylight."

Imar said to Coulig, "I will see that your men get some sack time. We'll break camp shortly after noon tomorrow. That should put us in Valekrie about evening time. Now that most of the army has left it should be easier to find lodging. Find us a place off the street where we can stay out of sight. Let's rendezvous at the Orca Inn. Safe journey and watch your back."

Coulig and Ian saluted and left without another word.

CHAPTER 27

Imar's party made it into Valekrie without too much difficulty. Most importantly, they were not captured and drafted into the Kandian Army. Vidar rode in the front with Imar and Kendal to smooth over discrepancies in their paperwork with a ready bribe. A few patrols were encountered and the sergeants of the first two were satisfied with their stories and their coins. However, the third patrol surrounded them and the sergeant in charge insisted on escorting them to the roadblock at the city's edge after refusing Vidar's bribe. Once at the roadblock the sergeant of the platoon, satisfied that the party was delivered to another authority, led his men out of town at a gallop to resume their patrol.

The men at the roadblock were more relaxed, even bored. Vidar passed the sergeant two silver coins along with the paperwork. "That sergeant that brought us in didn't have the usual business attitude. He even took offense when I offered a small gratuity."

"That was Kralik," said the sergeant. "He's as cold as a fish to everyone unless you're a member of his cult."

"Cult? Is he religious?"

"In the worst possible way," answered the sergeant. "Every few years some new religion pops up or a branch of an old one starts a new argument. They all claim they are the only ones that are right, and they all promise great rewards after you are dead, so long as you pay their priests regularly. This one came in about a year ago claiming worship to the nameless god. Kralik took the bait; hook, line and sinker."

"He wasn't real friendly to begin with and became colder after I offered him a tip. I take it fellowship isn't real high on the list of attributes for his branch of this religion."

"Only if you're one of them," replied the sergeant with a smirk. "The congregation doesn't give or take bribes, except the priests of course. They're taught to believe they are supposed to give up their pay to the church. The priests had to change that rule though when patron families began starving to death. Church members evicted from their homes began moving into the churches and cleaning out the clergy's pantries. The priests changed the required tithes so they could oust the people and go back to eating regularly while still making a profit. The members still give up half their pay to the thieving priests, and struggle to get by on what they have left. They claim their faith is based on love, but if you aren't one of them they can be as rude as a rattlesnake."

"They say love makes the world go round," Vidar said with a grin, handing the sergeant another coin.

"Yea, and money greases the axels," answered the sergeant, returning the papers. "Your papers are in order. You may pass." He signaled his men to let the party through. "A word of advice though," he said to Vidar as he climbed back into the saddle. "Your orders have you on the *Northern Demon*. Captain Rasher is as volatile as fresh naphtha. On his ship I'd sleep with one eye open and a hand on a sharp blade."

"Thanks, Sergeant," replied Vidar as he nudged his horse into a walk. "Good day to you."

"What was that all about?" Imar asked once they were out of earshot.

"I was curious. I noticed Kralik's medallion, so I thought I would get some details. I ran into some fanatics up north wearing the same symbol. I thought they were complete nut cases. Eating the red mushrooms with the white spots can make folks act like that and they were all carrying them like bouquets of flowers. I figured they were hallucinating."

"I've run across them in Sedar," added Kendal. "They are a strange bunch. The religion came out of the dessert of Hamaud. Everywhere else it has a pretty small following. No one really takes them seriously, but they are growing. They aren't very tolerant of nonbelievers and less so of believers that worship a different God or Gods. I personally don't understand religion. Most of the men in my company are nonbelievers and that keeps it simple. However, I do have a few men that practice one religion or another and that is okay with me as long as they keep it to themselves and respect the free thinking of their comrades."

After a moment Kendal continued, "This nameless god religion is not at all tolerant and causes discontent everywhere I have seen it practiced. I won't allow it in my company. I had one man convert to that religion. He stirred up more trouble than I cared to deal with. He really brought down the morale in the company, so I gave him the boot. I have a friend that is a member of Bertil's intelligence corps. He seems to think that the priesthood of the nameless god is a front for a spy network out of Hamaud. I don't know, but it would still be wise to beware of them."

Delayed due to anal patrol officers and talkative checkpoint sergeants, they met Coulig and Ian at the Orca Inn a couple hours later than planned. There was a scant two hours remaining till Dalla would call Ivan and consequently let Sumas know they were there. He knew they were coming to Valekrie. All he needed was Dalla's telepathy to know exactly when and where to strike. They had to make defensive preparations for that attack as well as ready themselves for the pending evacuation. The warehouse team was in the process of beginning their mission as Imar's party arrived.

Coulig was pacing nervously when he and Ian met Imar and company in front of the Inn. Obviously impatient, he barked at Imar and Kendal. "What kept you?"

Aideen's voice could be heard from the middle of the group. "Boy, someone's a little grouchy tonight."

Snickers followed, lightening the tension. Coulig's face softened slightly. He had to concentrate to keep from cracking a smile.

Imar suppressed a grin. "That will be enough, young lady." Then to Coulig, "Do you have a place for us to get off the street?"

"We couldn't find rooms available anywhere," answered Ian, "but since the departing army took most of the horses with them, there are a lot of vacancies in the barns and stables."

"Follow us," said Coulig. "We have one reserved."

The party dismounted, except Anisha, and followed the two men down the street a short way then turned off onto a small side street. The avenue was lined with shops and businesses that served equestrian needs, veterinary services, and wagon rental and repair. Due to the late hour, nearly all of the shops were closed for the day. They came to a stable with a dark wiry man waiting for them out front. As they approached he opened the large doors. It was well lit inside. Fresh water, hay and grain had been placed in the many empty stalls. Once everyone was inside he shut and barred the heavy doors.

"Greetings, travelers," announced the man to the group. "Once you have seen to your horses, I took the liberty of having food and refreshments prepared for you." He indicated a table against the wall with bread, cheese and smoked fish, as well as jugs of cold drinking water. There were also folding chairs against the wall next to the table. "Please help yourselves and seek comfort as best you can in my humble stable."

"This is less than adequate, Imar," said Anisha. "We have been on the road for weeks. We finally come to a city representing some semblance of civilization and you bring us to a stable. I want a bath, a decent meal that I can enjoy at a table and a glass of chilled white wine."

Everyone continued with tending their horses, ignoring Anisha's tirade. For the most part they were used to it, but there was some muffled muttering; 'not again,' here, and, 'gods, can't she ever just keep her trap shut,' there.

The stable owner was at a loss for words and was about to apologize when Imar whispered to him, "Ignore her."

Ian signaled Vidar over to where he stood with the man who had let them in. "Vidar, this is Chan," he introduced. "This is his stable. I only gave him a deposit to secure the place for us and with a *no questions asked* stipulation," explained Ian. "He is interested in buying our horses and tack as well as any other trade goods or equipment that we may have left."

"I am very pleased to meet you, Mister Vidar," said Chan. He was a short man with a narrow face. His piercing eyes implied cunning. "I am sure I can help you get rid of everything in short order."

"Mister Chan," replied Vidar coolly. "I am not seeking to get rid of anything. I know there is a shortage of horses and tack, since the Army just rode off with nearly all of it."

"You wish to make a sale quickly? There are no other merchants open for business at this hour. I will offer you thirty silvers for the lot."

"I would not part with half of our saddles for that price, Mr. Chan, much less even one horse."

"Please call me Chan," he insisted with a smile.

"And I insist you call me Vidar." The smile returned was genuine.

Both men had appraised each other like fencers testing an opponent with the first few strokes. The traders found skill in their adversaries, and seemed to anticipate the next step in their negotiations.

"I will give you one gold piece and fifty silver coins."

"Excuse me Chan, but I think I will go talk to one of your competitors." Vidar turned to walk over to a side door.

Chan's smile vanished to be replaced with alarm. "But you won't find anyone at this hour. All of the other businesses are closed."

"On the way here I noticed a number of empty corrals. I suspect the stables are just as vacant. It is a common thing when a military force mobilizes for a major offensive. I am sure that if I were to call on three or four horse traders, even at this hour, they would not turn me away for disturbing them. In fact, that may be a good idea. I bet we could get a little auction started with serious bidding before an hour has passed." Vidar resumed his move to the door, but Chan ran up and blocked the exit.

"Please, I beg you, don't do that. You need not go any further. I promise I will deal fairly." Vidar came back and he and Chan took chairs apart from the others and got down to serious negotiations. Rolf joined them to add his professional horse knowledge to the discussion.

Ian chuckled his way over to where the others were making plans. "Remind me not to buy anything from Vidar. I swear he could make a profit on a three legged dog."

"Even with some of the cut rate deals we made with those depressed villages up north," replied Imar, "he still managed to double our money." He turned to Coulig who was now wearing his chainmail, helmet and battle harness. "You're ready, I take it. We'll wait until the fire alarm sounds or an explosion erupts. Dalla will contact Ivan then. Maybe the confusion will slow down Bamsen or impair Sumas' mental hearing. That will be your signal to get to the dock. Kendal's men will try to have it secure before you arrive with the wagon. You may have to hide out until the pier is secure." He turned to Kendal. "I am leaving my family in your care. If you are discovered before our ships arrive, it could be a brutal fight. We will come as soon as we give Sumas the slip."

"Where are you going and who is *we* supposed to be?" Kendal inquired.

"Sorry my friend, I modified the plan a bit. I knew we were forgetting something earlier and it didn't dawn on me until Dalla mentioned it a little while ago. She thinks, since Sumas is so close, he will be able to get a fix on her exact location when she contacts Ivan. Because of that I think it would be best if we, Dalla and I, went to the other side of the city to make the call. Bamsen and Sumas will come for us there and we will lead them a merry little chase through the streets of Valekrie. It will take our ships some time to get here, so we need to keep them busy and away from that dock until everybody, along with our wagon load of stolen weapons, are aboard. I just wish we could get aboard that big ship and wreak a little havoc."

Kendal's jaw dropped. "Are you out of your mind?"

Imar smiled broadly. "Probably, I can't remember though. Maybe it was that bump on my head."

"You plan to play cat and mouse for two hours. The cat is probably a company of armed men and you and Dalla are the mice. You also entertain thoughts of the two little mice attacking what is probably the biggest warship ever built. One that is not only heavily guarded, but armed to the teeth with a new secret weapon that can shoot explosive fire. I'm glad it's at the other end of the dock. Otherwise you may ask me to try to capture it with a handful of men."

"No, that'd be biting off more than we can chew. Speaking of chew, have some cheese. It's very good."

"I'm out of here," said Coulig. Brin and Jax, now girded for battle, joined him. The three of them saluted Imar and Kendal then departed out the side door with many a 'Good luck' wished them by the other men as they left.

All the men were putting on mail shirts, buckling on greaves and fastening helmets. Weapons were checked and double checked. Imar pulled on his chainmail and his conical helm. He and his men donned their brown tabards displaying the hawk in the octagon in tan. Aideen wore her stout leather vest also bearing her father's emblem and carried her light katana on her back and buckler on her arm. Dalla had her shield with the many branched tree and one of the men handed Anisha and Missy a couple extra shields and daggers. The clatter of buckles, leather and steel was adding to the rise of adrenaline in the hearts of the warriors.

"Anisha," Imar said to his wife. "I know these past several weeks have been rough on you, especially since you are accustomed to a life of luxury and privilege." Anisha looked at him down her nose, expecting some sort of unreasonable demand, but she remained uncharacteristically silent. Imar continued quietly so that only she and Kendal could hear. "If all goes well tonight, you should be back in civilized Port Augustus within a couple weeks. You have wanted this for some time. If we are captured, you and Aideen may be ransomed or you may all be made slaves along with Missy and Dalla. The atrocities you would have to endure are unspeakable." Imar took a breath and sighed. "I must ask you to please stay together with Aideen and Missy. Be very quiet out there and please do everything Kendal says without question or argument. All of our lives could very well depend on it."

Anisha looked at him coldly as the seconds dragged by before finally answering him. "All right, Imar. I think I understand. I will do as you ask." She then went to a private corner to be alone.

"Thank you, Imar," Kendal said to his friend. "You may have just increased our chances of survival, at least if she sticks to her promise and doesn't start demanding tea service or a foot massage while we are waiting at the dock."

"When you get to the dock, if you can find anywhere to hide out of sight for a while, it will draw less attention."

"I was thinking that myself. Now back to you. Only one sword to hold off Bamsen isn't much. Why don't you take a few men with you?"

"No, I'd feel better if you had the stronger force to hold the dock and to protect the women."

Hager had been sitting in a chair listening while sharpening his sword. He spoke without getting up. "I'm coming with you." He said it in a matter of fact manner without ceasing to stroke his blade with the stone.

Imar discarded any thought of argument the moment he looked at his friend. He had come to know Hager fairly well over the past few weeks, and he could see why they had such a strong bond of friendship. It was still frustrating for Imar not to be able to remember, but when he looked in his friend's eyes he would sometimes see fleeting shadows of memories just beyond his grasp. He experienced the same thing with his daughter. Lately those shadows had become more vivid, almost tangible. "We will count ourselves fortunate to have your company as well as your steel."

Vidar came over, hefting a bag of coins. "We have our clothes, armor and our weapons and nothing more besides this," he said with a grin, handing the bag of money to his captain.

"You hang on to it," said Imar. "We did well?"

"We did well. I made arrangements to leave the horses and wagon at the dock.

"Good work. I'm sure Coulig will appreciate not having to bring them back here."

CHAPTER 28

The away team took up the same positions as before. Three support snipers, two men under the garbage wagon near the rear on the east side and five men in the shadows of the back street standing ready to penetrate the warehouse rear entrance.

The sentries had done this circuit many times, over and over again. They walked around the building dozens of times every night, night after night. Check the windows and check the doors—boring as hell. The only respite was trading off with front door duty, which was worse. Stand and do nothing while your feet went numb. At least circling the building allowed one to stretch out the kinks and give one the chance to drain the bladder out back out of public view. It was called a crap job. It wasn't as bad as cleaning latrines, but it was at least second on the list of the worst duty assignments. Complacency occurs with any repetitive duty and such was the case with the guards. If they had been new to the job they may have checked the shrubs and shadows across the street or looked under the garbage wagon. Huddled in their cloaks, wet and miserable and bored to death, they did their duty to the bare minimum and nothing more.

As they turned the corner to the backside, one of them said, "Hold up a minute guys. I gotta take a whiz." The guard turned, exposed himself and began to pee. "Ahhh, much better, my teeth were floating." The men under the wagon shot out and ran the short distance to strike. The man relieving himself caught the movement and shouted. His buddies turned in time to get bonked on the head. He reached for his sword and got it half drawn before he too got whapped on the noggin.

"Bastard peed on me," said Jessup, tucking his baton away.

Mackey started laughing. "It smells like he ate asparagus too."

The men in the shadows came across the back street to help drag the unconscious men out of sight. Gavin looked at the chortling crewman. "That shout didn't help, but you guys are making way too much noise. What's so funny anyway?"

"Jessup got hosed," replied Mackey wiping his eyes.

The other crewmen started laughing. "Phew, I'll say," said Pat. The comment started another round of chuckling.

Gavin tried to keep a straight face. He tried to be the stern and serious leader, but even Hawkins was nearly doubled over with laughter. His brows went up, his eyes grew large and he gritted his teeth. He couldn't hold it back any longer. The big man put his hand over his mouth and started cracking up with the rest of them.

Jax came over from where he left Brin and Coulig with the wagon in a side alley. "Coulig wants to know what's so funny. You're going to draw attention if you keep up this racket."

"He's right," said Hawkins. "Get these men tied and gagged. Hide them in the garbage wagon. And cover that poor guy up."

Jax looked down at the exposed man just as he was asking, "What's that smell?" Then it dawned on him as he recognized the odor on Jessup and started laughing which started the men all cracking up again.

"Just get back to your post," said Gavin with a grin.

Strangely enough, the sentinels standing watch at the front doors were not alarmed when they heard distant laughter. They assumed that their comrades had found something amusing. They could hardly wait for them to finish the circuit and hear the joke.

After about a half hour had gone by, Brin clucked the horses into a walk. The now loaded wagon pulled away from the back door of the warehouse. Jax sat on top of the load with his bow laid flat with an arrow nocked. Coulig sat next to Brin, his bow right behind his seat in easy reach. Jax waved a silent parting to Gavin as they headed down the dark back street toward the dock.

Gavin went back in and strode to the center of the floor. The men were just finishing up with pouring naphtha on everything and all over the place. He signaled with his lamp. They joined him by the back door and lit the torches. They all threw their torches and ran for it. Within a few seconds the fires were burning fiercely and spreading fast.

The guards at the front saw the red glow through the windows. They unlocked the doors and looked inside. They were terrified, knowing what flame would do to the powder kegs and ran for safety. Unlike the crewmen, they did not go quietly down a back street. They ran screaming up the main road sounding the alarm.

The first explosion woke the city. It blew out all the doors and windows of the warehouse. Burning debris flew out in all directions. Some of that debris was kegs of powder caught afire. Like a burning fuse they blew up randomly like giant grenades. Buildings surrounding the warehouse caught fire and the flames spread. One end of the warehouse collapsed and the entire building was engulfed in flames. More explosions followed.

Dalla, Imar and Hager sat their horses on a hillside in a well-to-do residential district on the north end of Valekrie. Imar was surprised at the magnitude of the explosions that erupted from the industrial district. It lit the night, coloring the overcast sky red. Hager watched the light show, but said nothing. Dalla wasn't the least bit surprised. She had seen the destructive power of far greater weapons in her time. Lights were coming on all over the city as well as in the houses along the hillside.

The explosions gradually ceased like popcorn just before it's done, a bang here and a boom there, then the noise of alarms and fire crews. Even the roar of the flames and the sounds of collapsing buildings could be heard on the hillside. Fires raged and spread, illuminating that portion of the city. But for the destruction it caused, it was a beautiful sight. They all dismounted. Imar took the reins of Dalla's mount. She still rode Bell and patted his neck fondly when she swung out of the saddle. He had carried her for some time now and she had grown attached to him. He belonged to Chan now, but Vidar arranged for using a few of the horses a few hours longer as well as renting the wagon now loaded with guns and munitions.

She walked a few paces and sat down on the ground assuming the lotus position. She began some breathing exercises as she relaxed her mind and body. She focused very hard on Ivan while putting up barriers to keep Sumas out, but she knew that would only prevent him hearing their mind speech. He would still know she was here and he would come.

Do you hear me? She thought.

I hear you. Ivan's thought replied.

I hear you too, came a different thought/voice.

Dalla and Ivan were both surprised. They could tell it wasn't Sumas. Ivan and Dalla had both set blocks to prevent intrusion from him. The thought speech was weak, but impish.

Who is that? Ivan asked.

Dalla's perception told her who it was. *Aideen, it isn't polite to eavesdrop.*

I can barely hear anyway and I just bumped into a lamp post.

Pay attention to what you're doing dear. We'll talk later.

Okay.

Ivan was curious, but a little agitated. *We're kind of busy right now. I assume you are ready. We heard the explosions from here and the clouds above the city are lit well enough to navigate by. We weighed anchor when we heard the first blast.*

Beware. Sumas is here and so is Bamsen. The Jarl has turned coat to join Drayden.

Fill me in when we are all safely underway. The marina is quite large as I remember. At what dock shall we meet?

Go to the pier on the east end. The dock tee's off of it and display's a green pennant. It is an easy tie up, so you can come right in without rowboat or tug assistance. There are no other ships on that dock. If the captain is skilled you won't even need to use the oars

Excellent and yes, Captain Beros is very good. Beware the assassin. We had him, but he escaped.

He found us. He got away with a decoy.

Clever girl.

It was Imar's idea, not mine.

Not bad. We'll talk about it later. Time to go.

Wait. One more thing; Bamsen has gunpowder and a ship at the west end big enough to carry seventy guns. I think they can fire five kilo cannonballs.

Ivan's thoughts resembled a stream of curses that could have sent sailors running. He was careful not to think the name of their adversary, but Dalla knew who he was angry with.

Careful Father, there may be a child listening.

Right, that is something else we'll have to talk about. So that's what caused the big booms. He gave them black powder and you blew it up. Good work, I am very pleased with you. You had better go. He's sure to be after you by now. Later.

Later.

Dalla opened her eyes. Imar gave her a hand to help her to her feet.

Hager swung into his saddle and spoke. "We'd better get moving."

Bamsen was livid. Word of his destroyed warehouse came to him at Drayden's palace minutes after he woke abruptly from the blast. The Jarl struck down the messenger with a savage back hand. He then destroyed his rooms in a fit of rage.

Sumas came to him in the middle of his tantrum and sternly said, "Grow up. We haven't time for this childishness. I know where the healer is. Where she is Imar is sure to be too. We must go now if we are to lay our hands on the octagon key."

Bamsen entertained thoughts of how well his advisor's head would look on a pike. They went to the courtyard where Sigurd waited with mounts ready for them. He had eighty mounted men ready to go.

The Jarl was still half drunk as he rode by the burning buildings where fire fighting crews struggled to prevent the fires from spreading. They were fighting a losing battle. Drayden ordered two companies of men to assist with the fires and two more to secure the streets in the industrial district as well as the docks. Bamsen and Sumas took thirty men and turned up the hill to find Dalla and Imar. Sigurd led the rest of the company to the docks.

The crewmen had barely gone a block before the night silence was rent with a deafening blast. Many of them dove for cover while others were knocked off of their feet before looking back at the fireworks erupting behind them. Shrapnel fell like rain. A burning powder keg fell on the roof of a building across the street. They dove for cover again as it blew the roof up and the walls out. More explosions followed, but they didn't wait around to watch the show. They ran on toward the docks.

Stepping into an ally, the crew moved toward the main road, but stayed in the shadows. They watched as a company of Kandian Red

Coats marched double time toward the fire followed by a water wagon.

"I have an idea," Jon said softly, darting back up the ally and calling over his shoulder as he went around the corner. "I'll meet you at the docks."

"Wait," replied Gavin's urgent whisper, but he was already gone.

Hawkins made a hand signal and moved back up the ally and the other eight men followed. This time they would not split up for the safety in numbers by staying together. They all wondered what the little thief was up to. Jon was very new to the crew and was well liked, but he had not been with them long enough to earn their complete trust. They moved stealthily down back streets and ally ways avoiding fire crews and soldiers.

They entered a yard diagonally across the lane from the well lit dock they hoped to be departing from. The lane intersected a road that came down the hill and ran straight onto the pier. The yard was dark and full of assorted gear associated with ships and fishing. There were piles of nets and buoys, masts, booms, yardarms and crab pots. Kendal's men were already there crouched low, spread out among the gear. Kendal and Ian were near the lane watching the pier. There was a building to the side of the yard that a roof extended out from: it was supported only by posts. There were nets stretched between the posts. Evidently it was where tradesmen hung nets and did repairs out of the rain. Kendal had placed the women there where they could stay relatively dry.

Gavin and Hawkins joined the mercenary captain and his lieutenant. After non verbal greetings were exchanged Gavin asked, "Where's Coulig?"

"See that gear shed over there with the barn like doors," replied Ian pointing up the hill a few hundred meters. "They backed the wagon in there. We helped them move stacks of sail cloth out of the way just before you got here."

"Okay, listen up," Kendal said to Gavin and Hawkins. "Your men aren't equipped with shields as we are. We will form a defensive shield wall at the head of the pier. I want your men to get the women aboard the ship when it comes in and get our wagon load on deck as quickly as possible. Have your men take our bows and crossbows. We will need suppression volleys to support our tactical withdrawal after Imar, Dalla, and Hager joins us. Any questions?"

Both first officers shook their heads. "Sounds like a good plan to me," said Hawkins.

Orders were being relayed. Bows and crossbows were handed to the sailors when the sound of hooves and the jingle of harness warned them that a large troop of cavalry was approaching. As they passed, Bamsen's blue was displayed on the livery of the horses and the occasional flash of blue exposed from under the cloaks of the men. Kendal recognized Sigurd's dark features in the street lights as he dispatched his men around the head of the pier.

Bamsen's commander ordered twenty men to dismount and form a shield wall in a crescent formation in front of the pier entrance. He placed five horsemen on each side of the shield wall then took the other twenty to patrol the area.

Kendal started to swear. "Son of a lice bitten whore. So much for plans. We're in deep dung now."

"Hey guys," said Jon from behind them. They all jumped.

"Don't do that," said Gavin. "I almost let the air out of you." Gavin noticed the red Kandian uniform. "Where have you been and what have you been up to?"

"Oh just having a little fun," answered the forger, as he pulled off the red coat.

"Out with it Sailor," said Gavin.

"Okay, okay, I just wanted to surprise you is all."

"That company across the street is all the surprise I can handle right now, so spit it out."

"All right already. I went back to the inn. I needed paper and pen. I wrote up some orders explaining that Bamsen had double-crossed Drayden and that any officer receiving this letter was to immediately seek out and kill anyone wearing Bamsen's blue and to take the Jarl prisoner. I signed it, *King Drayden.*"

"My Gods," said Ian. "That's bloody brilliant. How many did you make?"

"I only had time for one. By the time I finished and got back on the streets I could see Bamsen's horsemen coming, so I ran like mad. I took one of the uniforms that Pat and Muar had stolen then went to find that anal captain they told us about. As luck had it, his company was still here assigned to guard a fleet of support wagons set to leave tomorrow morning. The uniform was big and baggy on me. He thought me a teenage recruit serving as a runner. He tipped me a couple of coppers and read the dispatch. I lifted his coin purse while he read it. His eyes grew large, then he started rousting his sergeants and I came back here. Hey look, there they are. Boy that was fast."

They all turned. From up the hill came a phalanx of Red Coat Kandian infantry marching down the hill. As they approached orders were called out. The soldiers in the front two lines, as one, lowered their spears. Others drew swords and axes. More orders followed and raised shields ringed the company with armor. The sergeants in the Blue Coat shield wall, seeing that a conflict was imminent, brought shields up and swords ready. A cavalry sergeant rode up to the front of the phalanx and shouted inquiries to the captain as to what he thought he was doing. Bowmen in the fifth row fired at the mounted sergeant. Bristling with arrows, he looked like a porcupine before he fell dead from his horse.

"Wow," said Ian. "This should get interesting. What are we going to do now Captain?"

"Let us wait," replied Kendal. "Maybe they will thin their own ranks before we make our move. With a little luck, they will kill each other off before our ride gets here." He turned to Jon. "Do you want a job?"

"That depends. How much do you pay?"

"Forget it," said Gavin. "You signed on with us."

"But . . ."

"Forget it. We will discuss this later if we are still alive."

Bamsen's horsemen attacked the flanks as the phalanx clashed with the shield wall. A horse fell screaming and a rider was shot from the saddle. The horsemen had to use hit and run tactics and this slowed the force of the phalanx that would soon crush the outnumbered men in the shield wall. The ringing of steel and the cries of wounded and dying men joined the sounds of the flailing horse.

Sigurd heard the sounds of battle and returned with his patrol on a dead run down the hill. The rear of the phalanx turned to meet the charge as the blue shield wall broke. Sigurd's horsemen crashed into the Kandians and order was replaced with total chaos. Blood turned the muddy street red.

Coulig, Jax and Brin watched the madness from the gear shed. "Tie down the load," ordered Coulig. "It's going to get bumpy." He continued to watch while Brin and Jax lashed down the load. The horses were restless, stomping their feet, excited over the sounds of battle.

"Alright," said Kendal loudly. So he could be heard over the clash of battle. Everyone gathered around. "Bamsen's shield wall just broke. We need to get in there and replace it while the Red Coats and Blue Coats are fighting. We'll run two lines; I'll lead one on the right and Lieutenant Ian the other on the left. The sailors will shield the women in the middle. Once we take the pier, I want a V-formation shield wall to open briefly when Coulig comes with the wagon. I hope." To Gavin and Hawkins he said, "Get the women to the dock. Then come back and support us with arrows."

Kendal drew his sword and the others did the same. He raised his blade high and said loudly, "Honor and victory!"

His men, with adrenaline flowing in their veins and swords held high, shouted back, "Victory and honor!"

Off they went to join the fray.

"All secure, Captain," said Brin after a few minutes.

"Standby," answered Coulig without taking his eyes from the scene. Then he saw Kendal's mercenaries running to the pier with the sailors surrounding Anisha, Aideen and Missy. Within a few moments they broke in between phalanx and pier and established a shield wall. A few of Bamsen's wounded men from the broken shield wall thought Kendal's men were there to help, so they added their shields and swords in the wall against the Kandians. The sailors took the ladies to the end of the pier. Beyond the dock he saw the *Coastal Raider* two hundred meters out approaching the dock. Coulig threw open the door and said, "Time to go. Brin, you drive, we'll shoot."

CHAPTER 29

"This is the place my Lord." Sumas sat his horse almost in the exact spot Dalla had sat when using the mind speech to contact Ivan.

"Okay," growled Bamsen. "Where are they?"

"How should I know? I'm not a tracker. This is where the trail starts, far better than you would have done without my help. Now it's your turn."

Bamsen's head hurt and his stomach boiled. Sumas' sarcasm was getting tiresome. If he didn't need the black wizard, he would have had him impaled on the bowsprit of his new ship. Sumas smirked at him as if he guessed his thoughts. This infuriated the Jarl even more. He said to one of his sergeants with out taking his eyes off the wizard, "Follow their tracks."

Hager, Dalla and Imar rode a zigzag route through various residential areas of upper Valekrie. They did not want to loose the pursuit, so every now and then they waited for them to catch up after making sure their tracks were obviously visible. They kept up this cat and mouse game for some while before they heard the sounds of battle.

Imar took up his shield and drew his long sword, then moved his horse to Hager's right side. Then to Dalla he said, "Stay between us and slightly behind. It will be a measured pace, faster than a gallop, but not an all out run. Use your shield."

She nodded and took her shield from its saddle hook.

Hager, hands filled with sword and shield looked Imar in the eye. Imar didn't know why, but he knew the ritual Hager was wordlessly inviting him to perform. Together in unison they banged their swords against their shields twice. They both grinned broadly feeling the excitement the sounds of battle stirred from deep within their warrior souls. Adrenaline rushed through their veins. Pounding hearts beating like drums in their ears. They yelled a battle cry as they kicked the horses into a gallop.

Steering with their knees they rounded a corner and then another. They were then heading down the hill on the main road, the battle ahead and the pier beyond.

Bamsen and Sumas heard the battle sounds and gave up tracking their quarry. They rode fast toward the docks. Bamsen could see the battle when they gained the main road. His men were being torn up by Red Coats. The Kandians weren't faring much better. Half the men on both sides were down. He couldn't understand why they would be fighting when they were on the same side. If Drayden betrayed him he would have his revenge, but that would have to wait till he got to the bottom of this.

Sumas knew how to use a sword. He just had no intention of doing so. Others could do that. There was no sense coming within reach of a blade, he thought, so he gradually let the soldiers pass him until he rode prudently in the rear.

Bamsen didn't notice Sumas assuming the strategic position of 'way back,' but he did see Imar, the healer and the big bearded warrior ride out from a side street in front of them brandishing swords and riding toward the battle. The Jarl shouted encouragement to his men, held his sword out before him and kicked his horse for more speed.

Dalla saw Bamsen behind them and yelled a warning. They looked briefly back and grinned bigger, if that were possible. The healer thought they acted like foolish boys playing a new game. *Men*, she thought while riding for her life, *never truly grow up*.

As they drew closer, Dalla saw the ship approaching the dock. Then ahead of them, out of a building to the left came a wagon drawn by four horses. It turned toward the battle and picked up speed as it went. Perched atop the load were Coulig and Jax firing arrows as fast as they could load them. They slammed into Blue Coat cavalry and the fighting Red Coats. The horses rode down any man standing and drove other horses out of the way. Bodies littered the street and when the wheels struck them Coulig and Jax flew into the air. Luckily they came down on the load. They grabbed tie down lines and held on, no longer able to shoot from the bouncing wagon.

A swath now cut through the fray, Hager, Imar and Dalla followed the wagon through the shield wall that Kendal and Ian opened for them and closed up again as soon as they passed. The wagon continued on to the dock where the *Coastal Raider* was just bumping against the pilings. The rest of Coulig's men that had stayed aboard the ship along with a party of sailors were leaping off the ship and running toward the fight.

Hager and Imar pulled up short, swung legs over horse heads and landed on the wood pier at the same time.

"Get to the ship," said Imar to Dalla. He slapped her mount's rump and her steed ran down the pier. He sheathed his claymore and drew his short sword. It was more suitable for the close-in fighting in a shield wall.

Imar and Hager joined the fight with the support of Coulig's men and a number of sailors fresh from the ship. The shield wall was buckling against Bamsen's charge. Sigurd rallied his severely depleted company and joined his lord in attacking the shield wall. The Blue Coats that had joined Kendal's men against the Reds were confused and tried to rejoin their side. It went poorly for them. They did not survive long. The Reds and the Blues still fought one another and both attacked the shield wall.

Gavin and Hawkins along with the away team fired arrows to harass the enemy. Coulig, Jax and Brin went to support their comrades. A company of Red Coats was approaching from the industrial district. More were sure to come. No one was sure who they were going to attack first, but they had swords and there were a lot of them. Bamsen sent a rider off down to the west end of the docks toward his warship.

Some men stepped back to rest while fresh soldiers took the front line. Kendal yelled out to Imar as he stabbed under a shield into an enemy's foot. "We can't hold much longer. We must begin our withdrawal or we'll be ground into dog meat."

"Order it," shouted Imar. He spun his sword and grasped the blunt area just above the hilt. With sword reversed he hooked an enemy shield with the cross hilt and pulled it down and smashed the pommel into the face behind it. Hager slashed an overhand blow and split the exposed helmet and head like a piece of firewood. Imar spun the hilt back into his hand and thrust low through the opening where the man fell, stabbing another's knee. He raised his shield that softened a blow that glanced lightly off his helm and felt a slice to his calf. He couldn't spare time to look, but at least he didn't fall even though he felt blood run into his boot.

Kendal shouted the order to withdraw. Ian was injured and hauled to the ship. Coulig, with bloody shield arm, took command of the left flank. The shield wall slowly moved back step by step and condensed to accommodate the narrower pier. The pier improved the defensibility of their position, but both sides were losing men. Pat went down and Muar next, both with mortal wounds. Relief soldiers stepped in where wounded men fell. Both injured and dead were dragged to the ship. None were left behind.

The fighting stopped a moment and men on both sides were breathing hard trying to catch their breath. A few men fell to their knees exhausted. Then the enemy line parted and six horsemen charged in two by two close formation. The two in front carried lances. One of them was Sigurd.

They struck the shield wall and it broke. Two men were skewered and a third ridden down. A few enemy foot soldiers came through the hole, but Kendal and Coulig hastily closed up the shield wall. They kept the step by step pace toward the ship. Sigurd and another horseman were pulled from their saddles and the other four were shot down with arrows. Two horses died, one fell off the pier with a splash and the others ran to the dock. The infantry that broke through wreaked much havoc, but in half a minute they were all put to the sword.

Grenek was the one that pulled Sigurd from his saddle. Olsen joined his friend and placed the point of his sword to Sigurd's throat. "Remember us? We remember you."

Grenek put the tip of his sword to Sigurd's thigh and slowly pushed it in. Sigurd screamed. "It is war. We're soldiers."

Grenek's eyes showed pure hatred as he looked down on Sigurd. "We were not at war then, but we are at war now. All we did was ask about a friend. You have no friends and you're a sadist." He removed his sword and Sigurd screamed again. Then Grenek pierced the other thigh, careful to miss the artery. The backing shield wall was almost upon them.

Olsen made a slight cut in Sigurd throat. "And we will always remember your brutal hospitality."

"As well as your slow death," added Grenek. "If you do live, you will probably lose your leg." He gave one last hack to Sigurd's knee then joined the retreating wall.

The fighting shield walls walked over the screaming Sigurd.

The space on the pier was limited. The wood planks were wet and slippery from rain and blood. Battling soldiers had to step on or over bodies of men and climb over dead horses. Rear elements were going up gangways to the boat. The wagon was emptied and crewmen poured naphtha on it. Ship lines were untied, but for two and men stood ready with axes to cut them free. The ship strained against the line with one open foresail catching a breeze off the mountains.

The wagon was lit and it blazed as men shoved it toward the advancing enemy. Beros shouted at the top of his lungs. "Make a hole!"

Crewmen that knew that voice pulled comrades that didn't out of the way. A hole opened in the battle line and the burning wagon struck the advancing enemy. It stunned them to be sure. Men barreled over, some caught on fire and others jumped into the water. Several were thrown back or off the pier.

"Don't just stand there," shouted Beros. "Run for it or be left behind!" To the axe men he yelled, "Cut the lines!"

Imar, Kendal, Hager and Coulig were the last to leap off the dock and grab the rail as the ship pulled away from the dock. Comrades pulled them aboard just before three bolts struck the hull. Red Coats swarmed the dock once they managed to get around the burning wagon. There were still a few of Bamsen's men on the dock, but the majority wore red. The Kandian reinforcements were not aware of any false treachery. They fired arrows and bolts at the retreating ship while Bamsen yelled curses at the top of his lungs.

Once the *Coastal Raider* pulled away from the dock, the *Bedford Lee* launched three casks of burning naphtha at the pier. Two casks struck and engulfed the center of the dock in flames. That put an end to the arrows and the fighting. Men and horses jumped into the cold water.

The *Coastal Raider* turned south and unfurled all sails as did the *Bedford Lee*. Then they heard a boom, followed by a second one and then a third. A splash of water sprouted off the stern followed by two more. Each impact erupted with a geyser of water launching like pillars skyward. The *Sea Dragon* was firing cannons at them.

Longboats full of hastily assembled crews were rowing out to moored ships in the bay. Ships at the docks were preparing to give chase as well. The *Bedford Lee* and the *Coastal Raider* turned to starboard bearing west then loosed catapults. The *Coastal Raider* set flaming casks arcing through the night setting fires to three ships at wharf. The *Bedford Lee* launched buckets of stones and shot at the longboats causing most to return to shore for injuries if they did not sink. Two of the boats were obliterated.

Cannon fire rained around both of the Kalusian vessels, striking closer with bracketing fire, but without a hit. Both ships fired full broadsides of naphtha as they came abeam the *Sea Dragon*, first the leading *Bedford Lee* lighting the night with fiery death followed by a volley from her stern as she turned to port. Then, right on her tail, it was the *Coastal Raider*'s turn adding more fuel to the flaming *Sea Dragon*, then she too turned to Port to follow her sister ship.

Beros ordered another round fired from the stern as they made for the break water. He watched the flames from his quarterdeck. The cannon fire stopped. The flames roared on the *Sea Dragon* and the three other ships, but these seemed small by comparison against the backdrop of the burning city. The fires set in the industrial district had spread out of control and were now consuming business and residential areas.

"Pursuit will probably be small," said Beros. "They're going to need every able body they can get to deal with the fires." Beros seemed sad looking at the destruction that lit the night. "It's a mighty shame to burn a ship as fine as the *Sea Dragon*. I would have rather stolen her."

Ivan and Imar stood next to him. Dalla was below decks helping the ships doctor with the many wounded. She had no sooner stepped on deck when the first casualties began to arrive. It would be a long night for the healer. Wizard and warrior introduced themselves. Ivan felt something as he stared intently at the big ship. He saw the difference and was about to say something when Imar spoke.

"Look at the difference," said Imar. "Those ships are being consumed by the flames. The *Sea Dragon* is on fire, but she doesn't burn."

Beros peered hard with his one eye. "By all the Gods of the sea, you are right. Some of the gear on deck seems to be burning and the crew has evacuated, but the hull is not even scorched nor are the masts and spars suffering consumption from the flames." He shook his head, scratched under his eye patch then rubbed his good eye and looked again to be sure. "How can this be?"

"It is Sumas," Ivan replied. "He has grown very strong to be able to protect the ship like that. The naphtha is burning off, but the wood and cloth of the ship are not. Let me try to distract him and see what happens."

Ivan sat down on the quarter deck in the lotus position and meditated. Focusing only on his adversary he blocked out all others. He called out powerfully as if he were shouting in the mind speech, *Sumas!*

Ivan heard, almost distantly, exclamations from people near him on the deck. He felt Sumas put up barriers, but not before he flinched.

Ivan got to his feet and asked, "What happened?"

Beros answered him. "The sail cloth, furled though they be, burst in a flare of heat and burned to a crisp. Some of the spares are charred as well, but no more than that. It will be a while before she can give chase. They will have to change a few of the spars and all of the sails."

Ivan looked and saw burning rolls of canvas and lines falling to the deck, but other than that and some cooked yardarms, the damage was minimal.

The *Bedford Lee* was already beyond the breakwater heading south southeast. The *Coastal Raider* followed her into the dark and rainy night using all they could of the nor'wester to put distance between them and any pursuit that may come from the burning Valekrie.

CHAPTER 30

King Drayden stood by a large table cluttered with maps in his war room. He was a tall, lean, and serious man in his early twenties with shoulder length brown hair tied back in a ponytail. The king had just returned from the carnage at the docks. Drayden had been supervising the fires when word of a battle in his city came to him. He arrived at the burning pier just as Bamsen's huge warship began firing cannons on enemy ships wreaking havoc in the harbor.

The king was surrounded by advisors, and the usual flock of useless courtiers. He had half a mind to send them all out on bucket brigades. Most of his advisors he respected, but for the average herd of boot licking courtiers he had nothing but contempt. He would have loved to see the pompous peacocks covered with soot, packing buckets of water and manning pumps on the fire wagons.

There was a flow of messengers coming in and going out with dispatches. The King was looking at a map of the city as the fire chief pointed out to him the areas lost, the areas saved and the direction the fire was going. The wind was pushing the fire toward the docks.

"Scramble the fleet still tied to the quays." The young King had power in his voice even when he spoke calmly. "Move off any ships not on fire." It angered him that spies could walk in and set his city on fire then sail away unscathed. Drayden rarely displayed anger and he showed none now. "I want any craft still in dry dock to be launched immediately and anchored off in the bay, even if a pump crew is needed to keep it afloat."

"Yes my liege," answered both the fire chief and the harbor master.

"And I mean all craft, both public and private. If I hear of one fisherman losing even a dingy, you'll both answer for it. Now go." Drayden's green eyes had fire in them.

The two men exited the war room striding with powerful purpose. Drayden approved. He didn't like strollers, especially when business was at hand.

"Your Highness," Admiral Sven addressed the King,. "I have nine ships ready to pursue the two that are responsible for this attack. They can have their sails full within a quarter hour of your order."

"Admiral," replied the King calmly,. "I am less than pleased that your patrol boats let two enemy warships sail into our harbor without a fight, much less without any warning. They are the enemy; that is what the enemy does, so I don't see them as the responsible party. Those that allowed this to happen are to blame. I do intend to hold you at least partially responsible for this disaster. We now have to focus on saving the city, which will push our invasion plans back. How far back we can't even begin to guess yet. How you handle things in the next few weeks will decide whether or not I allow you to keep your head."

"But your Majesty, it was dark, and the weather . . ." stammered the admiral.

"No buts, Admiral," Drayden interrupted. "I don't want to hear whining excuses either; we haven't the time for it. I want results. Send four warships in pursuit of our pyro antagonistic enemy. You should have done that already." Drayden looked at the map showing multiple circles within circles, the largest encompassing one quarter of Valekrie. "There are only two enemy ships." A messenger approached, bowed, and spoke quietly to the king while pointing and gesturing at the map. Drayden handed the grease pencil to the man, who then proceeded to mark a larger ring around the existing circles. The king dismissed the man, gave orders to another who departed as quickly as the messenger, and then addressed Admiral Sven. "I expect my Chiefs of Staff to take initiative. My father discouraged it, but I am not him. You will learn this quickly or you will swing from my gallows. If those four ships have not intercepted their quarry in five days, they are to return. I want two ships on constant patrol outside the bay. Bring in the crews of the moored ships in the harbor to help getting dry docked vessels into the water and use all other available resources to assist with firefighting and disaster relief. The fire is spreading."

"Yes, your Majesty."

"That will be all, Admiral Sven."

The admiral saluted and left without another word.

Drayden turned to the man next to him. "General Khan, if I understand your report correctly, a company of our infantry attacked Bamsen's men because of a forged dispatch, supposedly from me."

"Yes, your Majesty," answered the general, handing him the letter. "It looks like your signature. I took the liberty of showing it to one of your clerks and he agrees with me."

The King looked at the letter, nodded, and then handed it back. "Excuse me a moment, General." Drayden turned to the audience. "Leave us," he said abruptly.

The room emptied in less than a minute, leaving the King and the General to speak in privacy. "Okay, go ahead Khan. You were saying?"

"It appears that the Jarl knew of the octagon key coming to Valekrie, but kept the information to himself. Bamsen launched a failed assault on Border City to get the relic. Then he surmised that the keeper of the key escaped into the Kandian wilderness with a platoon of mercenaries bound for Valekrie. Bamsen had to get out of the country before Thorson chastised him for assaulting one of his cities. He was supposed to bring his ships here anyway, so we saw his actions as nothing out of the ordinary. Jarl Bamsen had intelligence of enemy elements securing dock services for the

Kalusian vessels. That is why he deployed troops to the east pier. Bamsen hoped to intercept the key bearer named Imar."

"So Bamsen's spies spied on the enemy spies, and didn't tell us," Drayden mused while rubbing his stubbled chin. "If our city wasn't in flames it would almost be funny. It would seem that Bamsen isn't here to betray only Thorson. I should have known better than to trust a traitor. Bamsen thought he could get the octagon key for himself and use my resources to get to Eastonia with my army at his back. That is why he gave us these weapons. He figured if he didn't get the key he could still blast his way across the continent and into the underground fortress."

"It would appear so, my Lord. His wizard claims that he advised the Jarl against this deceit, but Bamsen wouldn't heed his council."

"What can you tell me about this wizard?"

"Well, your Majesty," replied Khan, "I think Sumas is the one that gave Bamsen the technology of black powder and taught his engineers how to make guns. He seems to have some genuine talent as well as being very intelligent."

"Do you trust him?"

"Not on your life, your Majesty," replied Khan evenly. "Bamsen is a hot tempered arrogant fool with far more ambition than is good for him. I think this Sumas was using the Jarl for his own means. The man is very clever." The general paused, his eyes distant for a moment before he continued, "But still, he could be useful. Except for that warship out there, that is more than I can say for Bamsen. I highly recommend caution, your Highness. Sumas is no fool. He probably used Bamsen's money and muscle to find the octagon key. However, Bamsen came to you with his offer of alliance about a year ago, not long after you were crowned. I think Sumas instigated that as a backup plan should he fail at finding and gaining the key. Also, if the stories are true about these new weapons that are supposedly in the fortress, he would need an army to use the weapons. I would not be surprised to find others in positions of power being manipulated by him as well. I just wonder what the wizard wants. Whatever it is, it's in that fortress, and he isn't going to share."

"Do you think this fortress is a hoax, General?"

"It would not surprise me, your Highness. If it isn't a hoax, it's imperative that we get to it first. Your father made every country on the continent enemies of Kandia. No matter who gets this power, if it isn't us, we will become a province after they grind us to dust."

"And if it is a hoax, what about the cost in blood and gold?"

Khan sighed and shook his head. "Keep your subjects too busy to talk and plot. Give them victories and keep the civilians at home working to supply the war effort. Have them build factories and plant more crops. The country will prosper and they will love you for it. Wars are good for the economy, your Majesty."

"Where is Bamsen now?"

"He and Sumas are under guard in the waiting room, my liege."

Drayden smiled. "Have them escorted in. I would like to speak with them now."

"Both of them?"

"Oh yes. I want the wizard to see how I deal with disloyalty."

"Yes your Majesty." Khan went to the door and passed some orders to the guards.

Bamsen and Sumas were brought in by two guards that stood flanking them and slightly behind. Two more guards stood at the door. The King came around the table and leaned against it, half sitting and facing them. Khan stepped up and stood by his king.

Sumas was calm. If he had any concern about his predicament, it didn't show. Bamsen, on the other hand, was red faced and grinding his teeth. The Jarl had been compelled to remove his weapons and armor and sit on a bench without refreshment while waiting for the king's audience.

"Can anyone write royal orders around here, Drayden?" Bamsen barked this out before thinking.

General Khan spoke up. "My Lord, I feel it my duty to caution you. A lack of respect when addressing his royal person is cause for immediate impalement."

The corners of the wizard's mouth turned up slightly, but Bamsen's face drained of color and he looked as if he were about to get sick.

"Actually," replied Drayden, "It was an excellent forgery. Even my advisors couldn't tell it was a fake. The forged signature looks just like my own."

"Please forgive me, your Majesty. I have lost a lot of men tonight and two of my ships burned to the waterline. I'm just a little stressed."

"You have caused all this stress, my Lord Bamsen. If I had known mercenaries carrying an extremely important artifact were coming to my city to meet two enemy warships at my docks," the king paused for effect, "we might have been prepared to meet the situation with some increased security. As I understand it, you even had men following two of the spies before they lost them. Why didn't you report any of this?"

"Your Majesty," Bamsen began, "You have been so busy with the troop deployment, and I thought I could handle it myself."

"Liar," Drayden snapped without raising his voice. "A quarter of my city has burned because of you and it still burns. The key to this hidden fortress on the other side of the continent just passed through our city and sailed away, also thanks to you. It will get there, I'm sure, before my army does. If whoever gets there with the octagon key can use these weapons, they will have the power to eliminate my legions. The campaign has barely begun and because of you Kandia has suffered a great defeat with heavy losses."

Bamsen bowed his head. Sumas looked at the King and raised one eyebrow slightly.

To the guards the king said, "Take him out and hang him." Drayden said it as calmly as if he were ordering a cup of coffee. "Bring me his head in a basket."

Bamsen's head snapped up, his eyes wide. The only one not shocked at the King's orders was Sumas, who prudently took two steps away from the Jarl. Bamsen roared his indignation. The two guards nearest him grabbed his arms and struggled to subdue the big nobleman. He nearly threw them off when the other guards put a sword to his throat and another to his back.

The Jarl ceased struggling and then seemed to accept his fate. "At least give me a warriors death," requested Bamsen proudly.

"You are a traitor to your cousin, the King of Abezda, and you are a traitor to me. You do not deserve to die by the sword." Drayden turned to the guards. "Take him away."

Bamsen struggled again, and this time a trickle of blood flowed from his neck while they got the shackles on his wrists. A minute later he was dragged screaming down the hall toward the gallows.

Drayden looked at Khan and said, "I want Bamsen's head sent to Thorson. I will write a letter to go with it. I believe he is presently in Seal Bay at a council of kings of the Western Alliance. I want a ship bearing flags of diplomatic truce to carry an ambassador to King Bertil requesting passage of our forces through Sedar. Bertil will deny us of course, but it would be discourteous of us not to ask before we invade. I want the ship to depart tomorrow."

"Yes, your Majesty," replied the General.

Drayden turned to Sumas and asked, "Do you want a job?"

Sumas smiled. "I thought you'd never ask."

CHAPTER 31

The glow of the burning city of Valekrie faded to wet blackness in their wake. They headed into a dark overcast night. It was a long night for all aboard the Bedford Lee and the Coastal Raider. The two ships kept close pace with each other by visual reference when they could. Then the light drizzle that had been plaguing them for days became intermittently heavy. In places the precipitation fog and the darkness hid them from one another. At times the navigation lanterns could barely be seen; red port, green starboard and white fore and aft. The lights of a sister ship would fade to nothing for a moment or two and reappear as an almost undistinguishable glow that would brighten as the features of hull, masts, spars and sail formed to solidity only to drift back into the swallowing gloom. When lost to view they could still hear each other through the curtain of night and fog. When those moments extended to minutes, the bow watchmen would hail one another to keep close yet prevent crashing. Under normal conditions they may have practiced light and sound discipline to evade pursuit, but safety required that they stick together in enemy waters and use lanterns and voice to maintain proximity.

The seas were fairly mild and the light nor'wester remained steady through the night. No lights of pursuit were spotted behind. As it were a ship's lantern would have been lost in the rain even if it were only five clicks away. At worst, an enemy bowsprit could have danced the swells a meter abaft without notice. The crews were fatigued and the watch was changed after four hours of stressful navigation. Both captains remained in charge through the night. Beros insisted that Gavin and Hawkins get some sleep since they would be needed to relieve their captains at daybreak.

Very few of the soldiers and sailors that had been on the pier escaped the battle unscathed. The ship's doctor and Dalla were busy treating the wounded within moments of the Coastal Raider tying to the dock. The sick bay was full and injured men were laid out in rows on the crew deck and in the fo'c'sle. Those with minor injuries performed triage, applied first aid and comforted their comrades while the healer and the surgeon tended the more serious of combat wounds. All too often battlefield surgeries were performed with a bone saw followed by needle and thread or a hot iron, but Dalla's skills kept the buckets from filling with amputated limbs. Alas, only a few brave souls lost an arm or a leg, but at least they lived.

Morning came and with it less rain and better visibility. When the gray dawn illuminated the iron overcast and silted seas, a call of sails aft on the horizon was shouted from aloft of both ships. The captains stood at their stern rails and glassed the four ships following them. The pursuit was spread out and sure to have their quarry in sight. Einar estimated them to be about thirty kilometers behind. He whistled across the way to Beros and caught his attention. He hand signaled that he wished to come aboard. He would have had a flagman wave out the request, as was proper, but Beros had already ordered the maneuver of a hull-to-hull transfer.

The Bedford Lee moved ever so lightly to starboard, as did the Coastal Raider drift gently to port. Soft buoys were hung out and tied to the rails to soften the kiss of hulls when it came. Without the buoys, the action of the ships on the rhythm of the moving sea would grind, gouge and tear at a vessel's bark to the great dismay of the ship's carpenters.

Lines were cast and heaved upon. The slack sucked up and the buoys mashed and rolled between the hulls as crewmen held lines fast with only a double wrap on the cleats. Einar and his surgeon stepped agilely from rail to rail and onto the deck of the Coastal Raider at the same time that Hawkins and his crewmates crossed over to their ship the Bedford Lee. The maneuvering took minutes, but the action of boarding only a couple of seconds. As soon as Einar was across, the men let slip the lines and the vessels parted and continued southeast making best possible speed. As it were, the

Bedford Lee was light and under burdened and had to trim back so that the Raider could keep pace. The Coastal Raider sat low in the water and was overcrowded. Einar went to meet Beros and the Bedford Lee's doctor went below to lend his aid in sick bay.

A meeting was held in the Captain's quarters. Folding chairs were brought in and set in a circle. Beros sat at his desk with Einar to his left and Ivan to his right. Imar sat next to Ivan with his bandaged leg on a stool. Next to him sat Hager with a bloody cloth on his sword hand and then Coulig with a bandaged shoulder followed by Kendal to finish the circle with his shield arm in a sling. Ian was in sickbay and did not attend. They waited for Dalla.

The healer came in with hair tied back and still in her travel attire, but with the addition of a once-white bandana and apron now bloody. Her blue top, with the sleeves rolled up, was stained dark red as well. She had washed her hands and face before coming topside, but no other part of her escaped the bloody painting of combat medicine. She was weary, the dark orbital circles and bags under her eyes made this obvious. Those that knew her were aware that her fatigue came from more than just working through the night without sleep. She was more than a doctor, physician or surgeon. She was a healer and an empath. So very few knew what that meant. She was a healer who used not just skill of hands and knowledge, but put the very essence of her mind and spirit into the healing of her patients. She saved more than she lost, but all took their toll. She would need rest soon or she would surely collapse.

The men stood up when she entered. All eyes looked at her with concern. Imar felt his heart skip a beat. This time his breath caught with worry. He had never seen her look so drawn out. Even when Gar's soul left his body under her care, she was emotionally drained, but this was different. Gar, she had known was gone; she helped him go by easing his pain before he departed. Imar could see, even feel, the difference as he looked in her eyes. Dalla had been fighting battles all night to keep souls from leaving the many battered bodies below in sick bay. She fought a different kind of war. After a battle, soldiers were tired physically, drained mentally and often emotionally. Many soldiers were wounded in mind or body, and sometimes both. Soldiers went through this fighting to wound, kill, maim, and all in order to live. Sometimes a soldier did this to profit, and just as often to save others, but in the thick of it, survival was everything. The terror of dying and the powerful desire to live escapes no one. Dalla fought too, but she fought to save life and limb. Terror came to her too, the terror of losing lives. She came from her battles wounded. Imar could see those wounds behind the windows to her mind. Dalla was exhausted. He was about to tell her to go get some rest when Ivan beat him to it.

"If you fall down in the middle of a surgery, my dear," said the wizard tenderly, "you could cause disastrous results for your patient. Captain Einar's surgeon can relieve you for a few hours and we can make do here without your council for now. Please go get some rest."

Imar could hear the caring in Ivan's voice when he spoke to Dalla. It sounded almost parental. He pushed that to the back of his mind for later. "He's right. You look beat."

"I can't," replied the healer. "Not yet anyway." She scratched dried blood off her wrist. The flakes fell like dull glitter onto the floor. "We are almost done with the most critical. I have to keep going for three or four more hours. With three of us working, and with the help of a few medically inclined volunteers, we can minimize our losses. After that we can transfer some of the wounded over to the Bedford Lee along with their physician."

"Okay," replied Ivan. "No more than four hours, then you rest. We have four ships chasing us, so we may not be past our problems yet. However, Captains Einar and Beros feel that we can outrun them once we can distribute the load."

Dalla considered that a moment then replied. "I will say this just to add my two coppers to the council, and then I will return to my work. We have more than a dozen men that will need a hospital if they survive the voyage. The severely injured must go to the nearest hospital, which is in Seal Bay." She paused a moment to let that sink in. "Imar needs to avoid all authorities. When he doesn't show up in Seal Bay he will be sure to have bulletins out and a bounty for his capture if there isn't one already. Imar goes where the key goes and I go with him, and that is to Eastonia. You gentlemen can figure out the details. Now if you'll excuse me." Turning on her heel she left the cabin and returned to her wounded.

Ivan sat down. Everyone else sat a moment later after looking at each other's expressions. Imar propped up his wounded leg. The wizard looked over at the two captains. "Which of these ships is capable of making the best time?"

Both captains answered at the same time, each claiming their ship was the fastest.

"With our present loads my ship is the fastest," said Einar. "But if the Coastal Raider were lightened up, she'd probably make the best speed."

Beros raised the brow of his good eye and said, "What do you mean probably? If my ship were as light as yours she would out run and out maneuver the Bedford Lee with ease."

Coulig and Hager were chuckling when Ivan raised his hand and said, "Gentlemen please, let us save manhood measuring for another time. We need to put distance between us and those Kandian ships. Not only that, when we get to friendlier waters we need to steer one ship to Seal Bay and the other to Port Augustus."

"Me and my men need to go to Seal Bay," said Kendal.

"Yes, I'm aware of that. Imar filled me in last night, or rather, in the wee hours of the morning. Yesterday and today seem to be blurring into one. I need to go to Seal Bay as well. As much as I hate it, I must go and speak with the kings. They need warning and advice, as well as a little education concerning the octagon key. I doubt that the idiots will listen, but I must try. The Abezdan and Kalusian monarchs are probably arriving there as we speak. I would not be surprised if they invite the magistrate of Renauld to the council as well."

"Renauld has always been neutral," said Einar. "They have no king and their politics is no more than a retired pirate acting as a judge to settle disputes. Other than a few basic rules, it is mostly a lawless land of offshore bankers and wreckers, not to mention a free haven for pirates."

"That's why I live there," replied the wizard. "Kings, councils, parliaments, and senates…Bah," Ivan curled his lip and spat. "Politics sour my stomach. The thieves I live with on Renauld are nowhere near as corrupt as the politicians running every kingdom I have set foot in. Not only that, Renauld's offshore accounts offer much better interest rates than any of the overtaxed kingdom banks. But that is beside the point. Renauld holds a strategic position for a naval war. If they remain neutral they can profit greatly, but either side could choose to overrun and annex their island. They may be forced to give up neutrality in order to keep their autonomy."

"I assume you have a plan," said Coulig. "There are four Kandian warships approaching our rear while we waste time with oratory. I'm starting to get an itch between my shoulder blades."

"I'm getting the same itch," added Hager in his deep voice. "And it gets stronger the closer those ships get."

"They're right," said Imar. "If you have a plan, I suggest you spit it out."

Ivan nodded agreement. He was well aware of his gift of gab. If no one had reined in on his oration he may have still been sharing his opinions when the ringing of swords announced the arrival of enemy boarding parties. "My plan is to jettison all nonessential material from both ships. We need all the speed we can get. I will go with Kendal and his men along with all the seriously wounded over to the Bedford Lee. We will take one of the cannons and half the samples of powder and muskets to the Kings of the Alliance in Sedar. The smaller cannon and the other half of the samples I want to stay on the Coastal Raider to go to Port Augustus and be given over to Akala Murdoch. If for some reason she is unavailable, then give them to her steward, Dorfin."

"We will need to bury our dead at sea," said Beros.

"I have three dead," said Kendal. "Two of them need to go with me or be cremated."

"We haven't the facilities to cremate and we are going to be dumping food stores to outrun the warships chasing us. I'm sorry, but our survival depends on a sea burial as soon as possible."

"I saw Dalla do it. She cremated two of my men without a whiff of smoke."

"It can't be done on a ship," Ivan said consolingly. "The process you speak of was done on earth, or stone. To attempt it aboard ship would burn us to the waterline. What is their religion to require burning?"

"They are not religious," replied Kendal. "It was just their preference. I try to see to the needs of my men even after death, whether it is spiritual or preferential. It is okay, their families will have to understand. I will take their personal effects to their relatives instead of their ashes."

"Good," continued Ivan. "I gave Dalla four hours to work with the injured. We can transfer loads then. We will have to move all wounded needing hospitalization over to the Bedford Lee at that time as well. In the meantime we can start dumping cargo."

"Let us wait till tonight to dump some of our cargo," suggested Beros. "We make for Renauld today, so our pursuit thinks we are pirates seeking haven. We can use repair materials to build rafts to put the rest of our cargo on after nightfall. Then we set red and green navigation lanterns on the rafts and set 'em adrift. Once that is done, we douse our lights and turn for Seal Bay."

"That's bloody brilliant," exclaimed Einar. "The Kandians will make for the rafts and we'll be lost in the dark. When they realize they've been duped, they will still slow up to take the cargo. No self-respecting sailor is going to pass up free profit that can be taken without a fight."

Beros smiled and scratched under his eye patch. "After they finish arguing over the two rafts of booty for four ships, they will most likely split up. They won't know whether we went on to Renauld or changed course to Sedar or Kalusia or if we split up. Either way, if we don't lose them we'll probably have fewer ships on our tail."

Imar had been thinking about his situation as well as the safety of his wife and daughter. Aideen's safety was paramount in his thoughts. His wife he would love to maroon on a rock if he could find one known for its abundance of sharks, but his duty to her and his morals wouldn't allow him the pleasure. He kicked himself mentally for wasting time on futile and frivolous thoughts and spoke his piece. "My wife and daughter shall go on to Port Augustus." He looked to Coulig, an old friend that he could not remember. The stout warrior had fought well at Valekrie and he knew he could count on that valor in protecting his family. Coulig reminded him of Hager. But for Coulig's trimmed goatee and Hager's big full beard, the two could pass as brothers. "I would ask Coulig and his men to escort Anisha, Aideen and Missy to the Murdoch estate."

Coulig put his fist over his heart and inclined his head. "It would be my honor. But where are you going?"

"I fear that I am a fugitive so long as I carry the octagon key. Anyone that travels with me will be in peril. If I go anywhere near Seal Bay or Port Augustus I will be captured, by either friend or foe, and relieved of the key. Even Thorson expects me to freely hand it over to him. If Bertil or Gerald get their hands on it the Alliance will dissolve; might as well burn the treaty. There would be war of everyone against all, just for the key. I will take a few of my men with me, but I think it best to keep our party small and travel under assumed names."

"You are right," said Ivan. "You will be hunted. It is important that you get to the fortress before you find an army blocking your way. You will need help. Dalla knows the way and the combination that needs to be used with the key to gain access. And she has some unique skills that could prove advantageous. Besides, there is no force on Earth that could tear her from your side."

Imar wondered how Ivan could know his and Dalla's feelings for each other. He hadn't said anything nor had there been time for him to pick up any gossip. Not that there should be any gossip. Other than a comforting hug on the outskirts of Valekrie, they had remained properly distant. Maybe the wizard had read his mind. When time allowed he intended to get all these mind readers together and establish a few privacy rules. One should not be snooping around in another's head without permission. It's just bad manners.

"Well you and Dalla are doomed for misery. It is tragic," Ivan muttered barely loud enough for Imar to hear. Then louder, the wizard continued. "I will join you on your quest after I finish my business in Seal Bay. We can discuss a meeting place later in private. I would have liked Dalla to explain some details to Akala's engineers, but I'm afraid you will need her help more, especially with your memory loss. A better guide you could not find. The engineers will just have to settle for some written instructions. She can write a manual and send it with Coulig."

"Alright gentlemen," said Ivan, standing up. "That should just about cover everything." Everyone stood and began scooting chairs to the side as the wizard spoke. "There is much work to be done, sea burials, rafts to build, cargo to jettison . . . Oh yes, before I forget. Don't toss any of the wine or grog overboard, and keep some cheese too. Okay, as I said there is work to be done, so let's get to it."

Coulig looked at the wizard with one of his nasty grins. "What are you going to do?"

"Who me? I'm going to take a nap."

The ships maneuvered for a ship-to-ship transfer. Einar stood ready at the rail in quiet contemplation. The mood on deck was somber as is often the way after so many are sent to the deep at one time. The wounded men to go over to the Bedford Lee waited on litters. One of them was Ian. The mercenary lieutenant had suffered an abdominal wound and was pale from loss of blood. Kendal waited with his lieutenant and what remained of his platoon. Another of his men had died since morning. He had lost six soldiers on this mission, four in the recent battle, and he carried that burden heavily upon his shoulders. Thirteen bodies were committed to the sea that day. Among them were Jessup of the Bedford Lee, Pat and Muar of the Coastal Raider, and Imar's friend and soldier, Rolf. Another ten or twelve men were expected to pass in the days to follow. Aideen and Missy waited with Kendal and his men to see them off. Anisha remained below decks. Coulig had lost five men in the battle. He and his men sat with their bed ridden comrades to see them off as well.

Imar and Dalla had said their goodbyes to the men they had come to know as friends. They excused themselves to meet with Ivan in private for a brief meeting in the Captain's quarters.

"I will meet you in Juana Napur," said the wizard. "Take rooms at the Mozar Abibi. If I am not there already, then wait for me."

"Where is Juana Napur and what is Mozar Abibi?" Imar asked.

"Dalla can fill you in. I have to go in a few minutes. I would recommend you have Beros drop you off at most any fishing village between Seal Bay and Port Augustus. Tell no one your plans other than hiding the key. Especially do not tell where we will meet. I would also avoid thinking about it. Your daughter seems to have some talent, so guard your thoughts well for her safety as well as ours."

"Everyone knows we go to Eastonia already, but no one knows which route," added Dalla. "Aideen does show some promise. I wish we could take her with us. She is at a good age for learning to exercise her natural talent."

"It is too dangerous," said Imar. "And her mother would never allow it."

"True," said Dalla. "I intend to work with you though. You have some talent yourself. It pops out from time to time."

"Me . . . talent . . . you gotta be kidding," responded Imar. Her comment surprised him.

"It is rather obvious," added Ivan. "Everyone has extra talents they are rarely ever aware of, some more than others. Aideen's are strong and she is easier to guide because of her age. She has not yet been corrupted by the world of narrow minded thinking or exposure to bigotry, pessimism and bias prejudices. You, on the other hand, are becoming aware of your gifts because of your amnesia. At least that's my theory. I think your awareness and perceptions are coming out because you have simply forgotten all the crap you have been fed throughout your life. That bonk on the head may have been the best thing that could have happened to you."

"Well it has been a living hell. I would rather have my memories."

"Anyway, back to your plans." As Ivan spoke they could hear the ships tying up together. "Find a coastal village and hire a fishing boat to take you to Menebeth. It is a fishing village south of Port Augustus. There is a good road from there to Juana Napur and those seeking you will probably be looking for you on more northern routes. Not only that, anyone looking for you will do their best to avoid Menebeth." Ivan raised a hand to stop Imar's question before it came out. "Dalla will explain. I have to go now." The wizard went to Dalla and they embraced.

"It has been too long and this has been too brief," said the healer.

"I'm sorry, my child, but it has to be. We will have plenty of time together on the blazing hot sands of the Hamaudi dessert."

Dalla and Imar followed Ivan out on deck. Everyone that was going over to the Bedford Lee had already crossed over.

Beros leaned over the quarterdeck's forward rail and called out to Ivan. "Come on Wizard, we haven't got all day to wait on you. Those ships are less than twenty clicks and closing."

Ivan hopped onto the rail with amazing agility and sprang lightly aboard the Bedford Lee. He turned and swept off his hat and replied, "I will miss you too, Captain Beros."

The ships pulled apart and made for the island of Renauld to the southwest as planned.

The two ships kept a steady pace all day and into the night. The four vessels following ceased to gain on them, but they did not fall behind either. Without the rain or fog the visibility was good and the continued overcast made for a dark night. The lights of the trailing ships stood out clearly.

The decoy rafts were built with a small sail and a fixed rudder so that the small vessels would hold a fairly steady course. It would not do to have the red and green lamps swapping sides as the rafts drifted, spun and bobbed randomly. That would be a sure giveaway even at a distance. A clear lens lamp was hung on each stern and lamps of red and green on the proper sides. The wicks were lit and the rafts launched at the same moment the real navigation lights were doused. The Bedford Lee and the Coastal Raider turned southeast towards Sedar. They watched the Kandian ships navigate toward the bobbing rafts, which held the last of their cargo. They were relieved that the pursuit vessels maintained their course. The ruse appeared to have worked. About an hour after the decoys were set adrift, the enemy ships closed on the bait. The enemy's lights seemed to remain in that spot until the distance caused the last of their light to wink out of view. No pursuit was spotted the rest of the night.

CHAPTER 32

The weather improved as the two ships traveled on a southeasterly tack. The winds had changed and brought clear skies out of the east. Because of this, progress was slowed. If any pursuit still hounded their trail it was well beyond the horizon. To catch the Bedford Lee and the Coastal Raider the pursuit would have to tack against a quartering wind.

The days passed, injuries healed and the more fit of the soldiers exercised at arms. Imar worked especially hard with his sword training. The wound on his leg required him to use a cane for the first few days after his injury, but he fenced anyway. He practiced with a variety of weapons, everything from cutlass to saber, axe to long sword. After being bested by Khaled and nearly killed, he decided he would practice thrice as hard to bring his skills to a higher level. The assassin's whirling scimitars impressed him. Because of that he worked extra hours each day with a pair of sabers. More than that, he was going to traverse a desert known for its hostile tribes and he was concerned that he might have to change his fighting style to adapt to the environment. The desert heat would make use of heavy armor a difficult burden as well as identify him as a soldier. He intended to travel as a merchant, not a warrior.

Imar also practiced with Aideen each day. The girl was truly talented and getting stronger. After one of these fencing sessions, Imar sat with his daughter in the bow and talked.

"Father," the girl said seriously. "I want to go with you to Eastonia."

"I know you do. Dalla said as much. She also mentioned your talent and that she would like to work with you some more."

"There you are then. How 'bout it Dad?"

"I don't think so. It's way too dangerous. I would rather you stay at your grandmother's house."

"Please Father, please?"

"No. Not only that, your mother would be very angry. She'd probably send soldiers after us."

"She'd get over it. Besides, there's something you should know. I can't quite put my finger on it, but she is up to something."

"What do you mean?"

"Well, it's kind a hard to explain. I can perceive her feelings and the direction of her thoughts, so to speak, but I'm not really able to read her mind. I can sometimes tell what Mother is thinking about and roughly where that thinking is going, but without detail."

"I don't suppose you would be willing to hazard a guess, would you?"

"I think she is planning on stealing the octagon key."

Imar tried to look surprised. He had already suspected as much. Now, with his daughter's help, his suspicions were confirmed. He had been meaning to lecture Aideen concerning the proprieties of listening in on the thoughts of others without their permission. However, her information was always useful, so he postponed his comments for now.

"Dalla told me that you were able to hear her and Ivan use the mind-speech. You were even able to talk to her in that manner. Why can you not pick thoughts from others?"

"That's totally different. They had prepared their minds and reached out with their senses to communicate. I am close to Dalla from her guiding me through perceptual exercises and my mind was daydreaming when they called to each other. She called him 'Father.' I've been meaning to ask her about that, but I keep forgetting for some reason. Anyway, I heard them, but it was faint. I probably wouldn't have heard them at all if I had been paying attention to what I was doing. As far as other people go, I can sense intentions and emotions. Everyone has a sort of glow about them and it is as if it changes colors with their moods. That assassin," Aideen shivered and paused. "His mood color was very black, with an outer layer of red."

Imar looked intently at his daughter. "You know, sometimes you really amaze me."

"You see? You should take me with you." She smiled.

"Sorry, not going to happen."

Aideen's smile faded. Imar saw the change and asked, "What?"

The little girl shook her head sadly. "I really hate to say this, but Mom's glow is dark too. It makes me sad. It also scares me sometimes."

Imar put his arms around his daughter and gave her a hug. After he ended the embrace he said to her, "Your mother just thinks differently than we do. Remember that no matter what she may be planning, she would not let any harm come to you." Imar sincerely hoped he was right.

"Okay. I will try not to let her scare me."

On the Bedford Lee Captain Einar and First Officer Hawkins stood on the quarter deck.

"I should really be going with them," said Hawkins. "I grew up riding caravans with my father. We traveled many times across the northern plains as well as the southern desert routes with loads of merchandise. Sometimes we used horses and mules and other times we used camels and llamas all depending on the terrain, the route, and the season. It is dangerous work and usually profitable, if you don't lose your cargo." He paused, and then muttered, "Or your life."

"Your services as a guide would be very valuable to them indeed," replied Einar. "I must admit though, that I would hate to lose you. I have been thinking lately about retiring. I was also planning on recommending you for the captaincy when I do. I think that if you wanted it, you could be master and commander of the Bedford Lee. It is a lot to think about and you probably don't need the added stress right now. However, this mission that Imar is embarking on is very important. If he fails, we could all be out of a job or worse, we could all end up dead."

"You have spoken of retirement before, and I look forward to the day when I can stand in your shoes. Not only that, this war could find just about every available ship battling at sea and my skills would be needed just as badly on the deck of a ship."

"I expect that the Coastal Raider will be turning south anytime soon. If you haven't decided by then, I would suggest that you stay aboard the Bedford Lee. I'm not sure how long this or any war is going to last nor am I sure how long Imar's quest will take, but I will hold off on my retirement for at least a year should you decide to go. The captaincy will be waiting for you when you return."

"Thank you, Captain."

The two ships spotted other vessels from time to time. At one sighting a trio of ships turned to intercept. The Coastal Raider and the Bedford Lee, light and agile, ran with filled sails and quickly outdistanced the curious trio. They made it a point to avoid both friend and foe for the sake of Imar's desired heirloom.

Sightings became frequent and when they came abeam of Seal Bay the two ships parted company with many waves to friends across the water. Hawkins had still not decided on whether or not to travel with Imar and company, so he stayed aboard the Bedford Lee.

CHAPTER 33

The Coastal Raider traveled south for two days without incident. They dropped anchor in the sheltered waters of a fishing village named Whale Cove on the border of Sedar and Kalusia. It was a small cove and even smaller village.

Earlier that morning when Imar rose and pulled on his trousers, his pouch felt different. He removed it from his pocket and looked in it to find his fake key had been replaced with a piece of wood. He shook his head thinking, Did she really think I wouldn't notice? Imar decided not to say anything. Fakes in the world would confuse his pursuers. He wished now that he would have had more made. Still, he thought it strange that she could steal the item without his noticing. He was usually a light sleeper, able to wake to a mouse fart. He shook off his heavy sleeping to fatigue and prepared his gear for departure after first checking on the real octagon key. He had recently hidden it in the hollowed heel of his boot.

A longboat was readied and farewells were in progress on the deck. Imar bent down and gave his daughter a big hug. "I will miss you, Aideen."

"I will miss you too," replied Aideen. Then she whispered in her father's ear, "You better check your pouch. I think she stole it. She has been acting like the cat that ate the canary."

Imar whispered back, "It's okay. Let's just pretend she got away with it." He pulled back and winked at her.

Aideen's brows went up and Imar could see the wheels turning in her mind. Then she smiled. "You know Dad, we're pretty close.

Sometimes I think I really can read your mind." She moved thumb and forefinger across her lips and said, "Not a word. You can count on me."

Imar smiled and went on to shake arms in the soldier fashion with many of the crew and fighting men. Anisha had come up on deck as was expected and embraced her husband perfunctorily, albeit coldly.

Imar picked up his claymore in its scabbard where he had leaned it against the rail and slung it across his back. He then went to Coulig. "From here on we will be traveling as someone other than who we really are. Our tabards, chainmail, and banner we will leave in your care."

"It will be well cared for, old friend," replied Coulig, gripping Imar's forearm. "Fare you well."

Imar, Dalla, Vidar, Hager, Aksel and Egil climbed over the rail and down a rope ladder into the waiting longboat. Gavin went with the rowers to see them ashore.

An hour later the Coastal Raider was out of the cove, catching the wind and heading south.

Vidar went off to find a fisherman willing to carry them south, while the rest of the party walked to the edge of the village and set up camp. The community of Whale Cove had no services. There was a road, more akin to a trail, that came down the hill from Coast Road. The village, being out of the way, got very few visitors. Most of the fishermen took their fresh catch to one of the larger towns by the sea at the end of the day. A few of the locals processed their fish by smoking, pickling or canning it in jars to haul out to town by wagon at their convenience.

Vidar spoke to several fishermen working with their families preparing fish for market. All responses were negative. The mercenary merchant, usually proud of his bargaining skills, went back to the camp feeling dejected.

It was a pleasant afternoon. The cove community was sheltered from the wind, but a few clouds could be seen scudding across a blue sky. Aksel and Egil were building a fire and Imar and Hager had just finished setting up the tent and planted their backsides on a log. Dalla was rummaging through the packs for the cooking gear when Vidar strolled in carrying a fresh salmon.

"At least I didn't come back empty handed," said Vidar.

"I take it you didn't have any luck," replied Imar.

"No, but there will be more boats in later this evening. I will try again then."

"You look troubled," said Hager.

Dalla said nothing as she took the fish from Vidar and handed it to Aksel to fillet.

"It is strange," answered Vidar. "Every time I mention Menebeth, people get either indignant or alarmed. One of the fishwives even went so far as to make a sign, say a prayer and then she threw a fish out into the water to appease one of her sea gods. I think it appeased an otter. Then she herded her children into the house."

Dalla spoke while setting a pot of rice by the fire. "Menebeth is a leper colony."

The comment was met with stunned silence. Everyone stopped and stared at the healer.

Vidar recovered first. "That little bit of information may have helped with inquires. Can we pick another destination?"

"We can," answered the healer. "But no one will go near the place, much less expect us to go over the mountains from that southern route. It is our best choice to avoid notice."

"Don't we risk catching the disease?"

"Not at all, there is nothing a healthy person need fear. Besides that, they won't come near us or have anything to do with us. There is a dock there. You may persuade someone to drop us off without tying up. There is a path from the village that climbs a bluff and then leads on to Coast Road. There are no roads into Menebeth. We will have to walk a ways south from there to a ranch where we can buy horses."

Dalla knocked the coals down and placed a wire grill over the fire. She took the fillets from Aksel and placed them on the grill. Nothing more was said on the subject.

CHAPTER 34

The Coastal Raider arrived at Port Augustus on a beautiful sunny afternoon. The trip from Whale Cove was uneventful, but for a couple of ships seen in the distance. Akala had received messages via pigeon from Captain Einar and from Ivan, so she had been expecting the ship's arrival. The vessel had been spotted as it entered the bay and word was brought to Akala. She and Dorfin came to the docks in a carriage to pick up her family. There was also an officer from the Royal Navy with a squad of men waiting for the ship as it tied up to the dock.

Akala had a fair idea of what the officer wanted. She asked him his business with her ship.

"I am Ensign Tremaine of his majesty's fleet," he said with a slight bow. "We had information that your son-in-law, Imar Amirson, was aboard the Coastal Raider. He is wanted for questioning. My superiors would also like a report on the battle at Valekrie. Any intelligence on the enemy city could be beneficial in the coming conflict."

Akala nodded her acquiesce, choosing to hold her opinion on naval intelligence to herself.

As soon as the ship was secured and the gangplank set, Akala went up on deck followed by Dorfin. Akala's foot no sooner hit the deck when Aideen slammed into her with a fierce hug.

"Grandma," exclaimed the girl. "I've missed you so much, and I have so much to tell you about horses, and battles, and ships, and . . ."

Akala squatted and interrupted her granddaughter's exuberance with kisses. "Later, dear," she flicked her eyes to indicate the officer coming up the gangway. Only Aideen and Anisha saw the gesture. "You can tell me all about it later when we get back to the house."

Akala stood and embraced her daughter. Anisha returned the hug with formal brevity. "Mother," she said, with a questioning looked of restrained emotions. "It has been a long time. It is good to be home."

Akala wanted to tell her daughter that home is where the heart is, but she knew that Imar and Anisha were not as close as her and Travin. Besides, the less spoken about Imar, the better.

Akala knew better than to wait for Anisha to introduce a mere servant, so she extended her hand to Missy when Aideen chimed in and proudly finished the formality. "Grandma, this is my new nanny, Missy." The girl was already moving to Dorfin as she added, "She's my friend too."

Anisha rolled her eyes impatiently then gave Dorfin a curt nod that was missed by the steward because of Aideen's exuberant hugs. Dorfin had some difficulty extracting himself from the child's embrace to offer a hand in greeting Missy.

Akala asked them to wait for her in the carriage, and said that she and Dorfin would be along shortly. She then met with Beros, Coulig and Ensign Tremaine in the Captain's quarters.

Tremaine's men began searching the ship on his orders after Beros told him that Imar was not on board. "Where is he then?"

Beros answered him bluntly. "How the hell should I know?" He did not like having his ship searched. In a roundabout way the Ensign insulted him by doubting his word. The captain did not like being called a liar.

"I am sorry," replied Tremaine. "I have orders to search the Coastal Raider for Captain Imar. These orders came down from the King. Would you at least tell me where you dropped him off?"

Beros really wanted to lie this time to protect his friends, but he knew the truth would come out eventually and there were some pretty severe punishments for people who lied to representatives of the King. Beros did not answer, but looked instead to his boss, Akala.

Akala nodded to Beros. "It's okay Captain, I'm sure Imar is long gone by now. Go ahead and tell him."

"Yes ma'am," answered Beros. He turned to Tremaine and said, "We dropped them off at Whalers Cove."

"Captains," Akala addressed Beros and Coulig. "Go ahead and brief Ensign Tremaine on the action and intelligence you acquired at Valekrie. We wouldn't want to be accused of not cooperating. Please come up to the house this evening and give me your full report. For now I am anxious to see my family, so please excuse me. Before I go, I do want to offer my condolences. Both of you lost men and I share that loss as well. I received word by pigeon and have notified their families and I'm sure that you'll want to pay your respects as well. Good afternoon, gentlemen."

Coulig followed Akala and Dorfin out on deck and asked Brin and Jax to escort her and her family to the house. He then went back to the meeting. Neither Coulig nor Beros missed Akala's word, 'brief.' Because of that the reports given Ensign Tremaine were the bare necessities. Nothing was mentioned about the octagon key and when asked, no knowledge of it was admitted.

Akala was brought up to date with the full report later that evening. She agreed that it was best that no one knew which route Imar's party would take.

Several days passed and Akala was getting anxious to begin her search for Travin. The project in the hills was nearly finished and she was packed and ready to go. All of the test trials had proved positive and production plans had been set.

It had been a long time since she had seen her daughter and her granddaughter. Her relationship with her daughter was somewhat strained and she did not really want to overtax herself with the stress of being around Anisha for very long. She loved her daughter, but she really did not like the person she had become. Her granddaughter, on the other hand, she did not want to leave. Akala, Aideen and Missy got along well and were nearly inseparable.

Missy was relieved that there were other servants at the estate that Anisha could abuse instead of her. The stable environment of a house allowed the nanny more effective time for Aideen's education. Much of the girl's reading time had slipped when they were spending long days in the saddle. At sea there were many distractions that prevented the concentration for studies, and reading with the ship's motion was not always conducive to keeping one's meals where they belonged. Most of Aideen's tutoring now took place in Akala's garden, which was ripe with vegetables now that summer was nearly gone.

Anisha didn't spend much time with her family. She stayed up late, often coming home at the early hours between midnight and dawn. She slept till noon and sometimes later, then she'd be off into town shopping and socializing. She claimed that because she had been gone for so long she wanted to catch up for lost time with old friends. Akala knew her daughter well, and knew that Anisha was feeding her a line of bull. Anisha did not have any friends. She only had acquaintances. When those acquaintances ceased to be useful she no longer had time for them.

Akala and Aideen were practicing with wooden swords one sunny afternoon on the South Terrace when Dorfin came out to watch.

He took a chair next to Missy and said, "She is really quite good for a ten-year-old."

"You should see her with a bow and arrow," replied the young nanny. "On our journey through the Kandian wilderness she put more grouse in the cook pot than any of the men."

"Impressive. Is she as good as Coulig?"

"Not yet, but she comes close."

Akala ended the practice session. She knew her steward well enough to know when he had something on his mind even though he showed no outward appearance of it.

"That is enough for me today," said Akala. "Besides, I have to catch up on some work and I need to discuss some things with Dorfin in private."

"No problem, Grandma. Would it be okay if I go raid the kitchen and get a snack?" Aideen was always hungry, but she was especially ravenous after sword practice.

"Of course you can, as long as you stay out of the sweets."

"Oh all right," Aideen answered dramatically.

Aideen and Missy left the terrace and made a beeline for the kitchen.

Akala sat down in Missy's vacated chair next to Dorfin. "What's up?"

The steward poured a glass of water and handed it to his boss. "Baker tells me that Anisha has been visiting Lord Townsend each day since their arrival."

"I personally find that disgusting, but she is a grown woman, and if I say anything to her about her indiscretions she will just bite my head off and tell me to mind my own business. Where is Townsend's wife?"

"Lady Lenora is at her family's chalet in the hills. She doesn't really like her husband. She has made it clear that she was less than pleased with the arranged marriage. He treats her badly, so she spends very little time around him except for social functions that require them to be in attendance together."

"Anisha's immoral forays are nothing new. I get the feeling that you are preparing me for unpleasant news."

"Yes, there is more. It seems that Anisha had some item of value that she offered to sell to Townsend," Dorfin paused.

Akala finished his sentence, "And he agreed."

"She refused to bring the item to him until he made a fairly large deposit into an account at the Royal Kalusian bank."

"How large of a deposit are we talking about? And what is this valuable item?" Akala was beginning to have a nasty suspicion as to the nature of the item in question.

"Baker wasn't able to find out the answers to those questions, but he did know that she only got half of the total sum. She is supposed to get the other half when she brings the item to him tonight. I did however bribe one of the bankers and found out that the deposit was a half a million in gold crowns."

"My good Gods," exclaimed Akala incredulously. "That is more than a king's ransom. She must have stolen the octagon key from Imar. This is not good. If it is the key we must steal it back. Make sure Baker is there tonight to observe the transaction and find out for sure what the item is and where it goes."

"I have already given him his orders as well as some misinformation about Imar traveling back up to Seal Bay to catch the northern caravan route."

"Good job, Dorfin." Akala sighed ruefully. "It seems every time I am ready to go search for Travin something dreadfully important comes up that keeps me here."

CHAPTER 35

Baker had found a narrow space between the walls where he could spy on Lord Townsend. It was conveniently located between a sitting room adjacent to the foyer and his Lordship's office where Townsend conducted most of his business. He had to access it from the wine cellar and climb up into the space within the wall.

Earlier, Baker made a small hole in the wall behind an old threadbare tapestry. From that position he could see the Lord's desk, but little else. Townsend was sitting at his desk while Anisha sat in a chair to the side of the desk facing his Lordship.

Townsend was very businesslike when he spoke. "Well," he began, "have you brought me the item for which I have paid you so dearly?"

Anisha had her hand in her purse. Her other hand she placed on Townsend's knee and slid it halfway up his thigh, saying sweetly, "Relax my dear. Of course I brought it. Do you have the rest of my money?" She pulled her hand back, letting her fingertips glide sensuously across his leg.

The Lord Townsend softened a bit and answered, "Of course I have your money. You'll need a cart to carry that much though."

"Just see that the money is deposited into my account tomorrow."

"You can trust me."

"I hardly think so. Just see that you don't cheat me and I won't have you murdered in your sleep."

"I would expect nothing less from you my dear. Now," he said to end any further delay, "The device please."

Anisha removed the octagon disc from her handbag and handed it to Townsend. He took it reverently, stared at it, and ran his fingers over the edges. He set it down on his desk. Baker sucked in his breath when he saw it and quickly put his hand over his mouth, hoping that he hadn't given himself away. Townsend took an ancient book from his drawer and placed it in front of him next to the key. The page he wanted was marked and he turned to it immediately and looked at the picture in the book.

"This is marvelous," he said breathlessly. "I have waited a very long time for this, and now I can hardly believe my eyes. I finally have it." He turned his head and looked at Anisha. "You have done very well my dear, but your husband must know by now that he has been robbed. He is probably on his way here as we speak."

"He is a fool. I tried talking sense into him. 'We could take this eight-sided key,' I told him, 'and access the world's greatest power.' He would have none of it. Then I suggested that we sell it, auction it off between you and Jarl Bamsen. We would have made a lot more money than the measly million gold crowns that you are paying me."

"That is true. Lucky for me that Bamsen is out of the picture. News has it that his head is decorating a pike in Sedar. By the sounds of it Bamsen had a lot more money and probably would've been able to outbid me. But you said Imar didn't want power, yet he travels to the east to unlock the fortress. Why?"

"That healer," she answered exasperatedly. "She has talked him into using the power of the fortress to destroy it and the fortress. What a waste. He is an idiot."

"I thought he was a strong man. It seems crazy to me not to grasp power when the key to it sits in your hand." Townsend picked up the key and marveled at it again. He then got a sly look on his face and said, "Let us celebrate our transaction."

"Let us do that," she purred in a husky voice.

Baker watched while Lord Townsend locked his book away in the drawer. He then stood and lifted a painting down from the wall. Behind the painting was a wall safe that Baker had not been aware of. Townsend told Anisha to turn her head while he applied the combination, but the man's head was in the way and Baker was unable to see the numbers. Once the octagon key was secure and the lock scrambled, Townsend replaced the painting. He then took Anisha's hand and led her away.

Baker figured he had seen enough. He would have liked to see more but he didn't have a secret hiding place or a peephole that would allow him to spy on the Lord Townsend in his bedchamber. He thought it best to get going and report his findings to Dorfin. He started wiggling and squeezed himself out of his place and down into the wine cellar. He grabbed a couple of bottles that he figured wouldn't be missed and was headed for the door when he heard talking in the room above.

Damn, thought Baker, back to work already. He set the bottles of wine back on the rack, much to his displeasure. He climbed very slowly and quietly back up into his place in the wall. He peered through the hole and saw Anisha taking her chair and sitting down, and Lord Townsend standing behind his desk. The view of him was partially blocked by a man wearing a black burnous with the hood up. All he could see was the man's back, but he knew immediately who it was. Baker suppressed a shiver and felt the hairs rise on the back of his neck.

Lord Townsend was talking. "You are late my friend. It is unfortunate that you failed in your mission. I will pay you for your time and expenses of course, but since you didn't bring me what you were hired to retrieve there will be no bonus."

Khaled briefly glanced at Anisha's smug face and then back at the man speaking to him. Lord Townsend was not easily intimidated, but when those dark, almost black, eyes bored into his, he nearly stepped back, but caught himself.

Khaled pulled his hand from his pocket, held up a gray octagon disc, and handed it over to Townsend. "I did not fail," he stated firmly.

Baker almost gasped. Townsend did gasp, and Anisha's jaw clenched so tight the cords in her neck stood out. The Lord took the disc and looked at it carefully, turning it over and over in his hands. He turned around and removed the painting from the wall again. He looked back over his shoulder and snapped, "Both of you turn your heads."

Khaled turned around and stood looking at the tapestry hanging on the wall—the one that Baker hid behind. The man appeared to be looking at him, right into him. It was all Baker could do not to pee his pants. Anisha turned her head as well. Her brows were knit and she looked as if she were in deep concentration as she stared at a low spot on the wall. Townsend removed the other octagon key from the safe and compared it to the one Khaled had brought. He turned around and sat down at his desk and placed both discs in front of him. Anisha and Khaled turned around and looked at the discs as well.

Townsend unlocked his drawer and removed his book and opened it to the marked page. He was not very happy. He carefully flipped the page and read. He had learned to read the language of this old script, but he was not proficient. He flipped another page and then another. The man read some more. Townsend began muttering quietly and making occasional groaning sounds.

He almost asked Khaled to draw his sword and thought better of it. He remembered that some religious fanatics have some strange customs and traditions concerning the drawing of their weapons. He drew a dagger from his belt and placed the blade on top of both discs then lifted it. Nothing happened. He opened another drawer and pulled out a magnet and stuck it to his blade. He pulled the magnet back off with difficulty and then placed it on each of the discs. Nothing happened.

Townsend's barely controlled rage was evident when his face flushed, but he spoke quietly with fire in his eyes. "These are fakes.

It seems that Imar outsmarted both of you. The authentic octagon key is magnetic." To Anisha he said, "Your husband, obviously didn't trust you and had some phony devices made in the event of a theft. I wonder how many he made." He paused and looked into her eyes. "I trust that you will return my money tomorrow."

"Yes, of course I will," answered Anisha sadly.

"See that you do and I won't have you murdered in your sleep."

CHAPTER 36

Akala laughed so hard her stomach hurt and tears were rolling down her face. Dorfin had just given her Baker's report from the previous night. She looked into her steward's eyes and saw the twinkle there that only a few people knew indicated amusement. Dorfin's face was just as impassive as always, but this time there were a few more wrinkles at the corners of his eyes, which for him passed as mirth.

They sat at the common table that was outdoors. It was late morning and the weather was pleasant even though the skies were mostly cloudy. A light breeze blew from the south and brought with it a hint of rain. Akala was having a breakfast of fruit and yogurt while listening to the news of the events that had taken place at Townsend's estate the night before.

It was ill news and Akala listened with foreboding, not liking the sound of any of it. As Dorfin spoke she was formulating a plan in her head for recovering the octagon key until he got to the part where the assassin arrived with a duplicate. She had just put a spoonful of yogurt in her mouth when her steward explained the part of both octagon keys being fakes and that Imar had duped Khaled, Townsend and her daughter. She spewed her yogurt all over the table and sprayed the sleeve of her fastidious steward.

Dorfin wiped off his sleeve with a napkin while Akala attempted to clean the table while howling with laughter. It took a little while before Akala got herself under control, but Dorfin's eyes sparkled from his straight face.

"That is just poetic justice," said Akala happily. "I am tempted to throw a party and have dancing in the streets."

"I knew you would appreciate the news. I did not bring it to you last night because I was afraid you would not get your rest."

"You are right Dorfin. I would've spent half the night laughing and probably would have given myself away by gloating when Anisha got home."

"Your daughter is already up and gone. I am assuming she has some business at the bank."

Akala slapped her leg and burst into another fit of merriment. As soon as she calmed herself down again she said, "This is excellent news. It also frees me to begin my search for Travin. I would like you to get word to Coulig that we will depart tomorrow morning. Send word up to Beros as well. Is his crew proficient yet?"

"From what I hear they are actually doing very well. It is too bad we had to pull him and his crew off of the Coastal Raider, but we had no one else available. I thought he was going to squawk, but when he saw the project he took to it like a duck to water. We are putting the Coastal Raider into dry dock and will begin making modifications for installing guns once they come out of production."

"Dorfin, you handle things better than I do, and I appreciate that. Travin and I couldn't have hired a better man. Now that Imar has gone inland, go ahead and deploy our ships and our troops however you see fit providing they don't conflict with Imar's mission. I would still like most of our fleet to keep working the southern latitudes and continue the search for any information on my husband. I will check in with our shipping agents from time to time for messages."

"Your granddaughter is going to miss you."

"Yes I know, and I will miss her too. She is in good hands here with you and Missy. I will make sure that Anisha knows you are the boss around here and that you speak with my authority. Don't let her get away with anything here and most definitely no parties. Do not hesitate to use the household guard to enforce that either."

The corners of Dorfin's mouth barely twitched with the hint of a smile and the twinkle returned to his eyes. "It would be my pleasure."

CHAPTER 37

Anisha was deep in thought as she rode alone in her carriage down the cobblestone streets of Port Augustus. She had told the driver to take a scenic route back to the estate. He now steered the carriage down a street near the wharf which was lined with restaurants that would not be open until later in the day. It was mostly cloudy outside and the smell of rain mixing with the scent of the sea blew in gently off the bay. Some of the restaurants, though not open yet, were preparing foods that added odors to the salt air. Anisha hardly noticed any of this and was barely aware of the clunking of the carriage wheels over the stone paving. Her thoughts were deep and her mood was black.

She had barely slept the night before. Her rage at being duped by her husband was overwhelming. It was small consolation that the assassin had been duped as well. She was also mad at Townsend as well as Khaled. If the assassin had not shown up she would not have had to return the money. She really had no reason to be mad at Townsend other than the fact that he wanted his money back. He was just as ambitious as her. She was mad at everyone and it was all everyone else's fault. She had tossed and turned through the night, and was still in a foul mood when she got up.

Having no appetite, and forgoing breakfast, she rousted the chauffeur and ordered him to prepare a carriage immediately. He got dressed and hitched up the horses as fast as he could, but she still snapped at him rudely and accused him of being too slow. She had him take her directly to the bank where she made arrangements to transfer the money that Townsend had paid her back into his account—returning that much money was more painful than pulling teeth. She was curt with the bankers, and she stormed out of the building to her carriage.

Even though she scowled at everyone she looked at, deep down she blamed Imar for all her ills. Why couldn't he see things my way? The fool, she thought. He was such a mighty warrior and a natural born leader. With her guidance he could rule the world. She had seen these strengths in him when they were younger. He had so much drive back then. That was why she chose to trap him with child. His ethics bound him to her and she thought she would be able to make him do her bidding by pulling the strings of his honor like a puppet. Her ambition had blinded her, and she knew now that she had chosen poorly.

She had to change things. Her climb to power would be greatly hindered if she divorced him. The black smear that would cause on her social slate would tear out the rungs of her aristocratic ladder. She intended to become royalty and society frowned on divorce in the upper classes. The only way out of this was for Imar to die.

Khaled had nearly completed the job for her outside of Valekrie. She had never heard of anyone ever besting Imar. If he had not been so insistent in training their daughter in martial arts, Anisha would be a widow now. She had to find a way to get Imar to give up the octagon key first, and then have him killed. She would have to be very careful that there was no evidence pointing to her involvement. After that she could sell the key, the real octagon key, to Townsend, but not for the pittance he was paying before. Oh no, he would pay much, much more.

Wait, she thought. Why let him have it at all? Townsend, if he had the octagon key, would have the power. He would have all of the power. Anisha thought hard and long, her brows knit together and her forehead wrinkled in concentration. The Lord Townsend's ambition was legendary. He may not be a warrior, but he is a leader and a shrewd businessman. Townsend usually gets what he wants, and he can be very ruthless in his pursuit to get it. Anisha was equally ambitious. With the octagon key, a partnership with Townsend could lead to great power. If they were married with such power she could be an empress. Of course, he would have to be the emperor for that to happen. Once they had the power of the fortress and vast armies standing at their beck and call, she could dispose of Townsend if he got in her way.

First things first, she thought. First she needed the octagon key. She would have to exploit Imar's weaknesses to get it. She would need help. Her brows relaxed and the wrinkles of deep thought in her forehead smoothed as a plan began to formulate in her mind.

Anisha stuck her head out of the carriage window and called to the driver. "Take me to Lord Townsend's estate."

CHAPTER 38

Khaled was humiliated. He was taught humiliation in his training and he hated it. He was also taught not to hate, but he never overcame that either. Emotions were supposed to be expunged from him through prayer to the nameless god. He was not supposed to be angry, but he could barely control his rage. He needed to relax, but he didn't know how.

He left Townsend's estate in the middle of the night. He was too angry and frustrated to sit still. Being told that his mission failed was bad enough, but being told of his failure in front of a woman was intolerable. The fact that he had carried a useless piece of metal for such a great distance all for nothing soured his stomach. Risking his life did not bother him, being deprived of killing a sword master because of a child did. Not just any child, but a girl child wearing boy's clothes and wielding men's weapons. The child was an abomination and the father created it.

Khaled rolled his shoulders, still sore from the child's arrows. The reminder of it drove him to intolerable madness. He walked into town keeping to the shadows, wanting a release, and needing it badly. He was not supposed to murder without purpose, but he felt his insanity would take him to unfathomable depths if his sword did not slake his thirst for blood very soon. The Lord Townsend had paid him for his efforts, for his failure. He carried a bag of coins that would have been ten times bigger had he succeeded in taking the real octagon key.

The assassin would go to a local temple of the nameless god and turn over most of his money to them. That was their way. He would also pray and rest. But first he would kill, and then give thanks for being the instrument of death. He would find a way to kill the skilled one called Imar. The weapons master was a worthy opponent. He also taught his girl child, to be more than just a girl. Blasphemy! Khaled decided he would kill the girl too. They both deserved to die. Maybe he would kill the girl first and make her father watch. Yes, that is what he would do. He would make Imar watch his daughter be slain, and then allow him to fight and die a piece at a time.

Khaled was deep in his brooding thoughts when he turned into an alley. Three men had just stepped out of a tavern side door into the alley to relieve themselves. Khaled came out of his reverie and killed all three in as many seconds. It happened so fast that none of them cried out. All that was heard was the sound of blades slicing flesh. He cleaned his scimitars on the dead men's clothes and calmly continued on his way, feeling much better. He wiped a spot of blood off his cheek and tasted it. He was happy now.

CHAPTER 39

Imar and Dalla rode side-by-side at the front followed by Hager and Vidar. Aksel and Egil brought up the rear, each leading a string of pack mules. It was a crisp morning when they set out from the ranch. The brown, grass covered hills had frost on them when they started out toward the mountains that day. They took it as a sign of an early winter, yet the leaves had not yet turned color in the lowlands. The high, distant peaks had termination dust.

When they had left Whalers Cove the day after the Coastal Raider dropped them off, the weather was still seasonally warm. Vidar found a fisherman to take them all the way to Menebeth, but it took hours of haggling and he had to dig deep into his coin pouch to secure passage for the party.

The trip took them a little over a week. It was a small boat, but not overly cramped for eight people. They didn't have accommodations for comfortable sleeping, so they stopped each night to camp on the beach. From time to time they saw other ships and fishing boats but none bothered them and they were left alone.

When they arrived at the leper colony the fisherman and his son would not set foot on the dock nor would they even tie up to the cleats. As soon as the passengers stepped off of the boat the son shoved off and his father rowed madly while the son hoisted the sail. They did not want to be anywhere near the leper colony, and did their best to put distance between them and it.

As Dalla had said, none of the inhabitants of Menebeth came near them. Everyone but Dalla seemed a bit apprehensive as well. Within an hour they had climbed the trail to the top of the bluff and shortly after that they were on Coast Road walking south toward a ranch that the healer knew about.

Dalla seemed to be familiar with the ranch; however, none of the family or the ranch hands acted like they knew her. They stayed there a few days buying horses, pack mules and tack. They also bought supplies for their trip and large amounts of potatoes and carrots for resale once they got over the mountains.

On the morning that they departed the ranch, they got up before the sun. The rancher's wife had prepared them a huge breakfast of ham, eggs, fried potatoes, and biscuits with gravy. They ate with gusto, especially the younger Aksel and Egil. They enjoyed their stay there, but were afraid of letting something slip about their mission. Conversation can do that when you spend time with people, and getting to know them. It was time to go, so the party left with many thanks and a farewell.

"I could be content being a farmer or a rancher," said Imar.

"Yes, it can be a good life," said Dalla. "It is hard work, but fulfilling."

"You've been here before?"

"I stayed here for quite some time, once."

"They didn't seem to remember you."

"The only one that would have remembered me was the old rancher and he was a very young boy at the time. It was a long time ago."

"Sometimes I forget that you have been around for a while. I never forget that you are special. You are certainly very special to me. It is just that you look so young and beautiful, I cannot think of you as being older than me."

"Flattery will get you everywhere," Dalla said jokingly with a smile.

As the sun climbed higher the morning chill was chased away to be replaced with a pleasantly cloudless day. Imar and Dalla loved being able to spend time together even though they were still properly distant. They were with close friends who liked seeing them together, but were sorry for them at the same time because Imar's marriage would not allow them to be mates. But at least they could be friends without Anisha's scrutiny and scathing criticism.

No one had mentioned Anisha since they parted company with the Coastal Raider. They spoke of Aideen daily though. Their moods were light, and they enjoyed themselves as if they were on a pleasure trip. Imar missed his daughter, but he was comfortable in knowing that she was safe at Travin and Akala's estate in Port Augustus.

They walked their horses at a leisurely pace traveling southeast toward the mountains enroute to Juana Napur where they would meet Ivan. From that Hamaudi city they would equip themselves for desert travel. To the east they must go. The answers to so many questions would be found in the far off underground fortress. For Imar the mission was still unclear. Dalla told him it was his duty to destroy the technology hidden deep below the ground. He thought this over many times and still did not know if that was the right thing to do or not. Open the fortress he would do, but whether to destroy it or use the technology was a choice he still had to make.

EPILOGUE

Journal of Imar Amirson

It is autumn of the year 5685. Dalla Ivanova explained to me that so many dark centuries have passed since humankind's near extinction, a rough estimate of the calendar from that time would place us at 8185, give or take a few hundred years. These numbers boggle the mind. The power that could keep people like her in frozen sleep for thousands of years truly amazes me. I do not think that technological knowledge such as that should be destroyed. Dalla fears the weapons of mass destruction, and Ivan assured me that we need to get there first to keep it from the wrong hands, but he seems to be against destroying the technology. Dalla would destroy it all, after taking as much medical technological data as possible before blowing it up. They both believe that taking the octagon key to Oldeisei is my duty, and my family's obligation. I once heard them call the place Washington DC. It is on the other side of the continent in far off Eastonia where few but merchant caravans have traveled. I have agreed to this, but what if I am the wrong choice? Could I be the 'wrong hands' that Ivan mentioned? Michael Ivanovich, the one we call Ivan, said that people with power of this magnitude caused deserts on the other side of the world to turn to glass with the heat of their nuclear dirty bombs. The radiation and the chemical weapons caused people and animals on the rim of that destruction to mutate. Even after thousands of years some of those places are still uninhabitable. I must ask; am I, an amnesiac, the right choice for the job?

I was born again a few months ago. I do not mean that in a religious way, like when a person decides to pursue a more pious way of life, but rather in a more physical sense. I was born a grown man—one without any memory before the moment I lost it. Since that day, that day my life began, I have been very busy, so I am taking this moment to write down some thoughts while I have this rare moment of leisure as we sit out a particularly nasty mountain storm within the dry comfort of our tent.

My friends tell me that I just had my thirty-eighth birthday a few weeks ago, but to me my existence only spans back to the day I awoke in a pit. That was near summer solstice. I wanted answers to who I was then. Dalla saved me. I was sure she was an angel. In fact, she is my angel. I sometimes wonder if she had not melded her mind with mine if I would love her the way I do now.

Dalla; if only words could express what saying, thinking, or hearing her name does to me. Each time I look upon her my heart hammers a little harder, I breathe a bit faster, and my soul sails upon a sea of love. Ah, Dalla; if only we could be one as man and woman should be. I would have her as my wife, but I am stricken with the sad duty to be already married to a woman I do not love nor even like. Perhaps it was luck, or maybe one of the gods gifted me with a smile the day Dalla came into my life. Of the many or even the one, the nameless god, I have seen nothing in my few months of recallable memory to indicate they exist. Dalla is silent on this subject, but I digress.

The shape of the octagon key was chosen for the shape of the structure it opens; the great Octagon military installation that delved deep into the earth, but climbed only eight levels above the ground. It was to signal a new era after war caused the destruction of the Pentagon, which previously stood where the new structure was built. It was a storehouse of knowledge in medicine, history, engineering, electronics, and astrophysics. It was also a warehouse of weapons, and that is what every king on the continent wants. Even that great structure was wiped from the earth, but only down to the first few levels. Below that the structure is sealed with alloys and nuclear powered energy shields impervious to our primitive tools. I am not so sure that the new development of gunpowder could not change that. I think it is King Drayden's plan to blast his way in, and with the aid Sumas can give him he just may do it. Now that the Western Alliance has the secret of gunpowder, perhaps they will leave me be and thus narrow my pursuers to those that don't have guns.

On guns, I wish we could have taken some with us when we disembarked from the Coastal Raider, but what few we had were needed as models to build more. After Dalla taught me to load and shoot a rifle, when we were aboard the Coastal Raider, I thought it wise to grab a pistol as well as some powder and ball. I have kept this a secret from my friends, including Dalla, so I have had no opportunity to practice with the weapon. If we are lucky it will never need to be discharged. What worries me most is when we get to the fortress and have to sit out Drayden's cannons and Sumas' cunning, while we learn how to use the defenses, I may not have time to convince Dalla not to destroy the knowledge. If that becomes our situation, then we will need to wipe out the weapons and the knowledge before it can be taken by a hostile force. Ivan and Dalla will know how to use the machines, and access the data. I can hope Ivan will side with me on this, and that I can win Dalla over, to using the technology for good purpose, without losing her love. Women are the best at creating secrets, but oh how they hate having one kept from them.

Dalla can read emotions in anyone and perform mind-speech with, she says, 'the open minded,' but except for Aideen, I've only seen her mind-speak with Ivan, and he is genetically enhanced like her. I hope I don't let anything out before I can tell her with words that I lean more keeping and using the technology. She is smarter than me; maybe it would be best if we did blow it up, but what a waste.

Ivan told me that I am more open to my perceptions because my amnesia pushes past the bullshit I've been taught that would prevent me from using it. He says Aideen is open-minded because she is young and hasn't been taught the negative beliefs yet. It makes sense I suppose. Either way, neither of them knew of anyone that is not genetically enhanced that could do this mind-speech, until Aideen came along. I'm not quite there yet.

About two hundred of these special people like Dalla and Ivan went into a deep freeze sleep. She calls it cryogenics. Of the four I heard of that survived the ages to be awakened in my grandfather's time, I have met three: Dalla, Ivan, and Sumas. Sumas got greedy—now he wants the octagon key to rule the world. What if there are more of these people? What if more of them want to rule the world? They lost many of these cryogenic sites from geographical shifting. Maybe more of them survived.

I can't help but think that there is a way that this technology, even the weapons, can be put to good purpose. This 'survival of the fittest' world has too much of the strong preying on the weak. The firearms we found in Valekrie may be the equalizer we need. A woman that can't wield a sword can defend herself against a stronger foe with one of those. I digress again. It has been too long since I could journal events in my very short life, and it may be a while before I have another chance.

We have just passed the peaks of the Western Range on our way to the desert city of Juana Napur. The rain sounds like it is letting up. We will be on our way again tomorrow. I doubt I will have another chance to add to this journal for some time to come. So for now, if the gods exist, let them watch and tell our story. They can help us if they wish, and if not, they should stay out of our way. For now, we have a continent to cross.

ABOUT THE AUTHOR

Brian K Kerley lives in rural Alaska with his wife and grandson. He holds a degree in aviation from the University of Alaska Anchorage, and studies literature and creative writing at the University of Alaska Fairbanks. Brian works seasonally as a bush pilot and has had a multitude of experiences from Army medic to ship welder and commercial diver on the Dutch Harbor crab fleet.

www.ingramcontent.com/pod-product-compliance
Lightning Source LLC
Chambersburg PA
CBHW062111170626
46813CB00002B/405